VICTORY?

"I will ride into battle myself," the medicine man said. "I lost the Sacred Arrows. I will regain them for my tribe."

"We are ready," a war-paint-smeared brave said to Gray Thunder.

"I have brought my greatest medicine to bear against the Comanche. No arrow will touch our skin. No knife will cut our flesh. No bullet will steal our lives." Gray Thunder chewed quickly on medicine root, then spat in the direction of the Comanche.

For a moment, the two warriors stared at each other, startled. And for his part, Gray Thunder had been too intent on regaining Sweet Medicine's legacy to the Cheyenne to anticipate opposition. He fired point-blank at the medicine man.

Gray Thunder gasped at the pain exploding in his chest, then let out another scream of rage and drove forward. His bloody knife found its target in a vile Comanche heart.

He felt his enemy die. Gray Thunder dropped to his knees, panting with exertion. The world turned dim around him, but he refused to surrender to his own weakness. Fire spread throughout his chest, consuming him. He tried to rise, then collapsed, falling into the tepee. Dangling from the rough-hewn center pole slowly swung a wolf-skin bundle.

The Sacred Arrows.

The medicine man felt a surge of power pass through his body that revitalized his soul.

"The medicine arrows," he said, a smile dancing on his lips. He grabbed the bundle with all his might and pulled the Sacred Arrows free.

In death he had restored the great magic of the Cheyenne.

BOOK YOUR PLACE ON OUR WEBSITE AND MAKE THE READING CONNECTION!

We've created a customized website just for our very special readers, where you can get the inside scoop on everything that's going on with Zebra, Pinnacle and Kensington books.

When you come online, you'll have the exciting opportunity to:

- View covers of upcoming books
- Read sample chapters
- Learn about our future publishing schedule (listed by publication month *and author*)
- Find out when your favorite authors will be visiting a city near you
- Search for and order backlist books from our online catalog
- Check out author bios and background information
- Send e-mail to your favorite authors
- Meet the Kensington staff online
- Join us in weekly chats with authors, readers and other guests
- Get writing guidelines
- AND MUCH MORE!

**Visit our website at
http://www.kensingtonbooks.com**

WARRIORS OF THE PLAINS

Karl Lassiter

PINNACLE BOOKS
Kensington Publishing Corp.
http://www.kensingtonbooks.com

PINNACLE BOOKS are published by

Kensington Publishing Corp.
850 Third Avenue
New York, NY 10022

All Kensington Titles, Imprints, and Distributed Lines are available at special quantity discounts for bulk purchases for sales promotions, premiums, fund-raising, and educational or institutional use. Special book excerpts or customized printings can also be created to fit specific needs. For details, write or phone the office of the Kensington special sales manager: Kensington Publishing Corp., 850 Third Avenue, New York, NY 10022, attn: Special Sales Department, Phone: 1-800-221-2647.

Pinnacle and the P logo Reg. U.S. Pat. & TM Off.

First Pinnacle Books Printing: April 2003

10 9 8 7 6 5 4 3 2 1

Printed in the United States of America

For Rabbit

Many years' experience has shown me that the dangers from which this Department [New Mexico under Mexican governance] suffers result from the various fortresses which North Americans have placed near this Department, the nearest of which is that of Charles Bent. . . ."

—Governor Manuel Armijo, 1840
letter to Mexico City

Outbreak

"Smallpox!"

The shiver went up William Bent's spine. He wiped his dusty hands on a rag tucked under his belt as he turned from the adobe-brick mud pit and stared at his good friend, Ceran St. Vrain, who had just ridden into camp from the south, down by the Arkansas River. The sturdy mountain man's aristocratic, broad face was pale under its usual weathered tan, showing how much this frightened him. From their long association, both as friends and business partners in Bent, St. Vrain & Company, William knew nothing frightened Ceran. The man had fought Sioux and Comanche and never shown so much as a bead of sweat from strain on his handsome face.

No longer.

"We can't stop," William said, turning and looking at how well construction on their outpost was proceeding. Mexican workers from Taos toiled to get the adobe blocks into place for the thick walls. William felt a fleeting desperation that the dread disease would slow or even stop construction. There were so many things to do, so many details to check. He had traveled through the Southwest along the Santa Fe

Trail more times than he could remember, but never had he known that the type of mud that went into the blocks mattered. The first batch of mud from along the Arkansas River had almost fallen apart, even baking in the coarse Mexican wool brought from Taos to put with the marsh grass. The foreman had moved the site for mining the proper type of dirt one mile north of the half-completed trading post, hauling the adobe south as needed. And so much of it was needed! The pits were filled with mud and workers as the pressure of time hung heavily on William.

A hundred Mexicans worked to haul water from the river and put it into the deep pits for the oxen to tromp around, mixing the clay to the proper consistency so the bricks could be packed into molds with the wool and grass before being placed out on wooden drying racks. In its way, making the bricks was as much commerce as anything William or his brother Charles had ever done.

William heaved a deep breath as he envisioned the post as it would be after completion. Fort William, the men were already calling it. It tickled his fancy to have it named after him, although Charles and Ceran were as responsible for the construction as he was. Charles made the long trip from St. Louis to Santa Fe over and over to keep the money flowing for construction. When this way station was completed, they would control the trade along the mountain branch of the Santa Fe Trail and extend their already vast trading empire just a little bit more.

A lot more. His grin at how well their plans went faded quickly.

Ceran had to be wrong. Smallpox couldn't interrupt construction of the trading post. He told him so.

"William, I've seen the men who came down with it.

Two Mexicans this side of Raton Pass. I was hunting when I saw them. They were with the last wagon train from Taos and got left behind."

"That means the teamsters might have brought it to us when they stayed last week." William stared at the Mexicans toiling in the adobe production and went weak in the knees. He was no coward, but how did anyone fight disease that spread like a prairie fire? An even more frightening prospect occurred to him. "The Cheyenne have to be told. An epidemic would wipe them out. Chief Yellow Wolf can move away for a few months, go to his camp at Big Timbers, until the danger passes."

Ceran smiled slightly as he said, "You didn't say anything about warning the Comanche." The aristocratic St. Vrain knew how his partner favored the Cheyenne over the plains marauders who ranged up from the center of Texas and contentiously fought the Sioux, Arapaho, Cheyenne—any tribe that didn't move out of their way fast enough. Only the Mexican governor, de Anza, had effectively fought them, and his methods were not those William—or Ceran—would ever endorse. De Anza had massacred women and children while the Comanche warriors were out raiding. Using their own tactics against them had convinced the Comanche of the ruthlessness of the Mexican governor, and had driven them from New Mexico Territory for years, but it had done nothing to prevent raiding along the Santa Fe Trail, which kept the cavalry on the move constantly, spread thin and getting thinner. As a result, the U.S. Army refused to send even one soldier along as protection for the large numbers of wagons Bent, St. Vrain & Company rolled along the trail. Even providing weapons for the freighters had proven ineffective, since few of them were trained hunters or fighters. William had come up with the idea of using oxen to pull their wagons rather than horses, to remove the primary reason for the Indian attacks. The oxen's more deliberate plodding pace had added a week or more to the trip, but had also stopped the Comanche raiding.

What Comanche warrior wanted to ride a stolen ox?

"We'll send a messenger," William said. "Their medicine man, Gray Thunder, has to know, too, so he can prepare the proper cleansing rituals."

"Better send several runners," Ceran suggested. "The Cheyenne and Arapaho are scattered all the way north to the Laramie Mountains."

"Only those around the post need to be warned so they won't come in, get infected, and then spread the disease." William took a deep breath and let it out slowly. There was so much work to be done on the fort. Another six months' construction might not see it completed if smallpox ravaged their workers.

"I can ride out, too," Ceran said. "I know the land like the back of my hand between here and Pueblo."

"I need your help here, Ceran," said William. "Your insight into the architecture is necessary. You know me. I'm a trader, not a construction engineer." He looked at his friend and saw that the pallor remained, made even more apparent by Ceran's bushy, jet-black beard. The grueling pace he had maintained on his ride to warn everyone was not enough to explain his pallid complexion. The man was as strong as a bear and twice as mean. "Are you feeling well?"

"The trip's worn me to a nubbin. A moment's weakness, nothing more," Ceran said, then sat heavily, putting his momentary bravado to the lie. Ceran looked up, his dark eyes forlorn and his usually impeccably groomed hair mussed. "I might have it already, William."

William shouted, "Kit! Get over here. We need a doctor."

"What is it?" A short, stout man with a huge mustache ambled over. Kit Carson's buckskins were old and faded but well mended. He pushed a beaver hat back off his forehead and peered at Ceran St. Vrain. "You need some water, Ceran? You're lookin' mighty pale."

"He might have the pox, Kit," William said.

Kit took an involuntary step backward, and William didn't fault him any for it. The short mountain man and scout had ranged throughout the West and had seen death of all kinds. None of them favored the high fever and pox and utter helplessness that went along with smallpox. Better to die a quick, clean death at the hands of a Comanche warrior or even endure a mauling by a grizzly. Those were understandable risks that an able man could face and match. But not the pox. It killed capriciously.

"That last buncha Mexicans from Santa Fe," Kit said, his voice choked.

"It might have been the Taos traders. Ceran said they left behind two men who had the pox."

"The workers," Kit insisted. "I thought they was layin' down on the job. Now I'm not so sure they wasn't already gettin' sick with the pox." He was the same height as William, but seemed to shrink until he was even shorter as the impact of their situation hit him fully.

"How many?" William asked. He had been so engrossed in finding building material and seeing to the layout of the large trading post that he had not paid as much attention to the workers as he should have.

"Half dozen, maybe," Kit said, his blue-gray eyes wide as he stared critically at Ceran. "Half a dozen Mexicans and Ceran, there. If he ain't got it, I don't know what's wrong with him."

William felt the shiver run up and down his spine again. Ceran St. Vrain had the pox.

Trade and License

St. Louis, Missouri
April 16, 1832

"You're plumb daft, Mr. Bent," the trader said, scratching his shaggy head as he stared at the list. "None of this will mean squat to the trappers. Hell and damnation, this is junk them Injuns'd want. Who wants to trade with the likes of them?"

Charles Bent shrugged, choosing not to explain everything he had observed in St. Louis over the past week. The traders had gotten rich in the past, but now they were only working harder to make their money as the price of beaver pelts dropped to half what they had been paid the prior season. Charles wanted Bent, St. Vrain & Company to plan ahead, anticipate new markets, and make even more money when others began to founder financially. All the magazines from Europe, some months old, showed the men wearing silk hats as well as beaver. A beaver pelt might sell in St. Louis for six dollars, but it wouldn't be worth spit if the winds of fashion blew off all those beaver-felt hats from men's heads and replaced them with silk top hats.

No more market for beaver meant the company had to find other products for trade. Charles knew he had figured it out. Buffalo robes would never find a saturated market, and the finest hunters were Indians.

Yellow Wolf had been helpful determining the location for Fort William, and had shown that cooperation with the Cheyenne was not only possible but profitable.

"Beads, calico, hell, Mr. Bent, you got so much tin here you could make gewgaws for every Injun west of the Mississippi. And German silver? What self-respecting Mexican in Santa Fe wants German silver when they got real silver from the mines down near Taxco? You want to trade with me for some of *that* and we can deal. But you won't stay in business a year if you buy this kind of junk."

Charles almost spoke his mind and told what he foresaw and how this dealer in beaver pelts would be out of business in a year if he didn't seek out other commodities.

"Think of me as a dimwit to be taken advantage of," Charles said. "I'm taking off your hands bolts of cloth—and the tin—merchandise no one else wants."

"But you're not bringing enough beaver pelts!" protested the trader. "I pay good money for them. I got folks back in Chicago clamorin' fer more."

"But you do want the buffalo robes?"

"Sure, of course I do. They sell at a premium in New York, but they're hard to handle. Beaver pelts ain't."

"That's so," Charles admitted. Only ten buffalo hides could be pressed into a single easily handled bale, but fifty beaver pelts occupied the same space. More.

The dickering went on, halfheartedly on the trader's part. He had ruined his own arguments, admitting he was moving merchandise from his warehouses that no one but Charles Bent wanted. As a result, Charles got two extra wagon loads for the price he had expected for a single wagon.

Rubbing his hands with glee, Charles stepped out into the muggy St. Louis afternoon and looked up and down the street. A horse-drawn trolley headed in the direction of downtown, and he had missed it. Rather than chase after it and get spattered with mud for his effort, Charles strolled along close to the buildings, picking out the dry spots along the boardwalk, his sharp eyes taking in the people thronging the trade district, what they sold and what they bought.

He was sure William could maintain good relations with the Cheyenne. His brother had an affinity for the Colorado Indians lacking in all the other traders. The mountain men and trappers like Kit Carson tolerated the Indians, even as they grudgingly respected them for their abilities, but William had virtually become one with the Cheyenne after the feared Comanche war chief Bull Hump had chased three Cheyenne into William's camp. William had hidden the three frightened braves and lied boldly to Buffalo Hump, something that took more than a modicum of pluck and courage. The Comanche had left after searching the camp without finding their quarry. William had given what supplies he could to the three Cheyenne and had won their tribe's enduring trust.

Charles selected his trade goods with the Cheyenne and their allies the Arapaho in mind. They were superb hunters and could supply buffalo robes for years to come in exchange for the white man's goods. Tin for making gorgets and arm bands. Kettles and iron Dutch ovens. Gaudy bits of colored stone and glass to mount in jewelry for both warrior and squaw. Cloth and rifles and ammunition and the German silver.

No one wanted German silver. Except Chief Yellow Wolf and the respected medicine man Gray Thunder and hundreds of other Cheyenne. A few trinkets of German silver traded for an equal number of buffalo robes.

Charles wondered if John Jacob Astor had noticed how fashion was trending away from beaver-felt hats. He hoped not. Let the American Fur Company continue flooding the eastern and European markets with beaver pelts and wasting time and money when the real market lay with the buffalo. If Bent, St. Vrain & Company could expand into the American Fur Company's territory in Wyoming and father north, they might supply travelers along both the Santa Fe Trail and the Oregon Trail.

The riches that would follow lay beyond Charles's astute reckoning.

Charles sauntered along and found himself heading for the government offices issuing trade licenses. The company had neglected to get the proper permits until now, but with Fort William being built, it would quickly become the center for trade along the Santa Fe Trail. That meant Charles had to have all the paperwork in order to maintain the trading post's status as being on American soil and deserving of American attention, even if it required paying American taxes.

Ceran St. Vrain was a Mexican citizen and had cemented ties with the authorities in Santa Fe. It was time for Charles to do the same at the other end of the Santa Fe Trail.

The clerk looked up with dull eyes as Charles swung into the close, stiflingly hot office. The confident short man seemed more impressive than his stature would imply, and this caused the clerk to drop his pen and push up his ink-stained sleeves.

"What kin I do fer ya, sir?"

"I'm here to take out a license to move freight, my good man," Charles said cheerfully. "Along the Santa Fe Trail's mountain branch."

"You're that Bent fella, ain't ya?" The clerk began digging through piles of paper and came out with a thick sheaf. He pushed it across the counter toward Charles. "Fill all that out, detail what yer likely to be haulin'—don't want none of them savages to get weapons or firewater, leastwise not much—and then you owe the U.S. Gummint two hunnert dollars for the license."

"And will this entitle me to protection by the military?" asked Charles, working quickly through the forms.

"Only if they want. They're busy chasin' down the Comanche, and if you ast me, they ain't doin' such a good job. Too many Comanche, not enough bluecoats. Ain't their fault. I betcha they'd like to ride along with a food wagon loaded till the axles creaked. Too good for them damned Messkins, if you ast me."

Charles let the clerk ramble on about his theories of how the United States had to expand, and if the Mexicans got in the way, they deserved to be pushed aside. He had heard it all, though usually couched in less belligerent terms. Still, Missouri's Senator Thomas Hart Benton had expressed his own views on Manifest Destiny, and they did not differ much from the clerk's, except in eloquence.

"There," Charles said, completing the last of the forms.

"You done 'em all right," the clerk said with some admiration in his words. "Now, pony up the two hunnert dollars and I'll put the official seal on this here license."

Charles fished out the scrip issued on a St. Louis bank. The clerk examined the paper money carefully, then nodded, stamped the crisp forms still damp with ink, and proudly handed them back to Charles.

"Hope you make a fortune selling to them brown

bastards. Take 'em for all you can, or they'll use the money against us. Mark my words, the Messkins are goin' to war with us soon enough."

"You might be right, but I hope to avoid any such unpleasantness," Charles said, tucking away the license in an inner coat pocket.

"There's war coming!" the clerk shouted after him. "With the Injuns and with them damned Messkins!"

Charles let the warm, muggy afternoon swallow him and wash away his distaste from dealing with the government clerk as he made his way toward the fancy hotel where he stayed for an afternoon repast. War and other unpleasantness were as far from his mind as anything could be. After all, he would return soon to Fort William, set up the trading post, and then wait for the money to come flooding into the Bent, St. Vrain & Company coffers.

Recovery

"You're a sight for sore eyes," William Bent cried, racing out to embrace his brother. Charles picked him up and spun him around, putting him down easily.

"You've been sick," Charles said accusingly. He reached out, his fingers touching the shallow pockmarks on his brother's face. "Was it—?"

"I'm afraid so," William said solemnly. "I came down with the pox right after Ceran."

"Ceran, too!" Charles looked around and saw their two hundred workers diligently lifting adobe bricks into place on the two-story-high walls of the trading post. The basic 142-by-122-foot outline that had been scratched into the dirt before he left had grown into a real building. Vigas were being placed for supports on inner rooms, and the turrets at each corner of the large enclosure were taking shape, spiraling ten feet higher above the ramparts. Another few months would see Fort William in operation.

But he had never heard that his brother and partner had contracted smallpox.

"All this and smallpox, too. You are quite the wonder, William." He stared at the twenty-four-year-old, who beamed at his older brother's compliment. "But what of Ceran? Is he here?"

"Kit took him to Taos when it was obvious we could not adequately care for him here. Kit got it, too, more's the pity, so wasn't able to look after Ceran. They found nurses there, though."

"Pretty ones, unless I miss my guess," Charles said. "Kit's well now?"

"Quite well, but so many of the workers came down with the pox that it slowed construction. I was hardly able to get around, though it barely touched me." William hesitated and then pointed to the south, in the direction of the Arkansas River. "We've started a cemetery before we finished the post."

"What of Ceran?"

"He is hale and hearty, Charles," William said solemnly. "He returned from Taos a few days ago and is out telling nearby Cheyenne encampments that the danger to them has passed."

"Did any of the Cheyenne come down with the pox?" Charles's heart skipped a beat as he considered how tragic in human terms that would be, loosing such a plague among their allies. Almost as bad would be the destruction of trade with the Cheyenne for years to come.

"Not a one. Our couriers warned them away in time. Gray Thunder stayed at Big Timbers, almost forty miles away, and performed his rituals every night. They escaped entirely. Only the Mexicans contracted it," William said. With a rueful laugh, he added, "And Ceran, Kit, and me, of course."

A dust cloud appeared to the north. A few workers stopped to watch, but their foremen quickly got them back to the job of lifting adobe bricks into place on the fort.

"It looks almost finished. I'm glad I brought trade goods," Charles said. "When do you think we can begin trading in earnest?"

"Let's ask," William said, throwing a rag to the ground after he wiped off his hands. "That's Ceran."

"William!" called Ceran St. Vrain. When he saw Charles, he jumped off his horse, hit the ground running, and threw his arms around both men, crushing them in a bear hug. "Charles! This is a surprise."

"William was telling me of your travails," Charles said, eyeing the mountain man closely. William showed only small scarring from the pox. Ceran's face looked as if he had been hit with a shotgun blast. Even his black, bushy beard failed to hide most of the pock-marks. Otherwise, the man looked to be in fine fettle, strong and sure.

"I suspect they are nothing compared to the tales you have to tell," Ceran said. "Look at that! Twenty wagons, if there's one."

"Twenty-four," Charles said. "And I didn't lose a single thread of cloth or ounce of tin along the way. We hardly saw any Comanche, and then only at a distance. William's idea of using oxen keeps them away from our wagon trains when there are others using horses for them to steal."

"Bloody red-skinned bastards," grumbled Ceran. Then he turned to William and said, "Yellow Wolf wants to meet with us right away. He's camped four miles off, near Timpas Creek."

"Would you like to come along, Charles?" asked William.

"My posterior aches from spending too much time in the saddle. Let me stay and see to the trade goods. You have a few rooms completed inside the post where I can store the most valuable of the merchandise. Unloading will take a while, and preparing for—"

"I get the idea," William said, holding up his hand to stop his brother. Charles could ramble on for hours about the deals he did and the dangers he faced along the trail. "Ceran and I'll be back before you know it."

"Bring the chief and some of his braves to trade," Charles said. "Maybe even Gray Thunder. I've got some herbs and trinkets I'm sure he can use in his medicines."

"Each worth a buffalo robe?" asked Ceran.

"At least," Charles said, laughing. It was good being back with his partners. It was even better finding they had eluded death from smallpox.

William put his fingers to his lips and whistled. A young boy saddled his horse and brought it to him. He mounted easily enough, but Charles was concerned that William still had not fully recovered, mild case of the pox or not.

"You worry too much. Worry about how to spend the profits we'll make!" With that William and Ceran wheeled their horses and trotted off in the direction of Timpas Creek and the Cheyenne waiting for the news that all was clear.

Three days later, Ceran St. Vrain and William Bent returned with more than 3,500 Cheyenne, who began immediately constructing permanent lodges and corrals near the fort. Charles was beside himself with joy at the trust Chief Yellow Wolf showed in the Bents and at the huge number of buffalo robes the Cheyenne had for trade.

Trade for the gewgaws the merchant in St. Louis had told him were worthless.

A Season of Trade

Bent's Fort
June 2, 1833

William Bent hiked his hand-tooled, mirror-shiny boots to the edge of the desk and leaned back in the comfortable chair Charles had brought from St. Louis on his last trip. He looked around his office and smiled. The trading post had been finished less than six months, and already it had become a crossroads for trappers with their pelts and Indians of all tribes coming to trade for the items and clever gewgaws Charles fetched from St. Louis. The only part that bothered him was the way the trappers refused to call it Fort William. To the man, they had decided on Bent's Fort, and nothing else passed their lips.

In a way, it was fitting, but William felt a small loss. This had been his dream and he had seen it through to completion.

"You're joking," Ceran St. Vrain said from across the room. He stood in the open doorway into the gravel-covered *placita*, vainly seeking even a puff of sluggish summer air to steal away the sweat on his forehead. The sounds of the buffalo-robe press in the middle of the trading post told of their real success. The giant screw drove down the wooden ram to compress the woolly hides into bundles of ten to make for easier transport back East.

"Numbers don't lie, Ceran," William said. "Over the winter and through the spring we made a profit of more than one hundred ninety thousand dollars. Does that surprise you?"

"I—no," Ceran said, turning from the courtyard heat to face his partner. He stroked his black beard thoughtfully for a moment, and then a huge grin split his face. "How could we fail with you pumping the Cheyenne for every scrap of buffalo hide and Charles skinning the traders back in St. Louis?"

"You've not done poorly down in New Mexico, either," William pointed out. "Your becoming a Mexican citizen has eased the entry of our merchandise. There is no importation duty for you, as there would be for an American citizen trying to trade there. Every cent—and centavo—not paid out in taxes is profit to us."

"Being Catholic has helped, also. The Mexicans don't trust you or Charles because you are Protestants," Ceran said.

"Charles keeps running into trouble because of that, but he won't convert, even if it is good for business," William said.

"He can keep his distance from Padre Antonio," Ceran said. "If he does, both Taos and Santa Fe are wide-open markets for our goods."

"They are as long as the troubles down in Mexico prevent regular supply trains from the south." William stared past Ceran out into the heat of the day. Trade had gone far better than they had anticipated, or rather, better than *he* had thought it would. Charles had been deucedly clever anticipating the collapse of the beaver-pelt market and the growing demand for buffalo robes. This had given them a trading advantage with the Indians other companies did not enjoy.

"The Mexicans trade in silver, the Indians in buffalo robes, and those in St. Louis cannot get enough of either!" gloated William.

"We have done well," Ceran said. "Part of it comes from building this fort." He stared out into the courtyard again where a farrier worked across the way to shoe a balky horse. To the west, just under Ceran's quarters on the second floor, a wheelwright struggled to replace broken spokes on a wagon wheel. More than forty men and their families lived within the tall, thick adobe walls of the fort, safe behind the metal-sheathed gates facing the tules to the east. Beyond the marshes the Cheyenne had built their lodges, affording even more security, and all around the fort commerce thrived.

"Most of it comes from the way we trade," William said, coming back to a sore point with him. "You know the trappers refuse to call this Fort William."

"I'll cut their throats if I hear them call it Bent's Fort," Ceran said. William wasn't sure if his friend was joking. "You deserve the honor. You built this fort, it should be named after you."

"Let them call it what they will," answered William. "As long as they continue coming here with their pelts." He was secretly pleased with Ceran's reaction. Here was a friend to the death, one he could trust with his life.

"Charles says there is no market left for beaver. Or very little."

"A good thing we told the trappers working for us. A fox skin fetches twice what a beaver pelt does now."

"Buffalo robes," Ceran said. "That's the secret to it."

"I've sent Kit north," William said suddenly. Ceran looked at him with narrowed eyes. William smiled and nodded agreement with his partner's unvoiced comment. "It's time to expand. Kit will talk to trappers selling to the American Fur Company and see if they won't deal with us. Astor is only now scaling back on how many beaver pelts he'll buy."

"This is a bold move. Astor is not likely to take kindly to us moving in on his territory."

"From the beginning, we agreed to go after the settlers moving along the Oregon Trail. This is our chance. Get the trappers to trade with us, then use them to steer the traffic to a Bent, St. Vrain and Company trading post."

"Not here," Ceran said, his arm sweeping about to take in the large post around them. "You'll need a new post. To the north, not far off the Oregon Trail."

"Fort St. Vrain," William said. "That has a ring to it, don't you agree?"

"Astor will fight if we try to move into his territory."

"Let him. We have plenty of money to supply such a fort. From what Charles hears, the American Fur Company is crashing against the reefs of bankruptcy. We might buy what's left in a year for a song and a dance."

"It's been a spell since I went to a fandango," Ceran said, jumping lightly into the air and clicking his heels. "But I can't build a fort a hundred miles to the north and maintain trade in New Mexico. I'd have to be in two places at the same time."

"Your brother Marcellin made a favorable impression on Charles when he visited your family in St. Louis."

"My younger brother aspires to be a ne'er-do-well," griped Ceran. "But he can work when he puts his mind to it. I'll send a letter to him and see if he is interested."

"Do so, Ceran. If he accepts and is half the man you are, Astor has already lost his grip on all the territory north to Canada!" William dropped his feet from the desk and stood. "I am going to smoke a pipe with Gray Thunder. Something big is in the wind."

"The dispute with the Pawnee? Has it come down to war?"

"That's what I fear. There is nothing I can do to stop the Cheyenne from going to war, but it would disrupt trade and cause untold trouble between here and St. Louis."

"We don't want to take sides," Ceran cautioned, knowing William had already decided to back the Cheyenne. "There wouldn't be any winner in such a situation."

"Bent's Fort is neutral territory," William assured him. "I've already contacted Colonel Dodge, should the matter come into question."

"Imagine that," Ceran said sarcastically. He made a face at William calling the post Bent's Fort, but said nothing about it. "The cavalry actually protecting Americans."

"You'd better get back to Taos," William said, "since you're not a U.S. citizen."

"Perhaps I can convince the *gobernador* to provide troops to protect our wagons in New Mexico," Ceran said. Then he laughed. "There's as much chance of that as Colonel Dodge stopping the Cheyenne from fighting the Pawnee."

"I'm afraid you are right," William said, humor draining from him. He scooped up his hat and put on his coat. He always presented himself formally to the

Cheyenne. They appreciated it, and it gave him added authority among them.

But not this time. William Bent smoked a half-dozen pipes and talked long into the night, but the Cheyenne had already reached an unshakable decision.

War.

Desperate Loss

Gray Thunder's ancient hands touched the wolf-skin sheath holding the Four Sacred Arrows given to the Cheyenne by the first medicine man, Sweet Medicine. Over the long years, these four arrows had been handed down from one medicine man to the next, and guaranteed victory for the Cheyenne in war and prosperity in times of peace.

"Are you ready to begin the ceremony?" asked Bull, the young medicine man chosen to take the arrows into battle against the Pawnee.

"No, not yet. We cannot begin too soon or the magic will be weakened," Gray Thunder said. "Only minutes before we attack should the ceremony be performed. Remember that and victory will always be ours."

More than sixty summers had passed since Gray Thunder's birth cries, and never had he felt more weight on his shoulders than he did now. The chiefs had declared war on the Pawnee. No more skirmishing. War. All-out, total, complete. Not since the brutal wars with the Crow had there been such preparation and anticipation. He looked across at his two lovely daughters, Owl Woman and Yellow Woman, and knew he would have to shoo them away soon. No woman could view the Sacred Arrows, and Gray Thunder took his role as Keeper-of-the-Sacred-Arrows seriously.

"But the scouts have found the Pawnee village and are ready to fight," Bull said.

"No!" cried Gray Thunder. "They must not spill any enemy blood. If they kill before the ceremony, we shall lose our most potent medicine. They cannot. They must not."

Bull looked uneasy, but Gray Thunder attributed this to the singular honor falling on the young man. If Gray Thunder's legs had not been bowed with age and hurting constantly, he would have ridden into battle with the Sacred Arrows and given the Cheyenne yet another victory, this time over the Pawnee. The Keeper-of-the-Sacred-Hat had already communicated to Gray Thunder his readiness, but he was an impetuous man. Gray Thunder had counseled for a change in Keeper-of-the-Sacred-Hat many times, but his pleas had fallen on deaf ears.

He had to show the chiefs the value of the big medicine of the Sacred Arrows—and patience.

"Go," Gray Thunder told his daughters. His wife did not leave the tepee with them, but turned her back and sat, head bowed, as was her place. She would accompany him as he took the four arrows to the battlefield.

Hands shaking more with anticipation now than with age, Gray Thunder took the bindings off the wolf skin and revealed the Four Sacred Arrows. Bull gasped at the sight of such powerful medicine. Even Gray Thunder's heart beat a little faster as he made sure all was in readiness.

"Gray Thunder, the fighting societies are here to escort us," Bull said.

Through the open flap of the tepee Gray Thunder

saw the leader of the Dog Soldiers sitting astride his horse, a fierce look on his war-painted face. This meant the other three soldier bands were already on their way to find the Pawnee. The Dog Soldiers always protected the rear and were the fiercest and most disciplined of the warrior societies. Gray Thunder appreciated that protection for such powerful medicine. The warrior shook his war lance in Gray Thunder's direction, urging him to speed. Still, the old medicine man did not allow the warrior to rush him as he dabbed more red paint onto his face, signifying he was Keeper. With solemn care, he folded the wolf skin back around the Four Sacred Arrows given them so long ago by Sweet Medicine, and rose. His wife trailed, head bowed. Bull pressed close to his side.

"Do not be too eager," Gray Thunder said softly to Bull. "Use your head and your heart and you will not go astray."

The thunder of hooves caused Gray Thunder to look around. He had been wrong. The Kit Foxes, Red Shields, and Elkhorn Scrappers were only now forming into battle formations. The brave from the Dog Soldiers had come directly from his society's camp, a few hundred yards separate from the rest of the Cheyenne village.

"What of the scouts?" Gray Thunder asked, remembering what Bull had said.

"The Kit Foxes are responsible," the Dog Soldier warrior said. "They chase after the Pawnee, as we should."

Gray Thunder nodded curtly and let his daughters lead his horse up. Never relinquishing the Four Sacred Arrows, Gray Thunder mounted, and winced as pain shot through his arthritic limbs. Once his horse had fallen into its ground-devouring trot, he felt better and the pain went away, as surely as the Pawnee would.

The longer he rode, the better Gray Thunder felt about the battle victory to come. The Sacred Arrows had been renewed, reflectched with new eagle feathers and their shafts rewrapped with fresh sinew. He looked left and right and saw how the tepee skirts had been rolled up to waist level in preparation for the fight to come. No one remained in the camp as they all, man, woman, and child, went into battle with the Pawnee.

It was as it should be.

The power of the four medicine arrows filled Gray Thunder with an exaltation he could not describe. This was his chance to be in touch with the greatest of the Cheyenne medicine men; he was merely the latest link in a chain stretching back into antiquity. He felt buoyed by the war songs given voice by the warriors around him as much as he did by the responsibility of his position and the certainty of victory over a hated enemy.

A commotion to the north distracted him, but the warrior riding with him took no note. Bull muttered something to himself and looked more ill at ease. Gray Thunder ignored him. His assistant should not give in to jitters, but he did not chastise him for that, remembering his own first time going into battle with the Sacred Arrows. Bull was a good medicine man, and would become even greater today with the Cheyenne victory over the Pawnee. They rode another half hour before coming to the crest of a rolling hill that looked over the sweeping prairie feeling the first touches of dawn from the rising sun.

"It is time," Gray Thunder said, dismounting. Again his legs almost betrayed him, but he ignored the pain as he began the ritual. Silence fell in the ranks of warriors, and the women all turned away so they would not witness the potent charms as he unfastened the wolf skin wrapping from the medicine arrows.

Gray Thunder faced the distant Pawnee, holding the notched ends of the four arrows as if he drew back on a giant, unseen bow. The arrowheads rested on his right forefinger as he aimed carefully, drawing a bead on the village. Bull popped a bit of medicine root into the old medicine man's mouth. Gray Thunder chewed and spat four times at the Pawnee.

"May they go blind!" cried Bull.

Gray Thunder's pulse hammered now as he lifted his left foot. The ranks of Cheyenne warriors responded with four loud war whoops. Gray Thunder hastily wrapped the Sacred Arrows in the skin sheath and tied it on the end of Bull's war lance.

"Stay behind the medicine man!" Gray Thunder bellowed. "Do not ride in front of the Sacred Arrows and they will protect you. The Pawnee are helpless against our medicine!" Answering cries came from the battalion headed by the Keeper-of-the-Sacred-Hat.

If the warriors fought well, the Pawnee would be caught in a trap and forced back to the river, where they would either swim away in retreat or die. Either was satisfactory for Gray Thunder.

Behind the warriors were arrayed the squaws and young children, ready to give whatever aid they could to wounded fighters. As the battle neared an end, they would rush onto the field and complete the killing begun by the braves.

"May the Great Creator guide our hands as they grip knives and our eyes as they seek out our enemies," Gray Thunder intoned. He handed the medicine lance to Bull, who took a deep breath, then mounted and let out a loud whoop. His horse rocketed down the gentle grassy slope in the direction of the Pawnee village. Barely had his first battle cry died when the warriors let loose their own cries and charged after him.

"Victory will be ours," Gray Thunder said confidently. He shuffled over and mounted so he could watch the battle from the elevated vantage point of horseback. For a minute or more, Gray Thunder was satisfied with the progress of the battle, then let out a shriek of astonishment when he saw how Bull led the attack, ready to count coup on a solitary Pawnee wandering about outside the village. Somehow, the Pawnee sat down as Bull raced up, the Sacred Arrows-laden lance ready to bring honor to all Cheyenne.

Bull thrust and missed. The Pawnee grabbed the lance and wrenched it from Bull's grip. The medicine man toppled from his horse and was killed with the lance bearing the four Sacred Arrows. The Cheyenne attack faltered, and this was all that was necessary for the Pawnee to mount and join battle. Disheartened and frightened that their most powerful medicine had failed, the Cheyenne were quickly routed.

"No, this cannot be. I performed the ceremony. Something is wrong! The magic has been broken! The medicine has been ruined!"

Gray Thunder wheeled his horse and galloped toward the small knot of women gathered a hundred yards away. On the ground at the women's feet lay a bloodied warrior, one of the Kit Foxes from his paint.

"What happened?" demanded Gray Thunder. "Why aren't you with your society?"

"We found them," the brave said, his voice cracking with strain. He tried to sit up, but blood loss made him too weak. "We attacked and slaughtered them!"

"What are you talking about? The fight's down

there!" Gray Thunder pointed in the direction of the carnage being wrought on the plains. His vision was as sharp as any young warrior's—he wished it were not so. He saw the Dog Soldier who had been his escort take a Pawnee arrow through the throat. As he struggled to pull out the arrow and before the brave could fall from his horse, two Pawnee fighters galloped up and grabbed his arms, each struggling to lift the scalp before casting the Cheyenne's body to the ground.

This was not an isolated or a unique death. Everywhere Gray Thunder looked he saw Cheyenne falling like stars from the sky.

"We found them. Six Pawnee buffalo hunters," the scout grated out. Blood flecked his lips, but he looked triumphant. "We killed them."

"No!" shrieked Gray Thunder, raging against the warrior's stupidity. "Not before the ceremony. You shouldn't have killed any of them! Not before the Four Sacred Arrows gave their medicine to our fighters. You ruined the medicine!"

"No Pawnee got away. They didn't warn the others. They died!" The brave weakly touched the bloody knife thrust into his belt.

"It doesn't matter," Gray Thunder said, hollow inside. Only he realized the immensity of this. "The medicine was corrupted. You spilled blood *before* the ceremony. The Sacred Arrows cannot give protection and victory if enemy blood has been shed before our attack."

Gray Thunder's rage grew again until it knew no bounds, but he could not take it out on the Kit Fox scout. The man had died, his hand on the knife that had destroyed the Cheyenne, thinking he had done well. He had killed a Pawnee—too soon. The tribe's most potent medicine was useless.

The ragged lines of retreating Cheyenne told how badly the battle was going against them. But Gray Thunder stared at a circular spot in the center of the fiercely raging battle, as void of warriors as if it had been swept clean. Bull lay facedown on the prairie, dead.

Thrust into the ground at his side was the medicine lance that had once held the Cheyenne's most potent medicine.

The Sacred Arrows had been captured by the Pawnee.

One of Four

William Bent took a deep drink of the water from the new well and smacked his lips in appreciation.

"That's about the sweetest water I've ever tasted," he told Ceran St. Vrain. "And I didn't have to hike down to the river to get it, either."

They stared down into the well, drilled in a room on the north side of the *placita*. Water bubbled from around the pump and formed a small pool. The well gave them the added security of not needing to fetch water from the distant Arkansas River for drinking and cooking, should the Indians attack. William wasn't worried about the Cheyenne, but the Comanche rode past, spotted in the distance now and then by sentries up on the fort's ramparts. So far, the Comanche had yet to launch an all-out assault on Bent's Fort, and William was happy to keep it that way. But the new well gave a guarantee that they could weather any such siege, even if it lasted for weeks.

"We don't want the well to get contaminated with marsh water from east of here," Ceran said, taking the dipper from William and sampling some himself. The day was hot, and cool water hit the spot.

"It's deep enough. We had to go down almost a hundred feet. I thought we were drilling to China."

"If we had, you'd've figured out a way to trade with the Chinese for silk," Ceran said, laughing. "That's after you finished the post, of course."

"I want to finish everything, but there is always 'just one more' niggling detail to look after," William said. The partners went into the courtyard and looked around. A small cannon had been fastened on the walkway to the east, dominating both the tules and any hostiles who might attempt to crash through the main gate. While a naval officer might consider it hardly more than a signaling cannon, Charles had brought it on his last trip from St. Louis and the first firing had frightened the Cheyenne. William wished they could have tried it out on the Comanche, and then decided it was just as well they hadn't needed to. The Comanche still gave them real woe attacking wagon trains out of pure cussedness, killing because they enjoyed it rather than out of desire to steal horses.

"Both bastions are about finished," Ceran said, pointing to the round turrets at opposite corners of the fort. "With the gunsmith able to repair and make about any firearm you want, we can stand off an army from here."

William eyed his friend closely.

"Are you thinking it'll come to that soon? You haven't heard anything about the Mexicans coming up to take us, have you?"

Ceran shrugged his broad shoulders and thrust his hands into his coat pockets. "It's not the Mexicans I worry about as much as the Texians."

"Them? They're always bickering among themselves too much to be a real threat. Besides, Santa Anna can control them. Can't he?"

"They're a rambunctious lot."

"We're too far north, and they'd have to cross the Arkansas River to reach us. Besides, the cavalry has been more active since Colonel Dodge was put into the field."

"I don't cotton much to him," Ceran said. "Or rather, I don't much like his commanding officer. Colonel Leavenworth is too old for a field unit. He moves too slow and he thinks too slow."

"That's why it's good that Dodge is doing most of the patrol. If only we could get him to protect our wagons as they come from St. Louis, we might double our profits."

"Mr. Bent, sir!" called a young boy from the parapet. He jumped up and down and pointed to the east. "Men's a-comin'!"

"Who, Diego? Can you tell who it is?" William called back. When he saw the boy was too excited to give a good answer, he went to the ladder and scaled it quickly, Ceran right behind. Using a small spyglass mounted on a tripod near their precious cannon, William studied the approaching riders.

"You've got good eyes, Diego," Ceran told the boy. "I can hardly make them out." He shielded his eyes against the morning sun and asked William, "Can you make them out? The golden glints lead me to believe those are soldiers."

"Cavalry," agreed William, straightening from the spyglass. "Speak of the devil and he does appear. From the banner, that's Colonel Dodge's unit."

"Diego, go to the kitchen and tell them to prepare a decent noonday meal for our visitors. We'll put the colonel and any of his officers in the main dining room and let the rest of his company eat as they see fit outside the walls," said Ceran.

William didn't dispute his friend's arrangements. When it came to elegant dining, there wasn't anywhere along the Santa Fe Trail that set a better table than Bent's Fort. But Ceran's aristocratic upbringing dictated strict social rules. For the most part, William did not object to the way Ceran seated their guests and insisted that most remain outside the fort's thick walls. Even after the trading post construction ended, William saw the benefits in keeping most of the Indians and traders outside where they couldn't get into too much trouble. Moreover, restricting entry into the fort for luxurious quarters and decent food made it a bargaining chip, a favor to be granted that might get them valuable concessions from the likes of Colonel Dodge and his junior officers.

They waited on the rampart until the colonel and his aide trotted up, skirting the tules and coming directly to the main gate.

"Good day, Colonel," called William. "Can I interest you and your officers in some dinner?"

"Mr. Bent, that's a mighty generous offer and one I'll be pleased to take you up on." Colonel Dodge was a man of about fifty, hair graying and his face like leather. He hesitated a moment before asking, "Can I make use of your farrier? My horse has a loose shoe."

William signaled for the main gate to be opened. The outer metal-sheathed gates swung wide, and he allowed the inner ones to similarly remain open in greeting. Dodge rode in, leaving his aide behind. William, and especially Ceran, appreciated this bit of manners.

"Diego, see to the colonel's horse," William said, dropping off the ladder to shake hands with the officer.

"Much obliged," Henry Dodge said. He stripped off

his canvas gloves and tucked them under his broad leather belt.

"This isn't a social call, I take it," said William. Ceran cringed at such bluntness. The former mountain man might have taken all afternoon before working around to the colonel's purpose in coming to the fort. That was his idea of politeness, but William saw no reason to pussyfoot around since he was anxious to get back to the myriad details that still required his attention. The well had been drilled, but the corrals outside the walls needed to be expanded and feed bins for the livestock had to be filled. Parts of the walls required reinforcement, and the storerooms were stuffed with merchandise to be inventoried and readied for barter.

Running the fort was akin to being mayor of a medium-sized town, and William felt the responsibilities acutely.

"No, sir, it is not. I've been out palavering with the Pawnee—" Colonel Dodge stopped when he saw how both William and Ceran stiffened. "I'm not meaning to get you involved in the squabble between the Cheyenne and the Pawnee, but—"

"Squabble, you call it?" said William, trying to keep his voice level. The ill-fated attack launched by the Cheyenne against the Pawnee had soured trade for more than a month. His sympathies lay with the Cheyenne since the Pawnee were too often allied with the Comanche, but his feelings certainly went further and deeper than that.

"To be polite," Dodge said brusquely. "I know you have contact with Gray Thunder."

"I do," William said carefully.

"I've recovered one of his Sacred Arrows and would return it, as a partial peace offering by the Pawnee."

"What?" Ceran's eyebrows arched in surprise as he stared. "They gave you one of the captured medicine arrows, just like that?" He snapped his fingers.

"Of course not. There was a considerable amount of dickering that went into it. And not a few threats, either. I am as sick of the Pawnee depredations as you—and the Cheyenne—are. They have returned one of the medicine arrows in return for a truce."

"Not a peace?" asked William. "Unless they got back all four of the Sacred Arrows, the Cheyenne would never smoke a peace pipe."

"I'm discussing the matter with the Pawnee. They are arrogant and know they hold the upper hand as long as the arrows are in their possession, but this is a beginning."

"What do the Cheyenne have to do to get back their Sacred Arrow?" asked William.

Dodge looked down from his superior height, pursed his lips, then said, "Merely accept the arrow and pledge not to raid the Pawnee village on the far side of the Arkansas River."

"No raiding," William said. "The medicine men will agree to that, and I am sure they can persuade the chiefs to, also."

"The Cheyenne lost so many men in that fight, they don't have a choice," Dodge said, his voice taking on a steely edge. "They agree or the U.S. Army will find itself in the most unpleasant position of enforcing a truce on them and perhaps even forcing them onto a reservation where they can be watched more closely. I do not want that, nor do you, I am sure."

William saw that the colonel had put him in the position of acting as negotiator with the Cheyenne. Dealing with Gray Thunder and the other medicine men would not be as difficult as getting Chief Yellow

Wolf to agree. Considerable ill feeling had built between the spiritual and military factions of the tribe as a result of the crushing defeat by the Pawnee.

"Very well. When can we arrange for the Pawnee to turn over the arrow to Gray Thunder? He is Keeper-of-the-Sacred-Arrows."

"Get them to agree and give them the arrow yourself," Dodge said.

"I don't understand," Ceran said.

William understood. The Pawnee had given one of the Sacred Arrows to the colonel, knowing full well its medicine would be ruined if a white man saw it.

"Give me the arrow and I'll return it to Gray Thunder," William said. "You've kept it wrapped in wolf skin and out of sight, haven't you?" The way he said it gave Colonel Dodge a moment's pause. Dodge might not realize the full extent of the Pawnee insult, but he understood enough to take the unsheathed arrow from the back of his saddle and hand it to William.

"No one has seen it," Dodge said, his dark eyes locking with William's. William took the arrow straightaway to the storeroom, where he found a wolf hide to wrap the arrow in before returning it to Gray Thunder. It wouldn't fool the wily medicine man, but maintaining what honor they could under the circumstances was more important than honesty.

And the Sky Falls

Cheyenne Encampment outside Bent's Fort
November 12, 1833

"Gray Thunder! Come quick!"

The medicine man looked up from the intricate holy pattern he traced endlessly in the dirt of the lodge floor as he sought spiritual guidance. The lookout outside the lodge was entrusted with keeping the Sacred Arrows safe. Gray Thunder glanced toward the slender wolf-skin bundle hanging to one side of the large lodge. The solitary medicine arrow returned by William Bent was still safe. Another, larger wolf-skin-sheathed package dangled from the top of the lodge, but Gray Thunder averted his eyes from it as if it were poisoned.

After the disastrous fight with the Pawnee, the chiefs had decided that losing the Sacred Arrows meant nothing. The potent medicine of the arrows would drain away in Pawnee hands and could never be used against the Cheyenne. Four new Sacred Arrows had been made and consecrated during an arduous ritual, but it was not the same. Gray Thunder wanted to retrieve the old ones, the ones handed down directly from Sweet Medicine. The new ones lacked the proper medicine, the proper power, even if the chiefs thought differently.

He got to his feet painfully and went to the door to peer out.

The Dog Soldier society guard carried the long pole for keeping away animals from the oversize medicine lodge. He paid no attention to what might be creeping up along the ground. He stared open-mouthed at the starry sky.

Gray Thunder craned his neck around, feeling the stiffness all the way down his spine. He had been sitting too long in one position as he thought on the Sacred Arrows and how he had failed in his duty as Keeper. Bull had paid with his life when the medicine had been vitiated. Gray Thunder lived to recover the three medicine arrows from their mortal enemy, the Pawnee.

The aged medicine man's eyes widened in shock when he saw a flaming streak across the sable dome of the night, leaving behind tumbling motes that fell like incandescent leaves. Before he could say a word, a second and a third and a fourth raked the sky, bequeathing similar glittering trails to the nighttime.

"The sky is falling!" the guard exclaimed.

"It's an omen," Gray Thunder said. He stepped out of the lodge to get a better view as more stars tumbled from their positions in the heavens. Gray Thunder whirled toward the north to see that the Seven Stars—what the white man called the Big Dipper—were still in place. For this he heaved a small sigh of relief. The seven brothers who had climbed the tree to avoid being trampled by a buffalo herd and had fired arrows into the sky, then followed those arrows to become the Seven Stars, wheeled about in the darkness.

This part of the world remained. But more stars fell, some splitting apart and spewing out luminous debris behind them.

"What does it mean, Gray Thunder?" asked the

guard. He gripped his pole tightly and seemed frightened. Gray Thunder had seen this brave in battle with the Pawnee and he had never shown any cowardice, but this was beyond his understanding. Gray Thunder sympathized with him—and wished it were beyond *his* so he could claim ignorance.

He could not.

"Catastrophe lies ahead for the Cheyenne," Gray Thunder said, his voice catching in his throat. "All the Sacred Arrows have not been returned by our enemy, the Pawnee. Until we again have the Four Sacred Arrows given us by Sweet Medicine, bad times will stalk us like a cougar tracking a fawn."

"War? Or starvation?" asked the guard.

Gray Thunder glanced into the medicine lodge. The single arrow that had been returned had been re-fletched and strung with new sinew to reinvigorate its medicine. He uttered a brief prayer of thanks to William Bent for his wisdom in returning it—and for how he had done so, obviously lying about the condition of the arrow and whether white men had seen the medicine arrow.

"One of two buffalo-arrows is ours. William Bent returned it to our medicine lodge, honoring us with his integrity. We will not starve, though times will be difficult."

"Then the falling stars mean we will lose in battle?"

Gray Thunder did not answer. Neither of the man-arrows guaranteeing success in war hung in the Cheyenne medicine lodge. He stared up at the sky, no longer filled with spectacular celestial fireworks. The radiance of the falling stars faded as quickly as the glory of the Cheyenne.

Competition

Ceran St. Vrain sucked on a blade of frozen grass as he stared down into the valley. He spat, plucked another blade from under a patch of icy snow, and then said, "We could burn it down. The sons a bitches trade guns and firewater to the Sioux, so who'd know the difference whether *we* did it or the Lakota?"

"We couldn't do that," William Bent said, leaning against his rifle as he studied the fort on the banks of the Platte River. "There's no honor in blaming the Sioux for something we did."

"I can blame them for everything that I don't blame the Comanche for," Ceran said. "What are we going to do?" He jerked his thumb in the direction of Fort Laramie. "They're cutting into trade along our northern boundary. All the Cheyenne say so."

"Bill Sublette and Bob Campbell are crafty," William admitted. "They built this fort in a good location on the Platte and get their buffalo robes from the northern Cheyenne as well as the Sioux."

"That's money out of our pockets."

"Times are changing," William said. "Charles had an escort of mounted dragoons on his last trip to Santa Fe, at least as far as the fort. The captain in charge said Colonel Leavenworth was crossing Pawnee country to make peace with the Comanche. We'll be far more profitable if our wagons get through unscathed. We can compete with Fort Laramie with the extra profits."

"Make peace? With the Comanche?" Ceran shook his head. "As likely to happen as Sublette sharing the wealth with us. All the Army wants is to train its soldiers for the fight to come with Mexico, making sure all their officers know the lay of the land. The fort is going to be on the edge of a major fight, William."

"Maybe so," William allowed. "The Mexicans can't hold on to New Mexico Territory much longer, not the way they treat their people there. The Navajo complain of Mexican slavers, the Texians are agitating for independence again, and not one in five wagon trains makes it up from Mexico along the Jornado del Muerto. We supply more goods to Taos and Santa Fe than any Mexican trader."

"That means more silver for us," Ceran said confidently. He stared down into the valley at the obviously prospering Fort Laramie. "But what are we going to do to make sure there're buffalo robes left for us? I hear stories of entire herds being destroyed. Thousands and thousands of the woolly beasts gone for good."

"We trade. We trade more fiercely than Sublette and Campbell ever could. They're mountain men first and foremost, not merchants." William saw how Ceran hesitated. "What's wrong?"

"This isn't to my liking," Ceran said. "Taos and Santa Fe can't be ignored with such opportunity there."

"Go back and make deals for everything Charles can ship you. You speak their language well." William smiled as he stared at the snowy peaks and the vast stretches of prairie around Fort Laramie. "And I speak Cheyenne better than Bill Sublette ever could. There'll be a mountain of buffalo robes at the fort in a month."

"And I'll see that every silver peso is milked from Santa Fe!" promised Ceran. The two men shook hands on their informal deal.

Ambushed

Sangre de Cristo Mountains
May 12, 1834

"I reckon I prefer the mountains," Kit Carson said, glancing behind at the sharp-edged, rugged pine-covered Sangre de Cristos and then across the table-flat plains draining into the Cimarron River. "There's not even a decent tree to be seen up ahead. Think we shoulda taken Raton Pass to get to the fort?" He was responsible for getting the mule train safely to Bent's Fort, and worried about the lack of water since the Cimarron was almost dry this year. They hadn't bothered with wagons, preferring to use pack mules for the goods being moved north. That let them move faster than with heavily laden wagons, but it also required him to be certain of water for the mules. If they got balky, they weren't going to budge an inch.

"And it's hotter 'n hell out there, too. Ain't even summer yet. Not really," said Kit's right-hand man, Edwin Clarke. "It's so danged hot, it'll melt the balls off a bull."

"Gonna get hotter, from ever'thing I heard 'bout the Cheyenne and Pawnee," Kit said. He chewed a bit more, then spat a gob. "That truce between 'em isn't holding."

"You said it," Edwin declared. "We'd better get on to the fort fast as we kin. I'll feel a lot safer having them thick adobe walls all around me."

"And Conchita's there to keep you warm at night," Kit said, joshing his friend. Edwin had taken up with the daughter of a farmer outside Bent's Fort.

"Not warm, no, sir," Edwin said, grinning ear to ear. "Hot. She's hotter 'n a pistol and—" The man grunted as an arrow whistled through the air and embedded itself in his thigh.

"Where 'n hell'd that come from?" Kit cried, standing in his stirrups and looking around the flat country. No trees or bushes afforded cover for the unseen sniper. Then he spotted a feather poking up over the edge of the eroded bank of a deep gully.

"There!" Kit shouted at the same time Edwin and two of the four others spotted the Comanche raiders. How the Indians had hidden themselves so completely was something Kit would worry about later—if he still had his scalp.

He clumsily drew his pistols and discharged them at the nearest brave, who chanced another shot. Both of Kit's bullets struck the brave in the chest, sending him tumbling backward. As if by magic, another warrior popped up and loosed an arrow in Kit's direction. The feathered shaft missed his head by inches. Kit pulled out his rifle, hefted it to his shoulder, and tried to keep his mule from shying as he fired. The heavy recoil built and then kicked hard against his shoulder.

"You got the red bastard," Edwin called. "I got me one, too."

"Get down!" Kit called, seeing what his friend hadn't. The arroyo where they had killed the Comanche was filled with more warriors, more than Kit could count. "They're gonna attack!"

He slid off the back of his mule and grabbed at the animal's reins, jerking the head around. The mule took the barrage of arrows and staggered. Kit grabbed his knife and quickly drew it across the mule's throat. His hand turned red from the hot blood gushing forth, but he had put the mule out of its misery. There was no hope for it surviving with a dozen arrows buried in its side.

"We need somewhere to take cover, Kit," called another of the men. "They got us surrounded. How'd they sneak up on us like that?"

"I hate to say it, but they're sneakier than we are," Kit said. "Kill your mules and take cover behind them."

"But how're we gonna get out of here?" demanded Edwin.

"On foot, if we're still alive. There's no way we're ever going to outrun an entire Comanche war party, not with them on horses and us on mules." As he gave orders, Kit loaded his rifle, fired, winged another Comanche, and then started reloading again. He could load and shoot three times a minute, as long as he had enough powder and shot.

Dropping to one knee, Kit yanked free what black powder he had. He heaved a sigh of relief. There was plenty since he had been taking kegs of it back to Bent's Fort from Taos. Now he needed the shipment to stay alive. Like a machine, he loaded and fired until his rifle barrel was too hot to touch. Kit changed to his pistols, the Comanche coming in screaming waves.

"How long are they gonna let us kill 'em like this, Kit?" asked Edwin. His rifle barrel had turned so hot it had melted, making it useless. But he had scooped up another dropped by the man to his right, who had fought hand-to-hand with a Comanche brave and lost.

"As long as any of them are left standin', from the look of it," Kit said. He had never seen such single-minded attacks from any Indian, much less a Comanche war party. They came at them on foot and not mounted. That saved Kit's party—for the moment.

"I knew there was a reason I hated 'em so danged much," said Edwin. "Now I know. They're the ones what'll be responsible for liftin' my scalp!"

"Not yet, they aren't," Kit said, discharging both pistols point-blank into the back of a Comanche who had crawled up and then jumped over the dead mule Edwin used as a sanctuary. The brave spun around, his lips drawn back in a grimace. He let out a cry that chilled Kit's soul and then leaped at the mountain man.

Kit was bowled over as the warrior hit him. Grabbing the Comanche's wrist kept a knife from driving down into his chest, but Kit felt the brave's strength fading as they fought. With a mighty heave, he tossed the brave onto the still body of the mule, and then turned the man's knife around.

Panting, Kit stepped back. The brave's own horn-handled knife protruded from his chest.

"Down, Kit, git down!"

Kit dropped like a stone as a flight of arrows cut the air where he had stood an instant before. Edwin fired, cursed at missing, then fell into a steady string of inventive and improbable curses as he worked to reload.

"They're goin' for their horses! We run 'em off!" shouted another of the trappers.

Kit studied the Comanche and knew that wasn't the way it was.

"Reload. Load every rifle and pistol you can. When

the Comanche come for us, stagger the shots. Half of you shoot while the others reload. That's the only way we're going to get out of this with our scalps where they oughta be, on our heads."

Even as Kit spoke, he knew it would take a miracle to survive. A solid wall of mounted Comanche warriors thundered across the plains toward them.

"Pick 'em off," Kit said, wiping sweat out of his eyes. The sun was overhead now and getting hotter by the minute. His mouth felt like the inside of a cotton bale and his rifle was as hot from the sun as it was from firing.

Three shots rang out. The others waited for the three who had discharged their rifles to begin reloading; then they fired. The Comanche galloped closer and closer. Kit fired and was reloading when he saw the miracle they had needed happen before his eyes. The Comanches' horses shied away, the smell of the slaughtered mules spooking them.

Try as they might, the Comanche couldn't force their horses closer. Kit fired, began reloading, and then there was a lull in the attack. He sank down, resting against the belly of his dead mule and keeping his head down should any Comanche try to take a shot at him.

"We done it, Kit. We chased 'em off."

"How're the others?" Kit asked. "How're the rest of you holdin' up?"

"Fine as frog's fur, Kit," called the trapper to Edwin's other side. Even the man who had dropped his rifle was still alive and able to fire a pistol with his good hand. Loading the black powder pistol was a chore for him, but so far none of them had been killed.

"They'll wait us out," Kit said. "How much water do

we have?" He didn't like the answer. They had filled their canteens as they left the Sangre de Cristos, but had been drinking steadily as they made their way to the Cimarron River, where they had intended to refill and water their mules.

"It's past noon, Kit. You think them savages'll keep after us much longer?" Edwin's question was answered with war whoops and more arrows as the Comanche launched another attack, which was again blunted by the smell of the mules' blood.

Parched and shaking from strain, the six men hunkered down behind their dead mules for the rest of the day. When the sun sank behind the mountains Kit so desperately wished they had never left, the Comanche made a final attack.

It failed, as had every other attack.

"They're leavin'," Edwin said, but it was more of a question than a statement.

"You're right," Kit said. "They *are* hightailin' it." He flopped down and rested across the bulk of his mule. "A good thing since we don't have that much more powder and shot. So much for William makin' any profit on *our* supply train."

"How many'd we kill?" Edwin stood and walked toward the nearest of the dead foe on wobbly legs. The others began the count, taking what they could use from the bodies of the dead Comanche.

"I make it out to be forty-two we killed," Kit said, marveling at the number. He and his friends had been shot up pretty good, but they had survived. Forty-two warriors hadn't.

"What do we do now?" Edwin stared at the dead mules, then into the night after the departed Comanche war party.

"We get to walking," Kit said cheerfully. "It's only

seventy-five miles to the fort. And what a story we'll spin when we get there!"

"Yeah," said Edwin, "but who's gonna believe us?"

Peace?

Bent's Fort
June 28, 1834

"I shoulda gone with him," Kit Carson grumbled. He sat in the trade room, watching as William Bent shoved goods through the small window at the end of the room, exchanging buffalo robes for trinkets. "The Comanche'll have all our scalps."

"You did a good job showing them who's boss," William said, closing the wooden shutters and sinking into a chair. He wiped his face with a linen handkerchief. "Besides, Charles can take care of himself. There's less to fear from the Comanche on the trail to Taos than there is from the Mexicans."

"Ceran has 'em boxed in," Kit said. "He's got 'em all eatin' out of the palm of his hand."

"I wish that were so. Governor Peréz is making noises about taxing our shipments, no matter that Ceran is a Mexican citizen."

"It's Charles who's stirrin' the pot to boilin'," Kit said. "Puttin' him and Peréz together's worse 'n puttin' a Comanche with a Pawnee. That's not even mentionin' his troubles with Padre Antonio. Now that fella, even for a priest, is a firebrand and is gonna be the death of us all."

"How are your feet?" William asked suddenly.

"Fine. They been fine ever since I saw the fort poking up its brown adobe walls. They're ready to go out and kill more Comanche."

"Forty-two Comanche warriors," William said, shaking his head in amazement at Kit's feat. "Colonel Leavenworth ought to turn you loose against them."

"If he did that, you wouldn't have any of them red devils to trade with. You still thinkin' on a post down in Comanche country?"

"I am. It'd be dangerous but profitable."

"You said a mouthful," Kit said. A warning shout from the sentry on the walkway overhead echoed through the post and cut off any more of Kit's observations on the stupidity of trading with the Comanche, no matter how much profit might be gained.

"Cavalry comin'!"

"What's this about?" wondered William. He heaved to his feet and, Kit trailing, went to the heavy inner gate and opened it into the vestibule where Indians came to trade through the shuttered window in the wall. The metal-sheathed outer door was open, an invitation for all Indians to come do business. William shielded his eyes and looked past the gently waving green stalks of the tules to the northeast, and saw the regimental banner of the cavalry column heading in the direction of the fort.

"Get some food ready for them," William called back into the post. To Kit he said, "See if Ceran might have left a bottle or two about before he went to Santa Fe. If I know cavalry officers, they've developed quite a thirst out on the prairie eating dust."

"Reckon I might know where there's a bottle," Kit allowed. He hurried off to fetch the liquor, leaving William to greet the soldiers.

To William's surprise, he had never seen the officer

at the head of the column before. He had expected either Leavenworth or Colonel Dodge. He hitched up his trousers, then waited in front of the gate for the soldiers.

"Good morning, sir," the lieutenant greeted. He held up his hand and signaled for his column to halt.

"Howdy," William said. "If your men want to go around to the south, they can put their mounts into the corral, get some feed for them, and even sample some of our fine water."

"Sergeant," the lieutenant ordered, "do as the gentleman has so kindly invited."

"How are you, Mr. Bent?" called the sergeant, wiping dirt and bugs out of his bushy mustache.

"Sergeant Denning, it's been a long time."

"You know each other," the lieutenant said stiffly, cutting off any response from the enlisted man.

"Sergeant Denning rode with Colonel Leavenworth, the last I saw. The colonel must think highly of you to trust you with such a good man." William actually thought the reverse. Leavenworth had put the experienced sergeant with a shavetail lieutenant to keep him out of trouble until he learned how dangerous it could be chasing after Pawnee and Comanche raiding parties. Too many officers newly arrived from West Point underestimated the Indians, and even held them in contempt as ignorant savages. If they lived long enough to get over this arrogance, they sometimes made decent officers.

"That is the news I bring. You are William Bent?"

"I am," William said, thrusting out his hand. The lieutenant shook it in a strong grip.

"I'm Lieutenant Cooke. Phillip St. George Cooke."

"Come on inside, Lieutenant. Kit Carson's hunting up a bottle of whiskey, if you'd care for a touch of firewater while on duty." William saw the expression on Cooke's face and knew the lieutenant needed the shot of whiskey, duty be damned.

"The situation on the prairie is desperate, sir," Cooke said. They went to William's office, where Kit waited with the bottle and three shot glasses. Introductions were made, but Cooke remained distracted. William motioned to Kit to keep quiet and let the officer say his piece before relating how he had been set upon by a Comanche war party and the resulting massacre.

"Colonel Leavenworth is dead," Cooke said, after knocking back a shot of genuine Kentucky bourbon brought on Charles's last trip from St. Louis.

"Killed?" demanded Kit. He glanced at William, who again motioned him to silence.

"The colonel was an older man and could not stand the hot sun and the poor conditions on the trail," Cooke said. He licked his lips and stared at the bottle, as if he wanted to down every amber drop. William made no move to stop him as he poured another shot. "Colonel Dodge has assumed command."

"Leavenworth had been patrolling to the south to bring the Comanche to their knees," William said. "How's Colonel Dodge fared?"

"He . . . he has negotiated a peace with the Comanche."

Kit laughed harshly and said, "Mighty warm for hell to be freezin' over."

"It, well, it was not what he wanted, but I do not think the colonel had much stomach for the extended campaign required, especially after Colonel Leavenworth died so abruptly."

"So there's an official peace with the Comanche?" asked William. His mind raced, all the possibilities turning over and over. "Would Colonel Dodge sponsor a trading party into Comanche territory, say to the Red River?"

"The Good Lord only knows," Cooke said truthfully. "Malaria has broken out among our dragoons. This forces us to patrol with even fewer soldiers than usual."

"So the Comanche have agreed to a peace, but going into their territory would be mighty dangerous," William said.

"Don't even think on it, William," cautioned Kit. "Tradin' with them redskins'll get you kilt dead."

"There's no profit without risk," William said. "I'll wait for Charles to return from Taos before going south with a trading party."

He stared at Lieutenant Cooke, and saw the man was stunned at the notion of any civilian riding into the teeth of such a trap. That was what separated them, William decided. Cooke saw only the trouble and *he* saw the opportunity, as dangerous as it might be.

Thievery

"We should have stayed in Taos," complained a grizzled, filthy, buckskin-clad mule skinner to Charles Bent. "Them Injuns are raisin' too much of a ruckus for us to make it to the fort for our scalps to stay where they ought to be."

"I've heard the same rumors you have," Charles said, "and there's no danger. William is waiting for the mules." He fretted over how few trade goods he had obtained in Taos, but the mules were needed more than silver or even foodstuffs right now. Bent, St. Vrain & Company had wagon trains on the Santa Fe Trail constantly now, requiring ever more animals to pull them. William's notion of using oxen had been a good one that had kept the Comanche from stealing horses used to pull the wagons, but the oxen had proved too bulky and needed too much water for the long pull from Missouri to the fort, and then getting them over Raton Pass to Taos and Santa Fe had required more fodder than was likely to be found, especially during the summer drought. Mules turned out to be stronger, more dependable—and harder to find.

"That peace Colonel Dodge dickered with the Comanche ain't worth the paper it's writ on," the muleteer declared. He spat, wiped his mouth on a grimy sleeve, and shook his head. "Truth to tell, I don't recollect hearin' that anybody in Washington ever even *signed* a treaty with 'em."

"A man's word is his bond," Charles said. "Buffalo Hump controls most of the Comanche raiders. I'm sure Dodge made the agreement with him." Charles worried that the others in the party would hear the lie in his words. The brief message he had received from his brother had told of Lieutenant Phillip Cooke's visit to the fort and nothing more. He made up details to suit the situation, and wasn't sure Dodge had even spoken with the powerful Comanche leader.

"There's more 'n the Comanche to worry about, Mr. Bent," the mule skinner said. "But if you say it's gonna be an easy trip, and that you'll pay us double, we kin leave right now."

Charles almost balked like one of the mules. The men were trying to rob him by bringing up trouble with the Indians when all they wanted was more money. He reluctantly agreed. If he didn't get the herd of two hundred mules to the fort within the week, precious bales of buffalo robes would sit around. It was getting late in the summer, and the hides had to be prepared for transport to New York and Europe once they reached St. Louis. Time closed in, and with it Charles felt the company's funds slipping away like sand through an hourglass.

"Done," he said, shaking on the deal. Better to pay a little extortion now than to miss the opportunity to sell a thousand buffalo robes in Europe, where the market was insatiable for the soft, fleecy-downed hides.

Charles climbed onto a mule and quickly fell into the rocking, swaying motion. He had spent enough time in the saddle to learn how to sleep without actually sleeping. An hour outside Taos, he jerked awake and looked around frantically.

"What's wrong, Mr. Bent?" asked the mule skinner. The man cracked his long whip to keep a dozen of the mules from wandering off. They were lightly roped together, and all he needed to do was persuade the one that had decided to be leader to return to the path and not go dine on a clump of grama grass near the road. Herding horses was easier. Herding cats was easier.

But that wasn't what bothered Charles. He swiveled around and studied the land ahead. They had entered a canyon leading north. From there they would swing out onto the plains north of Santa Fe and ride up through Raton Pass before reaching the fort. He had made the trip dozens of times, but never had he felt this uneasy.

"I feel as if somebody's walking on my grave," Charles said.

"We kin turn round and go back," the muleteer said. The man spat, wiped his mouth again, and looked not the least disturbed. After all, he was getting paid double wages, whether they pressed on to Bent's Fort or returned to Taos.

"No," Charles decided. The more he stared at the rocky terrain, the less he saw that posed any danger. However, the feeling in his gut refused to go away. He kept thinking of how the Comanche had so mindlessly attacked Kit Carson and his caravan of laden mules. He trusted Kit's abilities completely, and if the frontiersman had said the Indians simply popped up out of nowhere, that was gospel.

"We'll make camp early tonight," Charles decided. "There's an artesian spring free of sulfur not three miles off. We can water the mules there."

"I know the spot. Good place to watch the mules, too. We kin put 'em into a box canyon that's better 'n any corral."

Charles said nothing, but rested his hand on the pistol thrust into his belt. They reached the hot springs and saw to watering the mules at a pool where the water cooled to a bearable temperature. As much as he wanted to take a bath in the warmer water bubbling from the ground higher on the rocky slopes, Charles chose to stand watch over the mules. He had close to two hundred of the balky, braying beasts and every one was precious to him and the company.

Just past sundown the Shoshoni attacked.

Retribution

North of Taos
July 29, 1834

"Too bad Kit took off on his own," William Bent
said. "We could use him."

Charles Bent looked at his brother. They had made
good time from the fort returning to the spot where
the Shoshoni had stolen the mules. The fight ten days
earlier had been brief but fierce, encouraging Charles
to tell the muleteers to let the Indians take the animals. Better to lose a couple hundred mules than for
the men to be killed. That decision had not sat well
with anyone, least of all Charles, but staying alive to
trade again another day made more sense than fool-
ishly tangling with an unknown number of braves in
the dark and in their element.

"We've not done so badly on our own," William
said, leaning over to study the rocky ground for
tracks. Following a herd of mules didn't require Kit
Carson's skill, although it was surprisingly harder than
Charles had anticipated.

"You've learned how to track from the Cheyenne,"
his brother said. Then Charles grinned. "Are you im-
pressing Owl Woman by your skill?"

"Why'd you say that?" William asked too sharply. He
pointedly did not look up at his brother and kept his

face away, toward the ground and the tracks left by their quarry.

"You're sweet on her. I can tell by the way you look at her. Making excuses to see Gray Thunder doesn't hide what's obvious. Does she like you, too?"

"I think so," William said, dropping his facade of indignation. "But whatever tracking skills I have learned were all taught me by Ceran."

"He taught you well," Charles said, reaching out to put a hand on his brother's arm to congratulate him, both on his abilities and how things went with Owl Woman. Charles pulled back and sniffed hard, catching the scent of burning mesquite mingled with searing meat. A cook fire. The way the grassy meadow had been cut up showed that their stolen mules had been brought this way recently. Perhaps all the animals were grazing nearby under the watchful eyes of their thieves, but Charles couldn't be sure.

"How many Shoshoni do you think there are?" asked William. "The mule tracks obscure their number."

"When they attacked, it might have been a hundred. Or they might have relied on our confusion and been fewer than a dozen. I don't know."

"Well, I know one thing for sure," William said decisively. "We'll get our mules back or know the reason." He pulled two pistols from his belt and cocked them. He had two rifles slung over his shoulder. Charles was similarly armed from the ample armory in Bent's Fort. William lifted his hand and signaled to the three trappers who had volunteered to come with them from the fort.

The men were understandably nervous, but advanced bravely enough when William pointed in the direction of the clump of juniper where the cooking fire blazed merrily. William advanced quicker than the others, more the frontiersman than his older brother. And a good thing it was, too, that he was in the vanguard. He spotted the Shoshoni lookout perched in the crook of a limb before the Indian saw him.

William shrugged off his two rifles and thrust his pistols into his belt, then drew his knife. Moving like a shadow, he went to the base of the tree and looked up. The Shoshoni brave had fallen asleep when he should have been alert.

Slipping around the tree, William found a gnarled knob on the trunk that would support his weight. He judged distances, then heaved himself up. The surge caused long branches to rustle and woke the sentry— but it was too late. William grabbed a long braid of hair and jerked the man's head back. The knife flashed in the dim starlight and then turned black as the Shoshoni's lifeblood gushed out. He died without a sound.

William left the sentry dangling over the tree limb and retrieved his rifles. Charles saw the bloody knife and shuddered, but he knew the killing had been necessary. Until they learned how many braves they faced, they had to be cautious.

Advancing again through the clump of trees, they came to a small clearing. William counted quickly, then glanced at Charles, who held up both hands and wiggled his fingers. Both had counted ten more braves in the raiding party. They were outnumbered two to one, but had the element of surprise on their side.

From across the clearing William saw another man from the fort waving to catch his attention. The man gestured wildly, then showed he had found sixty of the stolen mules.

"Ready?" William whispered to his brother. He saw how Charles gripped his pistols.

Without waiting for an answer, William stepped out into plain sight and called, "Give us back our mules and we'll let you live!"

For a moment, there was no reaction in the camp. Then the braves went for their bows and arrows and rifles. William repeated his demand in Shoshoni. For an instant, the braves froze, and it seemed that William would get his way. Then someone fired wildly. He could not tell if the shot came from the Shoshoni or one of the anxious men from the fort.

William blazed away with both pistols, then thrust them into his belt and jerked around a musket, which discharged with a loud *pop!* and a flash that dazzled the eyes of the Indians. This gave William's allies a chance to fire, reload, and fire again.

By this time, the surviving Shoshoni had lit out and vanished into the night.

"Wait," called Charles to the others. "Let them go. We can get back our mules. That's what's important."

"Charles is right," William said, knowing the blood lust the others had shown wouldn't be easily quenched. Besides the guard he had killed, two other Indians sprawled across logs, dead by their campfire. "They know this country and would only try to spring a trap on us."

The others grumbled, but the surge of fighting spirit was already draining from them. Driving the recaptured mules back to the fort would take a considerable amount of skill and effort, and none of them fancied himself an Indian fighter, at least not like Kit Carson or William Bent.

"We showed them," William went on. "They'll think twice before stealing anything from Bent, St. Vrain and Company again!"

They left the braves where they had fallen, and recovered sixty-seven mules greatly needed to pull supply wagons across the prairie back to Missouri. Trade might be slowed for a few weeks, but it could never be stopped.

Victories

Bent's Fort
August 2, 1835

"You look all tuckered out, Colonel," Charles Bent said, eyeing Colonel Dodge from head to foot. The cavalry officer's uniform was a mottled brown from the prairie dust, and his face was caked with mud where the trail dust had settled in the rivulets of sweat that poured constantly from his forehead.

"My men have endured a considerable campaign this summer, sir," Dodge told the proprietor of the trading post.

"I've heard how you've been fighting all across Kansas. You've been running the Pawnee ragged." Charles saw the tired columns of soldiers, and wondered what it would take to get a government contract to outfit and supply the dragoons. He doubted it would be profitable to furnish saddle-broken horses, but food, blankets, and other items would be needed on a regular basis.

"And I've heard how you've been making obscene profits," Dodge said, grinning. "Is it true you buy the buffalo robes from the Indians for two bits and sell them in Independence and St. Louis for six dollars?"

"You're making it more profitable for us by the minute, Colonel," Charles said, not wanting to get into a discussion of the Bent, St. Vrain & Company finances. "Every wagon train that arrives in Missouri unscathed is that much better for everyone. And bringing back supplies keeps our, uh, friends in Santa Fe pacified."

"Pacified," grumbled Dodge. Both men knew the reports from New Mexico Territory were anything but peaceable. The colonel looked around and asked, "Is St. Vrain in Santa Fe?"

"Taos," Charles said. "He's a miracle worker when it comes to dealing with the Mexicans. He speaks their language as if he had been born there."

"He shares their religion, too, from what I hear. Where's your younger brother?"

"Do you mean William or one of the others?" Charles had brought George and Robert from St. Louis to help with the chore of running Bent's Fort. Both had proven to be godsends. Robert, the youngest, had taken to trading like a fish to water. George was more flamboyant, almost a copy of Ceran St. Vrain in the way he approached life with gusto, and a perfect companion for Marcellin St. Vrain at their northern fort.

"The crazy one who's causing such a stir down south. I can't believe he is trading with the Comanche."

"We've established a small trading post at Abode Walls," Charles said. "William is down there with Robert right now, making certain the right contacts are made. William says he'll be back home soon. I miss him since he's been gone for so long."

"Four months, is it?" asked Dodge.

"Nothing passes you by, does it, Colonel?" Charles ushered the officer into the *placita,* and from there to the dining room, where the table had been set with a linen tablecloth and fine china and silver. "Charlotte has prepared quite a nice meal for us."

Dodge licked his lips as he eyed the sumptuous food set out on the table. The black cook stood in the doorway, arms crossed and looking pleased at his reaction to her meal.

"Don't go insulting Charlotte by refusing to eat. We'll see that your men are well fed and your horses taken care of."

"There's no money for it. The Secretary of War cuts back our rations—and monetary allocations—constantly."

"Yes, yes, I know. Preparations for war with Mexico, now that you have so ably quelled the Pawnee and made peace with the Comanche."

Colonel Dodge snorted, knowing that the peace was as flimsy as could be. He hesitated, then sat at the table.

"We can discuss such matters over dinner," Dodge said. "Then I must go to the Cheyenne camp. There's been trouble with them raiding Pawnee villages to the north, and I want to be sure the war between the tribes isn't reignited."

The meal went smoothly and afterward, Charles and the colonel shared a fine cigar from the post stores. Their discussion rambled all over the prairie, ranging from trade to Indians to the probability of war with Mexico. Charles was almost sorry to see Colonel Dodge leave, having enjoyed a gentleman's conversation on topics not usually brought up among trappers and the Indians coming to trade. With some regret Charles watched Colonel Dodge mount his column and ride away in the direction of the Cheyenne village a few miles east. He shrugged and returned to his work. There were too many details to be dealt with if he wanted a successful trading season in St. Louis.

* * *

"Riders from the south, sir," reported Dodge's scout. "Not moving too fast, just sorta amblin' along."

Colonel Dodge took out his field glasses, wiped dust from the lenses, and turned them on the riders. He was afraid it might be Bull Hump or other Comanche raiders coming to ruin the peace with the Cheyenne. He had to keep the Cheyenne and Pawnee from each others' throats. Having the Comanche stirring the pot right now would be too much. The only outcome would be an all-out war that would engulf the entire prairie from Missouri to the Rockies.

He heaved a sigh of relief when he saw four wagons pulled by mules with white men at the reins. Dodge even jumped a little when the crack of a twenty-foot-long whip rolled across the land like thunder from the small wagon train.

"Mule skinners," he said. Dodge waited while the scout studied the men using his own field glasses.

"Might be the other Bent brother. The one what built Bent's Fort."

"William Bent?" Dodge frowned, then considered what this meant. "We'll escort them a ways. I want to hear what he has to say about trading with the Comanche."

"He might not want to tip his hat to you, Colonel," the scout said. "Might be there's no hair left after the Comanche finished with him."

Dodge had to laugh. If William Bent was returning from his trading post at Adobe Walls with such heavily laden wagons, that meant it was the Comanche who had been scalped. He passed the order along to his sergeant and wheeled the column southward toward the Arkansas River. In less than an hour the two parties met.

"Pleased to see you so hale and hearty, Mr. Bent," Dodge called.

"I wasn't expecting an escort, Colonel," William said. "Much obliged. Been too long since I've seen any white faces except these ugly gents." He poked his driver in the ribs with his elbow. The muleteer grunted and didn't look amused at the joshing.

"What's the situation like, down along the Red River?"

"Unpredictable, Colonel, that's the only way to describe it. But profitable for those willing to take the risk. I spent three months trading with the Comanche. They can be lying, thieving murderers, but if it's in their best interest to trade, they will. And they did."

"My company just came from your fort. I reckon you can find your way back safely from here," Dodge said, having learned what he wanted to know. The Comanche had not changed—and neither had they taken it into their heads to go on the warpath. Yet.

"I wasn't heading directly back," William said. "I was going to stop by the Cheyenne village at Big Timbers and see . . . how things are."

Dodge wondered at the slight hesitation. William Bent had no reason to be reticent about palavering with the Cheyenne. His good services had kept them peaceable when many hotheaded braves in the tribe had wanted to make war on the Pawnee and Comanche.

"Then it would be my pleasure to escort you there. I need to speak with Chief Yellow Wolf about keeping a lid on raiding. It's to no one's benefit if war erupts."

"My sentiments, also, Colonel," William said. He

gave directions to the driver and reared back as the wagon lurched off, the team of mules pulling strongly. Colonel Dodge watched the way the wagon wheels cut into the soft prairie shortgrass. Bent's trading expedition had been exceptionally lucrative, if weight meant anything.

They rode to the Cheyenne village, arriving in the late afternoon. Dodge frowned when he saw the frenetic activity. Dancers around the medicine lodge in the center of the village were decked out in full war gear. He deployed his men so that they could fight their way out, if the need arose. He glanced at William and saw the man's interest. But there was no sign of worry. This put Dodge a little more at ease—but not too much.

"What do you think is going on?" Colonel Dodge asked.

"It's not a war dance, if that's what you thought, Colonel," William said. "It's a victory dance, but it usually goes on around a bonfire. There's Gray Thunder. I'll ask. And his daughters."

Again Dodge looked strangely at William Bent. Then he sucked in his breath. William had detoured from a direct road back to his fort to see Gray Thunder's daughters. Or at least one of them. But which? Dodge smiled slightly, trying to figure that out. William turned formal and his eyes never left the medicine man as he approached, hands outstretched and holding shiny tin trinkets.

This told Dodge even more. William should have been able to trade the bracelets and beads he offered to Gray Thunder for a decent profit. That he offered them as gifts to the medicine man—and his daughters—convinced Dodge that William was sweet on one of the women.

William spoke at length to Gray Thunder, then beckoned the colonel over.

"Gray Thunder has good news, Colonel. He traveled far to the north and found a Pawnee village."

Dodge stiffened. No matter what William said, this was a victory dance of some sort.

"Don't worry so, Colonel," William said. "Gray Thunder is a great man, clever and wise. He found one of the Sacred Arrows stolen by the Pawnee and recovered it. There are now two medicine arrows hanging in the lodge."

"The Pawnee didn't object?" Dodge feared that the Pawnee who had possession of the Sacred Arrow might never complain, unless he could do it through a slit throat.

"Much wampum was traded," William said. He glanced at the nearer woman, then back quickly. "Gray Thunder is a great medicine man and has recovered that which Sweet Medicine gave his tribe so many summers ago."

"Excellent," Colonel Dodge said. He cleared his throat and began his lecture on how the Cheyenne were a responsible people and how he entrusted them with maintaining the peace in eastern Colorado. It wasn't long before the officer noticed his only audience was Gray Thunder, William having slipped away with both women.

By the time Dodge left the Cheyenne village, he felt better that Gray Thunder had succeeded in finding his tribe's sacred relic and returning it to the wolf-skin sheath. This afforded less reason to fight the Pawnee. Dodge vowed to find the two remaining Sacred Arrows and return them to Gray Thunder. That would increase his prestige with the tribe and give even greater leverage in keeping the peace.

It was lonely out on the plains, but Dodge preferred it that way. Fighting Pawnee and Comanche and Arapaho and Cheyenne every inch of the way alleviated the boredom by substituting constant fear.

Marriage

William Bent looked around the gathering and tried not to appear too uncomfortable. The high society of Taos had come to the villa to celebrate the marriage of his brother to Maria Ignacia Jaramillo, who stood on the far side of the room with her family clustered around her, her father in the forefront and gesturing firmly.

"There's no need for him to give her advice about her wedding night," Ceran St. Vrain said, coming up to hand William a glass of sangria.

"Where is Rumalda? I don't see her anywhere." William looked around for Ignacia's four-year-old daughter, but the young girl was nowhere to be seen.

"Perhaps her grandfather doesn't want her to see the marriage," Ceran suggested. "But no, that's ridiculous. Charles has been a father to the girl since her father died and she loves him dearly, as much as Ignacia. All the people of Taos love your brother."

"All?" William laughed harshly. "The parish priest would see him dead before marriage to a good Catholic like Ignacia."

"Antonio Martinez is a difficult man," Ceran agreed.

"But the good father can't stop the way everyone flocks to Charles when they have trouble."

"I wish Charles wouldn't pretend to be a doctor. He's going to kill someone someday."

"He knows more medicine than anyone else here. Hasn't he read widely and watched the Cheyenne medicine man gather the proper roots and herbs? And he never charges a single centavo for any cure. He is a saint to them."

"That might be true, but if they love him so, why does he have to call himself a surveyor? We should be honest in what we do. There's no shame in being a merchant. Company trading does more to keep them alive than Charles's half-baked doctoring skills."

"You're forgetting the law," Ceran said, sobering. "I can trade because I am a citizen—and a Catholic. You and Charles cannot because you are Americans—and Protestants."

"Father Antonio will never bless the marriage. The only way it could be worse is if Ignacia's husband had divorced her."

"But that didn't happen," Ceran said. "He had the misfortune to die and leave a young, beautiful, grieving widow who is prepared to marry the most successful 'surveyor' in Taos."

"Her father is arguing against it because Charles isn't of the same faith."

"Señor Jaramillo will have little to say about it. Look," Ceran said. "See the señora? If her husband weren't in the way, *she* would marry your brother, elbowing her own daughter out of the way. They love him, William. Don Francisco is protesting only to keep peace with Padre Antonio. He approves of Charles. Everything will be fine."

"She is beautiful, that I will say," William said, staring at Ignacia. Long raven hair fell down her back, jeweled combs holding it in place. A mantilla around her shoulders would soon be pulled over her head, in concession to Catholic practice, although the minister Charles had brought in was not of that faith. Ignacia's wide, dark eyes darted about, showing she tired of her father urging her to abandon this marriage. She was a strong-willed woman, although she was hardly twenty, and knew what she wanted.

She loved Charles.

"Papa, enough," William heard Ignacia say. She took her father by the shoulders, stood on tiptoe, and gave him a quick kiss, then flipped the lace mantilla over her head and hurried forward to stand beside Charles.

"The ceremony begins," Ceran said, pointing to Rumalda's dueña leading the small girl back into the room. "Let's not spoil this happy day for your brother."

"Never, Ceran, never," William said, though he wondered how it could end in anything but grief since Charles had already bought a house north of the plaza and intended to live there with his new family, rather than at the fort surrounded by friends and relatives.

Rebellion

Santa Fe, New Mexico Territory
June 7, 1835

"They want us to pay taxes!" cried the distraught Mexican serape merchant. "This is outrageous! How dare they let a man like Albino Peréz do this to us!"

"Yes," chimed in another sitting at the huge rectangular table in the main room of Manuel Armijo's home. Barely enough room permitted Armijo and his servants to walk behind the angry men gathered to complain about the injustice of the governor, but it was enough. The servants kept wineglasses filled, and Armijo whispered first to one and then another of the affronted men he had summoned to his hacienda.

"Peréz ordered me to leave my post," Armijo said when the men ranting about the injustice of taxes paused to suck in new breaths. "I am no longer collector of customs." Armijo tried to keep his voice with just the right touch of sadness, because he knew what moved these men. They were peasants who had become merchants and tradesmen, richer than if they had stayed in Mexico—richer than many of those ruling the distant province from Mexico City.

That was the crux of the problem facing them all. Governor Peréz had been ordered to begin the accursed taxation of all Mexican citizens because of increasing rebellion, both in Mexico and along the fraying edges of its far-flung empire. The Texians were closer than ever to gaining their independence, and the Mexican government needed money to pay soldiers, outfit armies, keep the peones in central Mexico in line even as Santa Anna crushed the seditious Texians, who had tasted freedom once too often.

"We had not heard, Don Manuel!" One man shot to his feet. "This is an outrage! You, who were governor, know our hearts and souls better than Peréz ever could, and yet they removed you."

"I cannot collect the levies from the American traders, because Peréz steals it." Armijo paused a moment, then held out his hands as if pushing away from a dinner table, distancing himself from his own remarks. His dark eyes flashed and he worked to smooth the thin tips of his mustaches. He was not a tall man, and his command came from presence. Whenever he walked into a room, men took notice. Armijo looked around and knew they would follow his orders, no matter what he asked of them.

Even treason.

"I should not be so bold," Armijo went on in a more conspiratorial tone. "Peréz might be an honorable man doing what his masters in far-off Mexico City tell him to do. But I am forced to ask a simple question: How much reaches the official coffers and how much goes into a hidden strongbox?" He shook his head sadly and said, "I cannot say."

"He is a thief, a pirate, a crook!" raged another of the merchants.

"I am only an ordinary citizen now, as are you all," Armijo said, waiting for the response he wanted. It came quickly.

"No, they cannot remove you! Who will keep the Americans honest? They try to sneak in their trade goods now without paying any duty! Let them pay so we can continue our trade untaxed!"

Armijo let the indignation rise against the Americans before he spoke again. It was always good to focus on a scapegoat other than the government. Santa Anna was not a forgiving ruler, and simply replacing Peréz was not enough.

"All you say is true, but what can we do?" Armijo said humbly. "I am no longer an official of the government, no matter what posts I have filled so humbly before."

"You should be governor again!"

"Are you talking rebellion against Santa Anna? He is a powerful general," Armijo said. "It would be foolish for us to openly call for rebellion against him—and Peréz."

"What are you saying, Don Manuel?" asked another, a gray-haired ranchero who had watched liked a hawk until this moment. Of all the men assembled, he represented true wealth and ties with Spain before Mexico had gained its independence. "Perhaps someone else affected by the laws Peréz chooses to enforce might rise against him?"

"The Pueblo Indians have no liking for our current governor," Armijo said obliquely, "but I treated them with fairness. Their stake in avoiding onerous taxation is as great as, perhaps greater than, ours. They are poor, and would become even poorer should these new taxes be collected."

"A good idea," the gray-haired rancher said, his lips curling slightly in a smile that was almost a sneer. "But they need a leader. Who might this be, Don Manuel?"

"Why, I have heard that they have come across a few

crates filled with muskets and ammunition enough for an uprising. Who better to lead the revolt than José Gonzales?"

"The Taos Indian? Isn't he a buffalo hunter? What does he know of politics? What does he care about taxes?" asked one of the slower members of the cabal, one who probably did not even comprehend that he was part of a conspiracy.

"He shoots straight. Should Peréz come into the sights of Señor Gonzales, none would leap to their feet in defense of our governor."

A few chuckled at the table, while several others looked perplexed and whispered back and forth among themselves, trying to make sense of all this. Armijo took careful note of those who understood fully the machinery he had set in motion, as well as those who did not. Both groups would be useful later.

"Gather your vaqueros and your rifles, señores," Armijo said. "I think I hear the rebellion beginning."

Manuel Armijo tried to keep from smiling. He had rallied more than one hundred armed vaqueros, all ready to follow him into battle. But Armijo knew he had to choose carefully his first fight.

"There!" he called. "Americans! They try to sneak into Santa Fe and avoid our taxes!" He charged forward, his magnificent stallion snorting and reveling in the heady feeling of leading so many other horses. Behind him Armijo heard the others, slower to respond, finally pick up the cry and advance on the traders' wagon train.

"Halt!" Armijo called. "Stop and be searched!"

"Searched?" called the muleteer with the long blacksnake whip. The man curled the whip, then let it uncoil slowly. A flick of his wrist caused it to pop softly. Armijo drew rein just out of reach of that dangerous weapon.

"You try to avoid paying taxes."

"I ain't doin' no such thing," the freighter snapped. "I pay at the customs office in Santa Fe. We been on the trail a powerful long time and I ain't in the mood to deal with . . . *bandidos.*"

Armijo laughed loudly, turned so his words could be heard, and then called, "He calls us thieves! He is the one trying to avoid paying the tariffs due on his goods."

"I brung these wagons along the Cimarron Cutoff straight from Independence. I fought Pawnee, I fought Comanche, I fought every damn inch of the way. I didn't get this close to Santa Fe to let a bunch of *bandidos* rob me!" He reared back, a powerful arm ready to send the whip lashing out. The freighter stopped when he heard a dozen muskets cock.

Armijo did not have to look to know the men behind him had drawn a bead on the teamster and the others in his wagon train.

"Pay your tariff now, Señor," Armijo said coldly. "Pay and be on your way, or refuse and die!"

Grumbling but acceding to the overwhelming force facing him, the teamster dug out a strongbox and began counting the money demanded of him. Armijo pushed him aside, slammed the lid on the box, and hefted the money aloft, his arm shaking under the weight.

"Let us go deliver our bounty to the governor!" Armijo called.

The response he received was all he could have hoped for. Passing the gold back to a vaquero, Armijo put his Spanish-rowled spurs to his stallion's flanks and rocketed off in the direction of Santa Fe. He knew what he would find there.

It was time to become a hero.

The sporadic, ineffectual fighting up and down the twisting Santa Fe streets showed the governor's troops were still trying to regain control. Manuel Armijo quickly took in the situation when he found a pike thrust into the middle of the town plaza with Peréz's head mounted on it. He stared at what remained of the governor and sardonically saluted him. Armijo rallied his small army and pointed out what happened to those who failed.

"The Indians scorn our control," he said, although the men with him knew Armijo would have done the same thing to Peréz should he have caught him first. "We must retake our fair Santa Fe! Death to the rebels!"

A ragged cheer ripped from the throats of the vaqueros.

Armijo rode to the customs shed and dismounted. He stopped in the doorway and with great fanfare cried, "This will be our headquarters. Bring me the tariffs collected from the American traders."

The heavy box rattled as it landed on the sturdy desk. Armijo pulled up a chair and sat behind the desk, opened the strongbox, and carefully stacked the gold coins so they were lined up in front of him like ranks of dragoons waiting for inspection by their commanding officer.

"Any soldier who once served the governor that joins our army receives one gold coin," Armijo said. "Tell them that. And if they do not rush here to accept this fine offer, shoot them. If you see any Indian rebel, shoot on sight!"

An uneasy stir went through the crowd of vaqueros as they realized they were caught in the middle of a deadly battle for control of the territorial capital. Then Armijo rallied them with fine words and honeyed promises and sent them rushing into the streets. He jerked as the first volley sounded like thunder, but the answering cries of pain and curses from wounded Indian rebels heartened him.

In two days, Santa Fe was enduring an uneasy peace. José Gonzales had been executed for treason, and Manuel Armijo was again governor.

Vigilance

"I wish Charles were off the trail," William Bent said, hands clasped behind his back as he stared from the ramparts of the fort. He didn't look at anything in particular. Rather, his eyes focused on distant events—fights he could not see, all the men dying he could never hope to save.

"He's safe enough," Ceran St. Vrain said. "It's our men in New Mexico that we need to worry about."

"Have you heard from Kit?" William began pacing along the narrow walkway, passing the small one-inch cannon and touching it from time to time. Its cool brass barrel calmed him a little. No matter what storm blew in from the south, the fort could withstand it as it had withstood Comanche attacks and other incursions. He had built well. Still, William worried.

"He's romancing that Arapaho woman, Waa-nibe," Ceran said in a neutral voice. William knew Ceran, with his aristocratic upbringing and French heritage, did not approve of Singing Bird. William had never met her, but if Kit loved her, that was fine with William.

"I hope he keeps out of trouble," William said. "Word came the other day that Armijo is making increasing trouble for Americans."

"Ever since he robbed the wagons to fund his rebellion, he's done nothing but harass us."

"Not us, Ceran, only Americans. Keep your Mexican citizenship and you'll be safe."

"I don't know about the company property, though," Ceran said. "Armijo is whipping up sentiment against everything owned by any American. Charles is a target because Padre Antonio rails against him so often. Armijo is a snake in the grass and will go along with anyone, even the priest, if it means he can consolidate his power."

"It's good that Charles is on the way back from Independence," William said. "I hope he hasn't heard of the trouble in Santa Fe. He could never stand seeing Ignacia put into danger, and would leave the wagons to ride directly back to Taos."

"Charles can take care of himself and the business of Bent, St. Vrain and Company at the same time," Ceran said.

William looked at his friend. "You're worried, too. I can tell."

"Of course I worry. If Armijo doesn't bleed us dry or hang us all because he needs a scapegoat, then the Texians will invade."

"I'm not that worried about the Texians," William said. "Houston doesn't have two pennies to rub together to finance any invasion, and his legislature can't raise taxes enough to even run their own government."

"You've heard the rumors Armijo's spreading about how we supplied the Pueblo Indians with arms so they could overthrow the Mexicans." Ceran turned grim and stroked his thick black beard as he talked. "He wants our scalps, William. Mark my words, Armijo is a dangerous man with more ambition than's good for anyone."

"I'd heard he was telling everyone the Texians had supplied the Pueblos with their muskets. I suppose people can believe both lies at the same time as easily as not believing anything Armijo says." William frowned and stared toward the south. "A rider's coming."

"It might be a courier," Ceran said. "I hired a half-dozen men to bring news, should anything important happen."

William and Ceran leaned over the battlement and peered down at the breathless rider.

"Mr. Bent, sir. Ceran!" he called. "They done got 'im. They throwed him in jail!"

"What? Who are you talking about? Kit?" demanded Ceran.

"No, Mr. Bent. Charles. He was headin' on home to Taos when he ran afoul of one of Armijo's patrols. They throwed him in jail!"

"We've got to rescue him," William said. "Ceran, get a dozen men. If that's not enough, I'll raise an army! By damn, Armijo's not going to get away with this!"

"Are you sure, man? Are you certain Charles has been imprisoned?"

"I seen him bein' led off with my own eyes!"

It took an hour to get provisions together, and another hour after that before the small rescue party hit the trail for Raton Pass. William rode in silence, his anger growing with every passing mile. Ceran plied the courier, who returned with them, with questions about the guard around Charles and how likely they were to need force to free him.

Ceran finally rode up to pace William.

"Armijo is jailing all Americans, but he was on the lookout for Charles in particular."

"Padre Antonio," William said, seething.

"I'm sure Armijo and Antonio Martinez are in

cahoots," Ceran said. "The padre never cottoned much to Ignacia marrying Charles."

"Negotiation won't work," William said, a hand resting on one of the pistols thrust into his belt. "We're going to fight."

"It'll be no good riding in brandishing guns," Ceran said. "Charles will keep his head. It's up to us to figure out the best way of freeing him, and taking on Armijo isn't it. Armijo is looking for a reason to seize all the company property. We've got stores in Santa Fe and Taos to lose."

"You're—" began William.

"I'm a Mexican citizen," Ceran cut in, "but he would force me to go to court in Mexico City to recover our stores. There wouldn't be anything left by then. Armijo is a dangerous fellow."

"Charles, Ignacia, and Rumalda will be safer at the fort than in Taos," William said, as if he hadn't heard anything Ceran said.

"Riders ahead! I see 'em coming out of the pass."

William reined back and stood in the stirrups to see what they faced. He did a quick estimate and said, "No more than three or four, all riding hell-bent for leather."

"We outnumber them two to one," Ceran said. "And that might be more of the couriers I hired."

"Get the men off the road where they can cover us if those are Armijo's men," William said. "Go with them, Ceran. I'm trusting my life to you."

"I won't fail you," Ceran said, positioning the men to catch the approaching riders in a cross fire, should it be necessary.

Less than ten minutes passed before the lead rider came around a bend in the road and William identified him.

"Charles!" William galloped forward. "You're safe!"

"William, you were coming for me. There's no need. I got away from that conniving bastard."

From horseback, they hugged awkwardly, and William reared back in the saddle and waved to Ceran and the others.

"You *were* coming to free me," Charles said, smiling now.

"How'd you get away?" asked William. "Are there soldiers after you?"

"Bribery," Charles said bluntly. "I bribed my way out. Ignacia's father took the money to Armijo. I wanted to threaten to burn Taos to the ground, but thought better of it."

"I would have, if they had harmed one hair on your head."

Charles looked back in the direction of Raton Pass, as if itching to return along the road he had already ridden.

"Ignacia and Rumalda?" asked Ceran.

"They're still in Taos. Safe, for the time being, but if Armijo—"

"Don't worry about them," Ceran said. "Go to the fort. I'll take a few of the men who've come this far with me and see to them."

"Her father isn't likely to permit them to leave," Charles said. "Don Francisco isn't an Armijo supporter, but he's not entirely on our side, either. What he did was for his daughter and granddaughter, not me."

"I'll watch over your women," Ceran said sternly. "If they won't go to the fort, then I'll stand guard at their door and no one will pass!"

"It's my place—" Charles began.

"It's your place to stay clear of Armijo for the time being. Why'd you abandon the wagon train? Where is it? In the middle of the Kansas prairie?" William turned into a magpie chattering out his questions and keeping Charles busy answering.

Ceran motioned for William to take his brother back to the safety of the fort. He would see to the Bent women in Taos. And God in heaven would not save Manuel Armijo if he had harmed even one hair on their heads.

Another Marriage

"I'm glad you could come, Charles," William Bent said to his older brother. "I see that you brought Ignacia, too. Wasn't the trip dangerous for her?"

"She is doing fine so far," Charles said, looking across the fort's *placita,* where his pregnant wife sat peacefully on a short stool, waiting for him to arrange for their quarters.

"Still, you lost the last child after the dustup with Armijo in Taos."

"But we have another, in addition to Rumalda," Charles said. "Armijo has left us alone, for the most part. It's to his advantage to get trade goods into New Mexico, since almost everything's been cut off from Mexico for the past several months. But enough of me. When is the wedding?"

"You're hoping it'll be within ten minutes, I see," William said, smiling wanly.

"No, no, there's no reason for us to hurry back to Taos. All that happens there is interminable harassment by Padre Antonio and the occasional military patrol sent by Armijo. I want to stay around long enough to throw you a fandango that'll be remembered like the old Green River Rendezvous."

"I wish you would move back to the fort, into American country at least, where you're safe."

"Safe? Hardly," said Charles with a laugh. "The Comanche are still raiding constantly. I hear you've even had to fire the fort cannon a few times to keep them at bay." Then he sobered and said, "Do the raids bother you enough to postpone your marriage?"

"Not at all," William said. "Owl Woman agrees this is a good time to get married. Gray Thunder is counseling the warriors not to go on the warpath."

"The Sacred Arrows," Charles said, nodding. "Any trace of the remaining pair?"

"Not so far, but there are always rumors that the Pawnee still have them. The replacement arrows ordered by the chiefs aren't the same, and the Cheyenne know it."

"Is that your dowry?" Charles pointed to a wagon laden with trade goods.

"Something for everyone in the tribe," William said. "And plenty for Gray Thunder."

"There's always so much going on," Charles said with a gusty sigh. "Ceran won't be here, will he? How's trade going at Fort St. Vrain?"

"He and his brother are finally completing construction. George wants to call it Fort George, of course, but I told him to be content with rolling our supply wagons along the South Platte."

"Our younger brother is quite a handful, but useful. From what Ceran says, they all get along famously."

"I almost forgot," said William. "Ceran sent a courier saying that he had finally bought Fort Jackson."

"Fraeb and Sarpy sold! Splendid! We control everything all the way to the Oregon Trail now. Especially after the repeated financial reverses of the American

Fur Company. Seldom have I ever wished a competitor ill, but for Astor I'll make an exception."

"We're doing well, brother," William said, nodding agreement. "Riches, a trade empire covering half the West, and women we love."

"When are you going to the village?"

"Now. I built my lodge at the western outskirts." William swallowed hard. He turned and shook Charles's hand. "I'll return in a few days with Owl Woman," William said. "Gray Thunder would have objected to the courtship by now if he didn't approve."

"You worry too much," Charles said. "You are an asset for any man's tribe."

"They haven't chased me away yet." William clasped his brother to him, then climbed into the wagon and got the mules pulling the heavy load. Outside the thick abode walls, fort wranglers tied forty head of horses to the rear of the wagon. William snapped the reins and got the mules pulling, feeling both excited and apprehensive as he drove for the Cheyenne village.

William almost stopped and turned around when he saw the lodge he had built at the edge of the encampment. Then it was too late to go back to the fort. Gray Thunder saw him and beckoned him forward, all his family surrounding him.

"Why have you come, Little White Man?" Gray Thunder called, using the name given William by the Cheyenne.

"I have come for your daughter, Mis-stan-stur," William said, his voice strengthening when he saw Owl Woman. She carried a wooden bowl filled with food. For him. For her husband.

Gray Thunder motioned for William to sit and discuss the matter. Gifts were exchanged and William bartered diligently, and finally had his offer of forty horses for Owl Woman accepted. More ritual exchanges, seemingly without end, were made and William's mind began wandering.

As he negotiated with Gray Thunder, William couldn't keep his eyes off Owl Woman. She wore buckskins tanned to the purest white, held around her waist with a brass-studded belt he had given her. The skirt hung lower on the right side than on the left, while the right sleeve of her blouse was short. The beaded, fringed material shimmered as she walked, red trade-cloth highlights and gleaming elk's teeth ornamenting her wedding dress. Her trim legs were encased to the knees in yellow leggings marked with bold black stripes. But choicest of all, in William's estimation, were the dainty feet in the lovingly made moccasins. Beads caught the light and turned all colors of the rainbow as she moved, her feet so light they seemed to float above the ground.

William looked up and saw the touches of rouge on her cheeks. As Owl Woman turned, long black braids swept around. Never had he seen a more beautiful creature.

"So it will be. Take this man his first meal as your husband," Gray Thunder ordered.

Owl Woman advanced, carrying the bowl. Her dark eyes shone and her lips were slightly parted, as if she had so much to tell him. William wanted to hear every word she had to say. Her younger sister, Yellow Woman, trailed along behind. By law and tradition, William had also married her. But he had eyes only for Owl Woman this day.

She followed eagerly as he led the way to his lodge and their wedding bed.

Massacre

In the Texas Panhandle
November 3, 1837

"The omens are against victory," Gray Thunder said. He glanced in the direction of the wolf-skin wrapping holding the two Sacred Arrows that had been recovered. Alongside was the other quiver, the one ordered by the Cheyenne chiefs holding four new Sacred Arrows. Very few of the warriors believed these held the potent medicine of the arrows captured by the Pawnee. Gray Thunder knew he might be part of the problem of their disbelief because he never spoke of the new arrows favorably, and always discussed recovering the two missing ones handed down as Sweet Medicine's legacy.

Only the warriors of the Bow String society took no note of the omens or Gray Thunder's reluctance to send the Cheyenne into battle before the stolen arrows were retrieved. They were hotheads and out to prove themselves the equal of any other fighting society.

"The only omen we need is a quick kill," Little Foot said, glaring at the Cheyenne medicine man. "The Comanche say they have a peace. With the white man, perhaps, but not with us. They lie! They raid our villages and kill our hunters. A quick foray into their territory and an even quicker scalping of their fighters will send the rest running south like scalded dogs."

"That is so," chimed in another brave from the same society. "We must drive them from our range. They kill our buffalo. They mock us with their presence!"

"Everyone kills our buffalo," complained yet another warrior. He was from the Dog Soldier society, and captured the immediate attention of those who were thinking on other things. "The white man kills our buffalo by the thousands. The Pawnee, Kiowa, and Comanche do, too."

"It is not good to go to war against them. Ever since the stars fell there have been few chances for victory." Gray Thunder's words fell on deaf ears. The warriors were whipping themselves into a fighting frenzy, and talk of bad omens had no place now in the discussion.

"There can be no victory if there is no battle," Little Foot said. That settled the matter in most of the assembled warriors' minds, no matter how vehemently Gray Thunder argued against this foolish act. Little Foot stared directly at Gray Thunder in open challenge. "Will you ride with us?"

"I will not risk the two Sacred Arrows," Gray Thunder said.

"That's of no matter to us," Little Foot said. "We will be victorious without Sweet Medicine's Sacred Arrows!"

The braves quickly stood and left the medicine lodge, Gray Thunder trailing as he wondered what he could do to protect this ill-omened foray.

"A Comanche village," Little Foot said with gusto. "See how cooking fires burn? Soon their lodges will be ablaze and they will all burn alive!"

Gray Thunder sat astride his horse, the pain almost

too much for him. His hips and legs throbbed, but every movement of his back sent lances of bright misery throughout his body. He chewed medicine root and spat to protect the braves and uttered invocations, but had no sense that any of the protections would work.

"Are you sure you want to attack them?" Gray Thunder asked.

"We will rush down and steal their horses, then slaughter them in their beds. The Comanche have grown arrogant and fat. Look! No sentries around their camp."

Gray Thunder studied the land and wondered if Little Foot had let his blood lust get the better of him. While there seemed no good place for guards to simply stand, the plain was crisscrossed with deep ravines from recent heavy rains. Any of those gullies could hide an army to go against the hundred braves that rode so boldly with Little Foot.

"I have done what I can to protect you in battle."

Little Foot sneered and then raised his war lance. He let out a whoop and led the charge directly into the camp. Gray Thunder started after the Bow String leader, but his horse balked and almost threw him. He fought to regain control, and found himself in the middle of a prairie-dog town. It took several seconds to guide the horse away from the leg-breaking holes.

By then the battle was almost over.

Gray Thunder gaped at the carnage wrought in such a short time. The Cheyenne had attacked a Comanche village. All the signs were obvious, but they had not seen what the medicine man had feared most: another nearby encampment.

Kiowa fighters swarmed up out of the deep gullies, as if they had been lying in wait for Little Foot. A cold shiver passed down Gray Thunder's arthritic spine when he saw the chief leading the Kiowa. Satanta. If there was any chief to rival the Comanche's Bull Hump, it was Satanta.

From the ferocity with which the Kiowa fought, they had obviously allied themselves with the Comanche and took special glee in killing Cheyenne. Many, many Cheyenne.

Gray Thunder never saw Little Foot or any of the other forty-one who perished in minutes of fighting. He shouted the order to retreat, and led those pitiful few stragglers who had survived Satanta's might away from the village.

All the way back to their village Gray Thunder cursed the loss of the Sacred Arrows so long ago. This massacre would never have occurred if he had not lost the medicine arrows to the Pawnee.

Birth

Bent's Fort
March 23, 1838

"Are you sure?" asked William Bent of the brave. "He's been gone for almost two weeks?"

The Cheyenne nodded once, then leaned against the opened outer door leading into Bent's Fort. William had not invited the brave inside. Few Indians, Cheyenne or from other tribes, ever received such an invitation, but he wished Gray Thunder could come now. He needed the old medicine man's magic to protect Owl Woman. Her pregnancy had gone well, but now that she was due to deliver their first child, William was not sure she was doing well. Charlotte, the black slave cook, insisted he knew nothing, worried needlessly, and that all would proceed according to nature.

William still wished Gray Thunder was handy with his medicinal roots and skill.

For all that, he would have shoved his brother Charles in the direction of the birthing room. Charles played at being doctor in Taos, doing what he could to help the people there. William had always scorned such pretense on his older brother's part, knowing Charles had no formal training and had learned little enough from Cheyenne medicine men during his stays at their villages. Now he wished for all the aid he could get for Owl Woman.

"Go back to your village," William told the brave. "Let Gray Thunder know his grandchild is due any time now."

The brave nodded, straightened, and shifted from foot to foot, but didn't immediately race back to the Cheyenne village. William knew why.

"Wait a minute," he told the brave. He went around inside the store room and found a bag of tobacco. Opening the shuttered window into the vestibule where he normally conducted most trade—but with the sturdy inner fort door secured—he handed out the tobacco as a gift. The brave sniffed it, grinned, and then took off on foot, his ground-devouring stride powerful enough to run a horse into the ground within five miles. William heaved a sigh of relief. He had made certain the message would be delivered properly to Gray Thunder and the rest of the village.

William went back into the center of his fort and looked around, his anxiety dying for a moment as he felt a sense of accomplishment rising. Activity on all sides told how vital Bent's Fort had become. A farrier worked to shoe three horses brought in by men from surrounding ranches, the cooks prepared a noon meal for the fifteen people inside the walls, and two clerks conducted an inventory from the most recent shipment from St. Louis. Business flourished on all sides.

"Charles, Ceran, Gray Thunder, why do you all have to be away now?" William wondered aloud. No one paid him any heed. He knew why Kit Carson was in Taos. Singing Bird was due to deliver their first child within the month. Somehow the notion that he would be the old hand at birthing and could tell the doughty mountain man all about it amused William.

The laugh forming on his lips died quickly when he saw the bustle at the door of Owl Woman's bedroom. The other women in the fort all crowded in.

"Charlotte!" he called up to the black woman. "What is it? What's wrong?"

A tiny squeal, followed by a loud cry, echoed through the fort.

Charlotte poked her head out. A huge smile split her face.

"Mr. William, nuthin's wrong. And it's a girl!"

"A girl!" William cried. He took off his hat and threw it into the air, spinning around in a dance wild enough to be noticed even at a mountain man's fandango. "A girl! Maria! We'll name her Maria!"

He hurried up the steps to the second story and went around to Owl Woman's bedroom. Almost hesitantly, he looked inside. Owl Woman looked drawn and pale, but held the tiny baby gently in the crook of her arm. Owl Woman looked at her husband, but Maria kept her eyes tightly screwed shut.

William vowed he would open her eyes to the world.

Death

"You are sure, my husband?" asked Gray Thunder's wife.

"I am certain," the medicine man said. "My shame will be erased after this raid."

"How did the Comanche get the Sacred Arrows?" she asked. She smeared more red paint on her face, signifying she was the wife of the Keeper-of-the-Sacred-Arrows. Gray Thunder had already renewed his vermillion markings, and looked like some wild beast, a dozen years younger than he was. For once, the pain in his joints faded and he moved about with a light step and a quick wit.

"The Pawnee gave them as a present. A trophy showing how superior they were to the Cheyenne," he said with some bitterness. "I found out when we captured a Comanche raider." Gray Thunder did not detail how the Comanche brave had come to impart this information. It wouldn't have mattered.

"The Dog Soldier society will not fail you, my husband," she said.

"I will ride into battle myself," the medicine man said. "I lost the arrows. I will regain them for my tribe."

"It wasn't your fault," she said hotly. "If the Pawnee buffalo hunters hadn't been killed before the medicine was invoked, our braves wouldn't have been slaughtered and you would not have lost the medicine arrows. How could you know the spell had been ruined because blood had already been spilled?"

"I lost the Sacred Arrows," Gray Thunder said doggedly, "and I will retrieve them." He hitched up his belt, where he had thrust a pair of sharp-edged knives, then settled the quiver over his shoulder holding the arrows for his bow. Gray Thunder had a musket, but preferred the ancient ways of killing for this raid. With his aching joints, he could not send an arrow flying as far as a rifle could shoot, but he could fire arrows faster.

And he could count coup with his bow before he stole back the Sacred Arrows.

"We are ready," a brave said to Gray Thunder.

"I have brought my greatest medicine to bear against the Comanche. No arrow will touch our skin. No knife will cut our flesh. No bullet will steal our lives." Gray Thunder chewed quickly on medicine root, then spat in the direction of the Comanche.

His wife mounted, ready to follow him into battle. Gray Thunder wheeled his horse about, let it rear, pawing at the air. This was the way he had ridden into battle before, when he was younger and undisgraced. It felt good to return to those days, those ways. He would again be spoken of around council fires with reverence and awe. With a loud cry, Gray Thunder put his heels to the horse's flanks and rocketed across the prairie in the direction of the Comanche camp along the Cimarron. Luck and torture had brought him the news that the Sacred Arrows were kept here. Skill and potent medicine would win the battle.

Lungs filled and then evacuated as he screamed his battle cry, Gray Thunder galloped at the head of the Cheyenne raiding party. He saw a few Comanche stir from their sleep, then realize they were being attacked. Unlike the ill-fated battle led by Little Foot, the Comanche had no Kiowa allies to save them. Gray Thunder yelped as he rode through camp, leaning down from horseback and swinging his bow.

The tip caught a Comanche brave on the cheek and drew blood.

Whooping with glee, Gray Thunder galloped past and counted coup on another Comanche too slow to raise his rifle and fire. At the far side of the camp, Gray Thunder reined in, jerked his horse around, and ran back into the camp toward the tepee where he knew the Sacred Arrows were being kept.

Rather than count coup this time, Gray Thunder nocked an arrow and loosed it as he galloped toward the tepee. The arrow went wide of its target, but still sent the Comanche brave he had aimed at scuttling for cover. All around the medicine man, the camp was plunged into confusion as the Cheyenne fighters slaughtered the milling Comanche.

"Steal the horses," Gray Thunder heard a Dog Society brave shout. Let the others gather horses. More important work lay ahead of him. He dismounted, walking resolutely to the tepee with the Sacred Arrows. From inside two braves rushed out to fight him. The first ran full tilt into Gray Thunder, knocking him backward.

For a moment, the warriors stared at each other, startled. And for his part, Gray Thunder had been too intent on regaining Sweet Medicine's legacy to the Cheyenne to anticipate opposition.

Gray Thunder dropped his bow and whipped out

his knife. He took a quick step forward and wrapped his arms around the nearest Comanche. Pulling hard toward him with the knife point, the Comanche's body pressed against his, he brought forth a flood of hot, coppery smelling blood that drenched the medicine man's hand. The Comanche fought for a moment longer, then sagged as life fled.

Gray Thunder shoved him aside.

And faced his own death. The second Comanche had had time to pull out a pistol. When his brother in arms had died at the point of Gray Thunder's knife, he'd found a good target. He fired point-blank at the medicine man.

Gray Thunder gasped at the pain exploding in his chest, then let out another scream of rage and drove forward. His bloody knife found a second target, this time in a vile Comanche heart.

He felt his enemy die. Gray Thunder dropped to his knees, panting with exertion. The world turned dim around him, but he refused to surrender to his own weakness. Fire spread throughout his chest, consuming him. The medicine man tried to rise, then collapsed, falling into the tepee. Dangling from the rough-hewn center pole slowly swung a wolf-skin bundle.

The Sacred Arrows.

Gray Thunder felt the knife slip from his nerveless fingers as he got his feet under him. Using the last of his strength, he stood on rubbery legs and reached for the wolf-skin wrappings. His fingers closed on the familiar sheath, and he felt a surge of power pass through his body that revitalized his soul.

"The medicine arrows," he said, a smile dancing on his lips. He grabbed the bundle with all his might, and his falling weight pulled the Sacred Arrows free.

Gray Thunder's wife found him curled up in the center of the Comanche tepee, clutching the precious bundle of medicine arrows to his chest. In death he had restored the great magic of the Cheyenne.

Pay—or Else!

"He's a thief," grumbled Charles Bent. "A thief and a bloody-handed murderer."

"Hush," Ceran St. Vrain said, looking around the small anteroom in the governor's palace where they waited to see Manuel Armijo. "The walls have ears." He glanced at the servants moving about in the next room. None paid the two merchants any notice, but he was worried. Ever since Armijo had engineered the coup that had seen Peréz killed and the Taos Indians discredited in the rebellion, the governor had struggled to find a new scapegoat. Armijo had to keep the Taos Pueblo in line, but couldn't afford to use them as his whipping boys any longer. To avoid rousing their ire, he had chosen the Americans as his bogeyman. Every impassioned speech the governor gave told of the hardships brought about by the greedy Americans and how they were to be feared as they spread with their doctrine of Manifest Destiny throughout the West.

He always added an additional message. They had to be taxed to keep them from consuming all loyal Mexican citizens.

"I wish there were more cheerful news," Charles

said bitterly, his jaw set. "You heard that Kit's wife died giving birth to their second child."

Ceran nodded brusquely, not wanting to discuss the matter. He had felt a momentary pang for Kit Carson and his loss, but not that much. Life could be hard on the frontier and death was inevitable, especially for a woman during birth. It was a pity the baby had died, too. It was now up to Kit to raise his surviving little girl alone.

"I don't know that I could have saved either of them, but I wish I had been in Taos to try. But no, I have to be tied up with Armijo and his senseless policies."

"You're making too many enemies, Charles," Ceran said. "Padre Antonio is still stirring up the Taos Indians against you. And Armijo would shoot you on sight if he thought he could get away with it."

"We'd cut off all New Mexico from trade if he tries to harm me. He knows the feelings in the United States about such shenanigans. And whoever controls Bent's Fort controls the Santa Fe Trail."

"What man likes the feel of another's hand around his throat?" asked Ceran.

"You have to choose—" Charles cut off his diatribe about Ceran's seeming neutrality in what could only be described as an all-out trade war when the door to Armijo's office opened and the governor's aide motioned for them to go in.

Charles stood, pressed away the wrinkles in his sharp, stylish clothing, then walked in, head high and chest puffed. He felt like a ram getting ready to butt heads, except the goal wasn't a female but trade for the entire territory.

Charles held his tongue when he saw Armijo sitting behind his desk only because Ceran whispered urgently in his ear to stay quiet. Armijo had built a small platform that raised his desk and chair up as if he sat on a throne. Resplendent in a uniform festooned with gold braid and jeweled medals, Manuel Armijo sneered slightly, pressed his mustaches down, and then spoke as if to peasants.

"You have a petition for the governor?" Armijo said haughtily, as if granting them a royal boon.

"You—" Charles bit back his retort as Ceran elbowed him.

"Excellency, we do."

"We? You and this Americano or you and your company?"

"Bent, St. Vrain and Company has done business in New Mexico for many years."

"Ah, yes, hiding behind the facade of your Mexican citizenship, Señor St. Vrain."

Charles saw Ceran suck in a breath, and knew any chance Armijo might have had to recruit the man for his schemes disappeared in that instant. The line had been drawn, and Armijo had forced Ceran to stand on the other side.

"I am proud to be a Mexican citizen, Excellency. And I am especially proud of my Catholic heritage."

"Yes, yes, your family is from Louisiana. French."

"Spain and France are at peace," Ceran said. "But we have not come to discuss European politics. Excellency, we are here to protest the five-hundred-dollar tariff placed on each of our wagons entering Santa Fe and Taos."

"Very well, protest. It will do you no good. The decision has been made. The wagons come from the U.S. and therefore must be taxed. It no longer matters what citizenship is claimed by the owners. Only the origin of the trade goods matters."

"This will force us to raise prices. We will have to charge more at our New Mexico stores. Do you want your citizens to pay more for the necessities of life?" Charles knew what drove Armijo to raise the customs duties. The governor pocketed the money, and would blame the traders when prices did rise. He got rich and generated hatred against the Americans with a single tax.

"And the luxuries," Ceran said, trying to coax a more favorable response from the governor. "We must cut back on the luxury items to concentrate on staples. Surely, having our fair ladies pining away because they cannot get the latest in fashionably patterned cloths from Europe or better implements for the kitchen or—"

"The tariff will never be revoked. The money is needed to build the military against possible invasion." Armijo tapped his fingers on the arms of his carved wood chair, obviously eager to end this audience.

"Invasion, Excellency? You still fear the Texians?"

"I fear no one!" raged Armijo. "I will not allow the Texians and the Americans who keep you under their thumb steal this land. There is no question how the U.S. eyes New Mexico Territory and covets it. I will fight to remain under Mexican sovereignty!"

"You are stealing from the treasury," Charles raged. "You want nothing more than to have the United States make a hostile move. It would give you reason for a mass killing of all your political enemies, American and otherwise."

"You, Señor Bent, would be high on that list." Armijo tented his fingers and rested his bearded chin on the tips. His cold dark eyes bored into Charles, who refused to be cowed.

"Don't threaten me, Armijo," growled Charles.

"You might collect your blood money, but if you touch one hair on my head or that of my family or friends, there will be hell to pay! And that's one tariff you'll be sorry to collect!"

Armijo shot to his feet and leaned forward, hands scattering papers on his broad desktop. A storm cloud of anger turned his swarthy face even darker.

"Get out of my office. Get out of my country!"

"Charles, come on. We're not getting anywhere," Ceran said, taking Charles by the elbow and pulling him from the office.

"Mark my words, Ceran," Charles Bent said when they left the Palace of the Governors and stepped into the Santa Fe plaza, "Armijo won't get away with such threats. The company has the funds to destroy him. Let him put a five-hundred-dollar tax on every wagon. We won't raise prices. We'll show him!"

Ceran took a deep breath, and wished Charles would tend to guiding the long trains of merchandise-laden wagons from St. Louis to Taos and let *him* deal with Armijo. Only trouble came from two such hot-heads trading insults.

Love at First Sight

Bent's Fort
March 17, 1839

Ceran St. Vrain felt his nervousness grow as he approached the fort. He had worked so long in Taos, keeping the company's stores running, maintaining trade in the face of increasing opposition from Armijo, that he needed the relative tranquillity and sanctuary of the fort to rejuvenate his spirits.

But it had been two weeks since his niece, Felicité, had arrived from St. Louis. Ceran had wanted to come immediately to meet her, but couldn't because of yet another scrape Charles Bent had gotten into with Antonio Martinez. The padre had insisted that Charles attend Mass, and rather than leave Taos for a few days to let matters cool off, Charles had publicly berated the priest.

That took a few days to soothe ruffled feathers. Then he had fought with Armijo's customs agents over the duties to be paid on a new wagon train just coming over Raton Pass. Every day had seen more than its share of time-wasting details when he wanted to return to the fort to see his sixteen-year-old niece. What would she think of her uncle ignoring her so long?

Such behavior wasn't gentlemanly, and it certainly

was not the way the St. Vrain family entertained valued relatives.

He put his heels to his horse and trotted the rest of the way to the fort when he got within view of its three-story-tall turrets. The horse was tired from the quick trip from Taos, but Ceran knew it could rest, getting the finest care in the fort's corrals. He would be caught up in a gala celebration for Felicité, showing her the best that the fort could offer.

Ceran smiled at the thought. Bent's Fort could offer the very best, even by St. Louis high-society standards. Ceran had ordered the best china put aside for use by distinguished visitors, and Charlotte Green was nothing less than a virtuoso when it came to preparing the food. No one left the table at Bent's Fort without commenting on her sumptuous meals, some fixed with recipes Ceran had found back East and others that she seemed to prepare instinctively.

"Ho, Ceran, welcome back!" the sentry on the wall called, waving to him. Ceran waved back, dismounted, and turned his horse over to a stable boy before hurrying through the vestibule into the graveled *placita*.

"Felicité!" he called. "Where are you, girl?"

From the second-floor guest room came an excited squeal and the prettiest girl Ceran had ever set eyes on. She pushed back her long, raven's-wing-dark hair and waved to her uncle.

"Uncle Ceran! I thought you'd never arrive."

"Business," he said in disgust, regretting the time he had wasted getting here. How could he possibly think Armijo was worth even one second of his time when a beautiful girl waited for him? "It's amazing how it can keep an old man from properly greeting his niece."

He took the steps two at a time and caught Felicité around the waist, spinning her about. Then he kissed her gallantly on each cheek and pushed her out to arm's length so he could look at her.

"You are so pretty. You must break the heart of every boy in St. Louis."

"Oh, Uncle Ceran," she said, blushing slightly. "You sound just like Mama."

"I hope not!" he roared, laughing. It had been too long since he had seen any of his relatives. He had worked diligently in New Mexico to maintain the flow of merchandise from the fort to both Taos and Santa Fe, and it had been almost six months since he had seen Marcellin. His younger brother, along with George Bent, ran Fort St. Vrain well, but there was little contact between Bent's Fort and Fort St. Vrain since Marcellin ordered goods directly from St. Louis to sell to those pilgrims making their way along the Oregon Trail.

And all his family was back in St. Louis. Ceran heaved a sigh. He missed them all.

"I'll have a table set for a big dinner and then we'll throw the wildest fandango ever," Ceran told his niece. "We have a good wine cellar, but there is one fine claret in particular you simply must try and—"

"And linen and crystal goblets and things I'd see only at the Planters House," Felicité finished for him, laughing. "I've poked around in your pantry. You do live well here, Uncle Ceran."

"The finest food and quarters between St. Louis and Santa Fe," he boasted. "And from the way things are going downhill in Santa Fe, I'd have to say better."

"You're the American consul, aren't you? Mama is so proud."

Ceran heaved a sigh. "I gave that up last year. The Mexican governor is increasingly anxious over trade matters, and it was causing friction with me representing American interests. I let Manuel Alvarez take over." Ceran saw his niece frown. He had to keep telling himself she knew nothing of the politics of the area. "Don't worry about it. He's a Santa Fe merchant and gets along well with Charles and the other Americans."

"I'm an American," Felicité said.

"Señor Alvarez would be as smitten by your charms as Governor Armijo would be insulted by your presence. That tells you much of what I think of the Mexican governor."

"Tell me all about Taos, Uncle. I want to hear every single detail."

"Why?" he asked, taken aback. Something about the girl's tone put him on guard.

"Oh, no reason," she said, opening her fan and fluttering it so she hid her face behind it. Dark eyes peered over the very edge as she said, "I might like to live there someday."

"I doubt that," Ceran said. "It is a dreary place with no amenities. What have you been doing to occupy yourself at the fort? I'm sorry it took me so long to get here."

"Oh, Uncle Ceran, stop apologizing so. I'm sure it wasn't your fault," Felicité said. "Besides, I've kept myself quite busy looking after Adaline."

Ceran went cold inside.

"Kit Carson's daughter?"

"Why, yes, Mr. Carson's. It is so tragic how his wife died. And he is working here now as a hunter. Kit's such a fine shot. He tried to show me how to fire a musket, but I wasn't very good at it."

Ceran heard more than a young girl's simple passing of the time in the way Felicité spoke of Kit.

"You've spent a great deal of time with Kit?" Ceran

tried to keep his voice level, but the steely edge alerted Felicité that something was wrong.

"Why, Uncle, don't you approve of Kit? He's a mountain man, just as you are, and he is a fine, upstanding man, honorable and brave and—"

"And he has a half-breed daughter," Ceran said with more venom than he intended.

"Adaline is sweet," Felicité said. "She is very bright, too. She was showing me how to do some simple weaving. I tried to show her how to crochet, but I lost my crochet hooks along the way. I promised her I would get her a set and—"

"Dinner's almost ready," Ceran said. "Come along and we can discuss the matter."

"What matter is that?" Felicité said, her jaw firming. "That I am quite taken by Kit?"

"What would your parents say if you married him?"

"Why, they would rejoice. He is famous. Everyone knows him in St. Louis. Lieutenant Frémont has even mentioned how great a scout Kit is and brags on him at every opportunity."

Ceran fumed as his mind raced. He had nothing against Kit or his frontier skills, but he would be damned if anyone in the St. Vrain family became responsible for raising a half-breed Arapaho girl. That would doom all St. Vrains in polite society forever. And Felicité certainly did not understand what it meant to raise a youngster. Her family had been wealthy enough to hire a governess while she was growing up, and she had no siblings. Right now, dealing with a small girl was a lark. Felicité had no idea how difficult it could be raising a family, especially when her husband would be off in the mountains hunting or scouting most of the time.

"Kit's out hunting right now," Felicité went on as

they entered the dining room, with its table set elegantly enough for kings and queens. "He won't be back for several more days."

Ceran turned the topic to family in St. Louis, and caught up on gossip and births and deaths, skirting the details of all the inevitable marriages. For Felicité, getting married would be both romantic and a way to establish her position among adults in the family. Ceran saw no way of convincing her that she would destroy her standing by marrying a rough-hewn, uneducated man like Kit Carson. Kit couldn't even write his own name, much less read or cipher.

Ceran excused himself and arranged for Felicité to return to St. Louis before Kit returned from his hunt. It was for the best.

Peace

Bent's Fort
April 1, 1840

"You did a good job, Kit," William Bent said, elbows braced on the western parapet as he leaned out to study the Comanche's nearby camp. More than a thousand Comanche had gathered, and for the first time in years, William did not feel uneasy seeing so many of them in one place—especially on his fort's doorstep. He had traded with them on their own territory at Adobe Walls, but there had always been a sense of tickling a grizzly. One misstep and a mouthful of teeth would clamp down.

But not now.

Even better, to the east along the Arkansas River camped the Cheyenne. William and Owl Woman had gone to their lodge a few days earlier, and had simply sat in front of it to watch all that happened in the village. Before Gray Thunder's death and the recovery of the Sacred Arrows, war parties constantly sallied forth against the Pawnee, Kiowa, and Comanche. Now there was only an undercurrent of excitement. Peace, true peace unlike the dubious one Colonel Dodge had managed years earlier, was within their grasp.

William felt a small glow realizing his part in the treaty process had been so successful. Kit Carson had ventured deep into Comanche territory and spoken with their chief, Old Wolf, and convinced him that trade with Bent's Fort was in his tribe's advantage. Raiding had become increasingly difficult as the Texians patrolled now, threatening rebellion against Mexico and shooting anything that moved on "their" prairie.

"Thank you kindly. Too bad Ceran's gone. He ought to be here for the final peace. He had as big a hand in it as anyone."

William wondered at Kit's sincerity about Ceran St. Vrain. After Ceran had sent his niece packing so abruptly, Kit had moped around for a spell, then taken up with a Cheyenne woman for almost six months. Eventually, she had thrown out his boots, signifying their relationship was over, and then Kit had become dour and withdrawn. William had hesitated sending Kit into the Cimarron region to parley with Old Wolf because of that, but the mission had given the scout purpose again and, to William's great relief, Kit had worked wonders. William's only other option would have been to send his youngest brother, Robert, out to offer the olive branch. Robert, as innately clever at trading as he was, needed the seasoning only experience could give in touchy diplomatic dealings among the warlike tribes.

"Peace will increase our business. We won't lose men and merchandise to Indian raids between here and Westport."

"And the profits'll pile up higher 'n the walls of this here fort," Kit finished with a laugh. "You and the rest of the company deserve it, William. The army's tried and failed to make peace with them Injuns. You succeeded when they failed."

"They used a whip. We're using a carrot. The carrot of trade."

A ruckus behind them caused the two men to turn. The guard at the big main gate on the east side of the *placita* argued with a man dressed in tattered Comanche garb.

"What's the problem?" called William.

"I think I recognize him," Kit said, grabbing William's arm. "That there's Jim Hobbs. Don't rightly know what he's doin' in that Comanche getup, though. Last I heard tell of him, he was workin' as a trader south of Adobe Walls."

"Let him in," William ordered the guard, then motioned for Hobbs to join them on the fort battlements. The man hurriedly climbed the ladder and faced William.

"I need help, Mr. Bent. Big help."

"I remember you now. You worked as a foreman making the adobe blocks for the fort walls a couple years back," said William. "Why're you decked out like that?" He had never seen a Comanche so poorly dressed. It was as if Hobbs had been purposefully clothed in worn-out hand-me-downs.

"The Comanche nabbed me, nigh on two years back. I was mindin' my own business down in the Panhandle, but they didn't see it that way. They took me prisoner, and I've been their slave ever since. I snuck out of camp whilst they was whuppin' it up. They think I'm down at the river fetchin' water."

"I recollect him workin' here, too," Kit said. "Jim here was a real good worker. We can't let him stay a slave." William heard the bitterness in Kit's voice when he spoke of slavery. It went against the stocky mountain man's nature, although he never said anything about Charlotte or her husband working in the fort.

William had to admit being the Comanche's slave

was a great deal worse than working at Bent's Fort.
The scars on Hobbs's face and arms showed how he
had been savagely beaten. Still, no matter what
William thought of the propriety of getting Hobbs
away from his captors, he saw problems looming. Old
Wolf wouldn't take kindly to losing a slave, and might
decide to return to the old ways.

The bloody ways riding the warpath.

"I don't know how we can help you," William said
slowly, mind racing. If Old Wolf or any of his braves
saw Hobbs inside the fort, there would be hell to pay.

"You got to, William. It ain't right for Jim here to be
kept like an animal."

Jim Hobbs looked at Kit with gratitude for taking
up his case. He knew when to keep silent, too, and let
William stew in his own juices.

"The treaty is too important to risk," William said.
He wasn't sure if he was trying to convince Kit, Hobbs,
or himself. "We can end twenty years of Comanche
raiding."

"He worked fer you," Kit said doggedly. "You owe
him somethin' fer that."

"There's another prisoner, too," Hobbs said. "John
Baptiste. You don't know him, but we've been closer
'n brothers the past couple years."

"You don't have any choice, William," Kit said.
"What danged good is a treaty with the Comanche if
they still hold our people as slaves?"

"Get on back to drawing the water for the Comanche," William said. "Use our well so you don't
have to hike the mile down to the river."

"William, what about—" began Kit.

William silenced him with a look. "I can't say anything about buying you from the Comanche. That
wouldn't be right, but Kit can. You get on back to

camp and tell your friend to stay alert, but not to do anything to upset the apple cart."

"Thank you, thank you both," Hobbs said, shaking their hands with a firm grip as if he mistook them for pump handles. He hurried down the ladder and found the well on the north side of the *placita,* then left with his load as William and Kit watched.

"What'll you pay to get 'im free?" Kit asked.

"Anything in our stores," William said. He went to prepare for the visit that night sealing the treaty.

"I knew it," grumbled William. "I knew there had to be more to it than Hobbs said." He sat heavily on the riverbank and stared at the Comanche preparing their gifts for the Cheyenne.

"What did you promise?" asked Charles.

"I told Hobbs I'd free him and Baptiste. He never told me that he was married to Old Wolf's daughter and had a three-year-old daughter."

"He never mentioned the two Brown girls, either," Charles said. "They were kidnapped from a wagon train on its way to Oregon years ago."

"How bad can this get?" muttered William.

"It can get a lot worse. Both of the Brown women're both married to Old Wolf's sons."

William grumbled some more, then fell silent when a loud shout went up amid the assembled Comanche. The shout died, became a drone like a million bees, and then rose to a disturbing volume. He got to his feet, worrying about what was happening.

"I've never seen anything like that in all my born days," Charles said in a whisper.

The thousand Comanche began herding horses driven down from hills south of the fort. William thought he had seen all the horses in the world as the Comanche began driving the massive herd down the river, and then the Comanche brought forth the second herd. And the third.

"The Cheyenne don't have rope enough for them. There must be forty head of horses for every Cheyenne," marveled William.

"I hope the gifts the Cheyenne have for the Comanche match this," said Charles. "I gave them five wagon loads, but compared to so many horses, that's nothing."

The thunder of so many horses galloping along the river died. Chief Yellow Wolf strode out dressed in his finest bleached-white buckskins, chest puffed up. He made grand gestures and all the Cheyenne began bringing out their gifts for the Comanche. At first there was some grumbling among the Comanche that this was all. But the Cheyenne did not stop. They kept bringing the Navajo blankets, the fine Zuni silver jewelry, the trade goods bartered from the white man, and in addition to that given them by the Bents, it all turned into mountains that toppled and formed new hills. And still the Cheyenne brought forth beads and cloth and every possible item to delight both Comanche warrior and squaw.

"Bells," William said. "I hear bells. The Cheyenne are giving up their brass bells." Among the trade items that brought the best return were the small bells, brought from Westport sewn to paper cards. The Cheyenne couldn't get enough of the melodious ornaments for decoration. Now every one William had ever traded to them was brought to go onto yet another mountain of tribute.

The Comanche grumbling had died, and now was replaced by joyous laughs and shouts of glee at the immensity of the Cheyenne gifts. When Old Wolf stepped forward, he reached for a few of the bells Yellow Wolf had put on the hill. Yellow Wolf stopped him and shook his head.

William caught his breath, then let it out when Yellow Wolf turned and pointed to the long tables set with food, still more gifts for the Comanche.

The two chiefs who had fought for so long went to the head of a table, which was creaking under the weight of so much buffalo steak and tongue, prairie chicken and pheasant, candied cactus, and items the Cheyenne must have stockpiled over the years.

"They set as good a table as we do," Charles said. Then, grinning ear to ear, he added, "Almost."

"Ceran wouldn't like being outdone. He's always bringing Charlotte new cookbooks and recipes, not that she needs it. Do you think she's helped Yellow Wolf prepare any of this?"

"I doubt it," Charles said to his brother. "Look. Aren't those oysters?"

"Canned," William said. "Not fresh, like the ones we have."

"That reminds me. We need to bring more ice from the mountains for the icehouse."

"Let's get out of the way," William said, "or we'll be trampled." They barely got behind a sturdy cottonwood as the Comanche rushed past, on their way to the extravagant feast in their honor.

"More," urged Yellow Wolf. "We need more."

"No more," William said firmly. "We gave you two barrels of beer. No whiskey." The sun had set and still the festivities built in intensity, drums hammering and the warriors of both tribes dancing together around bonfires. To give them alcohol now would ruin the tenuous ties being forged. William remembered how the Cheyenne leader of the Dog Soldiers, Porcupine Bear, had gotten drunk and killed one of his own tribe. If that could happen, William knew that if any of the Cheyenne got drunk now, they might revert to old ways and kill their ancient enemies.

"We need more," Yellow Wolf insisted.

"Bring Old Wolf here," William said suddenly, to his older brother's surprise. "We will give him a tour of the fort."

"William, are you mad?" whispered Charles. William silenced him with a hard look.

Yellow Wolf argued a little more for the whiskey, as much for himself as for his temperamental guests, then returned to the festivities. In a few minutes, Old Wolf rode up, head swiveling around as if he expected to be attacked at any instant.

"You do me great honor coming to my home, Chief," William said formally.

"You would show me your lodge?" The Comanche craned his neck, looking past William and Charles into the fort's *placita*. He dismounted and edged into the vestibule past where few Indians ever were permitted to venture.

"Our humble home is yours, Chief Old Wolf," William said, escorting the Comanche inside. Every step he took caused the Comanche to grow more excited. He studied the thick walls and the inner battlements with the small brass cannon. Seeing his interest in the armament along the rampart, William ushered the Comanche chief up the steps, to Charles's chagrin.

"We can kill many attackers with this cannon,"

William said, a hand resting on the cold brass barrel of the mounted gun.

"Fire it," Old Wolf said.

"No!" cried Charles, knowing what would happen.

William was more suave with his easy answer. "We fire only at our enemies. Do you see any enemies, Chief? I don't."

"No enemies," Old Wolf reluctantly agreed. They made a full circuit of the parapet, showing the Comanche how completely they defended themselves. William made sure the chief was impressed by their firepower before showing him the pool table next to Ceran's quarters. Old Wolf immediately spied the rows of whiskey bottles along the far wall. William poured the chief a shot of fine Kentucky bourbon, then joined him in a second.

"Come along, Chief," William said before Old Wolf could demand a third drink. "The Cheyenne have given you gifts. I want to add our own humble offering."

"You give me gifts, too?"

"We have traded before, Chief," William said. "We will trade more in the future to our mutual benefit. Even as we speak, my brother Robert is among your people trading." This stretched the truth a little, but not much. As soon as the treaty was sealed, William intended for his youngest brother to occupy the trading post at Adobe Walls and begin serious commerce with the Comanche.

"I like that cloth," Old Wolf said, a little tipsy from the two quick shots of liquor William had given him. The chief pointed to a bolt of calico.

"It is yours. Our gift to the great chief of the Comanche." William pushed it across the counter to the chief. Before Old Wolf could lift it, William took down a second bolt, this one of bright red cloth. "And this is yours, in exchange for a slave."

"Slave?"

"Jim Hobbs," William said.

"No, no, he is married to my daughter," protested Old Wolf, but both William and Charles heard the slyness in the chief's words. He was willing to be convinced this was a profitable trade, son-in-law or not.

"For your daughter," William said, measuring out an ounce of brightly colored beads. He made a great show of pouring them from a jar into a pan balance. Old Wolf watched as each and every bead tumbled and bounced around in the measuring pan. William poured the beads into an envelope and handed it to the chief.

"And this is for you," William said, handing the chief the almost full jar where he had gotten the beads.

"Done."

"What of John Baptiste?" asked Charles. "What is his price?"

"Who? Oh, him," Old Wolf said, dismissing the matter entirely. For a few more minutes they dickered, finally deciding that a broken-down mule was adequate payment for Baptiste.

"We have many more Two Gray Hills blankets," William said, showing the chief the result of a lengthy trade Ceran St. Vrain had conducted with the Navajo. The Navajo blankets were worth almost as much as a bale of buffalo robes due to the difficulty of obtaining them. "Will you trade for the Brown women?"

"My sons' wives? No!"

William and Charles dickered long and hard, but could not get the Comanche chief to yield on this point. They had to be content with freeing Jim Hobbs and Baptiste. Now.

"I would see more of your fine lodge," Old Wolf said, stacking his wares near the inner gate, now closed for the night.

"It would be our pleasure to offer you some of our food. Do you like fresh oysters, Chief?" Charles saw Old Wolf had never tried them. Old Wolf quickly developed a taste for them, gobbling a dozen. As the chief worked on a second dozen, almost depleting the fort's stock, gunfire outside brought both Bents to their feet.

"What's going on?" Charles called to the guard on the wall.

"Comanche. They're wavin' around their rifles and shoutin' somethin' I don't unnerstand," the sentry said. "They're lookin' mighty pissed."

Old Wolf got a sour look on his face, pushed past William and Charles, and hurried to the parapet, where he rested his hand lovingly on the brass cannon as he shouted to his warriors. For several minutes they argued. Then the warriors rode off, heading back to the Cheyenne feast.

"What was wrong?" asked William, apprehensive that the fragile peace might be in jeopardy.

"They worry that you kidnap me. I tell them I am eating oysters and to mind their own business!"

Laughing, the Bents and Old Wolf returned to the dining room and worked through the stores until the Comanche chief could eat no more.

Peace was a reality—and two men were freed from Comanche slavery.

Grant

"They are coming to kill us all. I know it," said Governor Manuel Armijo. "I feel it in my bones."

"It is the winter that you feel," Padre Antonio said, his words as cold as the wind whipping down the street in front of the Palace of the Governors. "Your bones are strong but your soul is weak, Manuel."

"I had to do it," Armijo said, his voice pleading with the priest to understand. "The law required it."

"You gave Charles Bent land! You gave away the sovereign territory of Mexico to an American!"

"I know your quarrel with Bent goes deeper than that," Armijo said uneasily. "I have no liking for him, either."

"You granted him land."

"Would you rather have the Texians swoop down on us and steal it away? If the land is registered, even they must observe ownership or risk having everyone sniping at them. And I didn't give it to Bent. He is not a citizen and cannot be given a land grant."

"You granted the land to Lucien Maxwell, who subgranted it to Bent. You knew Maxwell would do this, being such a close friend. This is wrong, Governor.

Wrong! It is an offense to the people of Taos, to the citizens of Mexico who remain loyal."

"Mexico City will never send troops to support us," Armijo said. "The taxes levied on American trade aren't enough to allow me to maintain a big army. We are at the mercy of the Texians, should they decide to attack us."

"Texians—always you speak of them as if they are devils! You need look no further than Charles Bent to find a real devil. He cannot be allowed to own any of the Maxwell land grant. Revoke the Maxwell grant, Manuel, my son, or there will be serious trouble—and you need not look to Texas for its source."

"Don't threaten me, Padre," Armijo said, bristling.

"There was one rebellion against the governor," Antonio Martinez said. "There can be another. And this is not a threat. It is only a simple statement of what will be." The Catholic priest whirled and left Armijo's office.

The governor shivered, and it wasn't from the winter wind blowing off the Sangre de Cristo Mountains. With a trembling hand, he reached for a pile of unsullied paper and began writing out a new decree revoking the Maxwell land grant. If this kept Padre Antonio happy, so be it.

Recruit and Invade

Bent's Fort
September 24, 1841

"It's the damned Texians," raged Ceran St. Vrain, crumpling a note he had just received. He tossed the balled paper into the corner of the room and tugged fiercely at his black beard until William Bent thought he would pull it off in huge handfuls. Ceran got to his feet, turned, then spun back, slamming his fists down hard on the table, causing their wineglasses to bounce. For once, the volatile mountain man took no notice of the potential spillage of his precious, fine French wine. His anger was too great.

"They will ruin everything," Ceran said. "We've got to stop them and their endless recruitment."

"I agree that the Texians are a nuisance, but they bother Armijo more than us. He's so afraid of them that he has all the priests out telling the people the Texians have horns and three heads." William had heard much more, but Ceran had, also. "The Texians know better than to attack our post. If they did, the cavalry would be on them in a flash and they'd be at war with the U.S."

"Colonel Dodge?" scoffed Ceran. "He wouldn't lead a sortie against them. Look at the way he made peace with the Comanche. Whatever's easiest is the

way he'd take. *We* had to get the Cheyenne and Comanche together for a permanent peace."

"Captain Cooke isn't likely to cotton much to the
Texians and their ways," William pointed out. "He has
no love for them. He's a decent soldier and knows the
pitfalls of dealing with the Texians."

"And where might Captain Cooke be patrolling?"
Seeing William's shrug, Ceran raged on. "You don't
know. I don't know. Nobody knows!"

"What do you want to do? Mount cannon on our
wagons and go after these scoundrels so Armijo
doesn't have to shoot them?" William was mildly
amused at the idea, but saw how seriously Ceran
took it. That sobered him fast. "I'm joking, Ceran.
We can't get involved in the fight. We're Americans.
We have to stay neutral when the Texians attack
Armijo."

"We can't just sit here," Ceran said. "How will the
Texians treat me? I'm still a Mexican citizen. We're
caught in the middle. Look at how Armijo treats
Charles. How many times has he thrown him into jail
this past year?"

"I lost count at four," William said, "but he always
gets out because Armijo needs the bail money."

"Some day the governor'll listen to Padre Antonio
and Charles will never be seen again," Ceran said.
"We have troubles coming at us from all sides. Armijo
hates you and Charles, especially. And if the expedition that left Texas reaches Santa Fe and throws out
Armijo, my life might be in jeopardy."

"All that is true, Ceran, but it is also built on what-
ifs. You'll always be safe here at the fort. If the Texians
drive out Armijo, let Charles run the stores at Taos
and Santa Fe until it's safe for you to go back. We're
doing well," William pointed out. "Our freight depot

at Westport is completed, and we can finally bypass the merchants in Independence."

"Thieves," grumbled Ceran, temporarily turned from his anger at the annoying Texians. "Westport is a godsend for us. At least we don't get scalped at the Missouri end of the Santa Fe Trail, even if Armijo demands his pound of flesh at the other. We were better off paying him tax on the goods sold rather than a flat five-hundred-dollar excise on every wagon load. He gets his money before we sell this way. Before, he had to wait until after we'd sold out our merchandise."

William took his wine and carefully mopped up the few drops that had been spilled. As he drank, he saw Ceran was not mollified. The man's face was still clouded with anger, and he left his wine untouched on the table.

"What should we do, Ceran?"

"I must go to Santa Fe and warn Armijo. There's no benefit to us if the Texians throw him out, in spite of how much I'd like to see his head on a pike. From the scouting report I just got, they're a ragtag band of half-starving ne'er-do-wells out on a lark. If it looks as if I'm on Armijo's side by warning him, he can defeat them without any trouble and think better of me—and the company."

"You underestimate the Texians, I think, since they did manage to pry themselves free from Santa Anna so handily," William said. "But since you feel so strongly about this, what do you need for an expedition against the Texians?"

"You're right about getting involved," Ceran said with a gusty sigh. "But I should be certain Charles is safe before I do anything. Armijo has whipped up so much resentment against the Texians, it is sure to overflow against Americans, too."

"See what Alvarez can do for us," William said, indicating that the American consul in Santa Fe who had replaced Ceran might be of service. "And watch your own back. Charles knows the risks of staying in Mexican territory, but you seem to think being a citizen is all the protection you need."

"I know Armijo hates me, too," Ceran said. "Anyone having anything to do with the company is a target."

"Send back a courier every day or two," William said. "I'd go with you, but I need to be here when the wagons from Westport arrive."

Ceran got to the door, hesitated, hurried back, and finished his wine in a single draught, then strode purposefully from the room.

William drank the rest of his wine, but found it bitter on his tongue.

Executions

East of Santa Fe
September 30, 1841

Manuel Armijo stood with his hands clasped behind his back as he studied the ebb and flow of the angry crowd outside his office across the plaza. Armijo smiled when he saw how the mob went after the Americans, and laughed as four men seized the American consul.

"Alvarez, you fool. You should never have opposed me."

"Governor, the troops are ready. Do . . . do you want to disperse the crowd first?" asked his aide-de-camp.

"How many soldiers have been mustered?" Armijo asked. He picked a minuscule piece of lint off his impeccable light blue uniform festooned with medals and dangling gold cords. He looked up. His dark eyes fixed on the young aide. The man looked hardly to be out of his teens, but Armijo knew this was not so. Diego had seen combat several times, and one day would make a good general. Armijo thought so, and so did Diego's father, a high-ranking officer in Santa Anna's army who had the ear of many important, powerful men in Mexico City.

"Two hundred, Governor."

"Not enough to waste on a crowd of this paltry size," he said.

"They will kill Alvarez, unless we go to his aid."

"A pity. Have them seize Charles Bent, also. That annoying *pendejo* is in Santa Fe, isn't he?"

"I believe so. I've been occupied with scouting reports of the Texians moving toward the city. I can find out if you wish, but the Texian threat is more—"

"Two columns, one nearing, yes, yes, I know all this," Armijo said testily. It irritated him that Ceran St. Vrain had been the one to deliver this intelligence to him. That meant he owed some small favor to the partner in Bent, St. Vrain & Company.

Armijo watched as the crowd argued over what to do with Alvarez. To Armijo's disgust, Don Guadalupe Miranda, carrying some slight authority as provisional Secretary of State, argued with the crowd until they released Alvarez. From his vantage point, Armijo saw a small cut on Alvarez's face and nothing more. If luck rode with Armijo, the peasants would find Charles Bent and dispatch him—permanently.

"We captured one of them," Diego said.

"What's this? An entire column?"

"No, Governor, pardon my imprecision. There is only one officer of the Texian army who surrendered. His name is Lewis and he seems inclined to cooperate."

"Bring him here. Immediately!" Armijo clacked his heels together and slapped his thigh to produce a loud sound. Diego jumped to it, returning in minutes with a ragamuffin. Two armed guards stood just outside the open office door, should Lewis present a threat to their governor.

Armijo looked the man over and came to a quick decision.

"Execute him," he ordered his aide.

"No, wait," pleaded Lewis, showing his true colors. The man's hands shook and he blanched in fear. Armijo wondered if the man had soiled his trousers. If so, it might require a peon or two for the cleanup of his office floor.

"Why? You are no use to me. You head an army come to steal away sovereign land and kill citizens of Mexico." Armijo watched carefully and saw that the man was putty in his hands. Lewis would agree to anything to save his own worthless gringo hide.

"I can tell you everything about the army. We . . . we've been on the trail since June. The Comanche jumped us at Palo Duro Canyon. We barely got away. The army's in no condition to fight."

"Yet it still marches on Santa Fe," Armijo said, as if it were of no interest to him. He thrilled at Lewis's revelation of hardship assailing the Texians. He had feared a real fight might force him to retreat into Mexico, but now it appeared that he could become the conqueror, the hero, the *santo de Nuevo Mejico.*

"I can convince the first column to surrender. They—they're not in any condition to fight."

"And the second?"

"A hundred soldiers could stop them," Lewis said. "They're almost out of ammunition."

"Yet they come to Santa Fe?" Armijo turned grim. He had believed the Texians to be invincible after their victory at San Jacinto. The Republic of Texas might be poor in money, but was rich in fighters—and fools.

"Please, Governor."

Armijo snapped his fingers and motioned for Diego to take charge of this weakling.

* * *

"So," Armijo said slowly, "St. Vrain was not lying." He laughed harshly. "Neither was our captured traitor."

The governor watched as three men astride gaunt horses rode toward the hamlet of San Miguel. He motioned to Diego to capture the Texian scouts. Diego dispatched a dozen soldiers, no more than this needed to take these invaders into custody.

"There," Armijo said, pointing to an abandoned adobe house. "Use that as a prison for the Texians." He imperiously gestured to bring Lewis forward. "Who are those three?" he asked.

Lewis swallowed hard before answering.

"Baker, Howland, and Kendall. Kendall's a newspaper editor along to record everything for people back in the Republic."

"He will have nothing to report except my victory," Armijo said, his lip curling. His troopers circled the trio and brought them directly to Armijo, who said nothing to them, but dismounted and led the way into the old adobe house.

Inside amid the ruins, Armijo spun about, hand on his saber as the trio, along with Lewis, were forced into the building at the end of leveled bayonets.

"You are invaders. You seek to overthrow the lawful Mexican government," Armijo said pompously. His anger grew as he shouted, "My government!"

"You got it all wrong," Baker said.

Armijo motioned. A soldier shoved Baker to his knees. The man tried to get back to his feet, but was shoved down again, his head banging hard against a crumbling wall.

"Execute him," Armijo said. The report from the soldier's gun filled the room, followed quickly by swirling acrid smoke and a stunned silence. Then Baker groaned and tried to force himself erect. The bullet had entered his back but had not killed him. A second soldier stepped up and dispatched the fallen Texian with a shot to the back of the head.

Howland opened his mouth to speak, but Armijo cut him off with another quick motion. The bullet from behind knocked Howland forward onto his face. He died before he struck the dirt floor.

"You monster!" cried Kendall. "You murdered them!"

"As you would murder my citizens, all of them loyal, peaceful Mexicans."

"Please, Governor," Lewis pleaded. "Don't do this."

"Imprison this editor person," Armijo said, walking past the bodies. "And bring Lewis."

Outside the adobe, guards posted themselves at the door and at the rear to prevent Kendall's escape. Armijo turned to Lewis and looked contemptuously at the man.

"Ride ahead and tell the Texian column that they face a thousand—no, *four* thousand—soldiers. Ride quickly because my army will be on your heels."

Lewis took off like a scalded dog. Armijo laughed and motioned to Diego.

"Let my nephew lead the soldiers. There is no reason to worry about the Texians."

"Very well, Governor," Diego said. "Will you return to Santa Fe?"

"Yes, I want to be sure that Charles Bent is properly . . . taken care of." Head high and whistling a jaunty tune, Manuel Armijo mounted his stallion and rode in triumph back into his city.

Defeat

East of San Miguel
October 1, 1841

"Comandante," cried the scout, out of breath from riding so hard. "They come! The Texians are coming!"

Governor Manuel Armijo's nephew licked his lips nervously, drew his saber, and looked around. His uncle had given him almost one hundred soldiers. With luck, Lewis had worked his lies on the Texians and they thought they faced four thousand trained, battle-hardened Mexican troops fiercer than any they might have faced at the Alamo, had they had the misfortune to be at that doomed presidio.

"Column, attack!" he shouted. His horse lurched, almost unseating him, but he recovered and found himself at the head of a ragtag band of soldiers racing across arroyos and down dusty roads in the direction pointed out by the scout.

The Texian troopers frantically grabbed for their pistols and got in their own way. Then their leader grabbed a pole and waved it wildly, a white cloth on the top.

"We want a truce!" the Texian cried.

"Surrender or die!"

"We surrender!"

The Mexican soldiers circled the starved, battered

invasion force and waited for the Texians to throw down their weapons.

"I accept your surrender!"

"We . . . Mr. Lewis said if we gave up you'd let us go. If we let you have our guns."

"Señor Lewis lied." He swung about in the saddle, waving his saber wildly. "Put them all in shackles. We'll march them to Mexico for trial!"

The Texians protested weakly, but they were in no condition to fight Armijo's force. They had been battered and wounded by the Comanche, and had endured cold and starvation as they made their way across the Panhandle into New Mexico Territory.

With a glee matched only by his uncle returning to Santa Fe as a conqueror, the *comandante* saw the would-be invaders chained together and started on foot toward the capital. From there he personally would see that they were taken to Mexico for sentencing after their trials. It was a good day's fight.

Arrested—Again

Taos
October 2, 1841

"You're sure you want to do this?" Ceran St. Vrain asked the large man with a face as pockmarked by smallpox as Ceran's own. "The flour mill is worth a great deal more."

"You call yourself a trader?" William Workman looked around, as if expecting to see the governor's soldiers coming after him. He turned his attention back to Ceran. "You're supposed to dicker for a lower price, not agree to my first offer."

"I want to be fair," Ceran said, "and the price you and Rowland asked for the mill is too low."

"We're not Mexican citizens. You are. They won't stretch your neck."

"You're leaving the territory?" Ceran heaved a deep sigh, and wondered how many other good men were leaving and what this meant for Charles Bent. The fewer Americans there were in Taos, the more Charles stood out—and the more he drew the ire of both Governor Armijo and Padre Antonio.

Armijo had canceled Lucien Maxwell's land grant because of the priest's protests, then reinstated it when he feared what might happen if the Texians seized the territory. Armijo tried to have it both ways, and Ceran knew the governor would end up having it neither way. Lucien Maxwell and Charles would never support him, land grant reinstated or not, and Padre Antonio would turn on him if it appeared that the Taos Indians were in danger from the Texians.

"We're headin' to Abiqui and then out to California. There's money to be had out there."

"Are you turning into prospectors?" Ceran began weighing out the gold dust to purchase the men's flour mill. The increased capacity to manufacture flour would give a real boost to Bent, St. Vrain & Company. This would let them stop shipping in less weighty material—the flour—and concentrate more on luxury goods where the real profits lay.

"Naw, that's for fools. We're openin' trade-goods stores."

"Might be we can make a deal later," Ceran said, passing over the leather pouch bulging with gold dust. "The company might expand out to the Pacific."

"You folks'll have your hands full here," Workman said. "If you do get out our way, look us up. We'll be the fat, rich men sittin' and drinkin' on big front porches."

"Good luck," Ceran said, meaning it. He shook Workman's callused hand and went to see him out of the office.

"We gotta go. Thanks, Ceran." With that, Workman rushed off, leaving Ceran to stare out into the plaza where a dozen Mexican soldiers milled about. He got a sinking feeling in his gut when he saw them, and went to talk with the sergeant in charge of the squad.

"Back," the sergeant said, lowering his musket and menacing Ceran with the fixed bayonet.

"What's wrong?"

"Orders," the soldier said, almost guiltily. "I don't

want to do this thing, but I must. The governor himself ordered it."

"Charles!" cried Ceran, seeing two soldiers dragging the man into the plaza. They held him by his arms between them so his toes dug grooves in the dusty street.

"See to Ignacia and Rumalda," Charles called as the soldiers shackled him and heaved him into the bed of a wagon. "Get Alvarez to post bail again."

Charles Bent didn't look worried, only irritated at behavior that had gone on for years.

"I'll do more than that if they don't release you," Ceran shouted as the rattling wagon circled the plaza and started on the road for Santa Fe. He ran a few steps, then slowed and finally stopped, cursing under his breath. Ceran veered and went to the company store and shouted orders, sending a courier to Bent's Fort and another to Santa Fe, with instructions to contact the American consul and free Charles.

Then Ceran set off to do some recruiting. Manuel Armijo finally had gone too far.

Fear of the Fort

"I have to protest," Consul Alvarez said, pounding his fist on the governor's desk. "You can't mistreat your prisoners like this."

"Why do you care?" Armijo said angrily. "They are rebels, invaders, scum!"

"They're human beings," Alvarez said. "You can't march them to Mexico City with iron shackles on their legs. They won't survive. It's hard enough making the trip along the Rio Grande on horseback with a supply train to back you up."

"They are Texians. They think they are so hard-bitten. But why are you pleading their case? They are not Americans. They belong to their vaunted Republic of Texas. Can it be that you wish they had succeeded in overthrowing my government?"

Outside in the plaza, the bugler assembled the soldiers who were entrusted with guarding the prisoners.

"You will pay for this, Manuel," Alvarez said. "If they succeed in taking over the territory, you'll be branded as a criminal." Alvarez paused a moment, then added, "I spoke with Lewis. He said you murdered two of the men who were with the newspaper editor."

"I had them executed," Armijo said, making a

dismissive gesture with his hand. "If the traitor says anything other than that, he is lying. Why do you believe him and not the great hero of New Mexico?"

"You? The great hero of the people?"

"Get out of my office. I have given you what you wanted. Bent is free, but not for long if he continues to flaunt the law. I will see him brought before the courts as a criminal!"

Alvarez started to say more, then grunted in disgust. He spun and stormed from the governor's office, going outside into the crisp New Mexico autumn air. A sharp wind off the nearby mountains evaporated the perspiration that had beaded on his forehead. Alvarez waved to Charles Bent, who stood at the side of the plaza watching as the dispirited Texian prisoners began their slow, painful shuffle toward distant Mexico.

The consul hurried to Charles's side.

"He refused," Charles said. "He is the great fighter, the greatest soldier in all history, and thinks he is invincible, so he won't grant leniency toward them." Charles watched as the prisoners left the south end of the plaza, their listless pace dictated by the slow tattoo of a drum.

"He'll pay," Alvarez said. "He talks big in public, but I can read Armijo like a book. He's terrified, Charles. He's scared to death of you."

"Me?" Charles laughed. "I spend more time in his jail than I do out. The company profits are dwindling because so much goes to paying my bail. What does Armijo have to fear from peaceable traders?"

"The fort," Alvarez said. "He is frightened that Bent's Fort will be used to launch an attack from America. He might capture starved Texians, but he could never fight even a small company of cavalry led, say, by your friend Captain Cooke."

"Cooke's not my friend. Not really," Charles said. He stared at the squad of soldiers lounging on the far side of the plaza. They eyed him suspiciously, but made no move to come arrest him. Again.

"Armijo is scared," said Alvarez."

"Maybe he heard that Ceran was talking to his old friends. Almost a hundred mountain men have said they would join him in an attack if Armijo kept me in jail, but he's not thinking of using the fort as a base. And that ragtag and bobtail bunch has no military discipline."

"They could topple Armijo, if they can fight. Armijo is an arrogant fool with no real political base in New Mexico. He can't even get Padre Antonio to support him all the time."

"Antonio José Martinez," Charles said, letting the name tumble from his tongue like lumps of burning poison. "He is his own man."

"When Armijo falls, who will the good padre support?"

"It depends on who removes the governor," Charles said. "If Captain Cooke is at the head of the column, you can bet Padre Antonio won't be any happier than he is now. The padre has said more than once he favors an independent country of New Mexico, free from Mexico and America. He would put some of his precious Indians in power, as figureheads only, of course, and he would be the power behind the throne. Mark my words, the good father has ambitions far beyond protecting the Pueblos."

"Charles, face one enemy at a time. Armijo fears you. He has scouts scattered along the Santa Fe Trail all the way through Raton Pass, ready to bring news of invasion from the fort."

"Perhaps that isn't such a bad idea," Charles said. "In fact, it's a mighty fine idea. I'll let Ceran know." He fetched his horse, ready for the trip back to Taos.

Scalped

Bent's Fort
October 30, 1841

"Good to see you again, Ceran," William Bent greeted his friend and partner. "I hope you're bringing good news about Charles."

"Good enough," Ceran said. "He's back in Taos and raising hell again. Ignacia is doing well, too, though she spends a great deal of time at her father's hacienda. Not that I blame her. I don't think we're going to be doing business much longer without keeping a gun close to hand."

"It's that bad?" asked William. He frowned. "I hoped the troubles would die down after the Texians were marched to Mexico for trial. If anything, the political situation is worse, thanks to Armijo's blundering."

"He thinks he is a great man and that the people worship the ground he walks on," Ceran said with a touch of bitterness in his voice. "We can overthrow him. His soldiers aren't well trained and with his aide, Diego, leading the Texians back to Mexico, his only able field commander is gone."

"We can't get involved like that, Ceran. You know that. We might threaten but we're merchants, not revolutionaries. We have to tend to business, and it's trading buffalo robes for items the Cheyenne and, yes, even Armijo need."

"That's nearsighted of you, William. You've stayed too close to the fort to get a feel for what's happening out there." Ceran lifted his bearded chin, indicating the open portal looking eastward across the tules.

"I listen to what the teamsters say, Ceran. I know what's wrong and what's right. We're in a dangerous position in New Mexico. I don't want Charles—or you—endangered by staying longer than necessary in Taos and Santa Fe."

"Without the company stores, our trade would disappear. We need them as much as they need us."

"The Cheyenne are a good market for us," William said. "And the Comanche."

"Have you heard from Robert recently?"

"No, but I'm not worried," William said. "It's hard to send messages from Adobe Walls, but Old Wolf is an honorable chief. The peace agreed to between the Comanche and the Cheyenne will hold, to our benefit."

"There isn't any treaty between the Comanche and America, or between the Comanche and the Texians, for that matter," Ceran said. "Unless you want to consider the peace Colonel Dodge forged to be worth more than a gob of spit."

"Old Wolf wouldn't do anything to jeopardize our trade. You saw how he took to the tour of the fort."

"He's the only Comanche who went through the fort," Ceran said. "There are other bands of Comanche who might not follow Old Wolf."

"Let's have a drink, Ceran. You worry too much."

Together the two went upstairs and to the far northwest corner, where Ceran had a pool table set up next to the bar. The men split one game each after a half bottle of whiskey.

"One more game. Winner takes all," William said.

"What's all?" asked Ceran.

"All the rest of the bottle." William held it up and sloshed around the two fingers left inside.

"I'll win," Ceran said confidently, chalking his cue. He turned and looked at the door when a guard came in. The man was pale and his hands were shaking. He glanced nervously from Ceran to William and then swallowed hard. He dropped his gaze to the floor.

"What's wrong?" William asked, reading the agitation as easily as Ceran. "Go on, man. Tell me."

"Mr. Bent, sir, it—it's your brother."

"Charles! Has Armijo arrested him again? I swear, this time I'll make sure that bloated pig is tossed out of office."

"Sir, it's not Charles. It's Robert."

"What happened?" asked Ceran, seeing William was struck speechless with dread.

"A buffalo hunter came up from Texas with the news just now. The Comanche s-scalped him. He's dead, Mr. Bent. The Comanche killed your brother!"

Trade and Trouble

Bent's Fort
July 2, 1842

"Who do you think it is?" Ceran St. Vrain asked the lookout, who squinted hard into the eyepiece of the telescope. Ceran had spotted the dust cloud to the northeast long before the sentry, but Ceran didn't fault the young boy for that. The boy had been struggling to clean his musket, and had spread parts out all over the parapet. A spring had gone bounding away, and he had chased it just as the unusual dust appeared on the horizon.

"Could be a dust devil," the boy said, "but I reckon it's more likely a whale of a lot of men."

"Friendly?"

"Ain't Indians, if that's what you mean. Looks like they're ridin' in a column. Might be Captain Cooke."

"I don't think so. He's still patrolling to the east, trying to stop the Texians from recruiting for another invasion of New Mexico."

"This smacks of military, Mr. St. Vrain."

Ceran pushed the boy away and spent a few minutes looking at the advancing column. The lookout was right. Military formation but not Captain Cooke.

"That's sure as hell and damnation not Charles Warfield hunting for Texian recruits. Indians would be spread out, Texians would be all bunched up together like they were sheep fearful of a wolf.

"Go tell William and Charles we're having company for dinner," Ceran said. He was glad both men were in the fort right now, although he wasn't too happy with the reason. His brother Marcellin had teamed with the younger Bent brother, George, at Fort St. Vrain to trade for buffalo robes from the Cheyenne and Arapaho, and the shipment was late getting out to Westport.

Ceran hung over the adobe wall waiting for the riders to come closer. He never bothered to load the brass cannon. There wasn't any reason since he recognized the dashing figure at the head of the column.

"Hallo, Lieutenant Frémont!" Ceran called. "Welcome to Bent's Fort. Have your men get around to the south and tend their horses. You can come inside and palaver at length."

"Excellent, Mr. St. Vrain," Frémont called from below. The young lieutenant dismounted, handed his reins to a grizzled-looking scout, and then strode inside, his pace military and precise.

Ceran slid down the steps and thrust out his hand to the officer.

"A pleasure to see you again, Ceran," Frémont said. He looked up to the second story and said, "And the Bent brothers, too."

"You on a vacation or are you doing somethin' useful?" came a joking voice.

"Kit!" Frémont went to the short mountain man, threw his arms around him, and hugged him for a moment.

"What brings you by?" asked Kit Carson.

"An expedition. I'm mapping the entire Colorado

area. And I need another scout. Come along, Kit. You're the best and I won't accept anything less for my expedition."

Charles and William Bent joined them and exchanged pleasantries, but Ceran was in no mood to dally and cut right to the core of the matter.

"You're not mapping the Santa Fe Trail, Lieutenant," Ceran said. "I've got maps better 'n anything you could draw. Why'd you come down this way?"

"To invade New Mexico?" Charles suggested hopefully.

Frémont sobered. "It would be my pleasure to lead an expedition against that despot in Santa Fe," he said, "but I spoke the truth. I am mapping trails to the Pacific, hunting for passes through the Rockies. On my way across Nebraska, I came across Baptiste Charbonneau."

"He ought to be at Fort St. Vrain," Ceran said, frowning.

"Your brothers, St. Vrain and Bent, sent him with a rather large barge load of buffalo hides to Kansas Landing, taking a route along the Platte River."

"We've built a small town at Westport—what you're calling Kansas Landing," Charles said. "It's a day closer to New Mexico than Independence, saving us that much in fodder."

"A day closer," Frémont said, chuckling. "You mean you don't have to deal with the thieving merchants in Independence. I know how they are. I had to go through several to outfit my expedition at a reasonable price."

"How'd you leave Baptiste?" asked Ceran. "What's wrong that you veered this far south?"

"While Miss Charlotte's cuisine is superb enough to draw me halfway across a continent," Frémont said, "you know how I feel about slavery. If you ever manumit her, I will hire her in an instant."

"But . . ." urged Ceran.

"But Charbonneau has run aground on a sandbar and is quite stranded, he and all his buffalo hides. I promised him I would inform someone at this fine fortress of his troubles."

"In exchange for one of Charlotte's meals," William said.

"If you want, I'll head on out and see to Baptiste's troubles," Kit said.

"I'll go with you," Ceran said. "I want to see if he has anything to say about Marcellin."

Charles laughed and said, "You want to check on your brother without seeming to. Very well, I understand." Charles hesitated, then grinned sheepishly. "I'll go with you, too. I want to hear how George is doing."

Beached

An Island in the Platte River
July 15, 1842

"There's fifty tons of buffalo robes getting mildewed out in the middle of that river," moaned Charles Bent. He paced back and forth along the banks of the Platte, hands behind his back as he agonized over the fate of the Bent, St. Vrain & Company property.

"Hey, Baptiste!" shouted Kit Carson, waving to the man sitting on the edge of the beached flatboat. "You goin' our way?"

"If you'll lend a hand, Kit," Baptiste Charbonneau shouted back. "You got the muscle to pull this here boat off? It's loaded with about the thickest bales of buff hides you ever did see."

"We have to dig under it," Ceran St. Vrain said, eyeing the situation critically. "We scoop out sand all around and try to get the river flowing under the entire barge."

"That's how they get riverboats on the Mississippi floating again," Charles said.

"Not exactly. They can use the paddle wheels to force water under the hull. We have to dig," said Ceran. He saw how firmly beached the boat was on the small forested island. He wondered if they might cut a few of the trees and roll the barge off, then discarded the idea.

As heavily laden as the barge was, the rollers would sink into the soft, sandy loam of the island.

"How'd you do this to yourself?" called Kit, stripping off his buckskins until he was bare to the waist. He tossed his shirt aside, then kicked out of his boots. He thrust a toe into the sluggishly flowing river and jerked back. "It's danged cold fer this time of year."

Before Ceran or Charles could answer, Kit took a step back, then ran flat out and launched himself into the river with a war whoop. He cut the water and surfaced halfway to the beached boat. He swam strongly until he got to the sandy island, then pulled himself up.

"It ain't half as bad as it looks," Kit shouted to Ceran and Charles. "I kin git it off inside of an hour."

Ceran threw up his hands, and Charles found a bit of shade alongside the river and waited for Kit and Baptiste to start digging. Kit was wrong. It took the better part of the day to dig a channel for the water, and even then it didn't lift the flat-bottomed boat off. In disgust the men swam to the shore and lay in the sun, stretched out in front of the two company partners.

"Water's down this year," Baptiste explained. "We were making good time, but I thought the current was too slow, so I kept in the river after sundown and never saw the sandbar."

"It'll take another day to get it free," Kit declared.

"We can hitch a line to your horses and have them pull, too," Baptiste suggested.

"No sense getting the barge off this time of day," Ceran said. "We float it in the twilight and run aground again—what have we gained?"

"Nothing but the chance to meet old friends again," Baptiste said cheerfully. He rolled over and looked at Kit. "What's this I hear of you finding yourself a fine lady?"

Kit grinned from ear to ear.

"I'm fixin' to be Charles's brother-in-law," he said. "Or somethin' like that. His wife's sister is 'bout the purtiest woman I ever set eyes on. We're fixin' to marry next year."

"Josepha didn't cotton much to Kit having a half-breed daughter," Ceran said, his voice level. "So he upped and sent Adaline to live with relatives in St. Louis."

"And Don Francisco wasn't too taken with the notion of having another non-Catholic son-in-law, but since Charles turned out so good, he didn't put up too much of a fuss when Jo said she loved me."

"I bet that'll be one wild fandango when you get hitched, Kit," Baptiste said. "I'd love to go. I remember stories my pa used to tell me of how he and Ma met during the expedition and the times after."

"Your ma, Sacajewea, was a fine lady. Shame she had to up and die so young like that," Kit said.

"My pa, too. Disease'll take you quick," Baptiste said.

"Didn't know him, but by all accounts Toussaint was a mighty fine fella," Kit said. "Heard the stories of how both Lewis and Clark talked good on him."

Charles stood and shielded his eyes as he studied the beached boat.

"Ceran," Charles called, "you seeing what I am?"

"No amount of digging and pushing or pulling is going to work," Ceran said.

"What's wrong?" asked Kit, sitting up. Then he saw what the others already had. "I'll be danged. The whole boat's split down the middle. You got fifty tons of buffalo hides beached fer good there."

Baptiste heaved a deep sigh, leaned back, and stared at the darkening sky before speaking.

"How many wagons can you fetch from the fort?"

"Kit," Ceran said, "first thing in the morning, head on back to the fort and see what you can rustle up."

"There'll be a caravan from Taos due any time now," Charles said. "We'll have wagons aplenty to move those hides to St. Louis."

"You gents mind if I don't come back with the wagons?" Kit asked. "I'd as soon go on to Taos."

"And Josepha," Charles said, a slight smile on his lips. "You get on back to Taos, then, and Ceran and I will see the wagons through to St. Louis."

"No point in going to Westport if we have to use wagons from this far north," Baptiste said. "You intend to stay with family, Charles?"

"I haven't seen any of my relatives there in a spell. It'll do me good to get away from William, too. He's still moping over Robert's death."

"I don't intend to mope, not in St. Louis," Ceran said. "I hadn't thought I'd see the best suite at Planters House for a year or so. Too bad I can't wire ahead and let them know I'm coming."

"So they can hide the women?" joshed Kit.

"That's what I like about Planters House. They know better than to try because the prettiest, most willing women will get away and come hunting for me," Ceran said. "Like always."

The men continued their banter until the sun finally set. A buffalo-chip fire was adequate for a small meal. Kit Carson left for Bent's Fort an hour before sunrise, and a week later the wagons rattled up to begin the tedious trip back to the St. Louis markets.

Arrested

Taos
February 2, 1843

"Please, Charles, leave. They are coming for you again," Ignacia Bent said, clutching at her husband's arm. "Armijo will kill you for sure this time."

Charles Bent shook his head. "The governor—and Padre Antonio—have tried for years. They want to annoy me, nothing more."

"Please, Charles," Ignacia pleaded. "For me. For our children. Go to the fort. You'll be safe there."

"The fort is at the heart of Armijo's fear," Charles said. "He thinks we'll use it as a base to launch an assault against him." He snorted in disgust. "For two cents I'd let Warfield and his crazy Texians use it to throw Armijo out."

"No!"

"I'm only joking. If the U.S. wanted to—"

"No, Charles, outside. Listen!"

Charles cocked his head to one side and caught his breath. He had heard the rattle of military gear too often not to recognize it immediately. He reached for a brace of pistols hanging from a peg by the door, then froze when the door crashed open. Charles stared down the bore of a large-caliber musket.

"Stop!" the soldier cried. Charles obeyed. Any show

of resistance now meant his death. The young soldier was frightened, and Charles didn't want to give him the slightest reason to pull back on his trigger.

"Get word to Ceran," Charles called to his wife as soldiers crowded into his house, escorted him outside, and poked and prodded him along to jail again.

Again.

Rendezvous

Raton Pass
February 5, 1843

"Whoa!" Kit Carson called, signaling the dozen mountain men with him to a halt. "I see someone comin' like their ass's on fire." He reached down and pulled out his trusty rifle, drew back the hammer, and laid it across his lap. He knew he should dismount for a better shot, but something told him this wasn't going to be much of a fight.

As he watched carefully, he made out a lone rider. Kit lowered the hammer on his musket and stowed it back in the saddle scabbard.

"Put yer guns away, boys," Kit said. "That there's the man we was supposed to rescue."

Charles Bent rode up, his horse lathered and its flanks heaving from the fast ride down the northern slope of Raton Pass. He took off his hat and waved at Kit as he rode up.

"I see Ignacia got word through to Ceran. Thanks for coming for me," Charles said.

"How'd you get out of the calaboose? Talk that son of a bitch Armijo to death?"

Charles laughed, more out of relief than from the weak humor. "I took a wad of money with me. They called it a 'fine,' I called it a bribe, but I spent eight hundred dollars to get out. I didn't even bother going back to my house because I'd only be arrested again on other trumped-up charges. I reckon Ignacia and the children are with Don Francisco."

"Her pa's a good place to go," Kit said. He still looked forward to a wedding with Josepha Jaramillo and having Charles as a brother-in-law. Charles Bent was an educated man and one Kit looked up to. "Don Francisco won't take anything off Armijo."

"I feel better on that score," Charles said, "but Armijo is mustering all his troops. He had me jailed because he wanted to keep me from helping the Texians. It didn't seem to matter to him that Ceran had told him about the prior Texian invasion."

"Now why'd he want to do a danged fool thing like that?" Kit asked. Then he shook his shaggy head. "Never mind. Armijo ain't thinkin' with his head right now. He wants somebody to rally his folks round him, but the Texians?" Kit laughed at the notion of a new invasion from the Republic of Texas.

"The Texians wouldn't make any better rulers than the Mexicans," Charles said. "It's reaching the point where America's got to move in or there's going to be real bloodshed in New Mexico."

"I heard tell there's a whale of a lot of bluecoats movin' round the area," Kit said, turning his horse and heading back up the road to Bent's Fort. "You think they're what Armijo ought to fear instead of them pesky Texians?"

"Armijo fears his own shadow," Charles said. "The Saint of New Mexico, he wanted to be called. The great liberator of the people. What a popinjay!"

Charles rode alongside Kit, his horse grateful for the slower pace. One by one the mountain men with them took different trails, the danger to their friend passed again.

By the time Kit and Charles reached the fort, it was obvious the soldiers in the area were all dragoons under Captain Cooke's command. The two men rode into the post and dismounted to find Phillip Cooke talking earnestly with William.

"That was mercifully fast," William said, clasping his brother to him. "What of Ignacia and the children?"

"Safe with Don Francisco," Charles said. He turned and shook hands with the cavalry officer. "And are we safe because we have a company of soldiers camped on our front step?"

"Your brother's been kind enough to provision my men," Captain Cooke said. "I'm patrolling the area, trying to run down Warfield. He and a handful of Texians are trying to stir up trouble by recruiting for their Republican Army."

"Are they havin' any luck at it?" asked Kit.

Captain Cooke looked as if he had bitten into a sour persimmon.

"Too much, I fear. Warfield is promising the moon and stars, and some men believe him. There's not a whole lot of jobs for men of that caliber."

"What's enlistment in the Texian Army worth now?" asked Charles.

"Land," Cooke said. "They don't have money, Sam Houston's been voted out of office again, and nobody outside the Republic will loan them a cent. But they have about as much desert and prairie as anywhere in the world, and Warfield is promising vast ranches for men willing to fight against the Mexicans."

"There's some mighty purty land in New Mexico," Kit said. "Too bad for the Texians that Armijo has already recorded the grants he's made." He glanced at Charles, who had been given a sizable amount of Lucien Maxwell's grant after Armijo had reinstated it, because of pressure from all sides except for Padre Antonio. If the Texians tried to seize the land, they would find themselves facing powerful landowning foes that would make the Mexican soldiers under Armijo's command look puny. The best Armijo hoped for was some semblance of loyalty to the regime that had doled out the grants, and fear that the Texians or Americans would not recognize the land titles.

"Warfield's not stupid enough to promise that to anyone, leastwise not that I've heard," Captain Cooke said. "What I fear is that Warfield's real target isn't New Mexico."

"You mean you think the Texians are intent on taking U.S. land?" William stared at the officer, aghast. "They wouldn't dare! They might win free of Mexico, or even think they could claim New Mexico as their property, but not one inch of American soil will ever fall to them!"

"Fine sentiments," Cooke said dryly. "I have three hundred dragoons to make certain it does not happen."

"You want to be sure we're not trading with them?" asked William. "We won't! No one in Bent, St. Vrain and Company will so much as give Warfield and his rebels a drink of water."

"Glad to hear it. Now I need to find where they are."

"Well, Captain," Kit said, "I don't have much to do now that Charles is safe 'n sound." The short, stocky scout shuffled his feet a little, like a young boy too bashful to ask for a sweet. "I'd take it as a real honor if I could poke around a bit for you."

"I can certainly use any information you can unearth,

Kit," Captain Cooke said. "What the Texians do in New Mexico doesn't interest me too much, though I am sure it does the Bents."

"We don't want the Texians invading America," William said hotly. "And Charles and Ceran can deal with anything happening in Taos or Santa Fe. We have many friends there, more than the Texians can ever win over."

"Reckon I'd better lay in some provisions and then hit the trail," Kit said. He hesitated almost shyly, then looked to Charles for approval. "After dinner, if Miss Charlotte's fixin' it."

Charles laughed and slapped Kit on the back. "If she isn't, I'll see that she gets to it right away and prepares something special for us." He looked at William, who nodded agreement, then faced Captain Cooke squarely and said, "It'll be something special for all our friends."

Reconnaissance

Bent's Fort
June 20, 1843

"You're risking too much, Kit," Ceran St. Vrain said. "You're a married man. What's Josepha think of you gallivanting around like this, spying on the Texians?"

"She don't mind much. Hell, Ceran, Charles is spendin' most of his time in jail. Armijo hasn't let up on him, so Ignacia and Jo pass the time together. Ignacia had to dig up their gold stash back in February when Armijo throwed him in the calaboose."

"That's not right," Ceran said. "You should see them moved out of Taos. There's plenty of room here at the fort for them. If what you say is right, Warfield has finally gotten enough men together to launch a good attack on Santa Fe. Heaven knows, he's spent time enough skulking here at the fort trying to enlist the hangers-on into his filibuster. I'm getting mighty sick of telling him to clear out."

"Never saw more 'n a handful of folks willin' to palaver with him," Kit said. "Too bad some of 'em's beaver trappers who can't sell their pelts anymore. I know them folks, and they're good people." Kit heaved a sigh. "Wish Captain Cooke had been able to round up Warfield and his boys, but it was like grabbin' a handful of water. Warfield was always where the captain wasn't."

"The danger's growing, I fear," Ceran said. "Warfield is backed up by Snively's forces from Texas. It won't be long until the pot boils over."

"Reckon so," Kit said, scratching himself. The fleas were bad this year, and nothing he did got rid of them better than scratching. "I heard tell of some massacres takin' place on Mexican wagon trains, one of 'em owned by Armijo. Cain't rightly pin it down, but it might be that Chavez—you remember him?—he was leadin' one wagon and got himself butchered by the Texians."

"There's too much bad blood building," Ceran said grimly.

"But the women'll be safe over in Taos, won't they, Ceran?"

"Not if Armijo takes it into his head to run like a yellow-bellied craven when the Texians go after him," Ceran said. He had dealt with Governor Armijo—too many times—and knew how the man would react. The hero worship he considered his due would quickly evaporate if everything Kit reported was true. Warfield had done more than recruit an army of rag-tag fools. He had found men with some military experience, both in Texas and from various Indian wars. No matter how Captain Cooke chased after Warfield, he had been unable to pin him down.

That told Ceran as much about Warfield's skill as anything else. Cooke was a good officer, and for some of the time had had Kit's expertise to draw on.

"I didn't think he was all he was cracked up to be, but from what you say, Warfield just might overthrow Armijo."

"Armijo's not got the sand in his gizzard for the

fight that's on his way. Can't rightly fix the number Warfield's mustered, but it's enough to worry Captain Cooke. Don't much think of him as a worrier."

"What's best for us, for the company?" mused Ceran, thinking aloud. He leaned against the adobe wall of the fort battlement and stared to the south, toward the Arkansas River. That presented a small impediment to invasion by the Texians, but not that much if they were determined. They had to see Bent's Fort as a handy base for their attack on New Mexico. Resolve hardened in Charles. They would never use William's fort for such a purpose.

"You think it might be a good idea to let them Texians smash into Armijo, then have American troops swoop in on 'em like a hawk after a kangaroo rat?" asked Kit.

"Do we do better dealing with the Mexicans or the Texians?" countered Ceran. "A new devil's no better than the old, and will probably be worse. The Mexicans aren't interested in expanding, only in hanging on to what they have. The Texians are showing how intent they are on conquest."

"Yep," Kit said, scratching some more. "If they push Armijo out and don't break a sweat, they'll be on our doorstep 'fore you can sneeze twice."

"They'd go from Santa Fe to Taos and seize the stores at the ends of the trade routes," Ceran said. "Then they'd come on north across Raton Pass. Warfield has already mapped the entire country while he's been sweeping back and forth hunting for recruits."

"Cain't say the Texians would treat a Mexican citizen too good," Kit said. "What do you want me to do, Ceran?"

"Go up to Fort St. Vrain and find out what George and Marcellin have to say about their shipments. I'm worried that another one might have been sent out and gotten beached along the Platte. And keep your eyes peeled for trouble, Kit."

"Trouble has a way of findin' me," Kit said with a gusty sigh. "I'm missin' Jo already, back in Taos. Still, even if them Texians win, they got to respect the land-holders, Mexican or Indian. Lucien Maxwell and Charles and—"

"And nothing, Kit. They're a foreign army invading an adjoining country. They won their independence from Mexico a long time back, and are smarting from the way Lewis turned traitor and helped Armijo defeat their first expedition. This is a war of conquest. They won't stop if they taste victory." Ceran wondered if the Texians knew his role in reporting their earlier invasion to Armijo. That wouldn't sit well with them, if they found out, and would jeopardize the company stores. Ceran knew they would take any excuse to seize Mexican property.

"I don't think none of the folks'll want to turn tail and run, 'specially Josepha and Ignacia."

"Then send word to them to barricade your houses and get ready for what might be a siege, if Armijo can't stop the Texians. But find out first what's happening up north with our wagons."

Ceran St. Vrain stared south and saw only trees along the river. But beyond that stretched grassland, and beyond that mountains and Santa Fe and the probable destiny for the entire region. As much as he hated to do it, Ceran knew where his duty lay.

Attack—and Die

Mora, New Mexico Territory
June 22, 1843

Ceran St. Vrain found Santa Fe bustling with news of the impending Texian attack. He rode to the office of the consul, but Manuel Alvarez was gone, his office stripped clean as if he had fled town. Ceran spent the next hour or so checking on employees at the Bent, St. Vrain & Company store, then knew he had to deliver his message to Armijo. The governor had rallied an army to meet the Texian threat before, but Ceran had to be sure Armijo understood what he really faced this time. If everything Kit had discovered was true, not only Warfield, with a well-trained army, but also Colonel Snively would mount their attack. The Texians had so far been more bluster than fight, proclaiming themselves the owners of not only New Mexico Territory, but also lower and upper California, with Arizona thrown in for good measure. With both Texian forces joined, that bluster would become a real threat.

Ceran felt like a traitor even thinking about warning Armijo, yet he had little choice. He had alerted the governor once before, and it had not really benefited the company, Charles, or Ceran personally. If anything, Armijo's harassment had increased. But

New Mexico under Texian rule was far worse than under Mexican.

"Better the devil we know," grumbled Ceran as he left the store, knowing he had to chase down the governor. He took a second horse from the company stable to make better time, and started riding for Mora, spending an hour on one horse before switching to the other to give the first mount a rest.

The hot wind blew against his face, but the sounds of battle reached him before the scent of gunpowder and death.

Ceran pulled down his broad-brimmed hat and kept riding. It was too late to warn Armijo of the size and composition of the Texian army he faced, but perhaps it wasn't too late to see how the battle went.

He reached a draw leading to a small town and paused. Beyond the town of Mora he saw the ebb and flow of the fighting. Ceran started to back away, but found himself caught up by the drama of the fiercely fought battle. The Texians were better armed and had reached high ground before Armijo's soldiers, but the Mexicans valiantly assaulted the superior position.

Ceran rode into Mora to the church, went inside, and climbed into the bell tower for a better view of the fighting.

Ceran's stomach churned when he saw how quickly the Texians overwhelmed Armijo and his forces. The governor had ridden out in his flashy medal-festooned powder-blue uniform, now stained with blood and streaked with black gunpowder from repeated nearby musket fire. Armijo rode around in circles, as if he had no idea what to do. He waved his bright saber about futilely, then did what he ought to have earlier.

"Retreat!" Manuel Armijo cried.

Only a handful of soldiers answered his call. They raced from the field, followed by sporadic gunfire and loud jeers from Warfield's troopers. Ceran watched as Armijo beat his retreat down the road leading to Santa Fe, and knew the capital lay with its belly exposed to the Texian threat. There was no chance at all the governor would come to his senses, rally another fighting force, and put up a decent defense of the city.

Ceran worked his way out of the bell tower and mounted. He knew that there was no point in following the routed governor. While he could ride north and probably avoid the Texians, he chose to go into their guns. He had to find what their strengths were and learn their intentions, if he could.

"Ho!" Ceran called. "Charles Warfield! It's Ceran St. Vrain from Bent's Fort!"

"Advance and be recognized," the Texian commander said, strutting out. He wore a bright red broadcloth sash around his middle where two pistols were thrust, cross-draw style. The man bled from a cut on his cheek and was grimy from gunsmoke, but otherwise looked like the cock of the walk.

"What's happened?" Ceran said, wanting to hear Warfield's report.

"We whupped up on them, that's what, Ceran. You come to join us?"

Ceran looked around and saw the Texians tending to their minor wounds. He also saw the Mexican dead. A quick count tallied up twenty or more, with ten times that rounded up and being held under the Texians' guns.

"You look to have struck a real victory today."

"That we have, Ceran. We captured all their weapons and supplies and danged near all of them, to boot!"

"What are you going to do with them?" Ceran saw Warfield stiffen at this.

"We ought to shoot the whole damned scurvy lot of them," Warfield snapped. "After what they did to our prisoners a couple years back. And they slaughtered three hundred of our finest down around San Antonio 'fore sneakin' back across the Rio Grande."

"Hadn't heard of that," Ceran said, still counting and trying to figure what Warfield intended to do now.

"Happened not more than a month back. That's why Houston finally got some spine and sent Snively to back us up."

"Doesn't look as if you killed many Mexicans," Ceran said. "More of the dead are from the Pueblos."

"Armijo can't get his own men to fight, so he sends them Taos Indians against us. It doesn't matter one whit to me. They poke their heads up, we shoot 'em off."

Ceran nodded slowly. Armijo had lost perhaps twenty soldiers, with another thirty Taos Indians who had been used as an advance guard to draw the Texians' fire.

"Like to jaw a while more, Ceran, but I got work to do."

"What might that be?"

Charles Warfield looked sharply at Ceran, then said, "If I didn't know the fuss Armijo makes over your partners, I'd think you was here to spy for him."

"I wish him nothing but ill," Ceran said truthfully. He had a cold knot in his belly from the way Warfield looked at him. The Texian was remembering how Ceran had been hostile to his recruitment and had chased him away more than once from Bent's Fort, never even allowing him to water his horses.

"That's what you say, but I recollect you're a Mexican citizen."

"For business only. Taxes are lower," Ceran said. "What do you intend to do with your prisoners?" He tried to distract Warfield from his suspicions.

"We can be generous," Warfield said. "We'll hold them for a spell, then let them go."

Ceran nodded in agreement, but knew why the Texians would probably do just that. There wasn't any way they could guard prisoners numbering damned near as many as they had in their fighting force. Even if Snively showed up soon, the question of the prisoners would remain a problem.

"That's mighty generous," Ceran said. He looked across the battlefield to where a few Texians moved bodies into an arroyo, and saw a rider approaching from the east. From the way the Texians greeted the newcomer, he wasn't one of theirs.

"Reckon I'd better let you get to your chores," Ceran said. He waited until Warfield saw the approaching rider, and from the Texian commander's expression, he knew this might be Snively's courier come to see how the fight had gone.

"Yeah, we'll see you at the fort real soon, Ceran," Warfield said, turning away. Ceran took the opportunity to ride off, trying not to gallop. The Texians had won the day and possibly New Mexico, and William back at the fort had to be warned. Ceran could not ignore Warfield's parting words.

". . . see you at the fort real soon."

Attack—and Rout

100th Meridian
July 30, 1843

"You have any news for me?" Captain Cooke asked Kit Carson. "The Texians have been bouncing all over, and I can use whatever information you've uncovered since you took off with that wagon train last month."

"I done what I tole Ceran I'd do, checkin' on his brother Marcellin up at Fort St. Vrain," Kit said. "Then I followed his wagons down along the Platte till I came across your column and the other wagon train bound for the fort. It was a godsend to me when you didn't offer to guard them all the way."

"Three hundred dollars," Cooke said suddenly. "I heard they offered you three hundred dollars to escort them."

"You heard rightly, Captain," Kit said, "but I got them to the fort just fine, hightailed it to Taos, and found the whole danged place in an uproar. The Pueblo Indians didn't cotton much to having Armijo send them into battle and get slaughtered the way they did at Mora. Padre Antonio is stirrin' up dissent."

"Dissent?" Captain Cooke laughed harshly. "Hatred is more the card he plays."

"You could call it that. He don't much like Armijo, but he don't like the Bents, either. The company store was looted and the manager sent me to fetch new supplies, but I ran into Lucien along the way."

"Lucien Maxwell?"

"He was comin' down from Fort St. Vrain. They ain't got more 'n salt and unbolted Mexican flour left. Rains been keepin' things mighty wet up north, too, and that don't do much for trade. That and the Ute bein' on the warpath."

Captain Cooke muttered under his breath, then said, "Is the whole of the West gone crazy? Armijo and Ute on the warpath and starvation along with Texians everywhere."

"Riots in Taos," Kit said. "That's what worried me. I done hired a trader to take the news to the fort so William can get ready. I want my family and Charles's family where they won't get hurt none."

"And you happened to come across my dragoons by accident?" asked Cooke.

"Well, not exactly, Captain," Kit said. "I was hopin' to meet up with Frémont. He's mounted a second expedition, but the rain and conditions kept me away. Just sorta happened I found you." Kit grimaced as a three-inch cannon went off. "Fact is, I *heard* you and came to see what the fuss was. I worried it might be the Texians since it surely wasn't like no thunder I'd ever heard."

"The men were practicing with the artillery," Cooke said a bit self-consciously.

"Looked to me like they was shootin' at buffalos."

"We needed the meat. Stew meat," the captain added hastily. "So will you scout for me?"

"You heard how Warfield routed Armijo's army. What is it you want me to do, Captain?"

Phillip Cooke looked around, then stepped closer to Kit before speaking. "I need someone who can't tell where we are."

"Beg pardon?"

"I am entrusted with defending the citizens and sovereignty of the United States," Cooke said. "Sometimes, that chore causes me to become a little . . . disoriented."

"You askin' me to keep you on your proper course or not?" Kit frowned. He didn't understand what the officer meant.

"No, sir, that is not what I'm saying," Cooke declared in exasperation. "I want you to scout and not ask too many questions. Just know that Mr. St. Vrain has given me important information, in the strictest of confidence, and I find myself duty-bound to act upon it." Cooke bellowed for his orderly. A corporal ran up carrying a tattered, yellowed map. Cooke unfolded it on the ground, using stones to hold the torn corners.

"We're about here," Kit said, after looking around the countryside and matching it with the map. He had an innate sense of direction and never experienced any trouble locating positions with a map.

"We are," Captain Cooke said, "and we're heading here."

"But that there's south of the hundredth meridian and out of the U.S.," Kit said. Then it dawned on him what the captain had been hinting at so broadly. "Well, maybe not. Maybe I read the map wrong by a few miles." He stared hard at Cooke, who did not flinch. "Think we should get some water along the Cimarron River?"

"An excellent idea, Mr. Carson. Will you do the honor of leading us?"

Kit and Captain Cooke looked downslope along the bank of the Cimarron River, well away from American soil.

"See yonder?" Kit said, pointing to the far horizon and a churning dust cloud. "That's another buncha men ridin' in. They ought to be no more 'n a day or day and a half's ride from Santa Fe."

"Snively," Captain Cooke said, "coming to join forces with Warfield. That settles the matter. We cannot let the two Texian companies combine. We have to take Warfield now before the others reach his camp." Cooke motioned for his bugler, who trotted to his side.

"Sound assembly, wait one minute, then sound the charge."

Kit saw the bugler's eyes widen. There weren't any men in Captain Cooke's company who didn't realize they were illegally treading on foreign soil.

Cooke unstrapped his heavy saber and fastened it to his saddle. He fumbled in his saddlebags and drew forth a second pistol, checked to be sure it was loaded, then unfastened the leather flap over his holstered weapon. Like most experienced cavalry officers, Cooke chose not to use the cumbersome sword in real combat.

"Come along, Mr. Carson," the captain said, mounting. "I'll need you to take orders back to my artillery battery. If we are not quickly victorious over Warfield's unit, the enemy must be destroyed by cannonade."

"As long as yer gunnery officers know the range," Kit said uneasily. Riding back and forth on ground covered by the artillery didn't suit him, but he realized Cooke meant to call down fire on his own head if they failed to capture or rout Warfield's men.

"Bugler, sound the charge!"

Kit tried to keep up with Captain Cooke as the officer galloped down the hill and across the grassland toward the encamped Texians. The charge caught

Warfield and his men by surprise. Kit held back; this wasn't his fight and he had an important job to do should Cooke's assault fail.

It didn't. Kit watched the wedge of cavalry cut through Warfield's camp, separating the Texians into disorganized segments. From what he could tell, all the Republic officers were on one side, and a goodly portion of the troops were cut out like calves from the herd on the other. This caused even worse confusion in the Texian ranks.

Cooke wheeled about and charged again, going for the clot of officers. A few tried to fire on him, but resistance turned out to be ineffectual.

Kit saw several spirited fights going on, but they quickly died when the Texians realized they faced an organized, trained cavalry that could destroy them as quickly as they had destroyed Armijo's detachment weeks earlier.

"Surrender, sir, surrender or die!" Cooke drew his second pistol and aimed both at Warfield, while clutching the reins in his teeth. Kit wondered how Cooke could ever hope to fight like that, but the sight turned Warfield pale.

"Don't go shootin'!" Warfield cried. He issued hurried orders for his men to surrender.

"Throw down all your rifles," Cooke shouted. The Texians obeyed hastily, seeing how they were cut into small flocks like sheep and were under the American guns. "Mr. Carson, go back to the hill and issue the order I have given you."

"But—" Kit saw Captain Cooke wasn't joking. He jerked his horse about and galloped back across the prairie, heading for the low rise where the artillery had lined up. Four cannon were trained on the area below, making Kit wonder what the captain had in mind.

"What's the order, sir?" asked the sergeant in charge of the battery.

"Fire," Kit said. "He wants you to fire at your target." The immediate discharge of a nearby cannon almost unseated Kit. He fought to keep his horse from bucking or rearing to paw at the air. Once it was under control, he turned and looked back at the Texian encampment along the river, thinking he would see it blown to hell and gone. To his surprise, the sergeant had elevated the cannon muzzles and lobbed shells to the far side of the river. Shell after shell exploded amid Snively's arriving force, throwing them into disarray.

Rather than attempt a rescue of Warfield's captured force, Colonel Snively beat a hasty retreat to the south. From what Kit could tell, Snively's men left behind a considerable amount of supplies as they raced away to keep from joining Warfield's men in American captivity.

After four rounds from each cannon, the sergeant ordered the batteries to fall silent. The smell of powder in the air made Kit's nose drip and his eyes water, but the cessation of firing was more palpable. It felt as if someone had grabbed him up and enveloped him in cotton wool. It took him a few seconds to realize he was deafened by the cannon's roar.

Then a ringing came to his ears and he slumped a mite, knowing the fight was over.

"Return to the captain with my compliments on a battle well won, sir," the sergeant called.

By the time Kit rode to the camp beside the river, Captain Cooke had stacked all the captured rifles and had stripped the Texians of their supplies. Warfield and the rest of his invading force were sent unceremoniously across the Cimarron and told in no uncertain terms to stay within the borders of their Republic. If

Snively had not been delayed and Warfield had pressed his victory over Armijo, the Texians could have taken Santa Fe within days. Instead, Warfield had waited for his superior officer—possibly ordered to do so because the colonel wanted some credit for the conquest of New Mexico. If so, that had been a terrible mistake and had cost the Texians a grand victory.

The second invasion of New Mexico had been turned back, this time by American forces.

Report and Away

Bent's Fort
August 1, 1843

"I'll give him this, Cooke is one helluva soldier," Kit Carson told William Bent.

William knocked back a shot of whiskey and poured himself another, stronger one. He held out the bottle, silently offering Kit more. The shaggy mountain man eagerly thrust out his empty glass for two additional fingers of the potent amber fluid.

"He sent them Texians a-runnin' like scalded dogs. There's no chance they'll be back."

"I've heard reports that there isn't much support for a new invasion, not with the trouble they're having within their own borders," William said. "That's a relief, but we still run a considerable risk here. The Ute are rampaging throughout the entire area to the west of us, and other tribes are threatening to join them. The post over at Pueblo is thinking on closing up entirely, and I don't blame them. They didn't build as securely as we did here."

"The Cheyenne, too?" Kit asked anxiously, loudly slurping at his whiskey.

"No, of course not, but they might get sucked into the war if the Ute continue their raids. Nowhere on the plains is safe from the Sioux and the Comanche."

William fell silent for a moment, his look distant and pained. "We know about the Comanche."

Kit saw that William was still pining away for his brother Robert. The youngest Bent's death had been especially vexatious because of the big show of peace between the Cheyenne and Comanche. Old Wolf had been taken by his exclusive tour of the fort, and had left everyone feeling that the blanket of peace spread over the Bents, too.

It hadn't.

"Armijo is cowering somewhere, because I don't think he's heard how the Texians were routed," William went on. He chuckled unexpectedly. "Is Cooke going to get into trouble for going into New Mexico to fight the Texians?"

"Don't suppose he's gonna keep that much of a secret from his superiors," Kit said. "He warned me not to talk on it, but ever'one knows already. Anyone with a speck of brains'd know what he done. They ought to give him a medal for it."

"We need to make a deal with Captain Cooke," William said. "I have to go north to palaver with some Cheyenne chiefs at a big powwow, but both Ceran and Charles will be here in a week or so."

"Cooke'll mosey up this way eventually. He's got a mountain of rifles he'll want to trade."

"He won't trade them for supplies," William said, running his finger around the rim of his shot glass as he thought. "He doesn't want to give rifles to rival factions among the increasingly violent Indian tribes."

"Could move 'em down to Taos. Charles needs to have an armory handy if Armijo gets out of hand."

"We don't have enough employees at the Taos store to make a difference," William said, turning grim. "Padre Antonio has stirred up the Taos Indians against us, too, and no matter what Charles says, this is the real danger. Armijo is on his way out, but the priest is a permanent fixture."

"Padre Antonio's brother's the danged magistrate," Kit pointed out. "Gettin' the whole law force on his side wouldn't take more 'n a snap of his fingers."

"We'll make do," William said. "We always have and we always will, even if the government is dead set against us. The company is too secure not to endure." He sat up straighter in the chair as he faced Kit. "You moving on? You have that look."

"Frémont ast me to scout for him. I heard what a success his first expedition was, and I surely do want to be part of anything that gent does."

"His wife certainly writes a lively piece," William said dryly.

"Fine folks. I truly do admire them."

"Go on, Kit. I've heard Frémont is camped down the Arkansas River not twenty miles west of here. The rains have kept him from making any progress on his scout."

"Thank you kindly, William," Kit said, shooting to his feet. "I don't mind workin' for Bent, St. Vrain and Company, but this is a chance I'd be a fool to pass on."

"Good scouting, Kit," William said, "and I expect to see you again soon—with your scalp where it belongs!"

Kit laughed at this and left William sitting in his room with the bottle on the table. William slowly emptied the whiskey bottle, growing more morose with every drink. Robert had been scalped, and Kit might be, too, if he tangled with the Ute. Those Indians were powerful, smart, and spread throughout Colorado, the very country Frémont intended to map. Worse, Charles insisted on spending too much time in Taos. If William had ever seen a powder keg, that was it.

"What about you, George?" William said, getting drunker. He toasted his brother up north, and then Ceran St. Vrain, wherever he might be. Then he started all over with his toasts until he fell asleep at the table, his dreams turning to nightmares of massacre and rivers running bank-to-bank with blood.

Bent blood.

Provisions
and Protection

"That's quite a troop you have with you, Captain," Ceran St. Vrain said, walking out to meet Phillip Cooke. The officer climbed down from his saddle, took off canvas gloves, and then rubbed his butt before turning to see if any of his men had noticed this momentary lapse of military bearing. They were in scarcely better condition.

"Mighty tired, Ceran," Cooke said. "We've been run ragged by the Sioux and even a Ute raiding party out on the plains. They are about the best horsemen I have come across, and I thought the Comanche were born astride their ponies."

"Come on in. Charles is in the kitchen telling Charlotte to whip up a meal for you."

"I see you just returned from St. Louis," the officer said, walking through the vestibule and into the fort *placita*. He looked around and saw the entire courtyard piled high with supplies.

"The wagons are on their way down to Taos with the remainder," Ceran said, seeing Cooke's puzzlement.

"You unloaded this much and still needed all your wagons? I didn't see any parked around the fort."

"Those were sent north to my brother," Ceran said. "We've had nothing but trouble with shipments to Westport and St. Louis from our post there. The Platte has been alternately flooded and dry, and we've beached too many barges for me to remember."

"I spoke with George Bent," Captain Cooke said. "He tells me much the same story."

"Did he also say we've got a real fear of getting across to Westport without Indians burning our wagons? They've stopped stealing from us and only destroy now, as if this will drive the white man off their ancient hunting land."

"That's a faint hope on their part," Cooke said. "We're here to stay. Ah, Charles, so good to see you!" The officer hurried over and shook hands with Charles Bent. They exchanged pleasantries, and then went inside where a table had been set with its finest cutlery, linen tablecloths, and crystal goblets.

Captain Cooke took one look and stopped in his tracks.

"What do you want from me, gentlemen? This is a meal fit for the president himself."

"Mr. Tyler is not likely to come. Yes, Phillip, all for you. Please. Sit down."

"I can take the place of honor in his stead, I suppose," Captain Cooke said, grinning. "I favor annexation of the Republic of Texas, also, even if it is not too popular."

The food was served, one course at a time, until seven were done and dessert of apple pie was placed in front of the captain.

"I know you want something from me. Ceran?

Charles? You don't dish out Miss Charlotte's fine pies to broken-down army officers."

"We could dance around it some more, Phillip, but why bother? You were busy chasing after the Texians when the wagon train asked for your protection."

"Kit Carson was paid three hundred dollars to escort them here. Safely, I am sure."

"Yes, Kit did a fine job. But that wasn't one of the company wagon trains. Bent, St. Vrain and Company requires more assurance that our cargoes will be delivered and that foodstuffs arrive on a regular basis."

"You want me to protect your wagons? In exchange for what?" Captain Cooke forked another chunk of the pie into his mouth, adeptly catching a crumb and popping it into his mouth.

"The army needs provisions. We are a devoted American outpost and unlikely to ever fly another flag on our pole. We will keep your troops in food and ammunition if you will send a squad along with every wagon train to keep them safe from the Sioux."

"And Ute and even Mexican *bandidos,*" Captain Cooke finished. He dropped his linen napkin on the table and pushed away slightly. "Well?" he said.

"Well? I don't understand," said Charles.

"You didn't fete me without a formal contract all drafted. Bring it on, let me look it over, and I shall probably sign it."

A few rounds of whiskey sealed the contract.

Grants

Santa Fe
December 8, 1843

"It appears that Christmas has come early this year," Ceran St. Vrain said, staring intently at Manuel Armijo. The governor barely endured a tic under his left eye, and his usually swarthy complexion had turned sallow. Ceran wondered if the man was well. From the way his hands shook and his dark eyes darted about at every slight sound, the governor was on the way to a lunatic asylum. "The winter snows are deep and give the land a deceptively peaceful appearance."

"You know I have no love for the Bents," Armijo said, his voice breaking slightly. He glanced out the narrow window onto the plaza, its cottonwood trees draped with feathery curtains of ice and the ground carpeted with almost a foot of new snow.

"You reinstated the Maxwell Grant, and Charles was given a portion of it by Lucien Maxwell."

"Padre Antonio was livid about that. I rescinded the original grant, but I had no choice. And I have very little in this. You are one of the most prosperous citizens of Mexico living in this territory. Are you loyal, Señor St. Vrain?"

"I find it difficult to support any regime persecuting my friends and those with whom I have no real quarrel." Ceran did not state his concerns about the way Armijo tormented the Taos Indians. In this Ceran found himself uncomfortably agreeing with Padre Antonio that great evil was being done under the guise of securing the territory against American invasion and occupation.

"They oppose me!" raged Armijo, jumping to his feet and knocking over his chair. His eyes were wild and he grabbed for the saber dangling at his side. He breathed heavily for a moment, then settled down. "I dare not allow the Americans a foothold in the territory any more than I did the Texians."

Ceran remained silent. He knew Armijo had written numerous letters to Mexico City detailing how Bent's Fort could be used as a base against both Santa Fe and Taos by the Americans. The governor knew Bent, St. Vrain & Company had also entered into an agreement with Captain Cooke—and the United States—to provision troops in exchange for protection from Sioux and Ute attacks. It had to appear as if they were conspiring with Cooke and the American government to seize New Mexico Territory soon, perhaps in the spring.

Ceran heaved a sigh. Always so much plotting and double-dealing. Would life ever be peaceable again? The Comanche had settled down again. For the moment. It amazed him how William spoke of renewed trade with them, in spite of the way a raiding band had killed and scalped his brother.

The matter of the Indians was taken care of. But Ceran wasn't certain what drove Armijo now. Shifting uncomfortably in his chair to squarely face the distraught governor, Ceran remained quiet and simply waited.

"I am sorry, Señor St. Vrain," Armijo said. "You have

done much to prevent the Texian conquests by your timely information. It is just that the pressures of governance are becoming so great."

"I'm sure," Ceran said dryly.

"You are a Catholic, no?" Ceran nodded in agreement. "You are a citizen, too. You would have much to lose should the Americans seize New Mexico."

"I can't say it is anything I seek. All I want is free flow of trade."

"As a Mexican citizen, they would imprison you and perhaps line you up against the wall, to execute you."

Ceran blinked at such ravings. What frightened him even more was that Armijo believed this would happen if the Americans took over New Mexico. More likely, the Mexican government's lack of support and Armijo's own policies would cause the territory to rot from within. If Padre Antonio and the Taos Indians he led did not openly welcome American soldiers, the rest of New Mexico might, simply to remove Armijo and his arbitrary orders.

Even the good Taos priest would not mourn Armijo's departure, seeing in the chaos of change a possibility for independence for the Pueblos.

"I wish to commend you for all you have done for the people of Mexico who reside in these lands."

"I do what I can," Ceran said carefully. This meeting had not taken the route he had expected. If anything, he had thought Armijo might declare him an enemy of the state and either arrest him or run him out of New Mexico.

"I have a deed prepared granting you a small property, which you must develop and defend against all foreign invaders. Accept it with the gratitude of a beneficent Mexican government." Armijo pushed an ornately lettered paper across the desk in Ceran's direction.

He took it and quickly scanned it. Amid the dangling red and blue ribbons, gold seals, and fancy signet imprints, he saw that Armijo had granted him more than a million acres of land.

Blizzard

Along the Santa Fe Trail
March 22, 1844

The heavy gray storm clouds slid as smoothly and silently through the sky to the north as if they were on greased rollers. Ceran St. Vrain tried to determine the direction of the wind, but felt nothing blowing against his chapped cheeks. He thrust his finger into his mouth, and held it up to see which side cooled from wind evaporation, but this summer trick did not work. His entire fingertip turned icy, without giving any clue to the wind.

"Try this," Charles Bent said. He jumped from his horse and scooped up a double handful of snow. He held it for a moment, as if weighing it like he might a pile of precious gold dust, then tossed it high into the air. The snow separated and created a miniature storm, the snowflakes twisting and turning brightly in the wan afternoon sunlight.

"No wind," Ceran said, watching the snow spiral directly back to the ground. "Or are you seeing something I missed?" He looked at the distant lead-bellied clouds sliding off the Front Range and hurrying across the Nebraska and Kansas prairie.

"I'm not sure this is good news," Charles said, sniffing hard at the frigid air. "That storm's coming this way, and we might not have long before the wind kicks up so we get some of that." He jerked his thumb in the direction of the clouds Ceran had studied so intently. Lightning flashed, but the thunder was swallowed by distance.

"We shouldn't have separated from the rest of the wagon train," Ceran said. "William doesn't have anyone but greenhorns driving the wagons he brought down from Independence."

"Sam Owens is experienced enough," Charles said, but Ceran saw his partner was worried, too.

"Owens is going on to California—and with a load of contraband tobacco." Ceran had to chuckle at that. If the new New Mexico governor got wind of two wagons loaded with illicit tobacco, he would sputter and storm about for days, maybe even calling out his dispirited troopers to stomp around and pretend they cared. Governor Mariano Martinez had decreed only shipments from Mexico. His shipments. Ceran considered buying the tobacco from Owen and giving it away, then decided they had trouble enough with the new governor without stirring the boiling pot even more.

"With twenty wagons, we can't make very good time, and there's nowhere to take cover." The grasslands stretched to a low line of rolling hills ten miles to the west in front of them. In all directions he saw only small ravines and gently sloping hills—nothing that would afford protection if the storm bit down hard on them.

"Maybe we should wait for William to catch up with us. It might be easier ride out the storm if we rejoined our trains. How far off do you think he and the rest of the wagons might be?" asked Ceran. He kept staring at the storm clouds, increasingly anxious over the approaching storm.

"Far enough that we can't see them, although this is about the flattest land between Westport and the fort." Charles heaved a big sigh. They had left the eastern terminus with thirty-four wagons and two dearborns. Sixty men or thereabouts worked as teamsters, but not all belonged to Bent, St. Vrain & Company. At this time of year, the army protection promised by Captain Cooke was lacking, and safety, mostly against the changeable weather, lay in a number of small wagon trains making up a much larger caravan.

"We'd better keep our wagons moving, then. There's no point heading back," Charles said. "William is more likely to find us by following our tracks than we are to find him, if he picked a different road. Besides, I don't like backtracking and losing precious time."

"The mules are up for it," Ceran said. "I wonder how William's oxen are doing."

"He's probably letting that Bill Boggs drive, if I know him. I like the boy, but William has taken a real shine to him."

"His brother Tom's been a good worker at the fort. The two of them together would be a real terror. William said he wanted to send the pair of them up to Fort St. Vrain and keep George in Taos to run the store there, or perhaps send him out as a wagon master later in the year to get some experience with shepherding wagon trains."

"George is as sharp as a whip," Charles said of his brother. "Leaving him in charge of the fort shows how much William thinks of him. I do, too, for that matter. It's a good thing for him to get all the experience he can since the company's bound to expand more, if Mexico ever releases its control of New Mexico Territory."

Ceran and Charles rode alongside the lead wagon

struggling on the deeply rutted ice and mud road, talking of how nice it would be to reunite the wagon train and eventually sit around a fire at Bent's Fort. But both kept their eye on the storm advancing from the north. From hard, bitter experience they knew how vicious such blue northers could be as they swept uninhibited across the flatlands.

"It's getting colder," Charles said an hour later. "No wind yet, but the temperature's dropping mighty fast. The lightning has died down, but that's not much of a turn of luck for us."

"Keep moving," Ceran decided. He craned around in the saddle, hoping against hope to spot William's wagons on the road behind them. Only ice-crusted prairie broken by their wagon wheels showed.

"Thanks for giving me so much of your land grant," Charles said unexpectedly. "Do you think Armijo ever knew?" He had to chuckle. Before they had started east with their wagons, Ceran had deeded over fifteen percent of the million-acre grant Armijo had given him as protection against American invasion. Santa Anna had quietly removed Armijo from his position and recalled him to Mexico City less than a month earlier. Neither Ceran nor the Bents considered it any loss, although they had to see what deviltry the new governor conjured up.

"He must have been sure the Americans would invade to be so generous to me," Ceran said. "I was worried about something happening to me, and you and your family certainly deserve some compensation for all you've put up with. With the section of land from Lucien's grant, you owned damned near as much New Mexico land as anyone, Charles."

"Don Francisco can manage the land," Charles said. "I'm thinking of putting the land in the name of the company, though that might not be such a good idea."

"I don't think the law allows a mercantile business to own real estate, only individuals," Ceran said. He knew Francisco Jaramillo would be an excellent custodian for the land, fairly dividing it and seeing that it was developed over the next seven years, as required by the law. It didn't matter that Armijo had lost his control of New Mexico, or even if the Americans took over, deposing the new governor. The land was securely in the possession of men who would put it to good use.

"Wind," Charles said suddenly. "I felt a gust against my face."

"Me, too," Ceran said, looking around. His heavy coat hindered him, but he saw how the storm track had changed. The dark clouds no longer sailed along a parallel course, but now showed an intersecting one. He made some quick estimates. "We've got an hour before the storm hits."

"Which wagon has the firewood in it?" asked Charles. "Gathering buffalo chips to ride out this storm's not going to be possible."

"I brought three wagons loaded with wood. It's expensive, I know, but if the storm is as fierce as it looks, we might need every stick. Too bad William doesn't have any." Ceran regretted saying that the instant the words slipped from his mouth. Charles turned glum as he began to worry in earnest about his younger brother.

Charles waved to catch the lead muleteer's attention and halted him. Clanking and rattling and creaking, one wagon after another reined in.

"Circle as tightly as you can," Charles told the driver. "We need to keep the mules near us and the fire."

"You want a bonfire?" the freighter asked.

"Not right away. Get a goodly fire started, and we'll see how much more wood is needed. Storms blow over in a few hours."

"Seen 'em last days," the freighter said, wiping his lips as he studied the ugly, black clouds boiling toward them. "This might be the worst storm of all."

"And then again, it might miss us," Ceran said, trying to put a cheerier face on it and alleviate some of Charles's worry about William. "The storm is going to pass to the east of us, if we're lucky. We might be caught on the edge, but the worst of it will miss us."

"Hope you're right, boss," the teamster said, putting his arm into cracking the long whip so it snapped right behind the ear of his lead mule. The balky animal started pulling and brought the wagon around.

Ceran and Charles scouted the area and found a shallow ravine. Getting the wagons into it proved a chore, but the two-foot-high dirt walls gave better protection than simply sitting out on the prairie.

"Bring the wagons with the firewood up close," Ceran called, motioning for the others to pull in tight. When the dozens of mules were released from harness, they snorted and bucked a little and kicked up their heels, but trapped inside the circle of wagons, could not go running away. By the time the fire blazed merrily, the mules crowded near to stay warm.

"We might have to worry about some of them settin' fire to theyselves," the lead driver said. "I seen a kitty cat get so close to a smithy's forge that her fur started to singe. Cat never noticed it." The driver laughed, a double plume of condensation gusting from his nostrils. "Then again, that mean old cat mighta liked bein' set on fire. Jist like some wimmen I know."

"Forget the cat and see to the rest of the men," Charles said irritably. The wind had whipped up into a real blow now. Tiny snow pellets sailed along like cold, wet bullets. One hit him in the eye, causing him to flinch and spend a few seconds clearing his vision.

"More wood," Ceran decided. Two teamsters had been assigned the job of keeping the fire fed and flaring cheerily.

"We don't want to burn too much wood too quick," Charles cautioned, settling down to warm his hands at the flaring fire. Ceran pressed close and warmed his hands, too.

"My hands are frozen lumps," he said, reaching up to brush snow off his coal-black beard. New flakes replaced it immediately.

"We can always burn the wagons we shipped the wood in," Charles said.

"Break out that keg of whiskey," Ceran called to the drivers. "Only a cup each. Save some for later on, when it gets really cold."

"Mr. St. Vrain," one driver said, "this ain't cold. You know it's cold when your words freeze in midair and nobody can hear what you done said till spring comes and thaws them."

The men set about telling tall tales, each trying to top the last. Then they broke into ragged song, trying to drown out the rising whine of the winter wind. Charles and Ceran huddled close to the fire, keeping their eye on not only their men for any sign of frostbite, but also on the mules. So far, the fire kept all of them from freezing.

By midnight, the snow had begun to fall. Ceran estimated an inch or two an hour, but it never let up. He brushed it off, kept the mules moving, and felt knives in his feet every time he took a step. Only thrusting his boot soles near the still-bright fire helped. When it became obvious the mules were beginning to slow and their hooves were freezing to the ground, he grumbled and poked a few of the teamsters awake to help him unload a bale of blankets intended for the army. He shook out the coarse woolen blankets and then began roping them to the recalcitrant mules.

It took a spell, but never had the gray, kicking animals looked better. With the warm blankets protecting them from the snowfall, they stood a better chance of surviving. Then Ceran poked through the pile of blankets and found one for himself, drew it snugly around his shoulders, and lay down near the fire. William wasn't as lucky, since his segment of the shipment contained canned goods and beads for trade with the Indians. A pile of beads might fetch a huge pile of buffalo robes, but in this storm shiny glass beads didn't do much to keep a man's bones from freezing.

Ceran drifted off to sleep, letting Charles stand the first watch. He stirred occasionally, not surprised to find several inches of snow on top of him as he turned over. He wiped the snow and cold from his eyes and saw the fire burning brightly. A fitful time ensued after he relieved Charles, checked on mules and men, then spent his time pacing about to stay warm before he was relieved by another muleteer and returned to his blankets. He went back to sleep, worrying about William and the others.

When he awoke in the morning, he found a stunning wonderland of white stretching as far as the eye could see. The snow had drifted from the ravine banks up over the wagons on the windward side. But the mules were noisy and braying for breakfast. He brushed snow off himself and stood, stretching cold, aching muscles. The teamsters already worked to feed the mules from grain brought along for this purpose. The grain gave added strength and energy to the noisy animals.

"What do you think, Charles? Are we safe?"

"We'll have a day or two of rough going," Charles said, studying the snowy road to the west, "but the main part of the storm missed us. It passed behind us."

"The luck of the St. Vrains," Ceran said.

"I hope the luck of the Bents holds, for William's sake," Charles said, worried. When William caught up with them two days later, they discovered many of his oxen had frozen to death at the height of the storm.

Ceran had to admit the luck of the Bents was greater, though. In spite of the deaths among the livestock, none of the teamsters had anything more than frostbitten toes, and Bill Boggs had suffered a frozen nose. After shifting loads, the reunited train moved out on the icy road to Bent's Fort.

Tentative Trade

Adobe Walls
June 10, 1844

"This isn't the kind of place to build a trading post," Lieutenant Abert said, looking around the desolate prairie. The land stretched endlessly hot, only a distant dust devil showing any movement other than heat haze. The blue Texas sky curved overhead without a cloud to afford relief from the burning sun.

"We've never had a real post before," William Bent said. "My brother traded out of tepees, when he had even that much. Earlier trade was conducted from the back of a wagon."

J.W. Abert signaled for his patrol to take a break, finding what shade they could amid the feathery-leafed, thorny mesquite bushes. He reached for his canteen, shook it, then looked around as if he would spot a cool oasis with flowing water. When he didn't, Abert shrugged, downed what tepid water he had, and then replaced the cork with a decisive thrust.

"You need to find a reliable source of potable water," the lieutenant said. "There's no way you can survive here without it. Those mesquite put down taproots for hundreds of yards before they reach water."

"There's a river a mile or two away," Ceran St. Vrain said, fumbling with a crude map made by Kit Carson the last time he swung through this desolate land. "We need water to make adobe brick, as well as to drink."

"Both might keep you alive out here," Abert said. "Dealing with the Comanche is dangerous."

"But safer now that President Tyler has agreed to take Texas as a state," William said. He dismounted, brushed the dust from his clothing, and walked around, getting the circulation back into his legs and posterior. Never had he seen such desolate terrain, but his nose twitched—and not from the sluggishly flowing stream Ceran had mentioned.

There was money to be made here trading with the Comanche on their home territory. Lots of it.

"You can rely on that if you like," Abert said somewhat testily, "but you won't find a cavalry column trotting to your rescue every time a Comanche brave kicks up his heels and shoots an arrow or two in your direction."

"I wasn't intending on that happening," William said, equally choleric and unwilling to put up with the lieutenant's sour attitude. He was pale and drawn in spite of the sun beating down, and his hands still shook the slightest bit. A few months earlier, he and Bill Boggs had gone to warn the Cheyenne of a diphtheria epidemic at Bent's Fort, and he had come down with the disease while on the mission of mercy. Cheyenne medicine men had nursed him back to life with their herbs, roots, and ceremonies, but he had never quite recovered full strength. William glanced at Ceran, who fought to keep the map from folding in on itself as a wind hotter than the breeze from hell began blowing. Ceran had argued against trading with the Comanche at all, but William knew the company had to do it before others moved in.

He knew he had to do it, competition notwithstanding. The loss of his brother still wore on him more than he liked to admit, because he had sent Robert into this fiery hellhole. Old Wolf's treaty with the Cheyenne was in force, but that hadn't stopped a band of Comanche from killing Robert. William had to prove to himself he hadn't been wrong.

"It'll take the better part of the year to establish a fort here," Lieutenant Abert said. "Are you going to build one as ambitious as Bent's Fort?"

"No, just a small one to protect the traders who'll man it year-round," Ceran said. "Adobe Walls, we'll call it, since that's what it mostly will be."

Abert shrugged. "This is a godforsaken place to die. Be sure to mark off a decent cemetery so other patrols will know where you wanted to be buried."

"Your optimism is overwhelming, Lieutenant," William said, losing his anger. "Thanks for escorting us this far, but we can go on without your opinion of our venture."

"No offense meant, William," Abert said. "The heat wears a man down, and I'm about worn to a nubbin. I see you are, too." The lieutenant peered closely at William. "You ought to let Ceran here do what he can so you can rest up. You never got over the diphtheria."

"I am fine, sir," William said, so stiffly that Ceran looked up, startled.

"See us to the river, Lieutenant," Ceran said. "We can go from there. If four wagons and a dozen men can't put up a decent defense, should it even be necessary, an extra dozen men's not going to make much difference."

"My soldiers are more than a match for any Comanche."

Ceran saw he had riled the lieutenant. "I didn't mean to imply they weren't. I was only saying we can put up a spirited defense, should the need arise. And I want to avoid fighting. We all profit by trade, Comanche and white man."

"Keep them peaceable and I'll owe you a great deal," Abert said.

"We'll see that they get everything they need so they won't go on the warpath," William said. "All we're asking is that you keep the whiskey runners and anyone else trying to smuggle firewater to them out of the state."

"Agreed," Abert said in a more equitable tone. "I have no love for any Comanchero."

Ceran, William, and their men began building their trading post the next morning, Comanche braves watching from the distance.

On the Mend

"I'll break your arm," the huge black man said, towering over the frail young man.

"Now, Dick, don't you go sayin' a thing like that to a guest," Charlotte said to her husband, stepping between him and Francis Preston Blair, Jr. "He a friend of the Bents."

"He cain't challenge me like that," Dick Green said, his powerful arms flexing. "He said it out loud, so's ever'body could hear."

"You're forgettin' your place," Charlotte said. "We nuthin' but slaves."

"My dear Charlotte," cried Blair, jumping to his feet. He was slight, pale, and his eyes burned with a fever born of more than sickness. "A slave you might be, but I am a slave to your fine peach pie. Never have I tasted better! And my father is mayor of St. Louis!"

The young man turned to the hulking Dick Green and looked up into his dark eyes.

"I challenged you, and I am a man of my word."

"Arm-rasslin'?" Dick tensed his arms, and the cloth of his shirt strained and threatened to rip. Charlotte hit him to make him stop.

"Don't you go bustin' any of them seams I worked so hard to put in."

"I'm still recovering my strength," Blair said. "My illness is fading away like a bad memory, true, but never on my best day at Princeton could I have matched you in arm-wrestling."

By now Blair and Dick had attracted most of the folks in Bent's Fort. They whispered among themselves, marveling at the way Blair talked to Charlotte's husband.

"Knives?" Dick asked tentatively. "Mr. Bent don't like people to get cut up inside the fort, but there ain't no way I'll shoot you."

"Banjos!" cried Blair. "We'll each play a song and whoever is best, as determined by the applause of these fine people, wins the challenge."

Blair grabbed his banjo and began a lively tune. When he finished, most of the people had been tapping their feet and were close to dancing.

"Your turn," Blair said, handing his banjo to Dick.

"He don't play," Charlotte said.

"Then I win!" Blair cried. "And I claim my prize."

"What's that?" asked Dick, realizing he was being put on.

"The first dance with your charming wife!" Blair caught Charlotte up and spun her around. "Who can play the banjo? A sprightly reel? A decent dance?" Someone took the banjo and struck up a tune, almost as good as the one Blair had played.

In a few minutes, Charlotte and Blair were twirling across the *placita,* an enthusiastic if out-of-tune song being sung by the onlookers. Panting with exertion, Blair came to a halt in front of Dick.

"Your turn, now that I've won the first dance," Blair said.

"I don't dance so much," Dick Green said.

"Then that is the prize I claim. You must dance with your wife. Strike up another song!" Blair grabbed his banjo back and started the tune. Soon enough Dick and Charlotte were dancing, surrounded by the others in the fort. Many of the men danced with their wives, but there were not enough women to go around and many of the men paired off among themselves, as they had done at more than one fandango during early all the Green River Rendezvous.

"He's quite a character," George Bent said to his brother, William.

"I had some misgivings about letting him stay here during his recuperation, but not now. Never have I seen Dick look so happy. He's taken quite a shine to Blair." William sat with his legs dangling over the edge of the walkway, his brother beside him.

"Francis has a way about him," George said. "I'm glad to call him my friend."

"You should get him to teach you some law. He's wasting all that book learning. We ought to hire him to run the stores down in Taos. Charles is locking horns with Padre Antonio again. If he gets thrown in jail any more, a lawyer on the scene is going to be a necessity."

"I don't think he would have any objection. Francis wants to stay since there's nothing for him back in St. Louis."

"When you think he's well enough, offer him a position with our stores in Taos," William said, coming to a quick decision. He liked the personable young man and, as his younger brother had said, George and Blair had become fast friends.

"As long as it's not Adobe Walls, that'd be fine with me. I'd even go back to Fort St. Vrain."

William laughed. "Even a year of trading in the Texas Panhandle without any trouble doesn't convince you how profitable that is?"

"It's desolate in Texas. And too cold up north. Besides, I think Francis would enjoy Taos and its people more."

"Who knows?" William said. "He might even get along with Padre Antonio."

The Bent brothers looked at each other; then both shook their heads at the same time as they simultaneously said, "Never!" They broke out laughing, then went down to join the next round of dancing led by Francis Blair.

Riots

"I'm so cold," Francis Blair grated out between clenched teeth. He looked over at his friend, George Bent. George swayed precariously in the saddle. Every time he did, a bit more ice broke free from his legs and body.

Blair twisted painfully to look in the other direction. For a moment he saw paradise ahead, the pass leading down toward Taos and civilization. Town. Food. Fire. A soft bed again. But mostly warmth. He needed to thaw out. Forsaking his view of heaven on earth, he kept turning toward the Mexican who had ridden with them from Bent's Fort and calling out to him. No response.

The man sat stiff and proud in the saddle, but something struck Blair as wrong. He guided his tired horse a bit closer and reached out to shake the man's arm. Blair recoiled when his fingers touched the cold silver concha decorating the man's sleeve. The heavy blanket slung over the Mexican's shoulders slid away, but the man made no move to grab it as it piled in front of him and then snaked to the snowy trail they followed through La Veta Pass.

"Are you all right?" asked Blair. He repeated his

question, shouting this time as his worried voice was swallowed in his own throat by the biting cold. Silvery plumes of condensation blasted forth from nose and mouth, convincing him that he actually spoke.

The man didn't move.

"Wake up!" Blair guided his horse back beside the Mexican and seized the man's right arm. It felt cold, as cold as death.

"George!" shouted Blair. "There's something terribly wrong with José." He strained to reach over, and grabbed the man with both hands and shook hard. "Wake up. Don't fall asleep."

George rode closer, ice caking his long eyelashes. He blinked it free, then maneuvered around to the far side so the two men had the Mexican trader between them. He reined back so he could take hold of the unmoving left arm.

"It's no good, Francis," George said. "He's gone. Froze to death."

"But he's in the saddle," Blair said uncomprehendingly. "How's that possible?"

"Move your own legs. Wiggle your toes. It's damned cold. We've been fighting the weather ever since we got into the mountains. José fell asleep, and it killed him."

"But—" Blair clamped his mouth shut.

"We keep riding. Don't try to bury him here. In Taos. Keep riding, Francis. We have to or we'll die, too."

Francis Blair tried to nod, but he was too stunned, too cold, shaken by the sight of a corpse riding alongside him and the snow that sneaked under his collar and the feeling that he had left the world he had known forever. Men didn't freeze to death like this at Princeton or in St. Louis.

* * *

"You got here at a bad time," Charles Bent told his brother. George stretched out next to Francis Blair on a bearskin rug in front of the warming fire Charles built up slowly as their bodies became accustomed to the warmth.

"Ah, Charles, you are so wrong," Blair said, sipping at warm wine that trickled down his gullet and puddled delightfully in his belly. His courage returned minute by minute. "We got here at the right time. What happened to José Contreras could have happened to your brother and me had we been on the trail one instant longer."

"You were foolish to come in such bad weather," Charles said, distracted. "Both passes are snowy and new storms rage through them daily. I'm surprised William let you leave the fort."

"We had to, Charles. Francis was feeling up to it, and William said you needed help. What can we do, now that we're here?"

"Keep from losing toes and fingertips," Charles said. "The fingers in particular, since they might be needed to curl around triggers to defend ourselves."

"Is it that bad, Charles?" George sat straighter. "Francis is capable of running the stores, if this would ease the friction between you and Padre Antonio."

Charles laughed harshly. "Nothing will ever ease the tension between us. He's out in the plaza even as we sit here, trying to rouse a crowd to lynch me."

"He's still disputing your claim to the land grant?" asked George. Seeing Blair's frown, George hastily explained how Ceran St. Vrain had given Charles a large portion of the land grant deeded by Manuel Armijo.

"That's at the heart of his antagonism, but he is

desperately hunting for other grievances, ones that will inflame the Indians. They neither know about nor care who owns the land, as long as they are left enough farmland for their own use."

"From the way you said that, the padre's found a rallying point. What is it, Charles? I am quite a good lawyer. I can argue any case, in any court, should it be necessary," Blair said.

"Thanks for your support," Charles said, "but Padre Antonio's grievances are like so many of the charges Armijo laid against me to throw me into jail."

"Trumped up," George said.

"Of course. This time, the priest says the company sold rifles and ammunition to the Ute."

"We'd never do that!" cried George, outraged. "I spent half my time at Fort St. Vrain stopping arms runners and whiskey runners. He ought to talk to William. He spends as much time dealing with the cavalry on this matter than in trading. Selling rifles to any Indian on the warpath is the last thing we'd do— the last thing we'd *want*."

"We know that, but the padre has a powerful argument, true or not. The Ute stole more than eight thousand sheep and drove off four hundred horses from his personal herds."

"Could one of your employees have sold the rifles to the Indians without your knowledge?" asked Blair, getting a feel for the evidence.

Charles laughed harshly and shook his head.

"Hardly. The padre says we sold the guns up north at Hardscrabble."

For a moment, the only sound in the room was the crackling fire. Then George asked, "How's that possible? We don't have a store at Hardscrabble. Besides, the traders from Pueblo claim that for their territory.

We don't intrude on them and they don't intrude on ours."

"I've checked. Wherever the Ute got their rifles, it wasn't from us or the Pueblo trading post. There's a steady flow of arms from Mexico. That might be where they got the rifles. Or even from a rather unexpected source."

"Where?" asked George.

"Manuel Armijo."

"I don't understand, Charles," said Blair. "He was removed as governor and sent back to Mexico City in disgrace. How can he be supplying the Indians with their firearms?"

"Nothing in New Mexico is like anywhere else," Charles said with a deep sigh. "Rumors spread by traders coming up from Franklin in Texas say that Armijo's star is rising once more and Governor Martinez has done a poor job maintaining order."

"He's letting Padre Antonio rouse the rabble against us," said George. "For that alone, Martinez ought to be recalled."

"I rather miss Armijo," Charles said, lounging back in a chair and thrusting his feet closer to the fire. "I never thought that'd be possible, but he was more amenable to discussion, even if he did shout and carry on like a pompous peacock."

"*That's* better than the current governor? My, my," said Blair. "Politics in New Mexico *is* different from other places."

"I suppose that might be so," Charles said. "But it's what we have to deal with. I—" He sat bolt upright when angry cries from outside filtered through the heavy wooden doors and two-foot-thick adobe walls.

"What's going on?" asked Blair, getting up.

"Grab a rifle," Charles said. "George, see that Ignacia

and the children are safe. You know where the bolt-hole is. Come along, Francis."

Blair hefted a rifle from a rack near the door, then took a second one, to be on the safe side. He followed Charles through the inner courtyard to the gate leading in from the street. The instant he stepped into the courtyard he heard the tumult, the angry catcalls, the one clarion voice inciting the crowd.

"Padre Antonio," Charles said, confirming what Blair had already guessed. "We'd better not open the gate. If they try to break through, be ready to fire. I don't want my wife or children caught up in this."

Blair nodded, looking braver than he felt. His clumsy, half-frozen finger curled around the musket trigger, and he assumed a stance where he could get the butt to his shoulder and fire.

Charles peered through a small knothole in the gate, then stepped back. He looked torn by indecision. Then he motioned Blair to one side, took a deep breath, and pulled back the locking bar on the gate.

Blair took aim, just in case. He swung around when he heard footsteps behind him.

"Don't shoot unless you have to. It would only inflame the crowd," George said. He carried a brace of pistols and held a third musket.

Charles Bent stepped forward and held his hands high over his head, trying to wrest the attention of the crowd away from Padre Antonio's inflammatory speech.

"Citizens, neighbors! Please!" Charles boomed, his voice deep and commanding. "What's wrong?"

"You're selling rifles to the Ute," the priest said accusingly, waving his fist in the air to emphasis his anger. "They stole my livestock!"

"Bent, St. Vrain and Company has done no such

thing," Charles said. "You know me. You know how we have only the safety of our dear friends and neighbors at heart."

He launched into a speech that quieted the angry crowd enough for Padre Antonio to lose control of them. The edge gone from their hostility, Charles slowly moved the grumbling men away.

"He is quite the orator," Blair said as he leaned against his rifle. "I'd be hard pressed to match his command of the language."

"It's the way he speaks even more than what he says," George said in admiration. "I've seen him quiet a frightened horse the same way. Let's hope it works now so that they don't bolt and try to stampede. We'd get trampled if they did."

An hour later, Charles stepped back inside the gate and swung it shut. The perspiration that beaded on his forehead took on a grainy look as it began to freeze. He wiped it off with a single swipe of his hand.

"That's taken care of," Charles said, slumping.

"For the moment," Francis Blair said. Although a newcomer to Taos, he knew the symptom had been well treated this day, but not the cause of the hatred aimed against the Bents.

One Wedding and Two Beatings

Taos
May 3, 1846

"Who'd have thought it?" Francis Blair said a little too loudly. He put down his cup, and sloshed a bit of wine onto the wood table and never took notice of it.

"It surprised me Charles approved of the marriage," George Bent said. "Rumalda just turned fourteen, after all, and Tom Boggs is a considerable bit older."

"I wasn't talking about the *wedding*," Blair said, laughing as he poured himself more wine. "I meant who'd have thought Manuel Armijo would be governor again!"

George heaved a deep sigh and shook his head. His friend was in his cups, and had been since the wedding earlier in the day. Blair had come West to recuperate from his illness, and had certainly restored his strength, first at the fort and then here in Taos, in spite of their treacherous journey over the mountains a few months earlier. As everyone had hoped, Blair had become a true asset to the company. His business sense was even more acute than George's, and George would have been the first to acknowledge that.

But if his business ability was greater, so was his thirst for wine and whiskey.

"Forget Armijo. Charles and he have patched up their differences, especially after Padre Antonio tried to keep Armijo from getting his old job back."

"Common enemies, a great cement for oddly matched fellows," Blair said. Then he spun about, spilling more wine. "I don't like the name Francis. It does not become me."

"Beg pardon?" asked George, startled at the drunken change of topic.

"Call me Frank. That is ever so much more rugged. Frank Blair. That is what a mountain man's name should be, not Francis."

"You've about drained Charles's wine cellar," George said, seeing the bottle Francis—Frank—held up as he waited for the final drop to slip into his cup.

"I have to wish the newlyweds well. To you, Thomas Boggs and Rumalda Boggs y Luna!" Frank Blair lifted his cup and downed the contents in a single gulp, smacked his lips, then threw the cup into the fireplace.

"Why'd you do that?" asked George. "That was a perfectly good cup."

"A formal toast requires it, old man," Blair said. "May they have many children who make their parents and grandparents proud." Blair staggered a little and caught himself. "And I had a second purpose, too, tossing the goblet into the fireplace."

"What?" George asked, wondering when Blair was going to pass out from his prodigious intake of liquor at the reception and later.

"A rebirth. My rebirth. Frank Blair's now burst onto the world, ripsnortin' and ready for whatever comes my way. Bring it on! Whatever 'it' might be!"

George wondered if part of the drunkenness on his

friend's part came from the distance to his own family or his lack of female acquaintances. Padre Antonio had continued telling both the Taos Indians and Mexican citizens what devils the Americans were, to the point where it was difficult to do business, much less socialize. Blair had made it clear early on that he did not favor visiting soiled doves, as much because of his perceived social position as out of personal prissiness. George did not much approve of loose women, either, but he had lived on the frontier too long not to accept what he could and not be overly fastidious about it.

"It's about time to go sleep off the wine," George suggested.

"Now is *not* the time. You say I've drunk all the wine? Then let's cross the plaza and find a dram shop for a nightcap." Blair hiccuped loudly. "Or two."

"I don't think so," George said. "I'm mighty tuckered out after the wedding reception. I can't remember when I've danced more and—"

"Then I shall go by myself. Point me in the right direction." Blair wobbled as he went to the door.

"Hold up," George said, giving in to the inevitable. "I'll go along and keep you out of trouble."

"Get me into more trouble, you mean, old man. You need to loosen up. Wet your whistle. Howl with the coyotes!" Blair leaned back and cut loose with a credible imitation of a lovesick coyote.

"Come on," George said, hustling his friend through the house and out into the quiet street. He didn't want to disturb Charles or Ignacia, much less Tom and his young bride. The only obvious way of quieting Blair was to let him drink until he passed out. Returning him to the house would be difficult, but better and easier than letting him create a drunken ruckus.

"There's a fine-looking cantina," Blair said, making

his way across the plaza, using the railing on the gazebo to support himself. He lost his balance, hung on to the rail, and sat down heavily on a step.

"It's quiet for this time of night," George said, to occupy his friend's mind with something more than another round of drinking. "It's hardly past sundown and everyone's home."

"Spoilsports," Blair said cheerfully enough. "We need to show them how a gentleman drinks. First, we have to find a gentleman! Point one out to me, George." He heaved himself to his feet and got to the far side of the plaza, not a dozen paces from the cantina.

"A gracious good evening to you, spoilsports," Blair called, waving to a trio of Mexicans coming from the cantina. "You should be ashamed of yourselves, not celebrating this fine day. And night. You are not pleasing me with your insistence on being so stodgy."

The men looked at one another, then exchanged a few whispered words. George saw them advance on Blair, and hurried to his friend's side.

"Excuse him, he's had too much to drink."

"And I'll have more, if foolish poltroons don't keep me from it."

"What did you call us?" demanded one man.

"A poltroon, a buffoon, a loon, all of those and ever so much more!"

One man rattled off a long string of angry Spanish, then grew increasingly belligerent when neither George nor Blair answered in the same tongue. He stepped up and shoved Blair hard. The drunken man staggered and fought to keep his balance. Blair stumbled over his own feet, and landed heavily in a mud puddle formed by overflow from a watering trough.

"There was no call to jostle him," George said. Before he could get out even one more word, another of the men cocked back his fist and let fly. George saw the blow coming from the corner of his eye and tried to dodge. He was only partly successful. The punch caught him on the side of the head and took him off his feet, to land on his hands and knees in the street.

The third man landed a heavy kick to his ribs, knocking the air from his lungs. Gasping for breath, George looked up through blurred eyes to see Frank Blair once more on his feet and swinging wildly. One blow landed on the man who had kicked George, and the melee began in earnest. Forcing himself to his feet, George joined in, and for a brief time thought he and Frank were getting the better of the other three.

Then a half-dozen Mexicans came from the cantina. The fight quickly became a beating. George saw Blair knocked down and savagely kicked by three men. He tried to pull free of the two holding him, but lacked the strength. Blackness circled his head like some evil vulture, and finally swooped down to seize his consciousness.

Justice—
New Mexico Style

Taos
May 5, 1846

"Those're sum a them," George Bent mumbled, his jaw not working properly because of the swelling on the left side of his face. He was bruised and battered, but had recovered enough to be angry all over again. At his side sat Frank Blair, his face likewise a mass of ugly purple and green bruises. Every time he moved, he let out a tiny grunt of pain, but otherwise sat stoically and let his friend do the talking.

"They are in custody and will be sent directly to the magistrate," said José Valdez.

"We want the trial moved to Santa Fe," Charles Bent said angrily.

"This is a civil matter, a local concern and nothing more," Valdez said, grinning broadly and spreading his hands as if to say this was out of his control.

"The magistrate is Padre Antonio's brother," Charles grated. "Two of the padre's other brothers were in the plaza and might have helped the crowd beat Mr. Blair and my brother."

"Oh, Mr. Bent, your concerns are understandable but misplaced. Justice Martinez is a fair man," Valdez said. "The evidence will be presented in open court and the proper verdict will be reached quickly."

"Charles," said George, tugging on his brother's sleeve. The simple act sent tremors of pain through his shoulder. "Witnesses. Who can we call as witnesses?"

"It should be obvious, even to Padre Antonio's brother, that you didn't fall down and do this much damage to yourself accidentally. Someone had to have beaten you severely."

"Get Consul Alvarez here," George urged. "We need all the help we can get."

"I can help," Blair said carefully. "I know the law." He winced as he shifted position. Simply talking proved excruciating.

"That doesn't mean anything in New Mexico," Charles said, forcing himself to keep a lid on his growing outrage. "I had the captain at the garrison send a patrol to guard my house. I don't want some hothead to get the idea all Bents are fair game."

"And Blairs," Frank chimed in. "Though they seem to have bagged me already."

"You're one a us, like it or not," George said, rubbing his jaw.

"That makes me feel a mite better, but not enough to make my bruises go away," Blair said, grinning lopsidedly.

"We have the accused men in custody," Valdez said. "If you wish, you may come to the courthouse now and we will see that justice is carried out."

Charles had to help George and Blair down the street. As they entered the one-story adobe that served as courthouse, they heard hooves pounding in the street.

"It's Ceran!" cried George. "How'd he learn so fast what's happened?"

"I don't know. Go on inside and take a seat. I'll talk to him," Charles said. He hurried to Ceran St. Vrain, and the two began a heated discussion.

"Ceran's a good man," George said. "He'll help us out."

"He's too late for that," Blair said, sinking down onto a hard bench at the rear. "I'll be happy if he escorts those animals to jail."

A half-dozen men sat in the defendants' dock, looking smug. One nudged another and pointed out George and Blair at the rear of the room. The men laughed until Justice Martinez rapped his gavel for silence.

"We have before us a case of assault," Padre Antonio's brother said haughtily.

"George, I remember him. He was there. He watched them hit and kick me and didn't do anything!"

George cautioned Frank Blair to silence. His vision was still blurred, but he thought that his friend might be right. For all that, he wasn't certain that José Valdez hadn't been part of the mob that had attacked them, too. Valdez hung over the rail of the dock and spoke softly to several of the defendants. There didn't seem to be anything but great friendship among the men.

"Where's Charles and Ceran? They ought to get in here," George said impatiently. He looked around for his brother and his business partner, but the pair remained outside, engaged in a heated discussion. He caught sight of Ceran gesturing forcefully and pointing. He couldn't see or hear Charles's response.

The magistrate droned on for a while, citing laws that might have been broken and possible punishment for anyone convicted of assault, but both

George and Blair turned restive when Magistrate Martinez continued skirting the issue.

"What's he waiting for? Get the trial started," muttered Blair.

"Silence!" rapped Martinez. "I will not tolerate any further disturbance in the courtroom. I now give my verdict."

"What?" Frank Blair shot to his feet. "There hasn't been any testimony. Neither George nor I have taken the stand. There have to be other witnesses, other than the defendants. You need to question them."

"Silence!" roared Martinez. "I have heard the charges and weighed the evidence. There is not enough to proceed. Case dismissed!"

Blair sat down, stunned.

"Welcome to New Mexico justice," George said. "The friends and relatives of the defendants are judge and jury. You can't expect them to convict."

"But this is a travesty," protested Blair. "We have to get justice."

"We did. The garrison captain has a guard on our houses to keep the mob at bay. And we weren't killed."

"No, this is wrong. Completely wrong. I won't accept it. Get your brother and Ceran. Tell them. They'll know what to do. Charles is friendly with the governor. This is definitely a matter of corruption in the judicial system."

The defendants left the courtroom, laughing and joking with Valdez and Martinez. Soon only George and Blair remained in the close, hot room.

Charles came in and sat beside his brother, looking glum.

"They acquitted them. The padre's brother let them all get off scot-free!" protested Blair.

"Never mind," Charles said. "Ceran's brought some important news."

"More important than letting bullies and thugs get away with their crime?" demanded Blair.

"Yes, more important. Far more important. We're all leaving Taos for the fort immediately."

"What is it, Charles?" asked George, knowing in his gut what the answer would be and dreading it.

"War," Charles said, his voice a hoarse whisper.

Preparations for War

Fort Leavenworth, Kansas
June 15, 1846

"Mr. Howard certainly brought the truth when he told you we'll be at war soon. I've never seen so many soldiers in one place," Charles Bent said as he and Ceran St. Vrain rode slowly toward Fort Leavenworth. The distant hollow boom of cannon told of constant practice by artillery units.

"If they used only half that firepower against the Mexicans, Santa Anna wouldn't stop running until he got to the South Pole." Ceran studied the troopers as they rode to the front gate.

"They won't use half," Charles said. "They'll use it all. I hope Armijo realizes how futile it will be to resist."

"I can't believe you've taken a liking to that sorry son of a bitch," Ceran said.

"After he was appointed governor again, he realized how fragile his hold on power really was. He might have whupped up on the Texians, but he has feared American power from the beginning."

"He fears Bent's Fort," Ceran said flatly. "If this force needs a staging point, it will be our trading post."

Charles was silent for a moment, then said, "Captain Cooke escorted only one or two of our caravans, but he certainly dipped deeply into our supplies every time he passed by. If this new general—"

"Kearny," Ceran supplied. "Stephen Watts Kearny."

"If General Kearny wants to use the fort and take our supplies, he must pay for it. We've lost a considerable amount of our profits by footing the bill for Cooke's dragoons."

"It might be worth a few dollars of trade goods if the Americans throw out the Mexicans," Ceran said.

"After what happened to George and Frank, you might be right," Charles said. He sucked in a deep breath as his mind raced. Ceran had put into words what he was thinking.

"We'd be even more profitable if we didn't have to put up with Armijo's excise taxes and all the other financial devilment he comes up with, too."

"That, and he is our chief competition," Charles said, distracted. His head swiveled back and forth like a clockwork mechanism as he tried to see everything all at once. The soldiers stretched out to the horizon, clumped into companies practicing their close-order drill and marksmanship. He tried to estimate the size of Kearny's army, but couldn't do it. A thousand. At least.

"I suppose I ought to get used to thinking of myself as an American," Ceran rattled on. "Since there's no way the Mexicans can stand against such a force, I wonder if it'd benefit the company for me to change my citizenship now, or wait until Kearny marches into Santa Fe and then make a public show of pledging new allegiance."

"Either, I don't know," Charles said, still distracted. A soldier stepped up and blocked their entry into the main parade ground of the fort. Fort Leavenworth had been constructed on a more traditional pattern than many other western military posts Charles had seen. The walls were constructed of stone with wood walkways inside, similar to the design William had used at Bent's Fort. The difference lay in the brick and stone of Fort Leavenworth's walls. Bent, St. Vrain & Company had used adobe; the U.S. Army had built using more expensive material not easily found nearby.

Ceran swatted at a mosquito and wiped his hand on his pants leg.

"Do these skeeters come out all day long?" he asked the guard.

"The river's not far off. Can't get away from them blood-sucking monsters," the guard said. Then he realized he wasn't supposed to talk to anyone he stopped. "Who are you and what's your business here?"

"Bent and St. Vrain to see Captain Cooke," Ceran said. "He's supposed to escort us to see General Kearny later this afternoon. That is, if these mosquitoes don't carry us off first."

The guard chuckled, then held up his hand to prevent their entry into the fort.

"Wait here and I'll see if I can scare up the captain." The sentry went inside the opened doors and yelled to someone on the far side of the fort. In a few minutes they saw Phillip St. George Cooke hurrying across the parade ground.

"Welcome, gentlemen," Captain Cooke said, shaking hands with them. He dismissed the sentry, and escorted Ceran and Charles to a spot of shade on one side of the dusty area where recruits were being drilled by a harried sergeant hardly older than any of those in his squad.

"We had word from St. Louis that war was imminent," Charles said.

"You must have taken it seriously if you came all

this way," Cooke said. He looked a little uneasy at this information.

"Mr. Howard is a credible source," Ceran said. "We've seen firsthand how civil unrest in New Mexico is becoming unbearable, mobs attacking American citizens on a regular basis, vandalism, constant threats. All that put together lends a great deal of credence to war being declared."

"Since you are here, your sympathies lie with America," Captain Cooke said.

Charles held down his anger. "You know that's true, Captain. Haven't we given you supplies in return for damned little support on your part? I am as patriotic an American as the next man, sir!"

"I've had my orders," Captain Cooke said uneasily. "If conditions had been different, I would have been better able to protect your wagons. But the Sioux drew my dragoons northward, away from the Santa Fe Trail."

"We know you weren't patrolling the road," Charles said glumly. "We lost more than our share of men and wagons loaded with merchandise to Kiowa and Comanche raiding."

"You should reconsider your trading post in the Panhandle," Captain Cooke said. "Deal with the Comanche and you'll get stung sooner or later worse than anything the Kiowa do to your wagon trains." He saw the expression on Charles's face, and then remembered how Bent had lost his brother. The captain murmured an apology, then said, "There's General Kearny. If we hurry, we can speak with him for a few minutes."

"We need to discuss supply routes," Ceran said, taking over as Charles still stewed over Cooke's inopportune advice. "And what trade goods might be required . . . should your soldiers come our direction."

Captain Cooke laughed and said, "You have a way about you, Ceran. I'd never accuse you of pussyfooting around, but you have the honeyed tongue of a diplomat."

They intercepted General Kearny and his aides as the commanding officer headed in the direction of the officers' mess. Cooke hastily introduced the two traders.

"Good to meet you. I've gone over the maps of the territory and decided Bent's Fort is an ideal base for our invasion."

Ceran and Charles exchanged glances. Kearny was a blunt man, and not prone to insult their intelligence by dancing around what they already knew. Why else would they have come to Fort Leavenworth if they weren't concerned over military action?

"When do you think war will be declared formally?" asked Charles.

Kearny turned his piercing eyes on the trader and said in a firm voice, "May twenty-sixth. It was declared almost a month ago."

"That explains why you have rallied so many green recruits," Ceran said. "We saw them drilling in close order all the way down to the Missouri River."

"They will be on the trail in a few days. Without trained officers like Captain Cooke, the invasion would be a disaster. I am counting on him, Captain Moore, and others who have spent years on the prairie to be the core of my force."

"I, uh, I spoke with Governor Armijo before I left New Mexico," Charles said. "He told me he expected up to five thousand troops under a General Urrea to march up from Mexico at any time to reinforce Santa Fe."

Kearny said nothing for a moment. He pursed his

lips, locked his hands behind his back, and paced about in a small, tight circle before looking up.

"Was he telling the truth?"

"I can't say, General," Charles responded. "Armijo is a gambler and has a tendency to bluff. This might have been told me in the strictest confidence, knowing I would relay the intelligence to you."

"I have eight hundred men already on the trail," Kearny said. "If they go against five thousand seasoned Mexican soldiers, there will be slaughter."

"Sir," said Captain Cooke, "with that many troops, they wouldn't simply sit behind walls and fight a defensive war. They would send a fast-moving unit up to get behind our recruits, cutting them off from supplies and reinforcements."

"Then they would attack. With so many soldiers lost, the Mexicans might think we'd yell 'Uncle!' and stop the war. Well, they are wrong!"

"General," said Charles, "I'm no soldier, but Captain Cooke's idea carries great merit. However, if you plan to use Bent's Fort, any dragoons reaching it would not be cut off from supplies. From reinforcements, perhaps, but not supplies. Ever."

"Thank you, Mr. Bent."

"There's more, General," Charles went on. "Ceran knows every mountain man in the West. If it came down to fighting for Mexico or the U.S., there's no question you could muster a company or two of rough-hewn, hard-fighting polecats."

"We can use their support, especially when it comes to working as scouts. Isn't that so, Captain Cooke?"

"They're the finest, sir," Cooke said.

They walked along in silence for a few more paces. Then Kearny declared, "Armijo is bluffing."

"How can you be so sure, sir?" asked Cooke.

"He would never have mentioned Urrea to Mr. Bent if those soldiers were actually on the way. Think how his political career would be enhanced if we walked into a trap. And have any of our scouts reported an attack against our columns?"

"No, sir."

"General Urrea would have attacked. News of the declaration of war must have reached Mexico City by now. The declaration was kept quiet, but not secret."

Charles held his tongue. Armijo was on pins and needles wondering if war would be declared, so he was still in the dark. That meant his superiors farther south did not share what they knew with their provincial governor.

"Urrea would also hog the glory, letting Armijo sit in his office and pout," Kearny went on. "Armijo might send Urrea to his death to bolster his own position, but he would never do it for any other reason. These men think highly of themselves and their own careers."

"Sounds reasonable, General," Ceran said.

"Good. Muster those mountain men, get supplies ready at Bent's Fort, and we shall use it as our base for the thrust into Santa Fe. The Mexicans won't know what hit them."

Before Charles could get down to dickering about what the army was willing to pay for the use of his trading post, General Kearny hurried off to speak with a clutch of colonels, all with the sharp-dressed look of men from Washington.

"War it is," Ceran said softly. "We'd better get back to the fort and prepare."

"Prepare to be bilked out of even more supplies," grumbled Charles, but he said nothing more. It was to the company's benefit, as Ceran had pointed out, for New Mexico to become part of the American West.

The Troops Mass

Bent's Fort
July 28, 1846

"I've never seen the like, William," George Bent told his brother. "If I use the field glasses, I can see even more of them. Fleas on a dirty dog's back wouldn't be thicker."

"Or eat more," groused William. "Why Ceran and Charles agreed to letting Kearny come to our fort is beyond me. Charles left, squealing like a stuck pig over how Cooke had eaten us out of house and hearth in return for nothing. Now Charles has invited the whole damned American army to drop in for dinner!"

"You have to admit there is a certain thrill to it, William," George said. "There must be ten square miles of tents, all with soldiers inside."

"The general told me to have fodder on hand for twenty thousand horses, mules, and oxen. I didn't find anywhere near enough to feed them. They are eating every blade of grass out on the prairie and have driven off the Cheyenne. If it rains like it did last year, the whole damned place will wash away into the Arkansas River."

"Think of the money to be made. Each of those soldiers has to eat."

"Think of trying to get paid for feeding them," William said glumly. "Worse than that, since we'll probably be paid eventually, is our trade being busted up. What Indian wants to come to Bent's Fort with an entire army of bluecoats on our doorstep?"

"I'd never join up," George said, "but a passel of young men from the fort are asking about it. They want to go down into New Mexico and pry Santa Fe loose from Armijo."

"I'd like to pry him loose from the governor's palace, too, but it's not likely to be done without a bloody fight."

"Ceran and Charles both agree that Armijo was bluffing when he said that general from Mexico City was on the way with so many soldiers."

"It wouldn't matter. Kearny's army is more than a match in numbers. But I've seen newborn kittens better able to take care of themselves. Look at that."

William cringed as the clumsy soldier's musket discharged when he tried to perform a close-arms drill. His sergeant hit the ground, hands on his head, until he realized the other soldiers were staring at him, some fighting to keep from laughing. The sergeant shot to his feet and dressed them down for not understanding what to do if they were shot at.

"You can ride out and talk to the Cheyenne. Big Timbers is only a day's ride off," George suggested. "I could go back to Fort St. Vrain and run our trade through there. Marcellin's doing a good job, but there's no reason we can't handle double or even triple the merchandise."

"Frank's all right down in Taos?" William asked.

"Reckon so. I haven't heard squat from him, but he knows business, and he learned a big lesson when the crowd beat us up. He's wary of more than a few men talking together now, and avoids the plaza entirely. I suspect he's even giving up drinking."

"When Kearny invades New Mexico, he had better make it quick, or the Mexicans will string up every American citizen they can find. Frank might be at the top of their list," William said grimly.

"Do you think we should tell him to get on back to the fort where he'd be safe?"

William mulled that over before answering. With Kearny disrupting trade at the fort, the company needed all the revenue it could get, and Taos was a big factor in generating a profit. But he wasn't going to risk Frank Blair's life for a few dollars. How they could ever explain to Blair's parents that they had sent their son out West to recuperate from his illness and he had ended up swinging from a noose was beyond William's skill. Francis Blair, Sr., was mayor of St. Louis and a powerful man politically, being close friends with Thomas Hart Benton, getting mentioned favorably and often by John Frémont every time he stopped at the fort. Political power and favorable notice by the famous made the elder Blair a very influential man, indeed.

He wouldn't understand that a minor priest like Padre Antonio had finally whipped a crowd of Taos Indians into a killing frenzy against his namesake and oldest son to avenge a land grant issued to Ceran and Charles.

"When do you think they'll move into New Mexico?" asked George.

"Soon, very soon. James Magoffin's wife, Susan, arrived this afternoon. I put her up in my bedroom."

"The pregnant woman? She is quite pretty. I wondered why she was traveling in her delicate condition."

"Her husband arrives tomorrow and will take

Kearny's demand for surrender to Armijo. Diplomacy first, then armed might," William said. "I hope and pray that this war is over soon." William heaved a sigh and added under his breath, "All I ever wanted was to earn a few dollars and live peaceably."

Neither seemed likely.

Ultimatums

Santa Fe
July 31, 1846

"Thank you for escorting me, Mr. Alvarez," James Magoffin said to the American consul. "The mission General Kearny has given me is of the utmost importance."

"We know," Alvarez said. He rubbed his hands down the outsides of his coat, feeling the bulges of the pistols he had holstered at his waist. A diplomat rarely went armed; it was bad for the image of peace. But now Manuel Alvarez felt he had to if he wanted to stay alive amid the constant civil unrest. "News traveled faster than the swiftest deer. War has been declared."

Magoffin said nothing, and kept his eyes fixed ahead, although he longed to look around as they rode in Alvarez's carriage toward the governor's palace. The Santa Fe plaza struck him as strange and wonderful, a place he might like to explore further with his wife. As he thought of Susan, he closed his eyes and tried to force all thought from his mind.

No distracting thoughts of family, no emotions to cloud his vital mission. If he succeeded, hundreds or even thousands of lives might be saved. If he failed, war was inevitable.

But the single life that forced him to fight so to

control his emotions had been snuffed out, gone as if it had never burned for even an instant. Susan had given birth, but their daughter had died within minutes. Whether the trip had proven too taxing for his wife, or whether the child had been doomed from the onset, Magoffin was at a loss to decide. Allowing Susan to accompany him had not been an easy decision, but one that had been dictated more by chance than careful planning.

"Here we are, Mr. Magoffin," said Alvarez.

Magoffin jumped as if he had been awakened from a deep sleep. For a moment he panicked when he looked out and saw a double line of Mexican soldiers armed with muskets. Then he settled down. He was a diplomat on a mission sanctioned by his government, operating under a flag of truce, as it were.

"Are you all right?" whispered Alvarez. "You look pale."

"I . . . I have other things on my mind. I want this over with so I can return to Bent's Fort right away."

"One way or the other," Alvarez said, his words trailing off when Governor Armijo strutted out like a peacock dressed in his elaborate light blue uniform covered with dazzling medals of all sizes and descriptions.

"Señor Magoffin, welcome to Santa Fe," Armijo said in greeting. He stood just outside the door leading into the Palace of the Governors, waiting for Magoffin to climb from the carriage. As the diplomat's foot touched the dusty tile of the portico, the sergeant of the guard barked a command. The soldiers snapped to attention and hoisted their rifles.

Again, Magoffin jumped as if poked with a needle. He felt sweat on his forehead, and hated such a show of weakness in front of the man he had to convince to surrender.

"For Susan," Magoffin muttered.

"How is that, Señor?" asked Armijo. "I am an old war horse and have grown deaf in this ear from too many rifles firing." As the governor turned, he made a show of rattling his saber and touching his rows of bejeweled medals.

"And I am an old man fatigued from a long trip, sir. Forgive me."

"You, an old man! Nonsense. You are young and sprightly," Armijo said. "With a wife who is even younger, no?"

Magoffin wondered if Armijo somehow knew about the death of his and Susan's daughter, or if he only tried to ingratiate himself with clever compliments. It didn't matter. The demands Magoffin delivered were graven in stone and could not be changed. No amount of bonhomie on Manuel Armijo's part could change what Magoffin was ordered to get.

And if diplomacy failed with this prancing mockery of a governor, General Kearny's army would triumph quickly over Armijo's.

It took less than an hour for James Magoffin to know he had failed to convince the Mexican governor of American intent.

"Magoffin is telling Armijo right about now to deliver the proclamation," General Kearny said to Ceran St. Vrain, leaning back in his chair and tapping his finger nervously against the side of his ceramic mug steaming with coffee.

William Bent came into the fort's main dining room, and pulled up a chair so he could sit near the general and talk without being overheard.

"You wanted to see me, General?"

"Ah, yes, I was just telling your partner that the fat is in the fire now. Magoffin was to offer amnesty for all Mexicans who surrender and pledge to be loyal Americans. If Armijo doesn't agree to all my terms, my army moves immediately."

"Magoffin can't get back until tomorrow at the earliest, General," said William.

"I am a careful man, Mr. Bent, and plan for every contingency. If Armijo does not see the wisdom in surrendering, I will need a constant flood of information from Santa Fe and anywhere else he might have hidden away his soldiers."

"What's that have to do with me, General?" asked William. "I'm just a shopkeeper."

"Oh, Mr. Bent, you are far too modest," Kearny said jovially. "Mr. St. Vrain tells me you have a pipeline into the Cheyenne tribe nearby and can do a reasonable job of sneaking about on your own."

"I'm not half the mountain man Ceran is," William said, not sure if he ought to be insulted. If this was a compliment, Kearny had much to learn about his delivery.

"Spies, Mr. Bent. I need spies in the midst of the enemy."

"Enemy? You don't know if Armijo is going to accede to Magoffin's demands."

"I plan ahead. This must remain a secret shared only by the three of us. The invasion will begin at dawn in two days. On August second, I march on Santa Fe with my full force."

"Which is it? Do you want me to recruit spies or scouts?" asked William. He still wasn't sure how he ought to respond. Kearny took everything for granted. That rankled almost as much as the immense cost of feeding and provisioning his five-thousand-man army.

"Call them scouts, if this soothes your conscience, sir, but they must report troop movements and give me a location for the governor. He will be the center of command for his army. Cut him off from his soldiers and the army will be headless—and helpless."

"I suppose we can ask around for men willing to do some scouting," Ceran said, staring intently at his partner. "What do you think, William?"

"I think we ought to see some money for the provisions we've given the general so far. The fodder for his livestock cost more than two thousand dollars. His soldiers are like a cloud of locusts devouring everything in front of them."

"Are you calling my men a biblical plague?" General Kearny put down the ceramic mug and glared at William.

"If you don't pay for what they are eating, yes."

"This is an outrage!" shouted Kearny.

"I agree!" William shot to his feet. "We're American citizens. You can't take our food and supplies and not pay for them!"

"Gentlemen, please," Ceran said, trying to keep them from coming to blows. In that he succeeded, but not in forging a truce between the affronted men. Kearny stormed out into the *placita,* and William went into the kitchen, ranting about how little they had left in their larder because of the army.

Invasion

Santa Fe
August 9, 1846

"He won't be pleased," the first scout said as they left Raton Pass far behind them and reached the road leading into Santa Fe.

"Should we even bother reporting to the governor?" asked the second. "We can keep riding. If we go to Taos, we can stay with my cousins."

"Taos?" scoffed the first. "That is not far enough away. We should go farther, past Navajo land to the coast. I've never seen an ocean and Pacific is a mighty fine name."

"Especially now," agreed the second.

They rode until they reached the governor's palace. Troops marched back and forth in front of the residence. The two scouts exchanged hurried glances. These soldiers were slow and clumsy compared to the ones they had seen earlier. And this company had been assigned to protect the governor because they were the best to be had in all the army of New Mexico.

"I . . . I don't want to go inside," said the second scout. "It serves no purpose. He sent you."

The first scout swallowed hard. He wanted someone to back up his claims, yet he counted this man as his partner, his friend, his comrade in arms.

"Go on to Taos. I won't follow that trail. My luck rides south, and I want to go along with it."

"Thanks," the second scout said, a wan smile on his lips. "Go with God." He jerked on his reins, got his lathered horse walking away from the soldiers, and vanished around a corner in a minute.

The first scout took a deep breath and wondered why he didn't join his partner. Then he knew. He was too honorable to back away, no matter what might happen. Their duty was clear, as was their fate. That thought allowed him to walk into the governor's office with his head held high, although he quaked inside.

Manuel Armijo looked up, smiling broadly. The smile faded when he saw only a grim expression meeting it.

"What is it? Report!"

The scout took a deep breath to calm himself. It did not work. He took a second and launched into his report.

"It's real bad, Governor Armijo," he said. "I rode almost to Bent's Fort. For miles around the fortress I saw American soldiers. As you ordered, I went from camp to camp, speaking with those who would talk. Many did, since they're bored with camp life already. They're champing at the bit."

"So? Get on with it. Are they marching to Santa Fe?" Armijo had gone pale. He knew the answer before the scout put it into words.

"More 'n five thousand soldiers, Governor. They stand at the northern side of Raton Pass as we speak. In only two days or three at the most, they will have their artillery lined up around Santa Fe. There are so many cavalry that escape from town won't be possible if they catch you here. The Americans are invading in force!"

Occupation

Santa Fe
August 12, 1846

"How long will it take for the cavalry units to circle the town and cut off escape to the south?" asked General Kearny.

"The report from Captain Moore says he ought to be in position by now," Phillip Cooke said. He stared at the map spread on the ground and held by small stones at each corner. The land seemed to jump up at him, moving from flat paper to the real contours of the terrain. How many times he had ridden into New Mexico, without authorization, waiting for this day, Cooke could not remember. Now it was different. He rode at the head of a huge invading army ordered by the president of the United States.

"There's no reason to put off taking Santa Fe," Kearny said decisively. "Captain Cooke, you will have the honor of leading the advance unit. I'll give support with artillery, both east and west of town. If you meet resistance too great for your force to overcome, I shall send word to Captain Moore and he will launch a pincers attack from his position to the south."

"That would force Armijo to fight on two fronts."

"And be bombarded from each flank," Kearny said.

"Do you have any questions concerning your orders, sir?"

"No, sir!" Captain Cooke snapped to attention, saluted smartly, and hurried to rally his men. For years, especially after Henry Dodge's death, he had ridden endless miles across the prairie chasing the will-o'-the-wisp Indians. The Sioux had been bad. The Kiowa were worse, but the Comanche had been the worst of all. Every time he was certain he had them in his sights, they drifted away like smoke on the wind.

That was not soldiering. Chasing raiders only to find they had left the field days earlier, plotting ambushes and killing only one or two old or wounded braves too slow to keep up with the rest of their raiding party, even finding villages populated with women and children—that was not proper soldiering.

Assembling his troops, marching them forward against another army, *that* was soldiering.

"We will be the lead element going into battle," Captain Cooke called to his assembled soldiers. "We will fight bravely this day, and we will triumph. Bugler, sound the advance!"

The bugler muffed the first few notes, then got his dried lips on the mouthpiece and sounded the call to advance. A shiver went up and down Cooke's spine. He drew his heavy saber and held it high so all could see it gleam in the morning sun. With a dramatic flourish in the direction of the New Mexico capital, he set off at the head of his dragoons. Now was the time to use the saber as a symbol of rank and command, even if it would prove to be a clumsy weapon in combat.

"Sir," said a nervous lieutenant who had joined only a few weeks earlier at Fort Leavenworth, "what'll it be like?"

"I have no idea," Cooke said honestly. "It might be

worse than pounding on the gates of hell if Armijo chooses to oppose us. The grapevine says a general from Mexico named Urrea has arrived with a force equal to our own."

"But our scouts didn't report that, did they, sir? That fellow back at the fort—"

"William Bent."

"Yes, Bent. I heard tell the general had him send spies, and they didn't see any big army."

"The diplomat, Magoffin, reported only minimal activity, too," Cooke said, "but we must be prepared to face the worst."

"Yes, sir," the lieutenant said, his voice quavering.

Captain Cooke looked at him and said, "It'll be worse in your mind. Wait until we attack to see if it matches what you fear at this moment."

"I understand, sir. I won't fail you, no matter how intense the fighting."

"I ask for nothing more, Lieutenant, and expect nothing less." Captain Cooke sat upright in his saddle, eyes quickly scanning the road going into Santa Fe. Traders had followed this broad path innumerable times over the years. This was the end of the Santa Fe Trail. The heart of Mexican control of the entire Territory of New Mexico lay ahead, waiting to be cut out.

Cooke had expected to see scouts racing into the city to report to Armijo. It was as if he rode into a ghost town. His heart raced as he arrayed his mounted troops and made certain the foot soldiers knew their orders.

"Fix bayonets!" he bellowed. Sergeants relayed the order to the infantry while the cavalry waited anxiously. "Infantry, advance, by the count!"

A drum began beating out a marching rhythm. Cooke was pleased to see the lieutenant's nerves had settled down and the officer rode alongside his infantrymen, looking like a commander in charge of both his men and the field.

"Cavalry," Cooke called, "prepare for attack." All around him men drew their six-guns and readied the pistols for the charge. He sheathed his heavy saber, then detached it from his belt, securing it under his saddle. Time for show was past; his men knew he would be at the front of the attack. Cooke took his spare pistol from his saddlebags and thrust it into his belt. Too many times he had seen greenhorn officers fresh from back East and West Point think they could use the saber effectively. He had learned firepower was better than a single slash at an infantry soldier as he galloped past.

Cooke sat anxiously, watching his infantry march forward, bayonets lowered and ready for the fusillade that never came.

"Sir!" the lieutenant yelled, waving from the line of adobe houses at the outskirts of Santa Fe. "No resistance!"

"Cavalry, forward!" shouted Cooke. His men raced off and quickly passed the foot soldiers. He rode at the head of the column, wary of a trap. All Cooke saw were frightened faces peering from doorways. Reining in, he called to a woman holding back two small children who wanted to rush out to look at the blue-uniformed soldiers.

"Are you well?" Captain Cooke asked. "Is anyone hurt?"

She shook her head, then pushed her youngsters back into her home.

Captain Cooke slowed the advance, making sure his infantry never lagged too far behind. He had not expected to reach the Santa Fe plaza without being challenged. But he did.

"Sir," the lieutenant said breathlessly, "is that the governor's residence?"

"It is," Cooke said. "Set guards. Stay alert. And have a dozen men accompany me." He dismounted, pulled his spare pistol from his belt, and walked to the portal leading to the inner courtyard. Behind him came the infantrymen. They entered the *placita,* the soldiers around their captain in a fan-shaped formation.

Cooke turned in a full circle. He had never been here before, but finding Armijo's office was not hard. With long strides, Cooke went to the door and kicked it open. Just inside cowered a Mexican soldier who thrust his shaking hands in the air.

"Private," said Cooke. He got a head bob in reply from the Mexican. "Where is Governor Armijo?"

"Albuquerque, *Capitán.* He left yesterday with all his troops."

Cooke stared at the man, looking for any sign of deception. He finally laughed without humor and shook his head. "I'll be damned. The son of a bitch turned tail, and we took Santa Fe without firing a shot."

Captain Cooke left to report his bloodless victory to General Kearny.

Celebration—
and Trade

Bent's Fort
August 17, 1846

Skyrockets arched high into the air, exploding with a cascade of dazzling blue and green sparks. Charles Bent reined in and watched as new rockets were fired from the ramparts of the fort. His horse shied when one rocket exploded directly overhead. There were few descending sparks, but the racket was enough to put anyone on edge, much less a nervous horse who had made the trip from St. Louis in record time.

Charles put his heels to the horse's flanks and urged it forward. A few minutes' trotting allowed him to reach the front gate and finally dismount. In spite of his expertise on horseback, Charles ached all over. He had to admit to himself, if to no one else, he was getting old and couldn't make the long rides as he once had.

"Here," he said, handing the reins to a young boy he didn't recognize. "See that she gets grain and a good currying."

"Yes, sir." The boy hesitated. "Who are you? You one of them?"

"Them?"

"Them diplomats comin' through here. Mr. Magoffin's back and with his wife. But you don't look like one."

"I'll take that as a compliment," Charles said, amused. "What do I look like?"

The boy shrugged, then grinned broadly. "Somebody who'll give me a dime to feed and curry his horse. We got plenty of oats right now."

"Done," Charles said, fishing out a coin from his pocket. He flipped it into the air and the boy caught it with a cat-quick grab.

"I . . . this is a quarter," the boy said in wonder.

"Do a really good job."

"Yes, sir," the boy said, heading around south to the corral with the horse.

"And son, I own this place. I'm Charles Bent." Charles laughed when the boy's eyes went wide and he started to stammer an apology. Charles waved it off and went into the *placita*, sure of what he would find.

At any given time, there were fifty or sixty men with their families in residence. The fort now overflowed with men, many drinking heavily, and women dancing to poorly played banjos and accordions. He looked around, but didn't see either of his brothers or Ceran. He took the steps up to the parapet, and found both Ceran and William fiddling with another skyrocket. Try as they might, they couldn't get the fuse at the back of the rocket to stay lit.

"Sit the candle under it. Maybe the entire backside will catch fire then."

"A good idea," William said, not looking up. Then he jerked around. "Charles! We didn't see you come in!"

"I thought all the fireworks and celebration was for

me." He clasped William close, then shook hands with Ceran.

"You must have guessed why we're celebrating," Ceran said. "Kearny took Santa Fe without firing a single shot."

"I suspected as much," Charles said. "You aren't usually this lax guarding the fort. And the boy who took my horse is a newcomer."

"A lot of them are," William said, positioning the candle directly behind the slender rocket. The fuse sputtered fitfully, but this time the entire end of the rocket caught fire. With a loud screech and a frantic wobble, the skyrocket blasted into the air, exploding prematurely and bestowing its glowing red sparks over the tules east of the main gate.

"They came flocking to the fort when Kearny left, thinking the fight in New Mexico would get bloody. From what I've heard, Captain Cooke rode straight into Santa Fe and never saw a single soldier. Armijo lit out like a scalded dog for Albuquerque and might still be running south."

"Then all of New Mexico is under American control," Charles said with some satisfaction. "I'd counted on this. I spent a great deal of company money buying merchandise. It'll be at Westport by the time we get back for the fall caravans."

"I'll head out this time," Ceran said. "I want to see my family and let them know all is well."

"You mean your room at the Planters House has been empty too long," William said, laughing. He set off a string of firecrackers, throwing them over the wall to dance and pop on the ground below.

"That, too," Ceran said. "We'll have the money now for a much richer life."

"No more tribute to Mexico," Charles said. "Armijo's

competition is gone, too. No Mexican taxes, no Mexican governor—we're on our way to a mighty fine year of trade."

"I wouldn't have thought it when Kearny came here with that army of his," William said. "He still hasn't paid us, but with trade restored and a virtual monopoly in New Mexico, we can make up the profits lost with a single caravan."

"Will you come back to Westport with me, Charles?" asked Ceran. "I can use the company. William's been out with the Cheyenne, assuring them Kearny wasn't after them. Besides, I need to find if there are any new restaurants in St. Louis. I'm sure you found all the good ones." Ceran patted Charles's ample belly.

"Not all of them. I had to leave some for you to ferret out," Charles said. He watched Ceran and William light more of the fireworks until the crate lay empty at their feet. They went to sit on the edge of the walkway and watch the festivities in the courtyard. At one end of the *placita* men and women danced. At the other, just below Ceran's quarters, serious drinking went on. Nowhere did they see anyone moping. America had won a striking victory in the war against Mexico and had done it easily and well.

"You look tired, Charles," his brother said. "Want to join the dancing?"

"I was thinking," Charles said. "Ceran can handle the wagon train back. I heard nothing about Sioux or Comanche raiders and with decent trade—untaxed—goods for Santa Fe and Taos, we'll show the biggest profit ever."

"But?"

Charles turned to his brother and said, "I should go to Taos to be certain everything is all right. Armijo might be gone, but Padre Antonio is a permanent fixture there."

"Frank Blair has things well in hand, Charles," William said. "He's a stout fellow and has a good head on his shoulders. And I'm not just saying that because he's George's best friend. It was our lucky day when he came West."

"I wasn't worried about him as much as I was Ignacia and the children."

"I should have mentioned it right away, Charles. There's nothing for you to worry about. They're all as fine as frog fur. George is looking after them, but the rioting has died down while everyone waits to see what it'll mean to be under American rule. Frank, George, and I did some scouting for Kearny, after a bit of dickering over what our services were worth; then we came back to the fort before the actual invasion. George and Frank left right away for Taos, and were there before Kearny even got to Raton Pass."

"I'm not worried, not now," Charles said. "But I should still go to Taos, and probably get on over to Santa Fe and pay our respects to General Kearny. I want to start on better terms with him than we ever did with Armijo."

"That won't be hard," William said. "If you promise him a steady supply line stretching back to St. Louis, he'll offer you the world."

"I don't want the world," Charles said, "but New Mexico would be good."

Lingering Danger

Charles Bent met Frank Blair on the outskirts of town. Blair had a jacket on, pulled around him strangely. As he turned, the coattails slid away from his body enough for Charles to see that Blair wore two six-guns, one strapped on each hip.

"You look like you're loaded for bear," Charles observed.

"What? Oh, these," Blair said almost guiltily. "I forget I'm wearing them."

"Six pounds of iron on your hips has to slow you down. How can you forget you're packing?"

Blair looked a bit defiant and then said, "I wear them all the time now. When I go to bed, one of them is on the stand. If I go to take a leak, one of them is with me."

"That's mighty cautious of you," Charles said, marveling at how Blair had changed. The young man had been pale and thin when he arrived at Bent's Fort. A few weeks' rest had improved his constitution immensely, but his disposition had always been cheerful to the point of giddiness. Charles remembered the times Blair played his banjo and danced with Charlotte and Rosita, enjoying life although his grip on it had been tenuous at first. Somehow, the stronger he grew physically, the more fearful and dour his personality had become. It made no sense.

"Are you happy with your position?" Charles asked. He had seen men who were uncomfortable working for someone else. Most mountain men fell into that category. One exception had turned out to be Ceran St. Vrain, who positively enjoyed the company of others and had worked ably and well as the Bent brothers' partner. Charles had been toying with the notion of allowing young Francis Blair a small stake in Bent, St. Vrain & Company, as much on George's recommendation as for the fine job Blair had done building sales in Taos.

But this suspicious, jumpy man rode a thin edge. Any sudden noise would set him off, or so it seemed to Charles. This wasn't the kind of man the company employed.

"Quite happy, Charles," Blair said. "Working at the store has broadened my experience immensely." He swung about in the saddle, his hand reaching for the pistol at his right side. Blair relaxed when he saw three women struggling along the road with their wash, heading for the river.

"What's wrong, then?" Charles asked.

"Nothing that hasn't been wrong before." Blair looked down and saw he had left his hand on the gun. He drew away. "You've been gone for a spell, Charles. It's worse than when you were here last."

"But the Mexicans are defeated. This is American territory now."

"The Mexican soldiers are gone," Blair said, "and with them all semblance of law in Taos. Padre Antonio tries to keep civil order—but not too hard, since unrest suits his purposes."

"He hasn't threatened Ignacia or the Jaramillos, has he?" Charles felt his anger rising at the mere idea the priest could put anyone at risk because of old hatreds.

"Not openly, but he stirs up the Indians every chance he gets, and there are plenty of them now, it seems. He has set up a small fiefdom of his own, with his brother and friends in power."

Charles snorted. "That hasn't changed. I remember all too well the outcome of the trial of the men who beat you and George." His jaw set as he asked, "Have they tried to harm you since Armijo was driven out of power?"

"Nothing overt," Blair said, "but I can't overstate it enough that you should always have a few men with you as bodyguards—and you should carry a gun, too."

"I dislike the weight," Charles said, patting his coat pocket.

"Then I'll assign a half-dozen men to watch your back while you're in Taos. It's for your own good. I hear rumors all the time, and it's possible a considerable number of the Mexican soldiers are hiding out, just waiting to cause trouble. Between that possibility and the good padre, I'm jumping at my own shadow."

Charles said nothing as they rode into town, stopping briefly at the company's store while Blair went off to run an errand. Charles cursorily examined the books, saw that the store was far more profitable under Blair than it had been when he and Ceran were running it, then sneaked off when Blair wasn't looking to walk to his house some distance away.

As Charles strolled along the familiar Taos streets, he noticed a small knot of boys trailing him. He turned and waved. They scampered away as if he had pointed a shotgun at them. He shrugged it off and picked up the pace, hurrying toward his house. He passed Kit and Josefa's house, turned down the street, and stopped short of the gate leading into the inner courtyard. Four men skulked about, trying to remain in the shadows and not doing a good job of it.

One poked his head up, and the sun clearly revealed it to Charles.

"Valdez!" he called, waving. The one-time constable scurried off like a cockroach. "José Valdez!" Charles shouted after him. The men with him also left at a dead run. Charles strode to the gate and looked at a pile of wood shavings.

He kicked it away angrily, wondering what was going on. If Valdez wanted to set fire to the house, burning down the gate was a sorry way to go about it. But then he had never given Valdez credit for much in the way of brains. Either the padre's brother or Padre Antonio himself told Valdez what to do.

Charles started to ring the bell, to get someone inside to open the gate for him, when he heard loud voices coming up the street behind him. He turned and went cold inside. A dozen Taos Indians waved clubs and brandished knives. Their murderous intent was clear.

Charles frantically rang the bell, but no one inside responded. He started to skirt the wall and go around to a side door when he saw that Valdez and two of his henchmen blocked his way. They grinned savagely now. He turned back, only to find retreat was cut off by the running, shouting crowd.

The Indians shrieked as they came for him. Charles stepped away from the outer wall of his house and looked up, desperately seeking something he could grab, something to pull himself up and get inside the house. Roof-supporting vigas that normally poked out were missing here, cut off flush with the wall to prevent a thief from easily scaling the wall.

"Kill him, get him!" cried the Indian leading the mob.

Charles braced himself for the attack, knowing he could never survive it. As the leader of the mob raised a club to smash down on Charles's head, a shot rang out. Then another and another. When the shotgun fired, its report echoed down the street all the way to the plaza. The bull-throated roar froze the crowd.

"Get out of here," shouted Frank Blair, riding up with four men. Two carried long-barreled shotguns, the muzzles smoking. The other two men had rifles leveled. From the set to their shoulders and the grim expressions, they were ready to shed blood. Indian blood.

"Them, too," Charles said, whirling around and pointing to where Valdez had blocked him. But Valdez and his cronies were gone like smoke in a breeze.

Charles pressed himself back against the cool adobe wall as Blair and the others rode through the crowd, breaking up the tight knots and destroying what control the leader had. In a few minutes, they were alone outside Charles's house.

"You should have stayed at the store," Blair said angrily. "I told you not to go off by yourself without a bodyguard."

"I'm sorry, Frank. I should have listened to you. Perhaps I ought to stay in Santa Fe from now on," Charles Bent said, meaning it. Taos no longer had the feel of home to him.

Governor Bent

"I feel like the conquering hero," Charles Bent said uncomfortably. His brother George, and especially Frank Blair, had insisted that he ride to Santa Fe with a guard strong enough to protect him against any contingency. He had protested that Blair ought to keep the men in Taos to protect the store, but Blair's lawyerlike arguments finally convinced him. As unlikely as it seemed, there might be pockets of Mexican soldiers left behind, stragglers cut off from their unit or even assassination squads sent by Armijo to remove the hated Americans permanently.

This was the argument that Blair had used, but Charles suspected the young man worried more about the Taos Indians under Padre Antonio's sway. In the few days he had stayed in Taos, there had been several small riots, mostly rock-throwing but still frightening. The disturbances had been quickly put down, both by the priest's fiery words promising eternal damnation and by the tight-knit band Blair had recruited as guards. Charles considered them little more than mercenaries since they were paid with company funds, but this was better than forming a vigilante band. Mercenaries could be fired by removing them from the payroll. A lynch mob was completely beyond rational control.

"It's good to see American uniforms again," Charles said to the man riding close at his side as they entered Santa Fe. Many emblems of Mexican occupation were gone or were being removed by surly peones. Many signs had already been painted over, Spanish replaced with crudely done English directions. But Charles saw no evidence that the people who lived in Santa Fe were being harmed or even showed any animosity for the bloodless conquest.

They weren't happy about the situation, but showed no inclination toward rebellion.

Before he reached the governor's palace, he spotted three or four burned-out or abandoned buildings that would make decent stores for the company. If he got the warrant to do business from General Kearny, he could open a half-dozen more stores to fill the void left by Armijo's wagons no longer supplying the town from central Mexico. A great fortune could be had in a short while, and everyone would prosper. Charles was certain he could deliver foodstuffs to Santa Fe and sell them for less than Armijo ever dreamed possible.

"Mr. Bent!" came the loud cry of recognition. Captain Cooke rode up, executed a smart salute, and then said, "I'm glad you came so quickly. I hadn't realized our courier had time to reach Taos."

"Courier?" asked Charles. "I don't understand. I decided to pay my respects to the general. No courier's reached me."

"Perhaps your paths crossed between here and Taos," Captain Cooke said, frowning. "It doesn't matter. I'm sure General Kearny will see you immediately."

"Excellent. I have some business to discuss with him."

Captain Cooke looked at Charles strangely, then called for an honor guard to escort their visitor to the general's office.

Charles signaled for his bodyguards to stay outside when they reached the Palace of the Governors. He wouldn't need them when he spoke with Stephen Kearny. As Charles entered the anteroom outside the general's office, the orderly saw him and hastily pushed his chair back, jumping to attention.

"Sir!" he barked. "General Kearny will see you immediately."

"Thank you," Charles said, wondering at the reception he received. If they were so eager to please, he could broach the subject nearest and dearest to his brother William's heart—payment for the huge army's provisions while camped outside the fort.

"Mr. Bent, you made excellent speed arriving. Thank you for such promptness. Am I to take it that you have agreed to accept?" General Kearny stared at him with flinty eyes.

"Accept?" asked Charles. "I just rode into town. What is it you're offering?"

"I thought you had read the dispatch. My apologies. After consulting with Mr. Magoffin and obtaining civilian approval from Washington, it is my proud duty to offer you the governorship of New Mexico Territory."

"Governor?" Charles was shocked at the suddenness. He had joked about being governor, but had not imagined it would happen this way, this soon, that it would be *given* to him. He had expected military oversight with an army officer to run the territory, followed in a year or so by a general election. That had been his goal, to become the first governor elected by the people of the territory.

"Who else? You know the people better than anyone else I know, your company can supply their needs, and you are an American citizen."

"Would you have considered Ceran St. Vrain had he been an American?" asked Charles.

"Perhaps," Kearny said slowly. "I am not impressed by these mountain men the way others back East seem to be. I prefer to appoint men of upstanding character, family men with roots in the area, dedicated men like yourself who have organizational ability and will not turn New Mexico into a personal fiefdom."

Charles felt almost embarrassed at the plans he had made as he rode into town about expanding the Bent, St. Vrain & Company's hold on commerce in New Mexico. Almost.

"This is a great honor, General. I accept!"

Kearny thrust out his hand and Charles shook it to seal the deal.

Governor Charles Bent. He liked the sound of that.

Gala

"Welcome, esteemed guests," Charles Bent said, standing atop a stack of empty crates in the courtyard. "We are gathered this afternoon to honor the man who has freed New Mexico from the yoke of a tyranny dating back to the earliest days." Charles waited for the sporadic applause to die down. "Join me in honoring General Stephen Watts Kearny, the liberator of New Mexico!"

This brought forth the applause he had expected. The general held up his hand to quiet the approval for his bloodless feat of driving out the Mexicans, then began his long-winded self-congratulatory speech. Charles began to shift from foot to foot, waiting for Kearny to slow down, but there didn't seem to be any end in sight. Charles wanted to tell the people of Santa Fe they could dance and sing, enjoy the food laid out on long tables, all furnished by Bent, St. Vrain & Company. There was much he wanted to say as the new governor, but until Kearny wound down, he wasn't likely to get the podium back.

Even then, Charles was astute enough to realize this might not be the time to give a speech of his own. People wouldn't listen, and the plans he had for New

Mexico were wide-ranging and important. He slowly edged around the *placita* and into a rear portion of the governor's mansion.

His mansion.

"Do you have enough?" he asked the head cook toiling in the kitchen. She stared at him, brown eyes wide.

"Why, yes, yes," she said.

"Is something wrong?"

"I have never seen the governor himself come to the kitchen unless something displeases him. Then, well, then people disappear and never return."

"You're all doing a marvelous job. Keep the food on the tables, both in the courtyard and outside in the plaza. I want the citizens of Santa Fe to appreciate that they are also Americans now."

He continued to wander through the maze of rooms that was his new home. Many of the rooms struck him as museums rather than living quarters. Charles made a few mental notes to himself to move the old Spanish and Mexican items to storage. He needed a staff, and these rooms would be perfect for the agents dealing with the various Indian tribes and pueblos.

As he returned to the courtyard, he saw that Kearny was just getting rolling. Many of the men and women crowded into the *placita* began to drink more heavily. Charles didn't blame them. He slipped away again, heading for the stables behind the governor's palace to be sure the livestock was being properly tended. At Bent's Fort he had noticed the stable hands often slacked off because they never expected the owners to come inspect their work.

Charles looked up when he heard a loud shout. He turned to see a man on horseback hunched over, galloping along the street. The rider whooped and hollered like a fool, then reined back and kicked up dust onto Charles's fancy duds. But Charles didn't care.

"Kit, you old son of a gun! You're back!" Charles shook hands with an obviously trail-weary Kit Carson.

"I heard over in Taos what'd happened. So you're Governor Bent, eh? Congratulations. I'da brung you some fresh meat to celebrate, but I never slowed enough to shoot anything."

"Kit, we've got plenty of food. When Armijo high-tailed it south, he left everything, including his spare uniforms."

"Them powdery blue jobs? He was a mite taller'n me, but I wouldn't mind gettin' one to wear for fancy occasions."

"It's yours. I'll have a servant go through the wardrobes and get the one with the most medals. Where have you been? I heard you signed on with Frémont's second expedition and then didn't hear a peep out of you."

"Been out West, along the Pacific Coast. Durned purty land. Been doin' mappin' for John Charles and even some explorin' on my own. If I didn't love Taos so much, I'd move out there lickety-split."

"I'm glad you're back. Right now, General Kearny's finishing a speech about what a great soldier he is."

"If I know him, and I heard plenty from John Charles, you ain't said the half of it. Kearny'll make himself out to be the finest soldier what ever lived, braver than brave, taller than tall, and mean as a grizzly with its leg in a trap."

"That's him," Charles said, laughing delightedly at having his old friend here to share the celebration with him. "Come on. You look tuckered out. I can get you some food. Then I'll have to see to my guests."

"If Kearny ain't bored 'em all to death."

The men swapped tall tales as they wended their way through the maze of the mansion. Charles introduced Kit to the kitchen staff, again surprising them by his personal attention, especially to someone as trail-dusty and shabby as Kit, then went to the *placita*, where Kearny had finally run out of steam.

The grateful crowd began working in earnest on the fine food spread on the tables. The general circulated among the people, shaking men's hands and gallantly kissing the women's, until he reached Charles.

"Didn't see you in the crowd, Governor. You didn't run out on my fine speech, now, did you?"

"I wouldn't have missed it for the world, General, but I was called back to the stables."

"Nothing serious, I trust. I can have a squad of men there if—"

"No, no, nothing bad. Kit just rode in from California, and I wanted a moment with him."

"Kit Carson? The scout that scoundrel Frémont stole away from me?"

"I didn't know the lieutenant had done any such thing," Charles said. "You were back East when he formed his second mapping expedition and—"

"I'd like to talk with Mr. Carson. Lead the way."

Charles bristled a little at Kearny's brusqueness, but pushed it aside, thinking the military man had yet to learn formal manners for civilian occasions. They entered the kitchen. Then Kearny stopped and faced him squarely.

"Your guests require your presence, Governor. Go see to them. You, Mr. Carson, come with me."

"Very well, General," Charles said. He saw how Kit reacted to these outright orders on Kearny's part.

"Kit, I'll talk to you later. Don't do anything you might regret later."

Kit glowered, hitched up his broad leather belt, and settled the two knives and the pistol there. He didn't respond, but seemed to be caught balancing on one foot, not sure if he ought to trail after the general or join Charles and to hell with the officer.

Kit made his decision and followed Kearny. Charles heaved a sigh, then went to enjoy the gala as much as he could.

"This looks like a quiet spot," Kearny said to Kit. He motioned to the scout to have a seat. Kearny perched on the edge of the desk, a long leg swinging nervously as he peered down at the much shorter, seated man. For a spell he said nothing, waiting for Kit to speak.

Kit was a trained hunter and knew all the tricks. He held his tongue, as Charles had suggested, and finally outwaited the officer.

"What I need from you, Mr. Carson, is some mighty dangerous duty. You will scout for my army as we make our way south."

"Wait up, General," Kit said. "I'm takin' dispatches from the West Coast back to Washington for John Charles Frémont. I don't rightly know what's in them letters, but they might be important to the folks gettin' them. I know they're mighty important to the people sendin' 'em."

General Kearny made a motion as if he shooed away flies. His lip curled a little as he spoke.

"They can't be too important, not compared with the duty you will be performing for me. We dare not allow the Mexicans to fortify any point to the south.

Texas is a state now, and can take care of its own defense along the Rio Bravo. New Mexico Territory, however, remains an open highway from central Mexico, a route that must be sealed off before Armijo can regroup and cause deviltry. He must not be allowed to retake Santa Fe."

"General," Kit said slowly, "I promised to do my best to deliver these dispatches. There's no way I can go with you, much as I'd like to, till after I hand these over in Washington."

"It's an order, Mr. Carson. I'm ordering you to scout for me. I need the best, and that's you."

"I said I *promised*, General. I never break my word." Kit smoldered at the mere suggestion he would drop his mission and go gallivanting off to track Armijo and his runaway army.

"I'll see that the dispatches are delivered. It's easier to find a courier than it is a good scout."

Kit hesitated now. He thought he had been insulted, but wasn't sure. The general had said he was a good scout, but he had also said any fool could deliver the dispatches. Kit didn't feel as if he had been scraped off the bottom of the apple barrel for the chore. Delivering mail was important.

"We will assemble and head out in two days, Mr. Carson. If you leave tomorrow morning, you ought to gather enough information to aid us on our way down the river to Albuquerque. I need to be certain Armijo has abandoned fortifications there and retreated farther south."

"You're makin' a heap of assumptions, General."

Kearny stared at him, never blinking. Kit thought on what Charles had said before leaving him, and then realized Kearny was likely to have him shot as a traitor if he didn't agree to the scout. For two cents he would simply up and ride for Washington and devil take the hindmost.

"Well, Mr. Carson. What'll it be?"

"Reckon I'll do some scoutin' for you if the dispatches are taken straightaway to Washington."

"I'll expect your first report in three days, sir." General Kearny stood, shook Kit's hand, and then strode out, whistling an army marching song as he made his way down the long, dim passages on his way back to the gala in his honor.

Dissent
and Rebellion

Santa Fe
October 20, 1846

"It's getting worse," Charles Bent said as he paced, hands locked behind his back. How easy it had been worrying about wagon trains and profit margins. Now he worried about those and the welfare of an increasingly rebellious New Mexico. Keep the peace, keep the people fed.

"You've told Kearny about this, I take it," Ceran St. Vrain said. Ceran lounged back in the chair, his feet hiked up onto the governor's desk. He reflected on the times he had come here to talk with Manuel Armijo and how he had longed to make this small defiance. Now Charles invited him often and he could do as he pleased, if it did not disrupt discipline among the staff.

"Of course I've written Kearny about it. He's too busy in the west, chasing Navajo raiders and fighting phantoms. I wish I had control of the army."

"There's no chance that will happen," Ceran said. "Colonel Price intends to hang on to his command like a weasel intent on ripping off your leg."

"An interesting comparison," Charles said, smiling a little. "Unfortunately, it's all too apt."

Colonel Sterling Price had arrived at Bent's Fort two weeks earlier with the Mormon Battalion, one of the most peculiar army units Charles had ever heard of. Brigham Young had forced a company of his men to enlist, in spite of his distaste for the United States and the brutal treatment of his followers back in Illinois. Charles had thought Young and his Mormons would have been more inclined to fight alongside Armijo, but it had not worked that way. The Mormon Battalion had been accompanied by forty of the men's wives and almost as many of the soldiers' children. By the time Price reached the fort, the Mormons were close to insurrection. The children were hard-pressed to maintain a military pace and the women were sick of the trail. Taken with men conscripted for duty they loathed, the Mormons were a bomb waiting to explode in the midst of the American Army.

Rather than court-martial an entire unit, Captain Cooke had seen the Mormons to Pueblo with the intent of escorting them into Utah and mustering them out of the army. But that left Price with only a handful of raw recruits who had come into Santa Fe, acting as if they owned the city. All of Charles's careful diplomatic overtures to Mexican sympathizers, winning them over to become American citizens, had been erased in less than a week.

How he wished for Phillip Cooke, or even the arrogant Stephen Watts Kearny. Sterling Price refused to do anything to discipline his men, and the soldiers laughed at Charles's orders.

"Price is acting on his own," Ceran said. "His superiors can't possibly approve of his actions."

"He isn't acting," Charles said glumly. "That's the problem. He thinks *he* is the great conqueror and the pitifully disciplined men with him are an army. They get drunk and rowdy every last night. I don't know if I've ever seen anyone under the rank of sergeant sober an hour after sundown."

"I've heard of a few nasty clashes with the citizens," Ceran said.

"Clashes? You call them clashes? Two rapes and a murder? And Price refuses to look into it, saying his men could not possibly have committed the crimes."

"Perhaps they didn't," Ceran said.

"We'll never know because he won't investigate. That way, he doesn't even have to cover up any misconduct by his recruits. I begged Kearny to put Colonel Doniphan in charge."

"That's not likely to happen. Doniphan is occupied in Las Vegas. Kearny understands how vital that part of the Santa Fe Trail is to his forays against the Navajo." Ceran saw how worried Charles was and asked, "You're sure Ignacia and your children are safe?"

"Of course," Charles said. "That was my first concern. And that makes me uneasy. My family is more important to me than what the U.S. Army is doing to the people of New Mexico. I'm governor and ought to have greater perspective."

"You're a husband and father. Those are your primary duties," Ceran said. "But you have more than the army to worry about."

"I know, Ceran, how I know," Charles said in anguish. "The Pueblo Indians—especially from the Taos Pueblo—and a large faction of Mexicans are beginning to protest."

"Not peacefully, either. I saw some houses being burned. I asked, and was told the mob thought the abandoned houses belonged to Americans. They didn't bother to find out they were abandoned months ago. They simply wanted to strike out."

"Kearny has to do something, about Price, about the unrest. I'm powerless to do anything but talk. My handful of lawmen aren't up to the chore of keeping peace in the face of such rebellion." Charles sat heavily in his chair. It creaked ominously under his weight. He tented his fingers under his chin as he lost himself in thought.

"Charles, talk is good for only so long. Your speeches are fine ones, but no one could stem the tide building in Santa Fe and Taos. For all I know, the rest of the territory is similarly aflame with resentment."

"There has to be something I can do. Kearny appointed me governor, but there's no power with it."

"California is well occupied now. Both Stockton and Frémont sent couriers saying that they didn't need more troops."

"Who told you that?" asked Charles.

"Kit. He was scouting for Kearny and not cottoning much to it. He had slipped away to see Josefa and his children."

"Is he still intent on returning to California to join Frémont?" asked Charles.

"I don't think so," Ceran said. "He worries about his family too much because, as bad as the crowds are here, they're worse in Taos. Padre Antonio is whipping them into a frenzy that'll lead to open rebellion any day now."

"For once, I can't find it in my heart to blame the padre," Charles said morosely. "What can I do, whatever can I do?"

Ceran had no answer. Worse, neither did Charles Bent.

Unruly Crowds

Santa Fe
November 10, 1846

The rock missed Charles Bent's head by inches. He ducked and threw up his hands to avoid a piece of adobe block thrown by another man in the crowd. The crumbly brick hit the wall of the governor's mansion and shattered into dust.

Charles knew how it felt. Every word he uttered turned to ash on his tongue. But he had to keep trying to bring calm to the turbulent city. He had lied to Colonel Price and sent the man on a wild-goose chase to the east of town, telling him Kit Carson had reported seeing a band of Navajo raiders trying to join forces with the Comanche. As far as he knew, Kit hadn't even spotted the elusive Lords of New Mexico ranging through their own country in the west. Every time Kearny—or Kit—came close to trapping them, they slipped through military fingers like sand and retreated to their rocky fortress in the Canyon de Chelly. It would take more than Kearny's halfhearted attempts to pry them out of their stronghold, but that continued failure on the general's part gave Charles a little respite.

He hoped Price and his brutish men went all the way to the Mississippi hunting nonexistent Navajo.

Charles straightened and faced another problem squarely.

"Citizens of Santa Fe," he called in a clear, even voice, "I am doing everything in my power to bring order to the populace."

"The Mexicans burned out my store," cried a man in the back of the crowd. A new rock arched upward, lobbed in Charles's direction. It fell short.

"The Indians stole fourteen of my horses," supplied another.

"Which Indians?" asked Charles, knowing the answer.

"What's the difference? It might have been the Ute or maybe it was Navajo. For all I know, the horses are pulling a plow at the Taos Pueblo now. They're a bunch of red thieves. What are you going to do about them, Governor?"

Facing a crowd in this way wasn't anything new for Charles, but he had never gained their confidence enough to turn their anger into more productive channels. He wished he had the gift of speech that caused men to listen, the presence that forced them to watch him—or lacking those, the military authority to put an end to the theft and open revolt shown by the Taos Indians and many of the disaffected Mexicans. For a brief spell, Charles had thought he could bring them over to the American view of how New Mexico could be, but Price, and to a lesser degree Kearny, had decisively ended that dream with their behavior.

Charles commanded only a few deputies, nowhere near enough to stop the worst of the agitators and arrest some of the looters.

He ducked another rock. The others had been thrown at him with lackluster intent. This one opened a gash on the side of his head and staggered him.

"I've written Washington," he said, knowing how lame this sounded. "I'm trying to bring General Kearny back to instill some discipline among his troopers."

"Write all the damn letters you want, it ain't doin' us no good. We ought to string up them Meskins!"

"And the Indians," shouted another. "They scalped my cousin over in Taos!"

"Quiet. Silence!" roared Charles, stepping up again. He ignored the blood trickling down the side of his face. The mood was turning ugly, and he had to stop them from taking the law into their own hands. "If Washington will not respond to my requests, I will write to Senator Thomas Hart Benton, the most influential senator in the West. John Frémont is a close friend of mine and Senator Benton is his father-in-law. I have his ear!"

"How's it gonna help us if another poly-tish-un makes a speech?"

"Senator Benton is a compassionate man and understands our troubles," Charles said.

"He's back in Missouri. How's he know what's goin' on here? What's he care?"

Charles launched into an impassioned speech that surprised even him with its vehemence and eloquence. Somehow, he quieted the crowd and got them to believe his letter-writing would produce results.

He hoped it would.

Charles watched the crowd disperse, muttering among themselves. At least violence had been averted this time. With a heavy heart, he went into the governor's mansion to find a servant who could patch up the cut on his temple. He knew stanching the flow of blood in the rest of the territory wouldn't be nearly as easy.

Cold Winds Blowing

On the Road from Santa Fe to Taos
January 15, 1847

"I feel abandoned," Charles Bent confided to an aide. The young man looked uncomfortable hearing such an intimate confession, but Charles had no one else to speak with. Kit was patrolling with Kearny, trying to track the elusive Navajo as they ranged across New Mexico killing and raiding at will. Ceran St. Vrain had returned to the fort earlier, and had found himself engaged with trouble at Fort St. Vrain and with his brother. And Charles's own brothers were similarly occupied. George and his friend Frank Blair were back East dealing for new wagons to replace those that had broken down during the fall caravans, and William was among the Cheyenne to whip up new trade.

"Senator Benton has no legitimate stake in New Mexico," the aide pointed out.

"That might be so, but we are a possession of the United States. If the politicians in Washington didn't want us, why did they go to war with Mexico?" Charles knew there were other reasons for the war, ones that had nothing to do with New Mexico. European powers were eyeing Mexico again, and a weak government in Mexico City invited their unwanted intervention. The

French and the Spanish and who knows what other Continental country coveted Mexico.

Charles almost wished Kearny's mission had been an abject failure, that Manuel Armijo had fought so well that the U.S. dragoons had been turned back at Raton Pass. Instead, Armijo had turned tail and run, leaving the entire belly of New Mexico white and exposed.

"White and exposed," Charles muttered. That was the crux of the problem. The Americans had come into Mexican and Indian country with no idea how best to govern. He had protested to everyone he could think of, begging for control of even a squad of soldiers, for a federal marshal's office, for some law-enforcement capability. Every request had failed. And every time he had tried to install lawmen on his own, Colonel Price had moved decisively to diminish their authority in favor of martial law administered by his own inept soldiers.

Charles had failed to whip up a strong civil authority in Santa Fe, but had inveigled friends to take the job of sheriff and deputy in Taos. Charles trusted Steven Lee and had known him for years. What he needed was a dozen more men as dedicated—and he needed them in Santa Fe, not only Taos.

The army wielded the real authority in this territory.

Charles Bent knew that might change soon unless something was done to quiet the displeasure among both Mexican and Indian citizens. He had heard credible rumors that a Mexican army under a capable, battle-smart general had formed in the mountains, intent on throwing the Americans out of New Mexico.

"Where's my heavy coat? Fetch it, will you?"

"Sir, you're not seriously thinking of going to Taos in this weather?" The aide stared at him wide-eyed.

"Why not? I've traveled in worse. A cold wind is nothing."

"The snows . . ."

"The snow will come when it comes. I'll take along adequate supplies for a week. It won't take me half that to reach Taos."

"Sir, let me see if I can't raise a few men to go with you."

"Nonsense, I'll be fine," Charles said. He was sick of looking at all the confused young faces around him. The only ones who sought a post with his administration were those too ingenuous or too young to understand what was happening. Try as he might, he could not convince them of the severity of the problems facing the government. They prattled on about trivial matters, and missed the real sources of antagonism against the occupying Americans.

"Well, I could go. . . ."

"Never mind," Charles said more sharply. "I'll take a spare horse. When one tires, I'll switch to the other. I can make fifty miles a day that way. I have in the past."

"But the storms are getting worse."

"I want to see my wife and children," Charles said, cutting to the heart of the matter. "I missed them at Christmas because of the unrest south of town." It had been more of a riot. Seven houses had been burned and four men's lives had been threatened. Only his persuasiveness had convinced the bloodthirsty mob to let the men and their families find sanctuary in Santa Fe rather than lynch them. A squad of soldiers would have brought the arsonists to justice and kept them from finding other homes to burn, but Charles didn't have that luxury.

He had waited through Twelfth Night to be certain the simmering pot did not boil over. And how he missed his family!

"I'll see that you have extra provisions, just in case of an added day or two on the road," the aide said, gratefully hurrying off. He felt he had done his duty to talk the governor out of such foolhardy travel in the middle of winter. Who could deal with the man if he wanted to ride a dangerous trail alone?

Charles finished signing the last of the trivial papers, and pushed them to the center of his desk for his aides to disperse later to the appropriate departments. He left his office then, not looking back. If he had not felt his duty so strongly, he would have tendered his resignation to General Kearny—if he could ever track down the man. Kearny moved about constantly, doing nothing constructive and avoiding the problems that he might have dealt with using his troopers.

The Mexicans and the Spanish before them had fought the Navajo and never gained more than an uneasy truce. The Navajo truly were the Lords of New Mexico, even pushing the Comanche out on occasion. Such a power had endured for too long for Kearny to erase it quickly. His time would have been better spent dealing with the Pueblos and Mexicans.

"All ready, sir," called a servant as Charles pulled on a heavy coat. He moved uneasily, a pistol strapped to his hip. He considered putting it into his saddlebags, then discarded the notion. No matter how uncomfortable it was at his hip under his coat, the pistol grease wasn't as likely to freeze. If he needed his sixgun, it would be awkward drawing, but it would fire when he did unlimber it.

"I'll be back within two weeks. Matters have settled

enough for me to take this trip." Charles wasn't sure he wasn't trying to convince himself it was all right rather than merely letting the servants know his intent.

He mounted and wiggled about. His rump had grown soft riding a chair rather than being in a saddle as he had once spent half his life. He found a comfortable position and snapped the reins, getting his horse walking out into the winter. Near the stables, he took the reins of the other horse, this one laden with his provisions. When the horse he rode began to tire, he intended to change loads. He could still throw a diamond hitch with the best of them.

Charles rode into the clear, cold Santa Fe morning, found the muddy, cut-up road leading north, and then angled to the northwest. In less than twenty minutes he had left the last of the adobe structures behind and reached the deceptively serene countryside. He sucked in a deep lungful of the pure, clean mountain air, and took in the full majesty of the rising sun splashing against the eastern slopes of the Sangre de Cristo Mountains.

The first part of the ride soothed Charles's nerves and gave him a sense of perspective on his position as governor. The razor-edged wind and the impossibly blue sky above sharpened his senses and cleared out the mental cobwebs as well as anything could have done. Added to this was the promise of seeing Ignacia again at the end of the trail.

Charles rode a little faster.

He was whistling a jaunty tune by midafternoon when he noticed a shift in the wind direction. The temperature dropped precipitously, warning him a storm might be brewing along the higher slopes. He reined back and looked around for a spot to spend the night.

It took him an hour, but Charles fashioned a crude lean-to for himself and a windbreak woven of branches between two ponderosa pines for his horses. He dug a small fire pit with his cold hands, and found enough pinecones to start the fire. It took quite a bit of skill to keep it going, but Charles was trail-wise and capable. He had built a fire adequate for both warmth and cooking by the time the storm struck with full fury.

Charles wolfed down his meal, then held out an empty tin can, which quickly filled with snow. He melted this near the fire and had fresh water to sip. But an hour later, the storm had not abated. If anything it had grown more intense.

Charles might have slept, wrapped in his fine buffalo robe and shielded from the cold ground by the stack of blankets he had brought with him, but he didn't. Too many men had frozen to death, although with lesser protection. Bleary-eyed but alert to any nip of frostbite on fingers or toes, Charles kept feeding the fire, a little less wood now to make his small supply last.

Still, the storm raged on.

Sometime during the night, the fierce winter storm died down a mite and Charles drifted to sleep. When he came awake with a start in the morning, the world had changed into a fairyland of dazzling ice crystals and an unsullied rippling comforter of pure white snow that stretched to the edges of forever.

The air carried the scent of his fire, but also pine and spruce and fir and a thousand other subtle scents he had forgotten living in garbage-strewn Santa Fe. He stretched his aching muscles and began shoving away the snow to tend his horses.

One had weathered the storm. The other had

frozen to death, reminding Charles of the thin edge between survival and death, even amid such pristine beauty. He gathered what supplies he could and packed them behind his saddle, then continued along the road to Taos.

Beauty and death. Such was the land where he was governor.

Revolt

Taos
January 19, 1847

Charles Bent knew something was wrong as soon as he reached the scattering of adobe houses at the southeastern edge of Taos. The quiet unsettled him. In spite of a heavy blanket of snow and the lateness of the day, there should have been people moving about. No one peeked through windows or from doors, no animals moved in corrals, nothing. It was as if everyone had simply up and left.

He fumbled to open his heavy coat. The chilly breeze whipping off the mountains sent a chill through him as the coat gaped open, but he wanted his hand near the pistol at his hip. He was glad now that he'd had the foresight to keep the gun close so it wouldn't seize up.

Charles's horse walked slowly toward the central plaza, now cloaked in long, slanting shadows. The dimness and occasional whirls of dancing snow made Charles feel even more isolated. It was as if he had ridden into some strange ghostly land where no one lived. He pushed back the coattail so he could draw his pistol when he saw thin curls of smoke rising at the far side of town not too distant from the plaza—the section of town where his home was.

The sound of a crowd suddenly, strangely echoed down one street, and then disappeared as quickly as it had come. Charles advanced, anxious now for his family. Exercising great caution, fighting with himself not to gallop headlong for his house, he rode in the center of the narrow, winding street. If it hadn't been for his alertness, he might have missed the boot soles poking out from an alley.

He stopped and stared. Much of the body was covered with snow, but the morning sun had drifted across the man's boots before moving on into the afternoon, sending shadows now instead of warming light. As a result, the man's boots had been cleared of snow while the rest of his body remained hidden.

Charles dismounted and gripped his six-gun with savage fury. The only explanation for the emptiness, the smoke, the silence, the one-time sound of a crowd was rebellion. Whether Padre Antonio led the revolt or whether the Taos Indians were running wild hardly mattered. Death stalked the streets.

Death itself lay in the street.

Charles nudged the feet and got no response. With his left hand he brushed away the snow while keeping his pistol trained on the body. It was a strange, silly thing to do, but he hardly realized it. When he cleared the snow from the dead man's face, Charles sagged.

"Lee," he said in a choked voice. Steve Lee had accepted the sheriff's job at Charles's behest, and now he lay dead, discarded like so much refuse.

Charles rocked back on his heels and stared at the body. Charles tried to figure when Lee had been killed, but couldn't. From the wounds on the back of the lawman's head and face, he had been beaten to death by someone using a rock or club, leaving him a butchered, battered mess. Charles looked up, and wondered if Lee had been on the roof above and had somehow fallen off. Even then, his wounds wouldn't have been so extreme. Steve Lee had been murdered.

Clutching his pistol even more firmly, Charles got to his feet and hurried down the street in the direction of his home. He slowed and stopped when he saw another body in the middle of the street. A dismembered body. Holding down his gorge, Charles sidled closer as if the body might miraculously reassemble itself and jump up.

"Oh, no," he said, turning the face up to the twilight. "Cornelio. They killed you, too."

He had persuaded Cornelio Vigil to become prefect of Taos. Another friend who had trusted him and answered his call to bring justice and stability to Taos had died horribly. Charles numbly pushed one arm back toward the body, as if this would somehow make Cornelio whole again. Then the shock wore off a little, and Charles saw that Cornelio Vigil had also been scalped.

Indians.

"Ignacia," he gasped, realizing how near he was to his home. Cornelio and Steve might have been trying to stop a crowd and been attacked and killed for their diligence.

Charles ran down the street, turned, and turned again, until he came to the lane leading directly to his house. He skidded to a halt and then stepped into the shadows. Only diamond-bright stars illuminated the street now, but a few in the mob worked to light torches. Charles couldn't tell if they intended to set fire to his house, or if they only wanted the light so they could see the men taking turns shouting curses and egging them on.

It didn't matter to Charles what they wanted to do with the torches. He had to find his family. The mob had already killed two good men, and maybe more lay dead in other parts of Taos. He backed off, found a narrow space between two adobe buildings, and eased his way to the next street. Here he went to the side door leading into his hacienda. It made him uneasy that the door had not been barred.

He slipped silently into the dark interior. A quirk of acoustics magnified the sounds of the crowd now. They might have been inside the hacienda shouting their curses.

Charles turned and hurried toward the back of the house, to the kitchen, where he thought Ignacia might go with the children.

"Alfredo!" he called, seeing a small dark shape. The ten-year-old boy turned and stared at him for a moment, then let out a squeal and rushed to him.

"Papa!" the youngster cried, clutching his father. "They killed Uncle Pablo. His servants betrayed him and they cut him up and then fed him to the hogs!"

"Quiet, there, there," Charles said. The sounds of the crowd grew louder, and some men began hammering on the gate. If they wanted to break in, nothing could stop them, but right now they only fired up their blood lust. If he could defuse it . . .

"Where's your mother?"

"With Rumalda and the other girls in the kitchen." Alfredo looked up at his father. "Are you going to fight them, Papa? I want to help!"

"To the kitchen," Charles urged. He followed his son through the maze to where two vigilant servants stood guard with wooden spoons and a fireplace poker. It would have been funny if the situation had not been so dire.

"Charles," cried Ignacia. She ran to him and hugged him. "The entire town is in revolt. I saw—"

She turned to be sure none of the children heard, Rumalda holding them close. "I saw what the Indians did to James Leal."

"The circuit attorney? Did they single him out for some reason?"

"They wanted him dead. Any American. All of them. They planned well. They divided into smaller groups and went after everyone they could find."

"Where's George?" he asked anxiously.

"He went north. He and Frank rode to Fort St. Vrain. And Tom Boggs is still with Kearny, scouting in the west."

"That's a relief," Charles said, seeing that much of his family was safe. "But what about Leal?" Charles had never liked the man much, but he had been a good attorney.

"They filled him with arrows, blinded him, and let him suffer. They poked and prodded him through the streets. They scalped him and then killed him. I saw this, Charles. I saw it." Ignacia's voice turned shrill, drawing the attention of their children. Rumalda moved to shield them, but Alfredo thought he was too adult and refused to be cut off like this. He adroitly sidestepped his half sister to watch his parents.

"We're trapped here," Charles said, his mind racing. "Can you dig through the back of the fireplace and reach the neighbors' house? There might be a way out some unwatched door once we get there since the crowd is intent on our gate."

"What are you going to do?" She looked at the six-gun at his hip.

"Take this. Hide it and use it only if you have to." Charles swallowed hard. Guns wouldn't stop the crowd. There were too many of them and Padre Antonio—or someone—had primed them for bloodshed. He had to find a way to derail that runaway train, and the six bullets he had in the cylinder wouldn't go very far.

"Don't, Charles. Stay and help us. We can get through to—" A loud crash told of the gate splintering and then falling inward.

"Dig," he said urgently.

Charles pushed his wife gently toward the kitchen fireplace and took a deep breath.

He stepped out of the kitchen and walked quickly to the *placita*, where dozens of Indians—all Taos from the look of their clothing—milled around, shouting and buoying up one another's courage with cries of how they would kill any American they found.

"What's the meaning of this?" Charles called to get their attention.

"Kill him!"

Charles ducked as an arrow sang past his face. He stepped back when he saw they were not going to listen to reason. Putting his back into it, he slammed the kitchen door and braced it.

"Leave now and I won't call the authorities," he said. He fumbled and reached for a chair to help him barricade the door. Hearing the wild roars, he changed tactics. "I'll see that you all get money. Lots of money."

The tumult died down for a moment. Then the door exploded into splinters as a half-dozen muskets fired. The lead fragments from the slugs tore huge holes in the door, sending Charles staggering back. He bled from a half-dozen scratches.

"Charles, are you all right?" Ignacia knelt beside him.

"The other room," he said, wiping away the blood. "Get everyone into the next room and try to dig through the back wall there. Hurry!" She hesitated, then rushed the others ahead of her like a sheep dog herding a flock. Charles forced himself back to push hard on the door as the Pueblos tried to break it down.

He looked up in time to see a section of the roof pulled back and two angry faces staring down at him. Charles grunted as one Indian fired an arrow through his upper arm. A heavy door panel fell inward and staggered him. A half-dozen more arrows came through the breach, four of them entering his body.

In pain, Charles doubled over, then stood.

"Money," he gasped out. "I'll pay you money. Take me and let the others go free. I know where you can get much money."

Two more arrows and a rifle bullet smashed into him, knocking him to the floor. He yanked out two of the arrows, but the others were in awkward positions for him to grab with his blood-slicked fingers. And for the rifle wound he could do nothing.

"Charles!" he heard Ignacia cry, as if from a great distance. "We broke through. Hurry, come with us!"

He stood, only to be spun about when another bullet struck his jaw. Charles let the force of the shot propel him toward the back room. He left a trail of blood as he made his way to the small hole they had clawed through the wall into the neighboring house. He dropped to hands and knees, but could not go anywhere.

Then he realized why. Strong hands held him. Indian hands.

"No, get away. Don't do this," he heard. Through blurred eyes he saw Rumalda scamper back through the hole to cradle his head.

He tried to speak, but the words jumbled strangely in his throat. The wound to his jaw must have affected the way he spoke. He made motions for Rumalda to get a pen and paper so he could write what he wanted. She didn't understand. He searched his own pockets and found a scrap of paper, but an inarticulate cry froze him.

An Indian towered above him, reached down, and picked him up as if he were a piece of kindling. The Indian spun him about and smashed him into the far wall. He hit hard and slid down, stunned. Then Rumalda screamed. Charles felt a strong hand grab his hair and pull his head back. A bowstring twanged and began sawing through his scalp.

Charles flopped onto the floor, his vision crystal-clear again. He felt the blood pouring from his body, turning him cold all over. A Taos Indian held his dripping scalp high and let everyone in the room see.

From the other house reached hands that dragged Rumalda through the hole, but Ignacia had come to him.

Charles heard her pleading for his life, for her children's lives. He was past feeling when cold steel began driving deep into his belly and ripping out his insides. He saw it but felt nothing, a curious calm settled on him. From a great distance he heard a voice telling the Indians they were fools to kill the governor, that he could have been useful as a hostage.

Charles smiled just a little. He would cheat them of that. He wiped away a new river of blood that threatened his vision. He wanted to see Ignacia once more.

"My darling," he said, trying to reach to her. It was as if she had stepped onto a fast-moving train that raced for some distant horizon. Her cries faded as creeping shadows devoured her.

Charles Bent, governor of New Mexico, slumped over, dead.

Sad News

Charlie Autobees wobbled in the saddle and almost fell off the horse. He caught himself, pushed back a scarf protecting his face to let the cold winter wind slap him awake. He had to get through. The ride from Taos through Raton Pass had been done in record time, but his horse had flagged and he considered tying himself into the saddle, lest he fall asleep and take a tumble otherwise.

The wind gave him a new vitality, and thinking about what had happened to Charles Bent and the other Americans in Taos lent fury that burned through his veins. He had seen Bent's body dragged through the streets—at least Ignacia and Rumalda had said it was Charles's corpse. It had been so terribly mutilated that he would never have recognized his friend. Getting the women and children to safety had taken some daring, but Autobees had been up to it after seeing how the other Americans were being treated.

He thought Ignacia and her family were hidden away where the raging mob wouldn't find them. He and his wife had gotten them out of town and into the mountains, where it would take diligent trackers to locate them. No one in the crowd Autobees had seen looked to have the patience needed to add a few more victims to their list of atrocities if it required any effort.

A thick column of smoke rising in the late afternoon caught on the breeze and turned and twisted like a vaporous gray snake striking at the heavens. Bent's Fort. He was close. This part of the mission to let everyone know of the Pueblos and Mexicans rising up against the American occupation in New Mexico chilled him more than the wind and winter ever could.

He had to tell William he had lost another brother. Autobees fought with himself on how to do it. Should he tell the details and horrify and infuriate William, or should the tale be more general, as if he had not seen with his own eyes the brutality of the mob?

Autobees still wrestled with this when he reached the closed gate to the fort. It looked solid and safe. Ignacia and her children had to get here eventually to be completely safe. Bent's Fort, with its cannon and limitless weaponry and ammunition inside the walls, could hold off a major attack for months. Water came from a well within the walls, and at any given time there was trade merchandise enough to live off until Captain Cooke or Colonel Doniphan could arrive, even if that took a month.

A safe place. A comforting fortress in the middle of a dangerous land.

Autobees swallowed hard, then licked his lips. His mouth felt as if someone had stuffed it with cotton and the words jumbled in his throat. But he called out his greeting to the sentries pacing along the walls.

"News for William," he called. "It's about his brother."

"George or Charles?" answered the sentry.

"Charles. It's real important and can't wait."

"It's gonna have to," the guard shouted back, not inclined to open the heavy gate leading to the courtyard. "William's out with the Cheyenne camped near Big Timbers. He's lookin' to build another trading post there."

Autobees wheeled his horse around and headed for the Arkansas River. He could follow it to Big Timbers. He knew William would have his scalp if he waited for him to return. William had to be told straightaway about what had happened in Taos.

He slowed the pace as his horse tired even more. Autobees knew he should have argued with the guard, maybe asking whoever was in charge of the fort to lend him a fresh horse. He began cursing himself when he realized Ceran St. Vrain might be running the fort. From the question posed by the guard, George was still up north at Fort St. Vrain. But Ceran had to learn of his partner's death, too.

Autobees put it off as fatigue—and he did not turn around and retrace his path to Bent's Fort. He kept riding. William had to know as soon as possible.

Sometime close to midnight, if his time-telling ability let him read the stars rightly, Charlie Autobees rode into the Cheyenne camp. A few horses whinnied at the intrusion, but no sentries challenged him as he rode to the big medicine lodge in the center of the camp. If William was anywhere, he would be here.

The tepee rose half again the height of the others, and smoke puffed tiredly from the air hole at the top. He dismounted, and his horse almost collapsed in response to having the weight that it had carried so long removed. Autobees dropped the reins, knowing the horse wouldn't go too far.

"William?" he called, not sure if he ought to barge on in. His dealings had been less with the Cheyenne and more with the Navajo. Their hogans were more solid and allowed a visitor to knock on the door frame to attract attention. "William, it's me, Charlie Autobees."

"Charlie?" The tepee flap opened and a sleepy-looking William Bent motioned him inside. After the frigid night, the heat inside the tepee felt oppressive.

"William, I don't know how to say this." He looked around and saw a dozen Cheyenne, including three or four medicine men and one he identified as a minor chief from the north.

"Spit it out, Charlie. You already woke me up. I'm not getting back to sleep soon, I'd wager." William saw the shock and revulsion on Autobees's face. William sank down cross-legged by the fire, and silently indicated a spot beside him. Autobees flopped down uncomfortably, his legs refusing to bend right after so long in the saddle.

"It's about Charles," Autobees said, tears coming to his eyes. Somehow, the man's name primed the pump and he spewed forth a detailed, bloody description of Charles's scalping and subsequent mutilation.

"What of Ignacia and the children?"

"I got them out of town." Autobees swallowed hard. "And I took Charles's body. The mob went off to kill somebody else—I don't know who—and I took the body. I carried it out of town in a cart and buried it in an unmarked grave. I didn't want those savages defiling him any more. I . . . I can show you where it is so you can give him a proper burial later." Autobees broke down and cried, from rage and loss, from pain, from exhaustion. "He was a good man, William. Such a good man! He didn't deserve this."

William sat, stunned at the news.

Then he said in a low, emotional voice, "No, he didn't deserve it." He looked up and saw a medicine man beginning a ritual of war. Beside him the chief stood and looked ugly.

"They kill our friend Charles. We declare war on them! War on the Mexicans! War on the Pueblos!"

With a loud whoop, the chief left the tepee and ran through the camp shouting that the Cheyenne were declaring war to avenge their lost friend.

Autobees still sobbed, and William wasn't inclined to dispute his Cheyenne friends' reaction. He wanted to kill, too.

Counterattack

Santa Fe
January 23, 1847

"Colonel Price," Ceran St. Vrain said in greeting. The military commander of Santa Fe looked as if he had bitten into something sour, then recognized Ceran and brightened.

"You are the very man I want to see." Price slapped Ceran on the shoulder in what was supposed to be a comradely fashion, but Ceran took it as a feeble attempt to win him over. From all that Charles had told him about Price, the officer was as responsible for the deaths in Taos as any of the mob. He had ignored Charles's pleas for protection, and had even diverted supplies and reinforcements intended to bolster Charles's position in Santa Fe.

But that was all water down the creek. Ceran had ridden like the wind from the fort, and had brought with him sixty-five mountain men who were as outraged about Charles's death as he was.

"I brought a few men with me," Ceran said, understating the effect of the rough-hewn men in the plaza. Price's green soldiers eyed the men with some trepidation, as if they might bare their teeth and take a bite out of a blue-coated arm at any instant. Ceran knew many of the mountain men cultivated this ferocity as a way of bragging about their own toughness without having to say a lot of words. But at heart, Ceran would not have traded any of the men for those in uniform.

He could take on every last rebel in Taos with only a handful of the mountain men. And would, if Price didn't give him satisfaction.

"So I see. I had no way of contacting you or I would have suggested some recruiting on your part. It's good that you took the initiative on your own."

"We'll root them out and make them pay for what they did to Charles. Steve Lee and Vigil and the others were friends."

"You'll not take the matter into your own hands," Price said sharply. "I have declared martial law, pending General Kearny's approval, of course."

"Of course," Ceran said dryly.

Price never noticed the implied contempt for his position, and rattled on. "I am taking a column directly to Taos. In a few minutes, actually. Would you and your irregulars care to come along?"

"In what capacity?" Ceran had a fleeting vision of Colonel Price ordering the buckskin-clad men to be nothing more than pack animals. There wasn't a man among Ceran's small army that wouldn't rip off Price's head and piss down his neck if he tried to demean their abilities that way.

"Well," Price said, thinking hard, "since you are a prominent man, I'll give you the rank of captain. Brevet captain, actually. I have already formed my column, so there's no place among my soldiers. We must quash this rebellion quickly and without missteps." Price swallowed hard. "I, uh, I've heard rumors General Tafoya has fifteen hundred men in the field between here and Taos. With only three hundred in my own command, such a fight would be . . . difficult."

"You've heard about the attacks at Mora. I'm afraid the rebels probably attacked my company's ranches, since they would be the best places to get fresh beef and other supplies."

"Supplies, always supplies," muttered Price. "You know about these things. You will be the perfect one to guard my supply wagons while I lead my men directly into Taos."

This was almost what Ceran had envisioned. Then he realized Price knew nothing about the way of the world—at least, not about the ways of fighting in New Mexico. His entry into Santa Fe had been accomplished without firing a single shot in anger. Whatever ammunition his men had expended had been either accidental or in celebration.

"You're marching right away to Taos? Cavalry or infantry?" Ceran asked.

"Both. The infantry departed an hour ago, with three howitzers as support. The cavalry is following within a few minutes. If you can keep the supply wagons rolling—something you are adroit at, I hear—you will provide us with much-needed stores after we have cleaned out the nest of vipers in Taos."

"You don't think it'll take your men more than a few hours?" asked Ceran, not sure if he was more amazed at the conceit or astounded at Price's stupidity. This wasn't Price's first command in battle, but he underestimated both Padre Antonio's shrewdness and the fierceness of the Taos Pueblo Indians. If General Tafoya reached Taos and joined forces with the Pueblos, the fight might be long and bloody.

"Hardly that. The mere sight of a company of soldiers marching smartly into town will disperse them.

Then it will be up to my men to find the perpetrators of these atrocities so I may summarily deal with them."

"How?" asked Ceran, fascinated at Price's stupidity.

"Possibly the firing squad, though I prefer hanging. That sends a message to other potential rebels what their fate will be if they don't go back home peaceably."

"I'll get my men onto guarding those wagons," Ceran said.

"Well done, Captain St. Vrain!" Price saluted. Ceran hesitated a second, then returned it. This pleased Price, who went off bellowing orders to his subordinates to mount and get on the road to Santa Fe.

"What's happenin'?" asked a scrawny, whipsaw-muscled trapper named Metcalf who had accompanied Ceran from Bent's Fort. He scratched himself and stared at Price as the officer bustled about at the head of the cavalry column. "He's a real pistol, ain't he?"

"More of a popinjay," Ceran said caustically. "He thinks the Indians will let him waltz into Taos so he can hang them all. The ones he doesn't stand in front of a firing squad, that is."

"Imagine that," Metcalf said. "You find out where he wants to be buried? There's a nice plot south of town where he can spend eternity."

"Get everyone together. We've got a real job to do, and I want you to be my lieutenant. Beckwourth might be a good choice, too, if you don't want it."

"Play loo-tenant to yer captain? Be my pleasure, Ceran. Ole Jim might be a good tracker, but he don't know squat about bein' an officer. Not like us!" Metcalf chuckled since neither of them was cut from military cloth. "I gotta get these miserable, smelly bears herded to the supply depot." With a shout, the man ambled off, bringing together the company Ceran had recruited.

Captain St. Vrain. He shook his head and laughed at the pomposity of it. His relatives had been French nobility. A mere captaincy hardly impressed Ceran. If he gave orders and didn't have the respect of these men, they would ignore him, no matter what rank Sterling Price bestowed. Ceran wasn't going to betray the confidence of Metcalf or Beckwourth or any of the others. Quite the contrary. He was going to show them—and Colonel Price—how to fight a real war.

"Look sharp," Ceran called to Metcalf, feeling edgy at the way the road curved before going through the rocky canyon. If General Tafoya or any of the other Mexicans supposed to be in revolt planned an ambush, this was the best spot along the trail from Santa Fe to launch it. Ceran had traveled this way more times than he could remember, and knew every rock and pothole in the road. This was the place.

Sterling Price had rushed ahead with his cavalry, riding hard to catch up with the infantry soldiers he had dispatched earlier. By now they were miles on the other side of the canyon, out of position for any action against *bandidos* intending to cut off the colonel's supply train.

"Stay down, don't let them see you," Ceran said. A dozen of the mountain men settled down amid the food and other supplies carried in the wagons. They might be spotted from the canyon rim, but not from anywhere lower. That was the best Ceran could do right now to lure the marauders in where he could shoot them.

If they even ventured outside Taos. The rioting and

mob law that prevailed might have burned itself out by now, but Ceran doubted it. He knew how long Padre Antonio had stoked the flames of hatred. Such loathing of any American wouldn't be sated by the deaths of a few men and women, even if the governor of New Mexico was counted among the mutilated, scalped dead.

If the mob still raged in Taos, some of the Taos Indians would have the sense to realize such brutality would not go unanswered. That meant army dragoons. And following such a force would be supply wagons. Ceran hadn't batted an eye when Price had assigned him to what must have seemed a tedious and demeaning job.

"Hey, Cap'n," called a man sitting in the rear of a wagon, his long musket across his legs. "You feel it?"

"What?" Ceran asked, dropping back so he could talk without shouting.

"There's a frizzy feel to the air, like 'fore a thunderstorm. Only this smells more like Injuns." Even as the man spoke, he pulled his heavy rifle to his shoulder, aimed, and fired.

Ceran's horse reared and pawed at the air before he brought it under control. He took a quick look over his shoulder, but knew what he'd see before he found it.

On the rocky ground beside the road lay a Pueblo Indian. The mountain man's shot had been quick and deadly. The man might have been spooked by a shadow or a deer poking about as it hunted for forage, but Ceran knew better. These men had nerves of steel and eyes keener than the average.

"To the sides!" Ceran shouted. "Both left and right, fire! Metcalf, stop the wagons and get the drivers shooting!"

The shouts and war whoops of the attacking Indians were drowned out by the fusillade Ceran had ordered. From the quickness of the fire, Ceran knew the men were already drawing beads and would have shot without his order. It still felt as if he had ordered their action, and they had obeyed without question.

Ceran drew his six-gun and guided his horse around in a full circle to take in the battlefield. The attackers might have read his mind about what to do. They came at the supply train from both sides, with a few Indians sneaking in behind to cut off retreat.

Seeing a Mexican poke his head out from behind a rock afforded Ceran his first good target. Three shots rang out. One sped past Ceran's head. Two from his pistol dispatched the attacker. He trotted back and forth along the line of wagons, seeing that the mountain men were doing him proud.

"We got 'em on the run, Cap'n," Metcalf declared. He reloaded his musket, leaned the cleaning rod against a wagon, then hefted his rifle, sighted, and fired in a smooth motion. Ceran saw Metcalf's shot bring down a Taos Indian intent on hightailing it.

As the echo of Metcalf's last shot died out, a curious silence fell. Ceran looked around, wondering if he had been struck deaf. Then he realized this was natural. The men had not yet realized they had driven off a spirited attack on the supply wagons. When they did, their shouts of triumph and glee were louder than any rifle shot.

Ceran let them celebrate a moment, then held up his hand for silence.

"Men, you've won a great victory! We drove 'em off." But Ceran stopped his congratulations when he heard distant shots quickly followed by the throaty roar of a cannon discharging. He cleared his throat and continued. "We've won here. Now we've got to go pull Price's fat from the fire."

The thunderous gunfire came from the far end of the canyon. It could only mean that Price had encountered the enemy and wasn't having as easy a time of it as Ceran's men. Ceran St. Vrain signaled for the drivers to get their wagons rolling again, then ordered his men to get ready for another fight.

This one might be a lot bloodier, especially if they had to save Price and his greenhorn soldiers.

Engagement of War

Outside Taos
January 23, 1847

"Metcalf, leave the wagons and be sure all the men are mounted," Ceran St. Vrain shouted, taking in the situation quickly.

"You sure you wanna do that, Ceran? We run them other devils off back there in the canyon, but they might take it into their heads to come back. They might hit us from the rear."

"We didn't leave enough of them in one piece to give us that much trouble," Ceran said, distracted. "Price needs us more than the supply train."

"He needs more 'n the likes of us," Metcalf said, scratching a nit. "He needs some common sense. Them big guns of his ain't gonna do squat unless the Indians attack straight up the middle. From the way it looks, both of his flanks are gonna get attacked first, squeezin' him out like a pustule." The trapper glared at the battle array and then spat, accurately hitting the center of a snowbank. The gob hissed and sizzled as it vanished into the white snow.

The gunfire from the battle rolled up the slope to where they had emerged from the canyon. Spread before them were blue-coated soldiers dug into positions, fighting what appeared to be a huge army. Price had positioned howitzers on either of his flanks. Without the deadly artillery fire laying down grapeshot every time the rebels tried to attack, he would have been overrun and killed quickly. Ceran realized Metcalf had sized up the situation perfectly. It wouldn't be long before the Indians and their Mexican allies figured out their best plan was to sneak up on Price's position, infiltrating rather than launching a frontal attack.

"He's doing the best he can with soldiers who've probably never even fired a musket," Ceran said. "Look. I make out several hundred Indians on Price's left. You see how they're coming together, like they're going to rush the cannon emplacement?"

"You figurin' to mess 'em up 'fore they can? There's damn near three hundred of them Injuns," Metcalf said, squinting critically as he evaluated the enemy, "and there's only sixty-five of us. That ain't fair."

"I know, but we don't dare take the time to let them bring up another couple hundred Mexicans to make a fair fight," Ceran said. This forced a laugh from Metcalf.

"You surely are a caution, Ceran." Without another word, Metcalf went to rally the mountain men. Ceran checked his pistol and made certain he had full chambers. Then he pulled out a short-barreled shotgun and broke it open to check that two fresh shells rested in the chambers, ready to take life.

Ceran thought of Charles, and felt all thoughts of mercy drain away like spring rain running down a sunbaked arroyo: A single rush and it was gone. He heard Metcalf, Beckwourth, and the others coming up behind him, and knew they would follow him into hell. He raised his shotgun high, then dramatically pointed in the direction of the Indians trying to mass for the attack that would destroy Price's left flank.

He held back a battle cry as he rushed forward into the fight, but Ceran heard the others with him giving voice to their frustration and need for revenge. Not a man here didn't think the world of Charles Bent, and not a man would leave the field until his memory was avenged.

Ceran knew his weapon was short-range, and held fire until he was close enough to see the Indian's lips drawn back in a fierce grimace, the bloodshot eyes narrow, and the quivering hand draw back before loosing an arrow. Ceran squeezed the shotgun trigger and was almost knocked out of the saddle by the powerful recoil. He had never fired the shotgun one-handed before. But the buckshot flew straight and true. He saw splinters from the Indian's bow arching into the air, along with a bloody mist—all that remained of the rebel's head.

Ceran galloped on and fired the second barrel, with less satisfying effect. He saw an Indian wince, but other than this, show nothing resembling a serious wound. Then Ceran was past. He shoved his shotgun back into a saddle sheath and drew his pistol, firing as he rode. He wounded another Taos Indian, and then passed completely through their formation. He wheeled about, swapped weapons again, reloaded the shotgun, and galloped back through the center of the rebel force.

This time he found less resistance. Ceran's men had scattered many of the Indians. Those who remained died as the mountain men's withering, accurate fire concentrated on them. By the time Ceran was ready for a third pass, the battlefield was empty of all but dead and wounded—and his men.

"Metcalf?" he shouted. "Where are you?"

"Right here, Ceran," came the weak reply. "One of

them red bastards got me with a hatchet." The trapper held his thigh, now bright red with blood. "But I got him good." Metcalf glanced in the direction of an Indian writhing on the ground, his throat slit.

Ceran didn't waste a shotgun shell on the dying Indian. It would have been too merciful.

"Get that leg patched up, or you'll die in the saddle."

"Can think of worse ways to go," Metcalf said.

"Die fighting them in Taos. Price will need every rifle he can muster. There had to be fifteen hundred against him, and I caught sight of a fair number of Mexican uniforms. I might even have spotted General Tafoya, though the distance was mighty big to be certain. This is a real uprising, not just a mob that's gone out of control."

"Reckon I got a few more left to kill then," Metcalf said. "You hold up ridin' on till I get myself a tourniquet."

Ceran saw that his small but deadly force had taken few casualties in their headlong attack. Those who had been cut down were put into a supply wagon emptied of powder and ammunition. When Ceran had finished with this grisly chore, he saw to Metcalf and made sure his lieutenant was properly sewn up and bandaged.

Then he went to pay his respects to Colonel Price. They had a powerful lot of fighting to do, and he wanted to make certain the officer was up for it.

Crushed

"What do you make of it, Colonel?" asked Ceran St. Vrain.

"I have my howitzers in place to make certain they cannot attack us head-on," Sterling Price said. He wore a bandage on his forehead and his left arm dangled limply, another wound sustained in the fight back on the trail. His soldiers had acquitted themselves well against five-to-one odds, even without Ceran's mountain men keeping a large group of the Taos Indians at bay. Ceran felt better about both Price and his men as a result of that fight, though other news had proven unsettling.

They had barely left Santa Fe when a rebel force had attacked in Las Vegas. The garrison commander was hard-pressed to maintain order, and held on by the skin of his teeth. Other reports of guerrilla attacks, mostly against outlying ranches, were about as Ceran had expected. The rebels sought to drive out the Americans and any Mexican sympathizers, but lacked a plan for doing so. Each group operated independently of the others, making them hard to find, but robbing them of the single powerful concerted attack that would have driven the American soldiers out of the territory.

By engaging General Tafoya when he had, Price had saved the territory. Now Tafoya had retreated to Taos, and had his back against the wall rather than sallying through the countryside, rallying the diverse elements to his banner.

"If I open fire, it will drive them deeper into Taos," Price said, sketching his battle plan in the snow with his saber. "My troops will advance on the double. Captain St. Vrain, I want you to take your mounted unit around to the north and cut off their escape. I don't want them returning to their Pueblo. It would be hell digging them out."

"Better to get them here," Ceran agreed. "Tafoya isn't likely to go with the Indians. He'll stand and fight since he has nowhere else to go. Do you have enough firepower to push them back as you plan?"

"Thanks to you protecting the supply wagons so well, I do," Price said. "Spare muskets and adequate ammunition, patches, and gunpowder are available to us."

Ceran saw the hardness in the man that had been lacking before. Garrison duty had softened Sterling Price, but now that he was in combat again, old— good—habits returned. He had become an officer capable of decisive action and bold attacks. Even better was the way Price's men followed him. Raw recruits had tasted the confusion of battle and come out experienced soldiers.

"When do you start the barrage?" asked Ceran.

"Thirty minutes. That doesn't give you much time, but I don't want Tafoya and the other rebels to figure out what your mission is. If they do, they might retreat immediately."

"This will break the revolt, Colonel," Ceran said.

"It'll go a long way toward that noble end, Captain," Price declared. "We'll still have to roam the countryside for a few weeks to clean out the pockets of resistance."

"Good luck." Ceran shook Price's hand, then fetched his horse to trot his men around Taos on their mission. As he waved to get Metcalf's attention, he saw Price pissing in the snow to wipe out the map. This act of defiance seemed to bolster Price's resolve. He began barking orders and getting his gunnery officers ready for the assault.

"Whatcha needin', Cap'n?" asked Metcalf. The trapper was a shade paler than usual under his grime from loss of blood, but hadn't slowed down because of his leg wound.

"We've got a fight to win," Ceran said. He explained quickly what they were to do.

"We might have our hands full, Ceran," Metcalf said. "We got maybe fifty men who can get around. The others are full of arrows or have had their horses shot out from under 'em."

"Price doesn't have any mounts to spare," Ceran said. The colonel's small cavalry unit had been wiped out, reducing his force to infantry only, with their mule-drawn caissons and howitzers. The colonel and a few of his officers still had horses, but there wouldn't be any extras to lend to the mountain men.

"We've had our hands full ever since we left Santa Fe," Ceran said. "This won't be any different. You and the boys have all the ammo and powder you can carry?"

"Wish we had a way to take along one of them mountain howitzers Price's so fond of. We could put it to right good use."

"Let's go fight," Ceran said.

* * *

The distant roar of Price's cannon firing methodically was drowned out by the screams of the men around Ceran St. Vrain. Price's plan to drive the rebels through Taos and into the mountain men's guns had worked beyond their wildest expectations. Ceran found himself facing hundreds of angry, armed Indians trying to fight their way back to their Pueblo.

The staccato snap of muskets slowed and the tide of rebels inched closer to where he had dug in with his men.

"We're runnin' outta gunpowder, Ceran. What do you want to do?" Metcalf's face was a bloody mask—not from his own blood but from that of two rebels who had penetrated their line. Metcalf was small and wiry, but a fierce fighter, and had dispatched both Indians using his knife.

"We can't run," Ceran said. "All our horses are dead or run off."

"We might try sneakin' away by slithering back east, outta their way. If they're intent on gettin' away from Price's guns, they might not notice."

"They'd see us and figure we were retreating for a reason. They'd be on us like ticks on a hound dog." Ceran didn't like the option: Stand and fight, probably dying. But it was better to hold their ground as long as they could and die doing it rather than getting an arrow in the back while running away.

"Some of the men's not so sure 'bout that."

"I'm not, either," Ceran said. "But if we're going to die, I want to face my enemy."

"Can't argue that. You got a knife for when you run out of powder?"

"Here," Ceran said, pulling back his coat to show a

sheathed hunting knife at his waist. It wasn't much against a brave armed with a bow and arrow, but he had a chance if the rebels he faced had exhausted their ammo and fought only with lances and knives.

"That's it," Metcalf said, firing four rounds at a Taos Indian who had almost reached the spot where they fought behind their fallen horses. "No more powder."

"And they sense it, like a buzzard smells a dying carcass," Ceran said in disgust. Two score rebels let out bloodcurdling cries and raced forward, waving their knives and hatchets in the air.

Ceran threw down his pistol and drew his knife. Let them come to him. They wouldn't be any more tired out from the run, but it gave him a few seconds to settle his mind for the fight—and eventual death—to follow.

"Who in the bloody hell's that?" asked Metcalf. "He sure looks familiar, and I surely do like the way he's fightin'."

"Dick Green," Ceran said, recognizing the black man wading into the right flank of the Indian mob. Charlotte's husband swung an iron rod with devastating effect. Every time that thin rod touched red flesh, a bone broke with a loud snap. It took only a few seconds for the Indians to realize they had a formidable foe coming after them and slowly turn from their attack of Ceran's position.

"Go!" cried Ceran. "Attack! Get 'em!" He swarmed up over the carcass of a dead horse, knife clenched in his hand. Ceran hadn't gone five paces when withering fire raked through the Indians' rank. Barely had the first bodies fallen when a second fusillade tore the life from a half-dozen more.

"Who's that?" Metcalf asked. "Whoever it is, we're gonna live to brag on this 'cuz of him."

"William!" Ceran staggered a little, then waved frantically when he saw William Bent and two dozen others from Bent's Fort and the company ranches. Lucien Maxwell fired with deadly accuracy, and Charlie Autobees had two six-guns, firing wildly at any Indian in front of him. As the rebels faded back into Taos to take refuge among the adobe buildings, Ceran reached William's side.

"You're a sight for sore eyes," Ceran said.

"You're a sight," William said, wrinkling his nose. "Not only do you need a bath, you need a doctor. Sorry, but I didn't bring along any of the Cheyenne medicine men, though they wanted to come."

"You told them this wasn't their fight?" guessed Ceran. It was the kind of thing William would do.

"No need to let another man do my dirty work," William said. The gunfire had died to intermittent sniping now, but the distant rumble of Price's howitzers remained to let them know the battle wasn't over. Yet.

"Did you come straight here? What took you so long?"

"I stopped by the Maxwell ranch and found they were under siege. I had a couple dozen men with me. We drove off the Mexicans trying to take Lucien's house, then checked several other ranches. The guerrillas had already burned a few, but we found the Mexicans and made certain they wouldn't do it again."

"You saved my hide today," Ceran said.

"Do you think Charles's murderers are still in Taos? I want them," William said. "I want to see them punished."

Ceran didn't respond right away. For a moment he wondered what was wrong. Then he realized the cannonade had stopped. That meant Sterling Price was sending his foot soldiers into Taos to clean up the pockets of resistance.

The fight was over. Now all that remained was getting justice. Ceran realized that might be the hardest battle of all.

Trial and Execution

Taos
March 10, 1847

"You've got to hand it to him," William Bent said, looking into the courtroom with some satisfaction. "Frank never hesitated when it came to doing his duty."

Frank Blair had begun prosecution of the Pueblo Indians and their Mexican cohorts before Colonel Price had ferreted out the last of the rebel resistance in Taos. The army had lost fifteen men, with forty more casualties, but the toll they had taken was far more extreme. Of the 150 Indians and Mexicans killed, Ceran St. Vrain and his mountain men had accounted for over fifty. But before the last scent of gunpowder had drifted away from town, before the echoes from Price's three-pound cannon had stopped ringing in everyone's ears, before the town realized what had happened, Francis Preston Blair, Jr., Esq., had begun to convene a court to try the rebel leaders.

"I'd protest if anyone else was on the bench or sat on the jury," Ceran said. "Padre Antonio's rigged too many trials for me to be much upset now."

William laughed without humor. A close friend of the family, Joab Houghton, presided as head judge. George Bent sat as foreman of the jury. Frank Blair acted as prosecutor and Ceran translated, when necessary. But the real power in the courtroom came from the rest of the jury. Charlie Autobees, Lucien Maxwell, Robert Fisher—who had worked for Bent, St. Vrain & Company as a trader for years, and the others who were still smarting from losses of friends and family, sat in grim judgment of the defendants.

That stacked the deck, but William knew it would hardly have mattered who sat on the jury as long as Ignacia Bent and Rumalda Boggs got the chance to testify fully. Their pathetic, moving story of the torture and death of Charles had left only the fifteen defendants unmoved. William had felt the tears welling his own eyes, and had felt guilty because of it until he saw so many others reacting similarly. Even Sterling Price, trying to maintain a stern military demeanor, had been visibly moved.

"The jury won't be long," Ceran said, pointing to the door where the men had repaired to reach their verdict.

"It's been fifteen days," William said. "I want this done." He heaved a deep sigh. Two brothers lost, both to violence. Robert had ranged into dangerous territory, no matter that Old Wolf had signed a peace treaty. The Comanche were treacherous and beholden to no single chief. But William had never thought Charles would die in such a gruesome, unseemly manner. Certainly not in front of his wife and children. That Charles was murdered in his own house made it worse, somehow.

"It will be finished soon enough," Ceran assured William. "Still, the people on the jury and bench bother me. They can't be impartial."

"If our friends—those who loved Charles—weren't judge and jury, our enemies would be sitting there in their stead. There's no such thing as impartiality in Taos. You know that."

"I know," Ceran said tiredly.

"Here they come," William said, sitting straighter.

"I suppose I ought to translate, but I think the defendants know the verdict."

William saw what his friend meant. All fifteen defendants whispered among themselves, then fell silent when Houghton banged the butt of a pistol on the desk for silence.

"Gentlemen of the jury, have you reached a verdict?"

George Bent stood and held up a scrap of paper. "We have, Your Honor."

"Read it to the court," Houghton said. He reversed the pistol so its butt would come easily to hand, should there be any disturbance among the defendants. The soldiers behind the fifteen men lowered their rifles to forestall any escape attempt. No one in the court doubted the verdict.

"Guilty," George Bent said.

"Muerto, muerto, muerto!" came the cry from those in the spectators' gallery.

"That'll be the end of it," William said more to himself than to either Charles's widow or his stepdaughter. He leaned back, feeling as if his entire body had gone boneless. One of the revolt leaders, Tomás Romero, had been shot down by an army recruit named Fitzgerald as soon as the infantry had marched into town. The young man had been avenging his brother, who had been killed earlier. But Fitzgerald had escaped from jail and no one, especially William and the men working for the company, had been too inclined to hunt for him. Even Colonel Price had not shown his usual predilection for following the letter of the law, and never sent a patrol after the escaped killer.

The other leader, Pablo Montoya, had been placed in front of a firing squad immediately after a hasty court-martial. William was hazy on the reason Montoya was executed by a military firing squad when the rest of his lieutenants were tried in a civil court, but the result was the same. Today's verdict guaranteed that.

General Tafoya had escaped, but Price was sure he would find the Mexican general before he escaped south and found sanctuary in his home country.

"I hereby sentence you all to death by hanging," the judge said. "And I hope God passes further much-needed judgment on you, because hanging is all I can do under the law of this American territory. Get them out of here," Houghton said, looking to Colonel Price for the guards to herd the convicted prisoners to the plaza.

"Are you going to the hanging?" asked Ceran.

William nodded tiredly. He had to see this through. Two brothers dead. There was no way to exact vengeance for Robert's death, but he owed it to Charles to see that his killers were brought to justice.

"Lucien Maxwell's headed back to the ranch to round up the cattle," Ceran said. "You might want to go with him to look over the herd."

"I'll witness the executions," William said doggedly. And he did. Every one of them.

Never-Ending Attacks

On the Santa Fe Trail
May 4, 1847

"Bill Tharp can't be more 'n a day or two ahead of us," said McGuire, scouting for the wagon train led by Ceran St. Vrain. "He got to Big Timbers 'fore us and then kept on goin'."

"We'll overtake him at Walnut Creek," Ceran said, every stone and dip in the trail perfectly etched in his mind. He tried to remember how many times over the years he had made this trip, and gave up trying to recollect. Too many.

"I'll ride on ahead and be sure he ain't broke down," McGuire said, putting his heels to his horse's flanks and getting the powerful stallion to a trot quickly.

"Tharp should have waited for us," Frank Blair said, looking apprehensive as their scout vanished over a low hill ahead in the road. "The Indians know we're fighting the Mexicans, and have taken it into their heads how this is a good time to attack any wagons out on the prairie. There's no cavalry to be had within a hundred miles. More. They're all with Winnie Scott at Veracruz by now."

"You've been talking to William too much," Ceran

said accusingly, half joking. Blair had decided after the trial in Taos that he wanted nothing more to do with the frontier. In a way, Ceran couldn't blame him. Frank was an Easterner by birth and education, and had come West solely for his health. Along with regaining his strength, Frank had found friendships stronger than any blood bond, but he had also found incredible savagery and death. Frank had been greatly upset at Charles's scalping. Almost as much as William had. Of the Bent brothers, George had taken his eldest brother's death the best, but this was only in comparison to William and Frank. When Frank had announced he was returning to his family home in St. Louis, George had curtly said good-bye, further opening wounds in all of them that needed healing.

Ceran felt a great void over Charles's loss, but oddly also, a paralysis that refused to fade. He ought to have felt more. He ought to have railed and ranted and moped the way William did. He should have looked upon Charles's death as proof that there would never be civilization in Taos, no matter how many company wagons rolled in laden with the accoutrements of polite society. All this and more should have boiled and burned in him, but instead he experienced a tiredness brought on by too many deaths and too much suffering.

He was emotionally exhausted and could do nothing about it.

Bent, St. Vrain & Company was the most successful business west of the Mississippi, and continued to grow and prosper with every wagon train out of Westport. It had made them all very, very rich. The Mexican War wouldn't last forever, and when it was over, Americans would flock to New Mexico Territory.

That meant even greater business for the company since there would never again be competition from Mexican shipments.

Somehow, Ceran couldn't care. Where William was morose and angry by turns, Ceran felt . . . weary.

"Are you going to look after Dick and Charlotte?" Ceran asked Frank suddenly.

"What's that? Oh, yes, of course. Dick's a brave man. I'm glad that William and George manumitted him and Charlotte. I wish I could convince them to come work for me."

"Charlotte's cooking would have you a hundred pounds heavier by Christmas," joshed Ceran.

"At least I would dine in peace, not waiting for some savage to shoot an arrow into my back or use a knife to scalp me."

"I'm glad they were given their freedom," Ceran said. "Dick fought well and deserves it."

"No one should ever be held in slavery," Frank said.

Ceran nodded quietly. Again he felt the dark emptiness engulf him. He remembered the arguments with Charles over slavery. The Bents were dedicated slaveholders, even if they treated the slaves decently. Ceran had grown up in Missouri, and had never gotten a taste of having slaves do his work for him. If anything, the freedom granted him by roaming the mountains, trapping and hunting, meant that he did everything himself. As a result, he knew his own skills and limits. Slaves had never been a part of doing for him.

"They're having a time getting used to the idea that they are free," Frank said. As if coming to a conclusion, he stated flatly, "I will do whatever is in my power to help them."

"You thinking on working for the company after

you return to St. Louis?" asked Ceran. "We need good agents."

"I don't know what I'll do. Get married and settle down, perhaps," Frank said. "Prosecuting Charles's murderers felt right. I might go back into the law."

"We'll miss you, especially George. I wish you two had parted on better terms."

"I understand his loss," Frank said. "He'll come around. Just don't keep him at the fort or up at Fort St. Vrain. Let him travel back to St. Louis once in a while. You can't monopolize all the rooms at the Planters House, Ceran."

Before Ceran could make light of his attachment to the fine suites of rooms at the fashionable hotel, he saw McGuire galloping back toward them, waving his broad-brimmed hat and yelling. His words were drowned out by the thunder of his horse's hooves

"We've got trouble," Ceran said, recognizing the signs. McGuire wasn't the sort to ride his horse into the ground unless there was a powerful good reason. "Get your rifles ready for a fight. Pistols, too."

He checked his own weapons. By the time McGuire reined in hard and kicked up a cloud of dust, Ceran was ready for anything.

"Tharp," gasped out the scout. "Not two miles over the hill. Comanche. They got him pinned down. Looks like they already run off most of his livestock. Horses, mules, oxen. They got him where he can't get away."

Ceran considered what to do. A few of his men rode horses, and could reach Tharp's embattled party quickly, but could they muster enough firepower to turn the tide against the Comanche? If they rolled on as a wagon train, he had no doubt they mounted more than enough firepower to drive off the Comanche. But if they took that long, Tharp and the others might be dead and scalped.

Or scalped and then killed, as Charles Bent had been.

"Time," he muttered. "Tharp doesn't have much, and we can't buy it." He came to a quick decision. "Whoever's mounted, get all your pistols ready. We'll go through those Comanche like a dose of salts."

"Ceran, are you sure?" asked Frank. Ceran had not seen the man so pale since he had come to Bent's Fort for his health.

"You don't have to come with us, Frank. You can lead the rest of the wagons to the fray."

"I . . . I'll come. I owe it to you."

Ceran hesitated, then said, "Frank, you don't owe me anything. We're friends. You and George are closer than blood brothers. But you're a passenger on this train going back to St. Louis."

"I'm ready, Ceran. Let's run those redskins off!" Frank Blair held up his rifle and waved it about, but Ceran saw the fear in the man's face. To order Frank to stay would be worse than letting him come along.

"Shoot straight and don't chase after the Comanche, if they hightail it. Stay with Tharp and his boys." Ceran knew the Comanche would try to divide the rescuers, then ambush them if they could. This was about the only command Ceran could give that would be understood—or obeyed.

With a loud yell, a dozen men brandishing their pistols and rifles galloped off in the direction McGuire had come from. Ceran found his horse flagging quickly, but gamely tried to keep pace. By the time he reached the rise looking down into the prairie where Bill Tharp had stopped to water his teams at Walnut Creek, a full-fledged battle was in progress.

Inwardly groaning at such odds against them, Ceran kept his horse headed downhill and into battle. He couldn't count the Indians, but they outnumbered Tharp—even with Ceran's rescuers—two to one. From the war cries on the lips of every Comanche, they meant business. Worse, McGuire had been right. All of Tharp's livestock was either dead or stolen, forcing him to stand and fight. Retreat was no longer a possibility.

An arrow sang past Ceran's head. He flinched, fired his pistol a couple of times, and then found himself in the middle of a melee that swelled all around him and threatened to swallow him whole. Ceran smelled rather than saw a Comanche brave behind him. He bent low, twisted hard, and fired three times into the man's chest. The Comanche tumbled from his horse and lay still. But as Ceran straightened, a war club crashed into the side of his head. He tumbled to the ground.

He lay stunned for a moment, then saw moccasins coming toward him at a dead run. He felt a powerful hand grip his graying hair and yank it back. Ceran waited for the knife slash that would separate him from his hair, but it never came. The grip weakened and Ceran rolled away, coming to his hands and knees.

Frank Blair stood over the fallen Indian, panting harshly. He had used his rifle as a club to knock the Comanche to the ground. From the way the rifle barrel was askew, he had smashed it with all his might into the brave's head.

"Thanks," Ceran gasped out. "I owe you."

Ceran lifted his pistol and fired as fast as he could. One bullet spat forth, missing Frank by inches, but finding a target in an approaching Comanche warrior's eye.

"We're even, Ceran," Frank said in a shaky voice.

Holding on to each other for support, Ceran hardly able to stand and Frank wobbly from a wound to his calf, they got to one of Tharp's wagons and rolled under it for protection. For a few minutes more the battle raged and then slowly died, the Comanche in the distance taunting and yelling at the Americans to come after them.

The men remembered Ceran's admonition before the fight, and returned the Indians' taunts with those of their own.

Ceran and Frank crawled from under the wagon. Ceran felt as if he had missed the fight by hiding, but knew that wasn't so. He had accounted for two of the fifteen Comanche killed.

"Jehoshaphat, Ceran, you took your sweet time comin'," a bloodied and battered Bill Tharp said, limping over. "And that ugly face of yours is 'bout the purtiest thang I ever did see." He thrust out his hand and shook Ceran's hard.

"They won't be back," Ceran said, eyeing the slowly disappearing Comanche, who still made obscene gestures in his direction. "They have their horses and what supplies from your wagons they could steal. When my train gets here, we'll be too big for them."

"Then git your asses movin'. I'm about fed up with bein' a target," Tharp said. Tharp hobbled off to see how his men had fared.

Ceran looked at Frank. Such a fight could change a man's mind mighty quick. Frank Blair was a hero, a fighter, someone who had saved a friend's life at the risk of his own. But all Ceran saw in the young man's face now was resolve never to be in such a position again.

Ceran St. Vrain didn't blame him.

Offer and Counteroffer

Ceran St. Vrain stood in front of the full-length mirror, turning from side to side to study his new jacket. The tailor had done a fine job shaping it to Ceran's increasingly portly frame. Ceran ran his hands across the fine material, letting it slip sleekly away without leaving behind any wrinkles. The coat alone had cost almost two hundred dollars, but he felt good in it.

He heaved a deep sigh as he remembered his childhood and the constant mention of nobility in his family. When Jefferson bought the Louisiana Purchase from France, all noble titles were erased, the St. Vrain family's included. Still, life in Missouri after they had moved from Louisiana had been good, and he always enjoyed returning here. It was as much of a home as anywhere for him.

Especially Planters House. In Ceran's mind this was the finest hotel in the world, although he had not seen any overseas. His uncle had boasted of the fine hotels in Paris, and his aunt had longingly spoken of those in London, especially Mivart's. She had a yellowed clipping from the *Times* of London plainly stating there were only three quality hotels in all of England. Thomas's at Berkeley Square, the Clarendon in Bond Street, and Mivart's. Ceran never knew if she and his uncle had stayed at all of them or only the Mivart.

He would probably never see London, but Ceran hardly cared. Planters House knew how to cater to his needs better than any foreign hotel ever could.

He made one last turn in front of the mirror and liked what he saw. When he met with military men, he preferred to be well dressed, especially if they were in uniform. Ceran laughed. In a way, this was a successful trader's uniform. He might not have brass buttons, but the silver ones were more expensive and more to his liking. And the silk jacket far outstripped the utilitarian blue wool jacket officers were forced to wear.

In such hot, humid weather, that gave him yet another advantage. He could remain cooler in his fine attire. Ceran picked up a portfolio and riffled through the contents before closing it. He hesitated now because he had not spoken to William about what he intended. Somehow, fighting off the Comanche along the way and hearing how Thomas Fitzpatrick, the new Indian agent bound for Bent's Fort with a wagon loaded with $350,000 in scrip, had been attacked by Pawnee had given birth to his notion. Fitzpatrick and his men had successfully fought off Pawnee attackers because the Indians had not thought the paper money was worth their effort. Ceran knew that opinion wouldn't be shared by the thousands of soldiers in New Mexico Territory fighting in the Mexican War. But Fitzpatrick had left Fort Leavenworth without any hint that he would be attacked.

After all the years, after all the treaties, the Indians

still preyed on wagon trains they thought too weak to fight back. Bill Tharp had been lucky, and Ceran realized he had been, too. The Comanche had stolen a few head of livestock, but had not burned Tharp's wagons.

But the attacks never stopped. Ceran grew tired of the fight.

Scooping up the portfolio stuffed with papers, he swung out of his suite, grabbing a gold-headed walking stick on the way. Ceran nervously twisted the locking head back and forth, making sure it would open to reveal the three-foot-long sword blade hidden inside, should the need arise. Then he stepped into the St. Louis street, and realized how different life was here than at the fort.

The people crushed together here hurried to their work and didn't look to rob him. He knew this was a decent section of St. Louis, but avoiding the ones that weren't was no handicap. Ceran hailed a passing cab and jumped inside, preferring this to the endless trolleys crisscrossing town.

"To the military headquarters, Department of the West," called Ceran.

The carriage driver snapped the reins and got his horse plodding along. Ceran leaned back and studied the buildings as he rode in comfort. Such a prosperous place, with a society that didn't include half-naked savages and food burnt to a crisp over a campfire. Ceran closed his eyes and imagined himself living in St. Louis surrounded by the finest things money could buy. The society whirl, the galas, the women all dressed in fine dresses trimmed with lace and smelling of the most au courant perfumes. To laugh at a sophisticated joke and not at crude japes out of place even at a Green River Rendezvous. Ceran sighed as he imagined it. So much had to happen before he could come to St. Louis to stay.

Leaving William and George and Bent's Fort would not be easy. Still, he could hire Charlotte Green. Her cooking and sense of culinary art had been the best there was between St. Louis and San Francisco. Ceran wasn't sure how he could employ her husband, but Dick was a brave man and deserved consideration.

"Here you go, sir," the driver called.

"Thank you, my good man," Ceran said, paying the driver and adding a handsome tip. He looked up the broad stone steps leading into the U.S. Army's Headquarters for all military action west of the Mississippi. It needed some repairs, but the large groups of officers hurrying along on their missions told Ceran this was the place he sought to make his proposal.

He strode up the steps, made a few inquiries, and finally reached the proper office. He paused outside and frowned. Only a colonel. He had expected to deal with a general about such valuable property. He shrugged it off. A colonel might be more inclined to agreement, having been in the field more recently than a general.

"Colonel Sampson will see you, sir," the orderly said, giving Ceran a once-over.

Ceran went into Sampson's office and looked around. He refrained from making any comment about such austere quarters. He wondered if the colonel had just walked in and sat down behind the desk. There were no personal effects on the desktop or on any of the shelves around the office. Most officers had trophies from their battles or letters of commendation framed to impress their visitors. The whitewashed plaster walls were bare, and nothing but a thin layer of dust rested on the shelves.

"So good of you to allow me to take a few minutes of your time, Colonel," Ceran said. Sampson grunted and pointed to the lone chair on the far side of the desk. The colonel had side-whiskers going to gray, sharp eyes buried in pits of gristle, and eyebrows that looked like caterpillars wiggling across his face. His sharp nose twitched, causing his bushy mustache to fluff up.

"I have limited time, sir. I understand from your brief letter that you have some small property to sell."

"It's more than 'small,' Colonel Sampson," Ceran said. "I understand that the Mexican War will not last forever, but the fight against the Plains Indians will go on for some time. The army needs a secure post along the Santa Fe Trail to wage such a campaign. Bent's Fort gave General Kearny a starting point for his invasion of New Mexico, and will afford you a safe post in your fight against the Comanche and Sioux."

"Bent's Fort, eh? I've heard of it, naturally, and read about the usefulness in Captain Cooke's reports. And Doniphan's and even General Kearny's. You're here to put in a bill for supplies? This isn't the proper department. I will—"

"I want to sell Bent's Fort," Ceran said curtly. "You need its adobe walls to protect your soldiers. You need it because it is the only safe spot between Fort Leavenworth and Santa Fe, and Santa Fe is hardly secure these days. There has never been a successful attack on the fort, and it is widely recognized as a point of stability. The reputation alone would be invaluable to you."

"Sell the entire fort? With all supplies?" Sampson's bushy eyebrows wiggled even more furiously now.

"A price of sixteen thousand dollars would be a bargain, Colonel. It would cost you far more to build such a sturdy fort."

"Why do you want to sell? I've heard rumors of disease. Bent's Fort isn't infected with some hideous contagion or pestilence, is it? The army has to watch for such things as slick entrepreneurs always on the lookout to skin us."

"There's no disease there," Ceran said, fighting to keep his anger in check. "Bent, St. Vrain and Company is seeking a buyer because the nature of our trade is changing. We see more profit now in supply at Westport and sales at Taos and Santa Fe than in transport."

"You'd let others run the risk of freighting?"

That was part of Ceran's plan, but the colonel's bluntness stating it irritated him.

"We would retain other outposts, such as Fort St. Vrain."

"Your namesake, eh?"

"If you're willing to make an offer for that fort, also, it will be considered."

"We have no desire for a fort in northern Colorado. There is no indication the region will ever be more than it is now, home to various renegade Indians and societal misfits."

Ceran liked Sampson less by the minute, and wished he had asked for more in return for Bent's Fort.

"The sale price is quite fair to all parties," Ceran said.

"Twelve thousand," Sampson said suddenly. "Not one cent more. Bent's Fort really isn't worth that much, but it might serve as a symbol to some of the savages. I understand the Cheyenne-Comanche peace treaty was ratified at the post."

"It was, and twelve thousand is absurdly low. My original offer is not open to negotiation, as it is already rock-bottom. I thought to make the army a decent, equitable offer for property that has been developed and is currently flourishing."

"If you are unwilling to accept *my* offer, Mr. St. Vrain, then you are wasting both our times. Good day."

Ceran St. Vrain stared at the colonel for a moment, then silently rose and left the office in the Department of the West, wondering where the army recruited such stupid, shortsighted officers.

On the ride back to Planters House, Ceran decided there was no reason for William to know he had even made the offer.

Precious Death

"How is she?" William Bent asked anxiously. The Cheyenne midwife made shooing motions to get him away.

"You would think you've never had a child before. You have three. Soon to be four. Go. Go away!" The woman made clucking noises like a chicken, and flapped her arms like a hen going after grain. This made William smile.

"Owl Woman will be all right, won't she? I couldn't bear it if anything happens to my wife."

"Didn't the medicine man say so? He says omens are good. Go away. Go, go, go."

This time the midwife pushed William from the room. Through the door leading into his and Owl Woman's bedroom he saw her on the bed, as pale as the bleached muslin sheet on which she lay. She didn't move, she didn't moan or tremble. She just . . . was. This bothered William more than he could say. The midwife was right. Three prior pregnancies and perfect children had not bothered him as much as this time.

In his gut he felt something was wrong.

Owl Woman's sister, Yellow Woman, waited for him

outside. The impossible heat of the day was more bearable on the fort parapet, a soft breeze blowing off the fragrant tules to the east. He leaned against the top of the adobe wall that had protected Bent's Fort for so long. Somehow, it didn't feel as secure to him right now. It couldn't hold back his fears.

"My sister will be well," Yellow Woman said. She came up beside William and laid her hand on his. "You love her too much."

"How is that possible?" he asked. William looked at his sister-in-law and saw so much of Owl Woman in her. After Gray Thunder had died, both women had spent less time with the Cheyenne and more here at the fort, until they knew the routine as well as he did. If it had been possible, William would have turned over much of the day-to-day routine to the women, but the roughneck traders and mountain men who passed through would never take orders from any woman, much less a Cheyenne squaw.

That didn't mean William didn't trust Owl Woman—and Yellow Woman—with his life.

"By law we are married, too," Yellow Woman said.

"By Cheyenne law, not American," he said. William hugged her close and felt her tears on his shirt. He tried to push her away, but his arms wouldn't let her loose.

"She will be all right," Yellow Woman said, but there was no conviction in her voice.

"If it's a boy we're naming him Gray, after your father. If it's a girl, we are going to call her Julia."

"That's a pretty name," Yellow Woman said.

"Mr. Bent," called the midwife as she came from the sleeping quarters.

William jumped back guiltily.

"What is it?" He saw the expression on the midwife's face. Yellow Woman rushed in without a word and William followed.

"It was sudden. She said nothing, gave no sign. The baby, a girl, is healthy but Owl Woman . . ."

William caught his breath. He heard the weak cries of the baby girl, Julia Bent. But his wife did not stir, showed no life. Yellow Woman began the loud laments of mourning. William wanted to join, but instead took his new daughter into his arms and held her close.

Another of William Bent's loved ones had died, and he was not going to lose Julia, too.

And Another Death

Bent's Fort
October 23, 1847

"You look so dejected, Ceran," said William Bent, "that I ought to buy you a drink. What'll it be?" William took a bottle of fine Kentucky bourbon from the shelf near the billiard table and held it out, trying to entice Ceran into a smile.

He didn't get the usual answering grin.

"Things aren't going well, William," Ceran said.

"I've gotten over Owl Woman's death," William said carefully. For months he had moped around, then had ridden off and fasted for a week, and gotten a vision interpreted by the Cheyenne medicine man as meaning he would find his true destiny with Yellow Woman. This had been difficult for William to accept, but he had. His sister-in-law had taken care of Julia as if the baby were her own. He could not have found a better nanny and, as Yellow Woman had pointed out, under Cheyenne law they were married. A man married not only the older woman but also her sisters.

For all the love and caring Yellow Woman had shown, she might as well be his wife. William had made it legal, marrying her in a ceremony more likely to be accepted by Americans.

He still missed Owl Woman, but so did Yellow Woman, and this bonded them together as much as caring for Julia and the other three children until he realized he did truly love Yellow Woman.

"You've lost so much, William," Ceran said. "Two brothers and a wife."

"But the company's still doing well," William pointed out. The trade wasn't as profitable as it had been, but the money still piled up.

"The Indians are making it difficult to get a wagon train from Westport to here. There's almost no chance of moving one from here to Westport without being attacked at least once. The cavalry isn't doing a damn thing to stop them."

"The war," William said, his mind drifting away. He felt that something wasn't right, but couldn't put his finger on it.

"They're off fighting the Mexicans when they ought to be here protecting Americans on our own soil," Ceran said. He stopped when he saw William's attention drifting. Cocking his head to one side, Ceran heard the heavy outer gates opening. At this time of night the guard let in only the most trusted members of the company.

Ceran went to the doorway and looked across the *placita* in time to see the heavy inner doors opening. For a moment he didn't understand whom the guard had let in. Then he let out a yelp.

"It's George! Something's wrong."

Ceran hit the stairs and took them three at a time in his rush to reach George's side. As fast as he was, William beat him. They stared up at George Bent, but the man didn't see them. Sweat beaded his forehead and his eyes were glazed over. He was flour-white and his hands shook as he gripped his saddle horn. He never looked at them or acknowledged their presence.

"Cholera," William said in a hushed voice. "Help me get him into the storeroom where we can quarantine and care for him."

Ceran and William grabbed George and pulled, only to find that he had tied himself into the saddle. Ceran whipped out his knife and slashed at the rawhide strips George had used. The bindings meant George had felt weak and dizzy enough to know he might not make it to the fort if he tumbled from his saddle. At some point on his ride to the fort, he had kept his wits about him enough to take precautions.

The two men wrestled George to the storeroom and laid him on a stack of buffalo robes. Without exchanging a word, the two went about tending him. They had dealt with cholera before and recognized the symptoms. When George became feverish a little before midnight, William tried to pour water into his brother's mouth. The liquid sloshed around and rolled off his cracked lips. None of it got to the man's desert-dry mouth.

George's eyes flickered. Those eyes blazed with fever, but he recognized his brother.

"Hello, Will. Been a while."

"Don't talk. Save your strength. We'll nurse you through this, Ceran and me."

"Ceran?"

"Right here, George."

"Thought you were Frank. Where's Frank?"

William and Ceran exchanged looks. George knew Frank Blair had returned to St. Louis months earlier. They had not heard from him since.

"He's not here right now, George," Ceran said gently. "I saw him in St. Louis. He says for you to rest and get better." The white lie was better than the truth for the enfeebled man to hear.

"That's Frank," George said. He stiffened and looked past them. A smile came to his lips and he reached out with a shaky hand. "Hello, Charles," he said, reaching for the darkness outside the storeroom.

George Bent sagged back to the soft buffalo robes, closed his eyes, shuddered once, and died.

William couldn't take his eyes off his dead brother. Ceran shivered a little in spite of the heat boiling into the room from the corner fireplace, and couldn't keep from looking out into the dark, as if he, too, might see Charles Bent.

He didn't. He took that as a good omen.

Troopers
and Arguments

Bent's Fort
November 15, 1847

"Another attack," William Bent said, shaking his head. "The Comanche won't stop. We need to deal with them decisively."

"It's not only them," said Ceran St. Vrain. "The Pawnee and Osage are kicking up a fuss, too. The Sioux moved farther north, but there's no evidence they are cutting back on their attacks, either. It's just that they affect those along the Oregon Trail rather than us."

"George ought to have been at Fort St. Vrain to deal with them," William said, turning morose. "Though fighting Indians is hardly a way to celebrate a birthday." William swallowed and closed his eyes, as if picturing George. "He would have been thirty-four."

"William, stop berating yourself over this," Ceran said. "There wasn't anything you could do to prevent George's death. The cholera was too advanced to nurse him back to health. Even the Cheyenne medicine man said so." Ceran knew how much faith William placed in the roots and potions offered up by the Cheyenne. For all he knew, they actually worked, but against cholera that had taken such a firm hold, only God Almighty could change the course of the disease.

Ceran worried increasingly about William. Losing two brothers and a wife in the span of less than a year took a toll on any man, much less one as attached to family as William. Even worse, William had lost all his brothers here. Somehow, Robert's scalping by the Comanche had affected him most powerfully, possibly because he had sent his brother into the heart of Comanche territory with the hope that the Cheyenne-Comanche treaty would bring permanent peace.

"It's not my fault," William said. "I know that. But I feel so helpless."

"We can hire more guards," Ceran said.

"You missed Colonel Gilpin this morning," William said.

"Gilpin? I'd heard there were soldiers in the area. What did he want?" Ceran spoke a bit too sharply.

William turned and stared at him. "Do you know Gilpin personally?"

"Of course not."

"You sound bitter, Ceran. The colonel has two battalions to supply. They've been sent out to put the Comanche in their place, them and their Plains allies."

"The army tried it before and failed."

"Ceran, we can't send enough armed guards with every wagon train to make a difference. It would eat into our profits too much, and we've been losing more and more to the raids."

"We're still making a slim profit. We won't earn a dime if we have to give this Gilpin all his supplies. We might even lose money if they eat us out of house and home."

"The army would purchase it. I propose selling whatever they need at a profit, true, but we wouldn't be giving away merchandise. If Gilpin stopped only a few raids on the wagon trains, it would be worth it to us."

"They'll steal us blind," Ceran said doggedly. "How much did we ever collect when we agreed to supply Captain Cooke? Nothing. General Kearny has yet to pay for any of the food we gave his troops. When Charles was governor, he could never get Kearny to come quell the revolt because the general was too busy chasing Navajo. When was the last time we had to worry about a Navajo attacking our wagons?"

"What's wrong, Ceran?" asked William. "It might be worth our while to give Colonel Gilpin the wares he needs to hold down the Indian threat. The war is going to keep most soldiers far to the south and let the Comanche range freely."

"Bent, St. Vrain and Company has a terrible record for getting the army to pay," Ceran repeated. "Why should we enter a new contract if we know we'll never see a red cent?"

"It's not worth arguing over," William said. "I've already authorized the quartermaster to draw against our stores."

Ceran fumed but said nothing. The army wouldn't buy Bent's Fort because they didn't have to. They could use it without penalty, never paying for the supplies they took and using the thick adobe walls to protect their officers should the need arise. Ceran saw the possibility of the Comanche chasing Gilpin back across the prairie and actually attacking Bent's Fort.

The army should have bought the fort if they intended to use it. And William should never have given approval for supplies to be released without discussing it with his partner.

Ceran St. Vrain left William wondering what ate away at him.

Burning Wagons, Wrong Trails

On the Santa Fe Trail
March 30, 1848

"I've scouted ahead and don't see any trouble," Ceran St. Vrain said, but in his gut he knew he had missed something. "I haven't even found any tracks left by Gilpin and his horse soldiers."

Lucien Maxwell shook his head, then took off his hat and slapped it against his thigh. He looked up and down the line of wagons, all laden with buffalo robes traded for over the last month. The spring was always the best time to get the buffalo hides since the Indians no longer needed them during the long, hot summer and would hunt more buffalo throughout the year, especially the spring and summer. If the wagon train got through, Bent, St. Vrain & Company stood to make huge profits. The voracious appetite for buffalo robes in America and Europe grew unabated.

"Ceran, I haven't seen the colonel on any of my trips to Westport and back. The man might as well be made of smoke for all the protection we get from him."

"William is still feeding him and his men," Ceran groused. He felt a momentary pang of guilt at trying to sell Bent's Fort to the army without telling William about his negotiations, but he felt even more anger that the army was getting the full use of the fort without having to pay for it.

"He's doing it out of guilt. We both know that," Lucien said. Ceran jumped, thinking Lucien had somehow read his mind. He settled down when he realized his friend was speaking about William. "He knows there wasn't much he could do about Charles and George dying, but it festers in his soul how Robert died."

"Letting Gilpin get all the food he can stuff into his mouth isn't the way to pacify the Comanche," Ceran said, growing more anxious by the minute. He had spent too many months of his life out on the trail not to obey his instincts. Right now, his sixth sense was screaming that something was wrong.

"Circle the wagons," Ceran said suddenly. "Get the rifles ready."

"What's wrong?" asked Lucien. He poked up his head like a prairie dog and looked around.

"Can't say, but something's eating away at me."

"Hey, Ceran, lookee there!" came the shout. A freighter had climbed to the top of his wagon and peered out at the horizon. "Dust. Plenty of horses kickin' up a fuss."

Ceran dropped to the ground and put his ear against the drumlike dirt. There had been considerable snowfall during the winter, but spring was dry as a bone. He listened for a moment, then jumped to his feet.

"What is it?" demanded Lucien, working to load a second musket.

"Too many hoofbeats for me to figure them all out. I swear, it sounds like they're coming from both north and south." He looked north again. "Get the wagons circled, Lucien. That's a Comanche raiding party!"

Ceran vaulted into the saddle and helped the teamsters swing their teams around. They didn't have time to unhitch the animals and get them into the middle of the circle. Worse, they had several hundred head of horses they were herding to Westport for sale in Missouri. These animals would draw the Indians like flies to shit.

And they wouldn't break off their attack until they had stolen enough to guarantee their position in the tribe. Warriors stole horses. Mighty warriors stole dozens of horses.

"Hey, Ceran, should we let the horses go?" shouted Lucien. "That might keep them from attacking us."

Ceran considered it for a moment, then shouted back, "No! They'd take it as a sign of weakness and come for us. Keep as many of the horses safe as you can. That way we'll know where the Comanche are."

"Yeah, coming straight for us!"

Ceran bent low and galloped in the direction of the advancing Indians. He wanted to take their measure and find out how many braves his wagon train faced. After a quarter mile, Ceran saw that they faced more than a hundred Comanche. He wheeled around and rode hell-bent for leather back to the wagons. A few warriors fired at him, but the range was still too great. Ceran didn't fear getting hit from a mile off. Soon enough, the Comanche would be nose-to-nose. Then he would have something to fear.

"Keep the horses inside the ring of wagons," he said, seeing how the drovers were having trouble getting the spooked horses into the loose circle of wagons. Ceran worried that the Comanche would shoot fire-arrows into a few of the wagons. It took a while for buffalo robes to begin to burn, but once they did, there was no way of saving wagon or cargo except to push it out of the ring.

When that happened, the horses were likely to bolt and escape.

Ceran hit the ground running and let his still-saddled horse join the others in the herd.

"We're in for it, aren't we?" asked Lucien. "I should have stayed in Taos."

"We all should have," Ceran said. "I'm getting too old to fight Indians. All I want is to run a store in Santa Fe and enjoy my dotage."

"I hope your dotage includes still having a scalp," Lucien said, hefting his rifle and firing it. The musket built muzzle pressure, then kicked him back a half step as white gunsmoke filled the air. Lucien wasn't the first to fire at the attacking Indians. He certainly wasn't the last, either.

Ceran began firing methodically. He had learned the rhythm required to fire, reload, and fire again as many as four times a minute. Not every shot came close to a Comanche brave, but with the others in the wagon train firing, too, the air was filled with deadly lead as the Indians rode into range.

Then arrows and lead slugs crossed in the air. An experienced Comanche warrior could fire three or four times faster with bow and arrow than a rifleman could with his musket. From the corner of his eye, Ceran saw one driver stumble backward with an arrow in his throat. The man threw up his hands, musket flying, then fell flat on his back, as dead as a mackerel.

A screaming brave loomed in front of Ceran, but he had expended his round. Ceran swung the barrel clumsily and caught the Comanche on the arm, deflecting his aim enough to avoid taking an arrow himself. Before Ceran could draw his knife and go after the Indian, the warrior wheeled about and retreated.

"Fire! Ceran, they set fire to three wagons."

"Push them out of the ring," Ceran called, knowing the Indians had done exactly what he had worried most about. There had been no way to stop them once they got close enough. There were too many of them.

Ceran dropped his rifle and ran to help two teamsters as they pushed the nearest burning wagon out of the circle. They had barely moved it far enough to keep the fire from spreading to adjoining wagons when a Comanche brave rode inside their defensive perimeter. The brave shouted and whooped and stampeded the horses.

"Out of the way!" Ceran found himself diving for cover under the wagon they had just pushed out. He scrambled forward when burning splinters fell onto his back. Then dust from a hundred horses' hooves and smoke from burning wagons obscured his view. Coughing, gagging on the air that had once been so pure, Ceran struggled to find a safer place.

"They got most of the horses," Lucien said. "But they're running. I don't understand it. They've got us. Why aren't they attacking?"

"Hey, Lucien, Ceran, look to the south." A teamster waved frantically, as if signaling.

"Get down, you fool. You'll get your head blown off," Lucien called.

"The Comanche are on the run," Ceran said, coming out to have a look. "He's waving to the cavalry."

"They are a tad late to help us, but maybe they can recover some of our horses. I surely do hate losing that many head. We had contracts for damn near a hundred dollars each." Lucien Maxwell reloaded his rifle, then hiked it to his shoulder and walked out, like a soldier on parade duty, to greet the cavalry.

"As I live and breathe," Lucien said to Ceran. "That's the colonel himself. I wondered where he was hiding out."

Ceran and Lucien waited for Colonel Gilpin to ride up. The column behind the officer looked uneasy at the obvious Indian attack that had befallen the company wagons.

"It was a Comanche raiding party, Colonel," Ceran said without any polite greeting. "If you get after them, you might get back some of the horses they stole."

"About a hundred, maybe 150 head," Lucien cut in. "We have a contract to supply the horses to the army back in Missouri."

"Good afternoon, gentlemen," the colonel said, watching the teamsters trying to beat out the fires in the wagons. He made no offer of his men to join their effort.

"We're fine, Colonel," Ceran said. "Get on after them."

"We are on the trail of some Osage raiders," Gilpin said stiffly. "If the Indians who attacked you are Comanche, they are not the object of our current campaign."

"They ought to be!" blurted Lucien. "You can get them, Colonel."

"I don't think the colonel has pursuit in mind, do you, Gilpin?" Ceran's bitterness boiled up.

"I have my orders, and they do not currently include going after a renegade band of Comanche. I take it you haven't seen any Osage. Or Prairie Apache."

"Just Comanche stealing our horses, setting fire to our wagons, and killing some of our teamsters," Ceran said.

"Do you wish for my men to form a burial detail?"

Ceran and Lucien said at the same time, "No!"

Ceran made no effort to keep the acrimony from his words when he said, "I prefer them to be buried by their comrades, by men willing to lay down their lives for each other. Why don't you and your soldiers just ride on off, Colonel, and leave us be?"

"Very well. But I do not understand your attitude, Mr. St. Vrain. Keeping the Osage and Apache at bay is a worthy mission."

Gilpin signaled his bugler, who tentatively sounded the advance. The colonel set off to the northeast, at an angle to the road and well away from the direction taken by the Comanche with their stolen horses.

Ceran St. Vrain had begun to dread the Santa Fe Trail, and wanted nothing more than to retire to Santa Fe or Taos.

Dangerous Trade

Bent's Fort
July 17, 1848

"You are going to get all our scalps lifted," Marcellin St. Vrain said angrily. "Stop trying to trade with those red bastards! All they do is kill whoever you send to Adobe Walls."

"There's a great market to be exploited among the Comanche," William Bent said to his partner's brother. "There's no reason the company shouldn't exploit it."

"You got one brother scalped by them. How many more good men are you going to sacrifice to make money?" Marcellin bit his lip the instant he said that. William glared at him, the piercing look going straight to his heart.

"Robert knew the risks. At the time, we all thought the Comanche would abide by the terms of the treaty."

"We aren't Cheyenne," Marcellin said almost contritely. "Even if you're married to one, we're not Cheyenne."

"The Cheyenne have had some new trouble with the Comanche, too. But we can make the Comanche dependent on us and our trade goods," William said. "When we do, we can control them by withholding luxury goods they crave most."

"You don't understand them, William. They aren't the Cheyenne. They aren't peaceable and never will be. The only New Mexico governor who ever dealt with them was de Anza."

"He killed Comanche women and children while their warriors were gone," William said. "That was brutal and uncalled for."

"It's the way *they* fight. That's why they stopped raiding in New Mexico."

"What's your point, Marcellin?" William felt an incredible exhaustion now that he had reached a decision to reopen trade with the Comanche. Adobe Walls had been closed, opened, and closed again so many times he couldn't remember them all. But it was a chance to develop trade and get a grip on the Comanche's wild spirit. He might not tame it much, but any lessening of their fierce raiding would benefit everyone on the plains. For whatever reason, Colonel Gilpin had been unable to quell them, concentrating more on their allies.

William tasted bile rising in his throat. This was one of the few points he had agreed with Ceran on lately. Stop the Comanche and their allies would also stop their depredations. William walked outside to the fort parapet and looked down. Ceran claimed he was making a big mistake trying to deal with the Comanche. Marcellin agreed that it was wrong, too.

But he had to try. For Robert's memory, he had to try. He couldn't have been so wrong that his brother had died in vain.

"They're coming," William called.

"Keep the gates closed," Marcellin warned. "Don't let the red bastards into the fort or they'll scalp us all."

William started to angrily order the gates opened for the Comanche, then settled down. He signaled the sentries to do as Marcellin asked. It couldn't hurt. Let the Comanche prove their peaceful intentions to trade rather than fight, and then he could open the trading post to a few of them. Only a few. It had been long years since Old Wolf had been given his tour of Bent's Fort. The Comanche chief had been impressed. Any new chief would be, too.

One guard went to the small brass cannon and rested his hand on it, anxiously looking to William for orders.

"Load the cannon," William said, "but keep your hand off the lanyard. If you fire accidentally, all I'm working for will be lost."

"Kill the bastards," muttered Marcellin. William angrily silenced him, not wanting the guards along the walls to get conflicting orders. He knew which they would obey—and it wasn't his more peaceable approach.

"Welcome!" William called to the dozen painted Comanche on their horses, still mounted and milling about at the front gate.

"Let us in!" demanded one, waving his war lance.

"Do you come to trade?" asked William. "That's the only reason to be here."

"We trade. Let us in!"

William caught Marcellin's hot glare and ignored it. He hurried down the steps and went to the storeroom with the small window cut into one wall. When the outer gates opened, the heart of the fort was still protected by the metal-sheathed inner ones. William could talk to the braves through the shuttered window without exposing himself.

He gathered the goods most likely to appeal to the Comanche and brought them close, putting them on shelves where he could pick them up without turning his back to the window. Then he pulled back the locking bolts.

The Comanche in the vestibule between inner and outer gates jumped. He had not expected William to deal with him through the small opening.

"What have you to trade?" asked William.

"Come out." The Comanche pressed his face inward, but couldn't get his head in far enough to look around the storeroom. He backed off, then poked at William with his lance.

"None of that," William said. "I'll close the shutter and you won't get to trade for any of this." William held up clear glass jars filled with brightly colored beads, cards of needles, lengths of cloth, and other goods valued by the Comanche.

"I want," the Comanche said belligerently.

"Then let's trade. What do you have to offer?"

The dickering began in earnest, with the brave's hostility dying down as he began to accumulate the items he sought most. Several times, William had to dodge to one side when the Comanche fired his rifle into the storeroom, angered by what he thought was a one-sided trade. William wasn't above taking advantage of the brave, but this time he played it straight. By the time William closed the shutter and got the Comanche braves outside the fort, he thought everyone was happy with the day's barter.

He left the storeroom and went into the *placita,* where Marcellin and a half dozen men worked on muskets, loading them and putting them into racks against possible Comanche assault.

"That won't be necessary, Marcellin," William said with some satisfaction. "Trade for the day is over and we've made real progress."

"Humor me, William," said Marcellin. "This preparation won't hurt, if we don't need the muskets. And if we do . . ."

"We won't," William said firmly. He turned at the sounds building outside the thick adobe wall. "What's that about?"

"Mr. Bent, sir, they want to talk to you at their camp."

"William, don't," Marcellin said. "They'll kill you."

William hesitated, his mind racing. He considered all the possibilities, and realized he had to agree with Marcellin.

"Very well. Tell them I am occupied with other business," William called to the sentry. It took only a few seconds for the guard to come back, looking uneasy.

"Sir, they ain't takin' it too kindly how you're not willin' to socialize with 'em."

"All right," William said tiredly. "I'll smoke a pipe or two and—"

"Wait, William. You can't. If they think you're lying about being busy, we'll never keep them under control. You've got to stay and not let them lure you out. I'll go."

"Are you sure, Marcellin?" He stared at the smallish man and realized there wasn't a cowardly bone in his slender body.

"I won't venture out past the range of the cannon. You keep a passel of sentries up there with the muskets I've spent the afternoon loading. And don't hesitate to open fire, if it comes to that."

"You don't have to," William said.

"Listen to the ruckus they're kicking up," Marcellin said. "I'll keep my temper. You see to it that I keep my scalp."

"All right," William said uneasily. The commotion outside grew.

Marcellin drew the six-gun at his belt, then tossed it to a guard and motioned for the man to get up onto the parapet. He fingered the knife sheathed at the other side of his broad leather belt, then removed it. No amount of weaponry would save him if the Comanche turned on him. He walked to the inner gate, then signaled.

The gates opened, Marcellin stepped forward, then vanished when the gates slammed shut and the locking bars slid into place. The outer gates opened. William hurried up the steps and leaned over, hoping the Comanche with whom he had traded didn't notice him amid the other guards. It was a risk he had to take to be certain Marcellin was safe.

Marcellin St. Vrain walked among the jeering, jostling Comanche, but never showed a speck of fear. He faced the one William thought was a subchief and spoke rapidly to him. From his vantage on the rampart, William couldn't hear what was being said. The Comanche warriors cheered and shouted, further taking away any chance of overhearing.

William heaved a sigh of relief when the Comanche built a campfire not fifty yards away and several braves sat down and took out pipes and tobacco. Marcellin joined them to smoke a pipe.

"It looks as if he's convinced them to stay peaceful," William said. "I'm going to get something to eat. If anything happens, call me right away."

"What about that?" asked one guard, pointing to the loaded cannon trained on the Comanche campsite.

"Stay away from it. If you fire it now and don't intend killing every last one of them with the first shot, Marcellin'll be a goner."

"Yes, sir. Uh, sir," the guard said, as William started down the stairs on his way to the dining room, "I don't know what's going on out there. They ain't smokin' no peace pipe."

William hesitated, then reversed his direction and went back up to see what the guard meant.

"Marcellin!" he called, but his warning was drowned out amid the loud cries from the Comanche. They had all stood as Marcellin and their chief faced each other. William didn't know what was going on, but Marcellin put his hands on the chief's shoulders and the Comanche grabbed one of the man's wrists.

A great shout went up as Marcellin and the Comanche began wrestling. Under other circumstances, this might have been great fun. All Indians enjoyed wrestling and other combative sports, but William saw the circumstances surrounding this bout as something other than a game played for everyone's amusement.

Marcellin held his own against the more powerful Comanche, then slipped. The chief moved like lightning, his brawny arm circling Marcellin's throat. William picked up a musket and aimed it, but the distance was too great for an accurate shot. At fifty yards he might as easily hit Marcellin as the Comanche chief.

"Whatya want us to do, Mr. Bent?"

"Wait, wait and pray," he said, his heart hammering in his chest.

Marcellin twisted, ducked, and reversed the hold. Then the loud snap of the Comanche's neck breaking echoed like a gunshot.

The silence that fell was absolute. No birds stirred among the tules. No human spoke. Even the wind had died.

William took in the situation, grabbed up the cannon lanyard, and yanked. The small one-inch gun fired. In the shocked calm, the report was startling.

The Comanche braves whirled around, going for their weapons.

"Get on back, Marcellin. Don't make us come for you," shouted William. On either side of him moved fort employees taking aim. William was glad now that Marcellin had loaded all the muskets. They might be needed.

The stunned lull that followed Marcellin killing the chief afforded him the chance to run for the gate.

"Don't shoot unless they chase Marcellin," William ordered. "Get the cannon loaded again. Grapeshot or chain. I want to take as many of them out as possible."

Frantic men worked to reload the small cannon. This wasn't lost on the Comanche as they milled about, whispering among themselves. By the time they began shouting curses and making threatening gestures, Marcellin St. Vrain was safely inside Bent's Fort.

"Don't fire. Wait. Hold your fire," William called as a solitary Comanche strode up, chest thrust out and looking like he could chew nails and spit tacks.

"He killed Little Dog. Send him back out!"

"It was a friendly wrestling match," William said. He pushed Marcellin back so he couldn't be seen from the ground. "It was an accident." William wasn't sure about that. It had looked as if Little Dog would have killed Marcellin, probably making the same claim he now was for Marcellin.

"Send him out!"

"I'll send him away," William said. "Far away to St. Louis. He will never be here again. Will that satisfy you?"

The Indian scowled and then spat. Then he looked up and said, "We will kill him if we see him again!" The Comanche spun and stalked back to the tight knot of braves, all clutching their weapons, looking fearfully at the small cannon trained on them. In a few minutes, they were mounted and vanished in a cloud of dust.

"Looks as if I've overstayed my welcome," Marcellin said. "It might just be time to find out why my brother likes Planters House in St. Louis so much."

"It's time," William said, feeling as if he had lost another relative. He had never been close to Marcellin, but George had. Together they had run Fort St. Vrain ably and well for many years. Now even this small connection with his brother was severed.

William shook Marcellin's hand, taking some consolation in the man's still being alive even if he had to leave Bent's Fort.

Gold Rush
and Slump

*Bent's Fort
April 3, 1849*

"It was a complete disaster," Ceran St. Vrain said to William Bent. "Nothing went well, and he lost not only his equipment but also eleven men. And still the fool wouldn't turn back. He went on through to California."

"John Charles is as bullheaded as they come," William said.

"The only consolation to this is that Kit refused to go with him. That should have told Frémont how the odds were against him." Ceran clucked his tongue and sipped wine from the crystal goblet. He looked up and saw William staring at him. "What?"

"This seems to be the start of something evil," William said thoughtfully. "The Indians are still attacking, no matter what peace treaties we sign. If it hadn't been for Chief Cinemo pleading with the Cheyenne from his deathbed not to go on the warpath, they would have joined the Comanche."

Ceran snorted in disgust.

"The peace treaty those tribes signed worked against us. Cheyenne and Comanche against the white man.

We were better off when the Cheyenne fought the Comanche."

"No, we weren't," William snapped angrily. "Peace is always better. At the least, Tom Fitzpatrick has worked long and hard to keep the peace and has done a good job of it. In spite of complaining all the time about Gilpin."

"I complain about Gilpin. The man is ill and not fit for command. But at least he has spent eighteen months chasing Arapaho and Kiowa and Comanche."

"To no good end," William said, finding himself arguing with Ceran although he agreed about Colonel Gilpin. He was tired of being caught between Fitzpatrick's carping, usually legitimate, and Gilpin not wanting to commit his dragoons for any good purpose. Fitzpatrick had wanted ten soldiers to go after a fugitive selling firewater to the Arapaho, and Gilpin had denied him even this small squad. The Indian agent had gone out on his own and brought the man to justice, only to have Gilpin boast back at Fort Leavenworth how he had captured the man.

William was sick in body and soul over the constant bickering. And sick of Ceran St. Vrain.

"I should get out to the village," William said. "Yellow Woman is doing well."

"And your new son?" Ceran asked. William wasn't sure if Ceran really cared. From his tone, he found more interest in the wine, admittedly of poor quality, than in any answer.

"Little Charles is doing well, thank you."

Silence fell again.

"Frémont didn't finish the mapping," Ceran finally said. "If he did, he lost all the work with his supplies over the winter, but this won't stop the men in St. Louis from planning a transcontinental railroad."

"It would go north, closer to Fort St. Vrain than here," William agreed.

"What difference does it make where it went? A railroad would put us out of business. There wouldn't be any reason to keep the fort open."

"There would, too," William said, irritated at such an attitude. "You've heard the rumors of gold out in California. Men will flock through here."

"They'll go north, along the Oregon Trail. If the railroad is finished soon, and a gold strike might speed up the construction, Bent's Fort will be a ghost town within a year."

"We serve a purpose, Ceran. We won't simply dry up and blow away like some autumn oak leaf."

"Oak leaves are colorful and pretty. All we have is a dried mud fort."

"Fitzpatrick runs his agency from here. Every year we make forays against the Ute."

"Bill Williams was murdered by them when he tried to recover Frémont's gear."

William's eyes went wide in shock. He hadn't heard.

"He paid for his foolishness leading Frémont," Ceran went on mercilessly. "We won't see his like here again. We won't see any of those mountain men. The army is building forts on the Platte and bought Fort Laramie, with an eye to protecting the Oregon Trail."

"They owe us," William said, his dander up. This time he railed at the army as much as Ceran. "They ruined our trade here when Dodge began taking our supplies, and continued throughout the Mexican War. They never paid for a quarter of the supplies they took, yet we still let them use the fort as a base."

"I told you that would happen," Ceran said. "And I'm telling you this gold strike in California will turn the Santa Fe Trail and trade along it to dust within a year."

"No, it won't," William said.

"The Oregon Trail is where the travelers will go, not south toward Santa Fe and then across to California. Kearny never broke the Navajos. Riding through Navajo land is a sure way to lose your scalp. No, the gold miners will go north where the army has forts to protect them from the Ute."

"We can make a profit," William said doggedly. The set to Ceran's jaw told him the arguments that had started months ago would only get worse. They had been fast friends once, but had slowly found themselves at opposite sides of any issue. The past year had been the worst.

"Do you," said William in a controlled voice, "want to dissolve the company?"

"Break up Bent, St. Vrain and Company?" asked Ceran. He took a deep breath, finished his wine with a single gulp, and said, "Yes."

"So be it," William said, anger burning in him even as he recognized how right this was. "What part of the company do you want?"

"The stores in Santa Fe and Taos. The rest is yours," Ceran said.

That suited William just fine. He had built Bent's Fort—William's Fort—and still had faith in the Santa Fe Trail as a profitable trade route. More than this, he had no heart to take over the stores in Taos where Charles had been murdered. It was bad enough for him now at the fort since George and Owl Woman had both died here, but it was a monument to them all. A stolid, sturdy, dependable tribute to the Bent family.

They dickered like experienced traders for another hour over the supplies, then stood, reached across the table, and shook hands.

Bent, St. Vrain and Company was officially dissolved.

The Death of Dreams—and the Fort

Bent's Fort
August 21, 1849

It was lonely in the fort.

William Bent walked through the dusty courtyard, taking a quick look into each of the empty adobe rooms that had once bustled with life. The wheelwright's room, the blacksmithy, the gunsmith's workshop, the storerooms, and the dining rooms where so many fine meals prepared by Charlotte Green had been appreciated. William stepped back to the buffalo-robe press in the center of the *placita* and scanned the upper floor. His bedroom. Charles's. The turrets at the opposite corners where sentries had stood their attentive watches for so many years. The billiard room and bar next to Ceran's quarters.

William held down a wave of bitterness over his former partner. Ceran did well in Santa Fe, from all accounts. He had not seen him in months. Kit Carson had brought word that all was well, and relayed messages between St. Louis and Santa Fe. Through the scout's rapid trips, William had learned George's son, Elfego, was doing well in Frank Blair's care. Dick and Charlotte were similarly well taken care of.

Lucien Maxwell spent much time raising cattle and sheep on his vast land grant, when he wasn't in Taos running a store for Ceran. All the old friends had slipped away, tending their businesses at opposite ends of the Santa Fe Trail.

The Trail.

William sighed. As much as he hated to admit it, Ceran had been right. The gold rush to California had taken miners north, along the Oregon Trail. What money there was here in the south lay at either end of the trail, not along it—and not at Bent's Fort.

William slowly climbed the steps and rested his hand on the small brass cannon as he stared out across the prairie to the east. He had tried to sell the fort to the army. The reception he had received was peculiar, as if they had already considered and rejected such an offer. After much haggling, he had gotten an offer from them that was so ridiculously low that he had turned them down flat. They had offered hardly more than the bricks alone were worth.

He turned and rested both elbows on the top of the adobe wall. Twilight slipped silently through the fort, casting long shadows. William looked hard for Charles's ghost. Nothing. Only the soft whisper of the night breeze building, blowing from the direction of the Arkansas River. Whatever George had seen before he died was denied William.

Try as he might, William couldn't see the ghosts of those who had died here. George. Owl Woman. Not even Robert's restless spirit had come back to tell him how futile it had been trying to trade with the Comanche.

The restless Comanche had turned more violent as the years wore on, until they ranged across all of Texas, creating a force that the cavalry had great difficulty containing. William smiled crookedly. Even using Bent's Fort as a safe base, the army could never contain the Comanche any more than they could a tornado. Only the inevitable, relentless spread of white-settled towns would steal the Comanche range and force them to find less violent ways of living. It wouldn't happen soon, but it would happen.

William heaved a sigh. Then, *then* it would be worth trading with the Comanche.

With deliberate steps, he went around the upper level, looking into each and every room. All had been stripped of their furnishings. Memories flooded out of each one, but no ghosts. Nothing he could touch or feel or speak to.

The cholera outbreak had caused the Cheyenne to leave the vicinity of the fort a week earlier, and slowly, by twos and threes, those who had worked in the fort had also left. Many had headed West to find their fortune in the California gold fields. Others, like Indian Agent Tom Fitzpatrick, had moved to Pueblo to be closer to the Ute and Arapaho. And the others? William didn't know.

He wished them all well.

"Will!" came the loud cry from outside the walls. "You 'bout ready to go?" Kit Carson waited impatiently for him.

"I'll be there in a minute, Kit. I've about paid my respects."

He went down the back steps, his mind turning over plans for a new fort farther south, over by Big Timbers forty miles away, where so many of the Cheyenne gathered. It would be better than this old fort. Bent's Old Fort.

With a deftness born of certainty, he went into the powder room and broke open a few kegs of black powder, then laid a long length of black miner's fuse out into the courtyard. It took a few minutes to light. The black fuse sizzled and popped, then began burning at its stately pace of one foot per minute toward the magazine.

If they weren't going to buy it, William was damned sure the army was not going to simply move in after he left. There were too many precious memories here for that.

He mounted his horse and ducked down as he rode through the portals for the last time.

"'Bout time, William. It's gettin' dark and you know how much I hate snakes. They come out this time of day." Kit Carson looked around anxiously.

"If I didn't know better, I'd think you were part Apache. Let's go, Kit," he said to the scout. "There's so much I have to do. I want to get a herd of horses moved up north to sell to the miners. And there's the new post to build."

Side by side, William and Kit rode toward the river. When the black powder in the magazine exploded, Kit ducked, looked back, and muttered, "Damn, what happened?"

William Bent said nothing as he left behind melancholy memories and rode on to a new beginning.

Epilogue

Bent's Fort was an oasis of civilization on the prairie, providing the only safe stopover along the Santa Fe Trail between St. Louis and Santa Fe. In only fifteen years, as the nature of the country changed, the fort became the central focus for this change. Trappers and mountain men gave way to buffalo hunters, then to traders and soldiers and finally gold seekers. Not only did the fort provide sanctuary from the various Indian tribes raiding on the plains, it was the site of the first irrigation acequia in Colorado. Livestock suppliers as well as traders and merchants, the Bents registered the first Colorado brand.

Until 1920, the fort had fallen into such ruin that it appeared to be nothing more than a dry field. In that year the La Junta chapter of the DAR began work preserving what remained. Restoration started in earnest in May 27, 1975, and for the Colorado Centennial year of 1976, after laying several hundred thousand new adobe bricks, the rebuilt structure was dedicated as part of the Bent's Old Fort National Historic Site.

Today it gives modern visitors a fascinating glimpse into an era that shaped and forged the United States of America.

For a sneak preview of
Karl Lassiter's next novel, *Sword and Drum*—
Coming from Pinnacle Books in November 2003,
just turn the page.

May 1, 1861
Jacksonville, Illinois

"You can borrow more money," Alice Grierson said.
She sat with her hands folded in her lap, a book of poetry on the small maple table beside her. She touched
her severe bun of dark brown hair, patted it firmly
into place and then stared unwaveringly at Ben, her
deep brown eyes not blinking.

"From whom? The banks have cut off all credit. My
brothers, John and Robert, are in dire straits, also. I
would never think of asking my sister Mary for money,
even if she had it to lend. You know she's not quite
right in the head. Your parents are kind enough to let
us stay here without paying room or board but have
no money to spare, otherwise. Who's left?"

Benjamin Grierson studied his wife and saw all the
signs that she was sorely vexed. Her jaw was set and
her eyes never wavered, as if they were spears impal-
ing him where he stood. He hated feeling as if he
were a school boy who had done something wrong.

"Your father," Alice said. "He might—"

"My father didn't want me to go into the dry goods
business in the first place," Ben said, exasperation
growing. "I wish I had remained a music teacher, but
we both know there's no money in that." Ben went a
little dreamy thinking of the earlier years when he
had been a band leader and had given lessons in both
piano and clarinet. None of his students had been

particularly good, nor had they paid promptly or fully, but he had enjoyed the challenge and the music.

"He won't give you the money because you didn't petition the governor strenuously enough to get that postmaster's position for John." Alice sat a little straighter in the chair and then made shooing motions to chase off their young son, Charlie, eavesdropping from the hall. "Go look after your brother," she told the boy. "He needs his diaper changed after his nap."

"Mama, that's all he does," Charlie said, lisping slightly. "Do I have to?"

"Go on," Ben said gently. "Do as your mother says. We need to talk." He waited for Charlie to go look after his infant brother Robert. Raising children, music—those were more important to him, but he had to deal with family and failure in his business.

"Since my father didn't want me to go into dry goods, it wouldn't behoove me to ask anything of him," Ben said, knowing logic would only make Alice angrier. "I don't like the turn of our fortune any more than you do."

"You spent far too much time campaigning for Mr. Lincoln," she said, as if this trumped all his logic.

"He won Illinois handily. I'm pleased I had some little part in that." Of all the men who had ever run for the presidency, Abraham Lincoln was, in Ben's opinion, the finest. But the elder Grierson was a dyed-in-the-wool Democrat and this had further widened the rift between father and son.

"If Mr. Lincoln's so beholden to you, why don't you ask him for a job?"

Ben Grierson licked his lips, then launched into relating the broad aspects of the letter he had received from Governor Yates. Ben had campaigned equally as hard for his friend Richard Yates as he had for Lincoln, but political activities had come at the expense of his business, as much as he hated to admit that Alice was right. If he hadn't left the day-to-day running of the business to John, they might still be raking in the profits. His brother was not much of a businessman.

"I received a letter from the governor," he began, skirting the issue until he found an indirect way to present the details.

"This doesn't have anything to do with all those awful books you've been reading, has it?" Alice looked across the small sitting room to the desk where Ben had spread out a fan of textbooks on strategy and tactics so he could skip from one book to another quickly. "When you were in the militia you were a trumpeter, not a soldier. Not a real soldier at all. Don't go putting on airs."

"I know I wasn't much of a cavalry soldier," he said. Ben closed his eyes for a moment and rubbed the side of his head. How he hated horses! When he was eight years old, he was kicked in the head by a horse and lay unconscious for two weeks, his despairing mother hovering by him the whole while. When he finally regained consciousness, he was partially blind for another two months. His mother kept him in a dark room until vision finally returned in his left eye. The only evidence of his mishap now was a huge scar on his cheek hidden by the thick, bushy black beard he sported.

"No, you're not much of a soldier. What does Governor Yates want of you? A position in the government? Clerking jobs don't pay well, but anything is better than having you around all day poring over those useless books and not earning a red cent."

His wife's condemnation stung, but Ben knew he

wouldn't feel as guilty if there hadn't been a kernel of truth hidden in what she said. Alice never minced words.

"Richard wants me to deliver messages."

"A courier? That's all? It cannot pay too well."

"Nothing at all, actually, but I can be of service," Ben said. "And I'll receive provisions and a place to sleep. That will relieve a little of the burden on your parents, if they don't have to put me up, also."

"Well, yes," Alice said, considering the matter. Then she eyed him critically. "You're not going to do something foolish like enlist in the army, are you?"

"Dear, I have no intention of sneaking off to smoke and carouse. You know me better than that."

"You smoked before we were married," she said, glaring at him as if he still enjoyed this vice. "And you talk of going to the theater often."

"I enjoy the music. You do, too."

"Not in such depraved surroundings." Alice sniffed and looked at the open book of poetry beside her, then began reading without another word. It was so hard being the moral compass with such depravity all about.

Ben heaved a deep sigh, went to her and kissed her chastely on the cheek. His wife mumbled some vague farewell, and he set off the carry documents for the governor, feeling a trifle sinful because Alice, again with her lightning-quick mind, had seen through to the real nature of the chore.

Ben picked up the dispatch bag from the governor destined for Colonel Prentiss, the commander of the Illinois Volunteers. He saw no reason to burden his wife with the added detail that Prentiss, with whom he had campaigned vigorously to get Lincoln elected, had offered him the position of lieutenant and aide-de-camp.

It was similarly an unpaid position, but with circumstances throughout the country moving in such a perilous direction, Ben Grierson felt more useful in the army than simply idling about his in-laws' house when he wasn't searching futilely for a new job.

He went outside and hesitated on the top step of the porch. His new position ought to give better opportunity to provide for his wife and young sons, but it required him to ride this accursed horse. He went down the four whitewashed steps, one by one in measured cadence to a silent drum tattoo, feeling as if he mounted thirteen to a gallows instead. Ben did his best to gentle the frisky beast, then hastily mounted and turned the horse's face in the direction of Springfield and Colonel Prentiss's bivouac.

It might not be so bad working as an aide-de-camp, if the job didn't require him to do much riding. After all, the Illinois Volunteers were infantry soldiers, not cavalry.

Benjamin Grierson gave the horse its head and struggled to hang on as it galloped away.

William W. Johnstone
The *Last Gunfighter* Series

__**The Last Gunfighter: The Drifter**

                       0-8217-5510-2   **$4.99**US/**$6.50**CAN

Known on the frontier as the Drifter, Frank Morgan has come to Colorado in pursuit of the *hombres* who killed the only woman he had ever loved. But two vicious outlaw gangs are running roughshod over the territory and now they've made an enemy of the Drifter by taking his son hostage. Suddenly one against one hundred makes for even odds.

__**The Last Gunfighter: Reprisal**

                       0-8217-5510-0   **$4.99**US/**$6.50**CAN

Once Frank Morgan had a wife and a future on the land, until a rich man with a grudge drove him out of Colorado. Since then Logan's taken up the one skill that always came easy—gunfighting. But there's nothing easy about two vicious outlaw gangs descending on the town, threatening to wreak havoc.

Call toll free **1-888-345-BOOK** to order by phone or use this coupon to order by mail.

Name_____

Address _____

City_____ State _____ Zip _____

Please send me the books I have checked above.

I am enclosing $_____

Plus postage and handling* $_____

Sales tax (in NY and TN only) $_____

Total amount enclosed $_____

*Add $2.50 for the first book and $.50 for each additional book.

Send check or money order (no cash or CODs) to: **Kensington Publishing Corp., Dept. C.O., 850 Third Avenue, 16th Floor, New York, NY 10022**

Prices and numbers subject to change without notice. All orders subject to availability.

Check out our website at **www.kensingtonbooks.com**.